THAT WOMAN

Beating the odds in Colonial New York

By Wayne Clark

Published by Wayne Clark YUL/NYC

ISBN: 978-0-9921202-6-9

Graphic design by Nell Chitty

Cover credits: Photo: jsteck. Painting: Willem van de Velde the Younger [Public domain], via Wikimedia Commons.

Printed by CreateSpace.

For Jeanine, Julia and Meghan

Acknowledgement

I would like to sincerely thank two people for their invaluable collaboration: my eldest daughter, Julia Clark-Combot, and my dear friend Anishella Jean-Baptiste.

CONTENTS

PART I

CHAPTER 1

A Lesson

"LISTEN," Gabriel Da Silva told his two children, Sarah and Jacob, "listen well because I am preparing you for life."

Over the years, Gabriel would sit his children down at a table in front of him and pass on what he called truths from his own life. He was a short man and always remained standing to add authority to his words. "I am preparing you for life." He said that many times.

In the end, he failed entirely. Throughout their lives Sarah and Jacob came to believe they were never truly ready for what happened next.

CHAPTER 2

What Happened Next

October 29, 1748
Bordeaux, France

IT WAS the highlight of Sarah's week when her father signaled for her and her older brother Jacob to prepare themselves to accompany him while he conducted business on the quays of Bordeaux. Preparation meant simply to spruce up, straighten up and, above all, look up. Show that you are someone, he would say.

Since his wife died two years earlier, Gabriel Da Silva had placed his children on the pedestal his wife used to occupy. His taciturnity at home still made the days long, but Sarah had her brother to chatter with as they worked in the shop, its little office upstairs and the warehouse on the third floor. When Jacob teased her, which he would find any excuse to do, she laughed. Since their mother had died their father no longer barked out their names when he caught them playing word games while supposedly doing his accounts, or playing hide and seek in the store room when they were supposed to be finding space for a new consignment of goods. Mostly it was wine from their father's best client, a producer in Pessac, a short distance southwest of the city.

Gabriel Da Silva was not a major merchant, so he was particularly proud of acting on behalf of the prestigious winery that had been in production for hundreds of years on the order of Pope Clément, a former archbishop of Bordeaux. Da Silva never had a problem with Catholics. Jews no longer had to pretend to be Catholic to get married. The King liked Jews when he profited from their commerce and borrowed their money to finance his fantasies of glory, first for himself, then for France.

Like many businessmen in coastal ports, Da Silva bought and sold whatever was at a good price, from fine silk fabrics made in Lyon to furniture made by the world-renowned craftsmen of Paris. Trade with the New World had made Bordeaux France's major port, and many a merchant and shipowner had made their fortunes. Compared to them, Gabriel was a small fish, like the sardines from his native Portugal. But, he told himself, "I am one of them."

Gabriel Da Silva was thin. His back was slightly hunched so he could not stand tall as he asked his children to do. Sarah, the youngest, was only 17 but she was already taller than her father, and almost as tall as her brother, two years her elder.

Sarah loved the days she spent on the docks of the great city. Though she knew only her little neighborhood, the streets around their shop on the Ruelle des Fosses, near the new Porte Dijeaux, she believed everything worth seeing in Bordeaux could be seen from the harbor, like the Église St. Pierre and the newly erected stock exchange, the Place de la Bourse, designed by the King's very own architect as a symbol of the city's prosperity. And she could gaze all day long at the ships anchored along the Garonne River. Even the river had come from far away, in the mountains of Spain, they said.

She and Jacob were not allowed to walk the quays alone. Her father said the press of men on the docks comprised men like himself, men with goods to offer, arrangements to conclude, or men of the sea, who seemed forever bent under the weight of the cargo they loaded or offloaded, or, if not bent, at least crooked under the effects of wine. And, said her father, there were men whose purpose on the docks was not declared, men who moved little else but their eyes. That only increased Sarah's excitement as she and her brother followed their father, watching as he nodded to people, stopping occasionally to converse, or occasionally even boarding one of the merchantmen, sometimes for an hour on end. When that happened she and Jacob would dutifully sit near the end of the pier, away from the crowded quays.

Though it was late fall, as reflected by the blue of the sky, which she found far richer than that of midsummer days, the heat was unseasonal. Men, masts, buildings and the waters of the harbor shimmered before Sarah's eyes. For a moment it caused her to lose sight of her father. He had grown smaller after the death of her mother.

As she hurried to catch up, Sarah instinctively stepped aside to evade the stench of a toothless man who'd tripped and stumbled toward her. She shielded her eyes with her left hand. Her father's long, thin grey hair lurched back into view. She hurried to catch up. Jacob was already at her father's side. On the docks, Jacob was never supposed to let his sister out of his sight. She realized she'd been too absorbed by the routine of chaos to notice she was lagging behind.

As she neared her father she thought she saw alarm in his eyes. He had been in intense conversation with a man she knew to be an agent. As she drew alongside, she caught a few words of the discussion. Finally the agent shook his head slowly, as if with regret. The hands he held up before his chest confirmed some kind of refusal. Her father sank down, coming to rest on a bollard. The agent turned away.

Sarah was at Jacob's side. They waited for their father to speak.

For long moments he remained silent, and swallowed a lot.

They knew a lot about his business of importing and exporting and the occasional retailing of wares locally. He had been training them for years to take over the business someday. After his wife died he added more and more responsibilities, which required more and more learning, not just the keeping of accounts and knowing about weights, measures and currencies, but also languages. Bordeaux traded with the world and, at least on the docks and in the inns and rooms that served as homes for the longshoremen and foreign traders, it was a world of many tongues. Sarah and Jacob could read and write French. As Jews, they knew Yiddish. And because the wine trade to the north demanded it, they spoke English and some Dutch. Her ear being more gifted than Jacob's, Sarah was nearly fluent in the tongue of her father's family, Portuguese. Sometimes by the fire late at night, when she saw her father's eyes growing heavy, she switched to Portuguese. Though her father was not much of a talker, it seemed to Sarah that hearing his own language freed his tongue, and occasionally, emotions. Her father loved her all the more for that gift for languages.

The sun beat down on them as they in turn looked down on their father, on the bollard, afraid he would say nothing and send them home burdened by mystery. At last, he mumbled something in Yiddish, something about "the end". Jacob and Sarah leaned forward to hear better, their young faces inches from their father's prematurely lined face. Suddenly he stood up, almost elbowing Jacob. He raised his right arm by way of invitation. "We shall talk."

With that the hunched little man strode quickly across the quay and up an incline past a balustrade built along the Chartron quays to allow Bordeaux's *haute-société* the pleasure of walking as they took in the joys of the jewel-like crescent port without having to mingle with the Dutch, Irish, English, West Indians and people from God only knows where who kept them rich by exporting their wines. Gabriel continued briefly up a narrow street that housed workers, then turned into an even narrower alley.

Their father's gait was weary but determined. The alley stunk of fried onions. He stepped through a door into a minuscule room. There was barely enough light to see the tables. When Sarah's eyes adjusted to the gloom, she counted four tables. At least darkness made it cooler. A moment after they sat down, three demitasse coffees were laid on the table by a wisp of a woman who said nothing.

Her father brought the little cup to his lips, almost an absent-minded gesture as his gaze fixed itself on the wall opposite. The desperation was still there, Sarah saw. When they had arrived on the docks a few hours ago, he had pushed forward with more purpose than usual. He was looking for someone in particular. Was it the man, the agent, the one who shook his head no?

As she sat at the little table and waited for her father to speak, Sarah replayed the fragments of the conversation she'd heard on the dock. "No," the agent said, "the captain has yet to come aboard." Her father had looked at the agent expectantly. "Regardless," said the agent, "the ship's departure will be greatly delayed. The captain is awaiting confirmation of a cargo more lucrative than the one he intended to take on. In the meantime, it is my understanding that the captain will profit from the delay to have repairs made to the ship."

The news clearly distressed her father.

"What remains in my store I must sell now," he told the agent. He was too proud to beg but the urgency crept through. "Otherwise I'm doomed. I can't afford to buy from my suppliers until I sell this load, and if I can't buy more of their goods they will go elsewhere." After a long silence he told the agent he was willing to reduce his usual profit if necessary. It was then that the agent began shaking his head slowly, regretfully. "No."

Her father sipped his coffee and stared at the wall as if he'd forgotten he'd just told his children he must talk to them. As she waited Sarah suddenly made a connection.

When her mother died two years before, of cramp colic after her appendix burst, her father mourned by not sleeping. He trembled at the idea of going to his empty bed. Would she ever feel that devoted to a man? In the following months, either Sarah or Jacob would frequently find him in the morning slumped in his chair by the fireplace. They knew he would want them to wake him. His first words were always about business.

Six months later, in the spring, he returned to his bed. Sarah was relieved.

After the initial sadness at her mother's death, Sarah began to feel hurt. It wasn't the same kind of passing hurt she felt when her father didn't laugh at one of her little jokes. At first, she felt this hurt had no source. It was just there, a kind of haunting presence. In time she defined the hurt. She felt betrayed by her mother. Immediately, she felt there was something evil about that thought. If it wasn't evil, it was certainly childish, she tried to tell herself. But the rationalization didn't make it go away. With the hope of banishing the thought, Sarah told herself that rather than think about her mother, she had to be strong for her father. When he started to distance himself from his grief, she started to feel safe again.

That lasted mere months, until the night her father returned home, face ashen, voice tiny. His eyes were so intense she felt they were trying to find answers in her own eyes. Later Jacob told her he had felt the same that night. They went to bed ignorant, in near panic. It was only the next morning that their father told them he had lost a great deal of money.

"A cargo, my cargo, has been seized by the British on the way to Ireland." He looked at each child in turn before continuing. "It was uninsured." He had gambled on a far greater profit and lost. It wasn't right, he said, that he was forced to take that risk. It wouldn't have been necessary if smaller merchants and townspeople hadn't owed him so much money. The excuse, Sarah thought, was probably true as far as it went. But as young as she was she couldn't come to terms with her father gambling with their very existence.

As she looked back, Sarah realized how simply they had been living since the uninsured cargo had been seized. They were spending more time working and less time eating. Watery soup had become a staple. The challenging and occasionally humorous discussions their table engendered when her mother was alive, and when her father was free to think of things larger than business, had vanished. They often sat in silence, as they were doing now at the café.

Finally her father put down his cup and spoke. "My children, I am ruined. I pray we are not all ruined." He paused. His eyes met Sarah's for a moment, as if by accident, then returned to the wall. He mumbled, "I will go to the *sedeka* tomorrow and ask if they can help us." The sedeka was a Jewish charity. Sarah had often seen her father putting coins in the pushke on the floor by the fireplace in their house. Her father placed coins in the box for the poor. Now the man she'd seen so often standing as an equal in conversation with wealthy merchants was saying they were poor.

That haunting presence returned. Sarah couldn't define it, just as she couldn't explain it following the death of her mother. But all the same it made her feel cold inside. Was it resentment? Then a wave of shame took her breath away. How could she resent the kind little man who sat beside her? Maybe the thought grew out of the frustration of having to sit on a thousand questions. The manners that she and Jacob had learned denied her the freedom to besiege her father with questions uninvited.

"I must return," her father said suddenly. "There's someone else I meant to see today. I didn't see him this afternoon. He has to show up at some point. He's the agent for a ship that's sailing soon. They're still looking for cargo. At least, I know they were yesterday."

Leaving the café, they turned toward the harbor. The sky had darkened. The glare of the sun was gone but the air was growing humid. It would rain, Sarah thought.

"Stay close by me," her father said after they reached the quay. As they walked, his head swiveled as he searched the passing faces. Sarah lapsed into a daydream she'd had many times before. She saw herself and Jacob laughing as they tried to keep up with their father, whose pace was fast but shuffling, sidestepping men, and raising his hand to acknowledge others like him who made the port thrive. He knew almost all of them, at least by name, from the nobodies like himself to the owners of fleets who never missed an opportunity to earn the King's favor in return for putting their ships at the disposal of the French Navy in its war with England.

In Sarah's daydream, she and Jacob were ushered aboard a ship with soaring masts. A crew member, a boy, would step forward to graciously show them where to stand safely, well away from barrels being winched aboard and stored below. The imaginary ship belonged to her father. Some day—in her daydream she knew this to be fact—her father would say, "My children, on the next tide we are departing on a journey."

At last her father stopped by the gangplank of a tiny merchantman.

"Is your captain aboard?" he asked a seaman. Learning that he was, Gabriel told the seaman to ask his captain for permission to board. Without urgency, the seaman made his way up to the deck and disappeared. "I may be a while," Gabriel said to his children." A moment later he was gingerly making his way up the gangplank. There were no ropes to act as rails.

More than an hour passed. Twilight had given way to night and a wind had started to blow from the east, signaling the arrival of a storm. Jacob spotted a folded tarp on the dock alongside the ship. "We can use that if it starts to rain hard," he told his sister. Neither had said much as they waited. They hoped the fact their father was below decks for so long meant he was working out a deal that would save his business.

Black clouds slid in front of the moon. Out of the darkness, strong hands suddenly closed tightly on the mouths of both Sarah and Jacob, preventing any sound from escaping. Jacob felt a knife blade press against his Adam's apple. For a moment, the pressure from the knife increased. Jacob got the message. Don't struggle. The soft skin under Sarah's jaw felt the same threat. The hands were rough. A hoarse voice ordered them to get to their feet.

"Slow now. And quiet. Otherwise..."

Rain started to pelt the docks. Either it was chance or the two men had timed it perfectly. The rain forced everyone to lower their heads as they pushed by. No one would notice the plight of the children. Their hands still gripping Sarah and Jacob's mouths, the men used their bodies to push them forward along the quay's edge. Sarah was immediately behind the caped man maneuvering Jacob. After what seemed like only seconds, the caped man stopped, twisting Jacob to the left. Sarah felt herself being shoved forward next to her brother. Momentarily, the hand dropped from her mouth, only to have it clamped firmly by the caped man, the one holding Jacob. Both children were forced to face the water. No one could see the hands covering their mouths. The second man slipped by Sarah on her right and turned to face them both, inches away. He held a pistol to Jacob's gut. Still pointing the pistol, he stepped backwards over the edge of the quay into a small boat. Sarah tried to turn to see her brother but the man tightened his grip on her mouth to keep her head from moving. The hand smelled of tar.

Once in the boat the first man waved the pistol to signal Sarah to join him. His free hand went to his mouth in pantomime, warning her to remain silent. She stepped down and was pushed forward by the bow. The boat rocked as Jacob stepped in. The caped man's knife grazed his face as he descended. A big hand forced him down beside his sister. Handing the pistol to his partner in the stern, the first man used an oar to push off from the dock. "Such obedient children," he whispered, dipping the oars into the water. The rain fell harder, so hard Sarah didn't see the big ship until the side of the little boat bumped against its hull.

CHAPTER 3

Questions

SARAH imagined that her whole being had dissolved into a speck of tar in the pitch-blackness of the hold where she sat, propped upright by another body. Sarah had been blind and immobile for what seemed like hours as the ship followed the late-night tide toward the open sea.

Suddenly, she defied panic with the only means left to her. She opened her mouth and forced sound into the darkness. At first it fell out as a gasp, as if she'd been punched in the stomach and rendered too breathless to howl against the pain. She tried again. A clear pitch, a single note. She strained to hear it above the sounds of terror that surrounded her. Again she opened her mouth, and sucked in the stench until her diaphragm ballooned. She opened her mouth so wide it hurt, and let the note escape, this time even louder. She hung onto it for dear life, sustaining it until her breath failed her. There was nothing left to do. There was nothing left to vomit, neither food nor bile. Again, her mouth opened. How long had she been doing this? She would never know. It had become a trance, a self-imposed spell. Had she been able to see herself, she would have seen that she sat clinging to her knees just inches from the hull, her face almost brushing it.

The deep moaning of hull suddenly stuttered as the ship's motion changed, now writhing and corkscrewing. The abrupt change in motion broke her concentration. Sarah had forgotten the fear that had impaled her body since the kidnapping. Quickly inhaling another breath through her mouth to escape the smell, she pushed out the note again. There was nothing to hold onto except the bodies pressed against hers. By their sounds, she knew there were men, women and children. In that inky gloom, when they began to be tossed about, they groaned, wailed and retched. The more Sarah focused on the note escaping her mouth, the hellish harmony that surrounded her slowly shrank into a single dissonance. It was no longer the sound of human beings. It was just a sound, one that accompanied her note. If passengers could hear her note, she thought, would they know it was a lifeline to hold onto?

Wedged next to her was her brother Jacob. Would he understand that? Would he know to let the same note pass through his vocal cords? They used to sing children's songs together. That was long ago. A horrendous thud from on deck took her breath away. A moment later Jacob's voice picked up where she left off. She knew it was him gently grasping her left arm with both hands. His young man's voice, richer than hers, was more promising. Sarah turned her head toward Jacob. Like a feather, her right palm scanned his face. Tears. She felt a crinkling of the skin beside the right eye. He continued to sing the note. He sensed her touch. Instinctively they adjusted their voices until they eased into consonance. The sound joined them physically.

Their despair dissolved into a child's game, like the one they used to play to conquer pangs of hunger on nights when their father had not asked them to set the table.

Their father, seated by the fire, would be as hungry as they were, and irritable. But he never stopped them. Sarah always wished he would join in but he was too serious a man to add his voice. He did not look at his children but Sarah believed he was listening. Sarah used to think that their father chose to believe they were making a childish attempt to chant, to pray. Jacob liked Sarah's theory because it would mean he had earned his father's praise.

A few other passengers added their voices to the darkness. Most did not, but comforted by the unified voices it seemed their cries had quieted. Not one person knew the name of another, except those in families, but they were less alone now for having clung collectively to the note started by that woman.

Finally, a seaman backed down the companionway. Stopping before the last step, he turned to face the passengers, a lantern glowing beside his head. He had to fold his body almost in two to avoid crashing his head against the beams of the main deck above. Even Sarah had been unable to stand upright the night before when she was shoved into the compartment.

Apart from a muffled retch, the passengers became silent in the shadows created by the boy's lantern. He had a pleasant face until the ship yawed abruptly and the lantern lurched, re-carving the youth's expression into alarm. He steadied the lantern as the ship swung round before stumbling into a trough. Sarah was thankful her stomach was empty, its former contents spewed on the deck's planking under her feet. He said his name was Charles.

"In case you didn't hear," Charles announced as if speaking above a gale, "it is seven bells in the morning watch. On land that would be 7:30, not that you have anywhere to go or anything to do." Sarah couldn't tell if he meant that as a simple statement of fact, or whether it was empathy, pity or sarcasm. Before returning to the deck, Charles hung the lamp from a beam.

Since the ship had left the long Gironde estuary and

collided with the open sea, its motion contrived with her churning gut to empty her mind. During the endless night nothing registered. She was later to realize it wasn't seasickness that prevented the facts of her sudden forced departure from Bordeaux from aligning themselves into something even remotely explicable. It was the desperately irrational notion that their father had been involved.

There it was again. The readiness to blame both her mother and father for nameless crimes, for nothing more than a feeling she had, a feeling she feared. It was like an ice-cold premonition. She felt it when her mother died. In an instant, her affection had vanished. Its absence had become a presence in Sarah's soul. She felt it when her father became imperfect and vulnerable, when he confessed that financial desperation had led him to gamble with the family's future. The insecurity she felt from that moment on was silently undermining all the wisdom her father had passed on to her and Jacob, the lessons that would prepare them for life. Sarah had loved her life, her family. Now it was disintegrating. She was too young to put a stop to any of it.

Jacob was almost a man, so he didn't talk of such things. But Sarah remembered what she saw in his eyes when their father announced that his cargo, the family's future, had been confiscated by the British Navy and that he had not insured it. She recognized it because that look echoed in her gut where she already knew she was alone in the world, even when she was with her father and Jacob.

Charles descended the companionway again. He said the rain had stopped and they would be permitted to go on deck briefly, in groups of no more than four at a time. Sarah grabbed Jacob's arm to be sure they went together. Once everyone had their turn on deck, the young man said they would be fed.

Though she had grown up seeing sailors on dry land, on the docks and in the streets of Bordeaux, no one in her family and no one she knew had ever been at sea. This was not how she imagined it.

As soon as she had taken Jacob's outstretched hand and stepped on deck she rejoiced in the salt air after the stench below. But it was cold. She wore only a light dress. The day before in Bordeaux had been hot. Quickly her eyes scanned not the grey sea that had swallowed up the ship, leaving all signs of France behind, but the crew. Who were the men who'd kidnapped her and Jacob? Would she even recognize them in daylight?

When they had exited the lower deck they found themselves near the rear mast. The proximity to the stern explained the haunting sound that did battle all night long with the tormenting silence. To Sarah, the rudder's gears and cables were the screams of the tongue-less many who must have come before them.

"Near the mainmast. Go!" A sailor next to them pointed forward. Jacob led Sarah forward but off to the leeward side where they could hold on to rigging at the point it joined the bulwark. It meant they could look out over the swell of gray water with their backs to the wind. With no land in sight, they had no idea whether they were sailing up or down the coast of France or headed to lands shipping agents had described to their father and rated according to their profitability. Sarah used to think these men had no imagination.

The sails seemed hardly half full. Wherever they were going, it would take forever.

Though they'd never been to sea, the leagues of rigging seemed to make sense now as they watched sailors adjust sails. On the quarterdeck, a stout sailor, standing next to a sharp-nosed man wearing a black tricorne hat and a gray broad cloth coat, had just ordered more sail be put on. Was the man wearing the tricorne the captain? Jacob could not make out the words he was now saying to the stout man who, like most of the other sailors, wore a wide-brimmed hat and what appeared to be an outer shirt made of canvas. The tarred breeches were baggy and brown.

Fatigue and the chill of the sea air had won out over the

horror of the hold and the kidnaping at knifepoint. Sarah and Jacob clung to each other in silence.

Sarah was thinking about her father. Did he now know what had happened to them? Was he trying to find them? Had he been attacked, too? Jacob, as was his habit, focused on the tangible, the immediate, the ship, the crew, the sea that bore them somewhere with such indifference. The ship had two masts. The one nearer the bow had two sails, one of them triangular and vertical, the other square, like the one on the other mast behind them.

Pointing to the companionway, the stout man who'd stood beside the captain told them:

"You two. Back down. Go." He spoke in English. The young sailor who had first told them to go on deck had spoken French, but with an accent. Sarah and Jacob had heard voices like those all their lives on the docks.

He repeated the command pointing at two other men who'd been let on deck at the same time as Sarah and Jacob. They'd been speaking French and Sarah and her brother had gone silent to eavesdrop, hoping they'd get an answer to why they'd been forced aboard the ship.

One of them was young. His clothes looked like they belonged to someone else, someone less muscular. He had come on deck with an older man in greasy clothes still damp from the previous night's rain. The young man was excited.

"This changes everything," he said, not trying to hide his words. The words tumbled out. The older man's eyes didn't move from the deck the whole time the young man talked.

"I'm going to be indentured," the young man said. "I don't really know what that means."

Without raising his head, the older man said, "Nor I."

"Whatever it means," the young man said, his voice tinged with joy, "it doesn't mean the gallows."

"You have a point," said the older man, raising his right

finger to the side of his nose.

From what Sarah and Jacob could pick up, the young man had been caught carrying a weapon, a pistol. He said he'd picked it up from the ground where it had fallen when a nobleman was getting down from his horse. When the nobleman didn't deign to even acknowledge the youth's presence, and walked away, the youth tucked the pistol in his trousers. He had never touched one before, he told the older man. "It was beautiful."

The older man finally looked at the young man's face. "Caught with a fire arm, I'd have thought you'd already have had your neck stretched, lad. A middle-class gentleman carries a cane to protect himself, and a nobleman carries a sword to do whatever the hell he wants, and to boot, he can carry a bloody cannon if he has the horses for it. But riffraff like you… A gun? Let me ask ya, have you ever tried a thing called thinking in your life?"

The boy laughed. The sound came out but the skin on his scarred face barely moved. Encouraged, he added that he been charged with killing a man with a blow to the head from a table leg during a street fight involving a score of men outside a Bordeaux tavern. "I don't remember hitting anyone with a table leg," said the boy. The lower court convicted him, mostly based on the information gathered from the other brawlers.

Weeks later, a priest visiting the jail stopped and took in the boy's hideous face. "It is clear that God has already reprimanded you." He took up the boy's cause and sought an appeal from the Tournelle chamber under the Bordeaux parliament. The court could not help but take note of the boy's appearance. Because the boy often tried to turn away the repellant side of his face when being spoken to, all his physical movements appeared awkward. To that fact, the court added acknowledgement that the dead man was a known ruffian. Consequently, a case was made that the young man suffered from a state of imbecility. The court ruled that he bc released from the prison at the Palais de l'Ombrière and sold into indentured service in the French West Indies.

"What's happening?" Sarah asked once they'd returned below. "Are we going to the West Indies?"

"I don't know," said Jacob. "We'll find out soon enough." He meant his words to offer a little encouragement, but the resignation in his voice won out.

The compartment was tiny, barely four feet high, no more than 10 feet in length. They numbered 11. Less than a foot per person. It was made even less because of the casks that lined each side, planks of wood beside them to keep them from rolling about in high seas. On the other side of the forward bulkhead they could hear voices. Jacob said that had to be the crew's quarters. Judging by the numbers he'd seen on deck, there must be a lot of them because the ones in their quarters now would be off duty.

Several of those in their compartment had a tiny valise or a cloth bag. Basically, they'd all come aboard with the clothes on their backs. A few had Bibles. Others had scraps of writing paper.

"Think they were kidnapped like us?" Jacob asked.

"Why would anyone kidnap us?" Sarah asked.

"I've heard stories."

"What kind of stories? Are we going to be ransomed?"

"By the looks of these people," Jacob said, "they have nothing. What's to ransom?"

"We have something," Sarah said.

"Had something," Jacob corrected her.

Before continuing, he waited until he could bring himself to digest the past tense he himself had used. The word left a bitter aftertaste.

"Even if we are ruined, as father says, we have more than most," Jacob told his sister. He always thought before he spoke. Formulating the next idea left pauses, and he was used to his fast-talking sister invading those pauses.

"If people are so poor they can't be ransomed, how do

they pay for their voyage to the New World?"

"They don't."

"It's free? If it costs nothing, why couldn't Papa, you and I go and start over? Why didn't he suggest it yesterday? Papa could leave his debts behind. The authorities would sell the house to pay them off."

Jacob almost smiled. His sister's mind was happiest when finding solutions, to the leak in the ceiling that allowed water to drip on the bread, to creating plausible fabrications to placate a customer impatient for his commode from Paris. She was also good with sums, not just calculating but remembering them. In her spare time she would figure out how they could shave expenses to save money to buy goods for which there was a suddenly high demand. She kept her ears open on the docks and, to her father's delight, was on the road to becoming an encyclopedia of investment and trade possibilities.

"He didn't suggest it because free isn't free," Jacob said. "You pay your way by selling them your freedom. For years. Three, five years, whatever the buyer insists on."

"You become a slave?"

"Yes. You sign an indenture, a contract. It would state that in return for the voyage to the New World you agree to work for someone for the stated time. You don't get paid. They would tell you the wages you don't get are used to pay for your voyage, to pay to house, clothe and feed you. You have to do whatever they ask for all those years."

"And then," asked Sarah.

"They free you then, supposedly."

"What if the man who bought your freedom was a good person?"

Sarah, despite her moods, was an optimist at heart, or maybe just young, thought Jacob.

"Would a good person treat another like a slave?" Jacob knew his sister was probably quicker than he was, and probably brighter than most people, but he was training himself to think like the philosophers. He had read only one such work, *Passions of the Souls* by Descartes. He had been deeply impressed. He turned the pages respectfully as he read and re-read passage after passage. The treatise had been among papers and books a client wanted his father to have shipped, along with cases of Burgundy, to Saint-Domingue. The trunk containing the papers had been damaged en route to Bordeaux. The contents sat in their third-floor stock room while the trunk was being repaired.

Sarah and Jacob made themselves small by squatting against the barrels as the final four people came belowdecks. They were followed by two sailors, both young. They carried tools. They pushed their way through the passengers and began removing the forward bulkhead. Jacob had been correct. The crew's quarters were behind it. The men of the previous watch slept in the hammocks, which swung erratically as the ship was now knifing through waves rather than cresting and sinking on the swell that met them shortly after leaving land behind.

The division between compartments had been makeshift all along, made only of canvas. The two sailors made their way further forward, past the hammocks in the next compartment. Half an hour later they returned, one with a large, blackened kettle that was obviously heavy. The man held its handle with two hands and walked with his legs spread wide to avoid letting the pot bang against his shins. The other man had already reached the passengers. From a canvas bag he removed wooden plates, mugs and a spoon for each person.

"Maybe the voyage wouldn't be too bad," a man said. "Smells better than anything I ever ate on land."

"It's pea soup," said a gaunt woman, tall enough to have to bend as if bowing before an aristocrat.

The sailor maneuvered the pot to the center of the compartment.

The soup was thick and hot. Most of them had not had a chance to have their evening meal the day before.

Fear, despair, cynical resignation and, in the case of the adolescent boy with the scarred face, relief had replaced hunger.

As the soup was being ladled out, the boy, emboldened by his earlier talk with the grimy older man on deck, blurted out: "They're fattening us for the slaughter." Again he uttered his expressionless laugh. He felt eyes on him and lowered his head to the bowl in his lap.

"What's the boy talking about?" It was an English voice, accented, Irish, that of a wiry man in his late 20s. Blood clotted the black hair on the upper left side of his head. He switched to French. Sarah concluded that he must have been working on the docks, or was a crew member from an Irish ship. "Who are they?" the young man wanted to know.

Before anyone could attempt an answer, the seaman named Charles descended the companionway, stopping just before the floor of the hold. Turning to his left to face the "passengers", he pointed to Jacob and Sarah. "You and you… Follow me." For the rest of them, he added: "Make way for the sailors coming down in a moment. They're going to rig your hammocks. You'll be two to a hammock, so if you're alone find a partner. You'll keep yourselves warmer that way. If we have enough, you'll each get a blanket. If you stay on the floor you'll get run over by a runaway barrel some night in a storm."

CHAPTER 4

The Negotiation

THE young sailor was already far ahead of Sarah and Jacob when they reached the deck, where they saw that the sun had come out. Jacob kneeled to help his sister up the final steps of the companionway. Before Jacob had taken his first step, the ship lurched and sent him sprawling against his sister. This time she helped him up. They grabbed each other's waists and staggered to the door where the sailor waited, amused, below the quarterdeck. He opened it and impatiently waved his left hand beckoning them to follow. "Make sure the door is well closed behind you." With that he knocked on another door.

"The children, captain," he announced. He hadn't waited for the captain to invite him in.

"Go," the captain ordered, not looking up at Sarah and Jacob.

The stern windows were divided into two-foot-square sections by strips of lead. Through them, sunlight glinted like minuscule explosions in the ship's wake. The carpentry of the cabin was no more than functional. The captain was not a man for frills. His hat sat on a globe on a small table to the right of his desk. Without his tricorn hat, Jacob thought, the captain's nose took full possession of his face. He was reading. Finally, he tossed the paper onto the desk. His eyes followed its trajectory. When it landed, he looked down the table's length and saw Sarah and Jacob. The desk was large and rectangular. The captain sat at its top end, stern windows to his back. Before him, more papers, a goblet and a sword. The table served as both desk and chart table.

"You of course have fathomed why you are aboard my ship."

"No sir," said Jacob, answering the captain's French in kind.

"I'm disappointed. You have an air of intelligence about you. I thought you'd spare me explanations."

Neither Jacob nor his sister spoke. His condescension hung in the air.

"At least you have manners," the captain said after a long, evidently deliberate silence.

"I don't expect you to rejoice about the... the... the... I was going to say the offer I was about to make you. It's not strictly an offer. That word was simply in deference to your apparent manners. The truth of the matter is we have a business matter to agree upon."

Jacob couldn't believe his ears.

"Sir, you cannot call this a negotiation." Jacob's voice grew bolder. "We are not here by choice. We were grabbed from the docks at knife point and thrown on your deck like bales of hemp."

"So much for manners," said the captain. He stood up. Jacob realized how much shorter he seemed here than when they'd first laid eyes on him standing on the quarterdeck talking with a sailor who passed on orders to the crew.

The captain reached for his sword. Jacob swallowed

hard and edged himself in front of Sarah.

After gazing at Jacob for a moment, the captain slowly bent to retrieve the sword's sheath from the floor. After inserting the sword he turned and hung it by a hook on the bulkhead.

"I don't much care how you came aboard," said the captain. "We have set sail for Britain's American colonies, a city by the name of New York. If you spent time on the docks at Bordeaux you undoubtedly know of the place."

Returning to his chair, the captain opened a drawer and withdrew two pieces of paper, which he placed in front of him, aligning them. He was a pedant, thought Jacob. Sarah had once accused him of being one when he refused to store even low-value coins he suspected of having been shaved with coins that were clearly intact. Sarah was not opposed to making every centime count but she and her brother had been charged with hurriedly stocking their small storeroom with countless bottles of wine just arrived from three different wineries on the very same day. Priorities before pedantry, she had said. Jacob remembered the little smile that appeared a moment later. She liked her turn of phrase.

"Though you dispute that you came aboard by choice, a complaint that cannot now be investigated because we are far from the supposed sight of the aggression, witnesses, so on and so forth, you nevertheless, both of you, must pay the cost of transporting you, and all that it entails."

"We have no money," exclaimed Sarah, almost shoving aside her brother who had continued to shield her from the captain's eyes, and hopefully to keep her quiet while he negotiated with calm. "We were kidnapped. This is preposterous."

When the captain failed to reply immediately, she stepped directly in front of Jacob and leaned on the end of the desk, looking straight at the captain at the far end. "I suspect that the kidnappers are aboard your ship. Unmask them and make them pay." She added: "And make them pay our return journey. Surely there's nothing left to discuss."

Gently, Jacob placed his hands on her shoulders and eased her upright and away from the desk.

"One other thing," said Sarah. "Our quarters need to be mopped, and mopped well. They're foul."

The captain stared steadily at her. Finally his face twitched and a second later he erupted in laughter. Sarah faced him, unblinking.

"Child, child, child," said the captain. "Do you wish to root yourself on my bridge as well and set a better course? Or perhaps you want to tell my mariners how to trim a sail. Or would you like to trim them yourself to make sure the task is done to perfection?"

As arrogant as the captain was, he could read character. Jacob squeezed Sarah's hand, begging her to be silent.

"There is an alternative," said the captain. He let the possibility of compromise linger for a moment, as if preening in the pretense of being a reasonable man. "I can furnish the voyage free of charge if you consent to work off the considerable cost your predicament imposes upon myself."

Seeing that he had their attention, he let the pretense dissolve.

"For example," he said, his voice cutting, "you, mademoiselle, you could tend to mopping your quarters. Would that suit you? I can also guarantee you that this long voyage will require the setting of a sail or two. I assume you have the skill. As for your gallant brother, perhaps he could climb the rigging on your behalf and you could simply tell him what to do."

Neither Sarah nor Jacob spoke. They suddenly realized there was no battle to win. The nose behind the desk would have its way no matter what they said.

"I shall tell you how you will repay me. You will agree to pay off your voyage by working for a certain number of years for no wages once we reach our destination. You will fulfill this agreement in the service of whomever I see fit when the time comes. The length of time you will be required to work to pay off this debt will depend on the skills you have to offer. It could be three years. It could be five, or nine."

Again his gaze singled out Sarah.

"For example, mademoiselle, if mopping floors represents the height of your future achievements, you might find yourself thusly engaged for five years before being free of your debt to me." Sarah felt faint. The captain's face, the nose, the fish eyes, repulsed her. Worse, the period of enslavement was unimaginable. She was 17. Five years would be almost a third of her life. She took Jacob's hand, hoping it would stop her trembling.

"The two of you have wasted a great deal of my time. We shall now conclude our agreement." The word was absurd, Jacob thought again.

The captain slid the two pieces of paper forward, towards them.

"Come around the desk and put your mark." He pushed a dirty inkwell and pen toward them.

Jacob went first. The captain handed him a pen. With an angry flourish, Jacob signed his name. Sarah stepped up and did the same, gladly copying her brother's gesture. Jacob pushed both pieces of paper toward the captain but not enough to allow him to retrieve them without standing up.

They expected another outburst. Instead the captain, now standing, seemed intrigued, glancing up at them, then returning to the signatures.

"Well, well, well. You seem to be literate. Or is this just a monkey's trick you've been taught?"

Before they could reply, the captain stood and turned his back on them. While he appeared absorbed by the wake his ship was generating, Sarah and Jacob stared at each other. They didn't dare speak.

It was many minutes before the captain returned to his chair behind the desk.

"Literacy gives me options," he finally said. "It can make you more valuable to the person who buys your contract from me in New York, and that means I can sell you for more money. It also will mean that your period of servitude will probably not exceed three years. Some buyers in New York might find the price, my price, prohibitive if the contract were for more than three years."

Turning back to Jacob, Sarah exploded:

"By what right does he sell us!" She said it in Yiddish. Jacob's eyes pleaded with her to stop.

"What's that?" the captain demanded. "Explain yourself, girl."

Jacob nodded to his sister, indicating that she should tell him what she said.

She related her words in French, adding that she had spoken in Yiddish.

"You're Jews, then," the captain said, not displeased. "Both of you?" he asked.

"We're brother and sister," said Jacob.

"Pray tell, do you speak other tongues?"

Sarah answered. "English and Portuguese. That is my father's language."

"And your father, what is he?"

"A merchant," Jacob answered. "We were with him on the quay when you kidnapped us."

"For the last time, I did not kidnap you. You would do well to never utter that accusation again. Should you do so, either of you, your final port of call will be bottomless waters that bear this vessel."

He let the threat sink in, then asked, "What exactly was your father doing that kept him from keeping an eye on his children? Docks are dangerous places… But I guess you know that now," he said with feigned sympathy.

"He was trying to find a buyer for some goods."

"You and your hot-headed sister, I imagine you work for your father. Your dress tells me you are far from rich, therefore you labored for your father."

Sarah had already grasped that the more skills she had, or could say she and Jacob had, the better their chance of avoiding eternal hell in the New World. The captain may be a foul being but in the end, she thought, he was just a businessman, just like the merchants and agents and suppliers who lived on her father's stage. She thought of it as a stage because she knew nothing of the world beyond the world her father inhabited. He may not have been rich, or big, or strong, but he was the center of it. Until now.

"We are skilled in keeping accounts, complicated ones because we buy goods of all kinds, from the best wines to the best carpentry France has to offer, and countless other goods. We sell to other merchants and to agents who represent the world. That is why our father insisted we learn all the languages spoken on the docks of Bordeaux."

Though she was doing her own selling job, Jacob recognized the pride in her eyes. She loved pleasing her father, as he did. How could he ever find them? The thought darted through his mind but left a trail of hopelessness. He had to fight to regain his focus on the moment.

"You can say what you want, girl," said the captain but there is no earthly reason for me to take your word. It was just moments ago that you gave me the impression that your skills stopped at mopping."

Again, a glance from Jacob stifled the exasperation Sarah was about to give vent to.

"You will have to prove yourselves before we arrive at our destination," the captain said. "You will work for me. You will toil for my quartermaster. You will work for my cargo master and for the carpenter if needs be." He had spoken in English, so well neither Jacob nor Sarah could guess which was his first language. Again the captain read their minds and seemed to smile. The flat lines of his lips merely stretched horizontally, as if pulled by fingers to make a funny face for a child.

"If, if, if I am impressed," he added, "I might make a mop and a bucket available to you. Who knows, you might even find yourself more warmly clothed than your fellow travel companions. When we arrive in New York winter will be on the horizon."

In the following silence, Sarah realized she could not begin to imagine what lay ahead.

"Now leave me," the captain interrupted. "I have other… how shall I put it… negotiations to conduct."

CHAPTER 5

A Pressing Matter

THE HMS Justice, a snow-rigged Royal Navy sloop-of-war, sat abeam of the Yorkton, rising in the morning swell while the Yorkton curtsied. Each ship creakingly echoed the propriety on the next swell.

The Justice had appeared from nowhere, thought Sarah. Unable to stomach the stench below, she had silently made her way to the deck before sunrise. She had wrapped her two hands around rigging in the ship's waist. When darkness gave way to a mist that clung low to the sea, she spotted the masts of the other ship. Like dirty fingers, 10 black dots now pointed at her, at the Yorkton. Cannons.

Sarah peered over the side as a boat bumped against the Yorkton's hull. She counted 11 sailors. Several held pistols, all seemed to have cutlasses. A wide-faced seaman standing in the boat's stern clutched the Yorkton's ladder, dangling freely from the ship's side. A boy at the boat's bow hurled a line aboard. It was caught by a long-faced man with thinning hair. His forearms and hands danced.

In seconds, the rope was secured to a stanchion. Sarah thought she had memorized the movements. She took three steps aft and knelt down to examine the knot. She would learn to make that knot.

The long-faced man pushed her aft and out of the way as an officer in a blue coat climbed aboard. At his side was a sheathed sword. His hair was blond, the line of his features clean and regular. He stood a head taller than the Yorkton's captain, who raised his tricorn hat, stating his name for the British officer. His mouth barely moved as he did so. He made no effort to duplicate the formality the British officer had displayed when introducing himself.

In unison, they walked toward the cabin door. Sarah's heart beat fast. She wanted to fly below and wake Jacob, but he had barely slept during the three days the gale had shaken the ship like a corpse in a lion's jaws. Countless times, frigid water exploded into the compartment despite the closed hatch on deck. Sarah began to think it was a blessing that the wail of the storm muted the screams of her fellow passengers, but when her panic got the upper hand the shrieking wind smothered even her own thoughts. She was nothing, just a body attached to Jacob with a death grip that never let go even when his bigger body was tossed halfway across the deck. Finally all became silent, or maybe she had become deaf. The hatch was lifted but no light entered. It was still night. Jacob had succumbed to sleep. She released his arm and unsteadily stepped toward the companionway. Once there, she looked up into the darkness and breathed.

When the captain followed the British officer into the cabin, several of the ship's crew uttered quick curses and exchanged nervous looks. One of them slowly slipped in behind the others. Sarah then saw him crawl forward, then disappear behind the foremast. She watched for several minutes, but he didn't re-emerge. Was he hiding? She turned and saw that the British seamen had mounted to the quarterdeck. Most faced forward and stared down on the crew, pistols and cutlasses at the ready. All Sarah could identify in the crew's remarks were the words "press" and "limey bastards". Earlier she had determined that a good number of the crewmen were English. Why would they speak of limey bastards?

A sailor who had accompanied his lieutenant to the captain's quarters, suddenly appeared on deck.

"Masterson," he yelled, turning to face the quarterdeck. "Take two others and follow me. We've got three volunteers."

Two broad-chested sailors leapt down the stairs to the main deck. The Yorkton's crew resentfully stepped aside to allow them to pass. The British sailors disappeared down a hatch before the foremast.

"It's the fuckin' Irishman," said the long-faced man who'd shoved Sarah out of the way when the British boarded.

"What Irishman?" she asked.

"Padraic. Mean bloke. Just plain mean."

"But why..." Before Sarah could finish asking her question, the seaman replied:

"Shoved the master. During the gale, two nights ago, the day she started to blow. Around eight bells. Master told him to go back up to finish taking in a sail. Said he'd already done it. Complained he'd spent the whole watch doing it. 'The sail is dowsed well and good,' the Irishman said, all defiant like. Master told him straight out that the lightning had shown him to be the lying bog-jumper his is. 'Aloft!' he ordered. That's when the Cat-lick shoved him. He's been chained up in the orlop, keepin' the cables company."

Twenty minutes later the three British sailors reappeared. In front of them, chained at wrist, three sailors, not just one.

In the captain's quarters, the Royal Navy lieutenant barely allowed the captain time to sit down at the end of his desk before announcing what the captain had guessed anyway. "I have the unfortunate duty of having to impress whichever seamen aboard your ship who strike me as suitable and enter them into the King's service."

"Impressment?" replied the captain, with cold-eye calm. "In a time of peace?"

"We are at war, sir," said the lieutenant, "and have been for the past eight years, since 1740 to be precise. No doubt you've had occasion to notice."

"Yes, yes," said the captain, outwardly ignoring the British officer's sarcasm. "That rather silly business about Marie Theresa and the Habsburgs. Eight years already. My goodness, lieutenant. You have been busy."

Realizing the captain was not about to cooperate, the lieutenant took two quick steps around the side of the desk, approaching the captain.

"Present your entire crew on deck immediately, Captain, so that I may inspect them."

"Lieutenant," said the captain, not in the slightest intimidated. "The war is over. You have obviously not had occasion to notice. The guns are silent. Perhaps you've been at sea too long. The peace treaty was signed last month, the Treaty of Aix-la-Chapelle, I believe it was called. The lady has her throne, and a pretty one it is, Archduchess of Austria, Queen of Hungary."

"Until I receive official word," said the lieutenant, red-faced but standing taller than before, "I have no choice but do my duty. Assemble your men."

"Wait a moment, sir," said the captain. "I am eager to get underway. The gale has thrown me off course. Were it not for that tempest, who knows, we may never have encountered each other. I have an idea that may allow us to settle this matter quickly, to the satisfaction of both parties."

"Pray continue," said the officer.

"One of my crew has shown himself to be a mite

disrespectful. I've just had occasion to imprison him below. It is my understanding that the Royal Navy is quite adept at removing disrespect from any equation. Let me add, the lad in question is strong and able."

"One will not suffice, Captain."

"More sherry?" The captain stood to hold the bottle up to the lieutenant's glass. The offer was accepted. "Takes the chill away," said the captain, his mind churning as he sat back down.

"I need men as well, sir," said the captain. The lieutenant, still standing and looking down on the captain, merely nodded.

A shrill voice sounded on deck. A woman's voice. Heavy footsteps. The voice fell silent.

"Captain." A knock at the door.

"I am busy. Come back later."

"We have a problem."

Excusing himself, the captain squeezed by the lieutenant and made his way to the cabin door. The master's eyes beckoned the captain to step out.

"It's the girl, the young one," said the seaman. "We had to throw her below. With all the crew standing there on deck, all assembled as ordered, she started screaming something about a man who kidnapped her. She ran right up to him and pointed her finger in his face, him and another one. She was fit to be tied. Kept screaming, 'They're the ones! They're the ones!'"

"Keep the girl below. I'll deal with this." The master was dismissed.

"My apologies, sir," said the captain, taking his seat. "A misunderstanding on deck." As he spoke to the British officer his eyes were fixed on the table. An idea was forming, a way of killing two birds with one stone, but he had to handle it right. He needed time to think.

"My sincerest apologies," he said to the lieutenant. "I must again speak with the master for a brief moment." He was halfway past the officer when he said it and beyond the cabin door before the British officer could reply.

The master jumped down from the quarterdeck the instant he saw the captain.

"Take Peterson and Almeida to the orlop." Don't alarm them. Just tell them you need them to take care of something. Take the carpenter with you. When they see him they won't be curious. Once you've got them in the orlop, chain them up with the Irishman."

"Why, Captain?"

"Just do as I say. Opportunity is knocking," said the captain, turning and reentering his cabin.

"Everything's settled on deck," the Yorkton's captain said, slipping by the lieutenant. "Now let us settle affairs here."

The captain smiled his flat smile but it was genuine. He was pleased with himself.

"Sir, though the Royal Navy is not at war at this moment, I respect your needs. I have already offered you one man, who has many years of service ahead of him. If I were to sweeten the pot with two more, one of them an able seaman, could we bring our discussions to an agreeable conclusion?"

"Indeed we can," said the lieutenant, turning to the cabin door.

"Master!" bellowed the captain as he followed the officer onto the deck. "Arrange to have the prisoners brought to the waist."

The Irishman had to go, thought the captain. As for the two other men, that woman, the French girl, Sarah, had identified them. She had the bull by the horns and from what he'd seen of her, she would never let go. She couldn't do anything on board except drive him crazy with demands for justice, but once ashore she could prove to be an embarrassment. She can write, which means she could write the authorities. With her manners and languages, she could pretend to be from a respectable French family. She could drag me into it. She could drag the man who buys her into it. It's too late to throw her overboard on a stormy night. The whole crew knows that woman by now. In fact, she and her brother had become useful to him over the weeks of the voyage.

"Bring up the girl," he ordered. "But tell her she will have to keep her mouth shut no matter what. Bring her brother, too. Tell him to make her keep quiet."

Sarah and Jacob climbed on deck just as the British sailors were marching prisoners to the other side of the ship, where their tender was tied up. The captain watched Sarah's face closely. When one of the two men he'd paid to kidnap people to indenture was about to be handed over, he thrust his right foot against the bulwark, momentarily keeping him on deck. "Captain, Captain…" The captain turned his back and faced Sarah. Jacob had her arms pinned.

"To the Justice." It was the booming voice of the Navy lieutenant commanding his oarsmen to push off and return to ship, three men richer.

The captain bid Sarah to approach him.

"In the weeks you have been aboard," he said, puffing out his shallow chest, I've been conducting my own investigation. It became apparent that you were speaking the truth. The two men you recognized today as your kidnappers had acted on their own. They had hoped to sell you to me, so I could sell you in turn once we arrived in New York. They had been misinformed. I do not work that way. Yes, I provide passage to the penniless and in return have them sign contracts of indentureship to compensate me for my costs, but I take no one against their will. Under British navy discipline, you can be assured, those two will suffer a worse fate than any jail can offer, in France or the New World."

Not knowing whether to believe him, but relieved to see the kidnappers taken away in chains, Sarah thanked him. Just a simple, soft-spoken "thank you", no "sir" attached.

"Master! It's time we were underway."

CHAPTER 6

Born To Die

THE tall black-haired woman with the cruelly pinched face and missing left forefinger had been ranting for five nights, in fact five days and nights. There was little difference below deck for what the captain called the "passengers". For those well enough to climb up on deck the universe of grey that greeted them day after day offered no reason for hope. At least while on deck the wind and waves suffocated the woman's ranting.

In a phlegm-tinged voice that was occasionally silenced by the creaking of the ship, the woman was telling stories of the people who had passed through her life, even if only for a moment on a street corner, and how she had redirected each and every one of them towards the glory of God by citing passages of the Bible, which she said were indisputably written by the hand of God himself with their very sins in mind. This morning the rant had become a wordless wail.

Sarah, huddled with Jacob, did not want to open her

eyes. As much as the ranting had threatened her sanity, the wailing was worse. Was the woman being tortured? Sarah opened her eyes. Beside her, Jacob sat upright. In strongly accented French, a man said: "She's giving birth! She's giving birth! What do we do?"

No one budged.

Finally Sarah, on hands and knees, climbed over the motionless body of a man to her right. His eyes met hers as she raised her knee to pass over him. He did not try to sit up to see what the commotion was. Nor did he even blink.

After crawling to the port side of the little compartment, Sarah could make out the woman, half raised, the upper part of her torso leaning against the bulwark. A big young man hovered over her. One glance at his unshaven face told her he had no idea what to do. Nor did Sarah but the way the screaming woman held her hands over her lower belly meant only one thing: she was giving birth.

Sarah clutched a fold of the woman's broad black skirt and tried to remove the vomitous slime that caked her hands as she crawled to the woman. Sarah had never seen a woman give birth. She reached under the skirt in the near darkness, finding the woman's upper thigh and working her fingers upwards. Then she felt the little head, already free of the womb. Did she dare gently pull on the head? She had no idea. Feeling blindly down each side of the child's cheeks, she reached the woman's labia and edged her fingertips inside. The baby edged further forward, towards her. The baby's head and now its shoulders and chest were directly below her face. She could feel the warmth of the infant, not yet succumbing to the deathly chill of the compartment. When Sarah dragged her way across the deck her fingers were almost numb, as they were every morning. Now they tingled, thawing, as she maneuvered the infant.

Sarah had become oblivious to the woman's screams, her head beneath the woman's skirts and her whole being focused on the tactile communication between her hands and the baby. The baby slid out. Sarah felt one little foot. Her fingertips sought the other. Finding it, she eased both out. Now lying flat on the deck, cradling the infant as best she could, Sarah demanded, "Get that dress off me." After the baby came out, the woman involuntarily let her legs slide to the deck, her dress covering Sarah and the baby. At last the woman was silent.

"Knife!" Sarah called out. When coming on board everyone had been stripped of any arms they may have had. "Hurry!" Sarah, now lying on her side, clutched the baby to her. At last a man knelt by her side with a small blade. "Cut it," Sarah told him. He hesitated. Sarah now held the baby against her chest with one arm and with the other grabbed the man's wrist. She pulled it down next to the umbilical cord.

"Cut it!"

Rising to her knees, Sarah placed the child, a girl, on her mother's chest, then removed her own canvas shirt to cover both of them.

She and Jacob were the only passengers with the waterproof, wind-cutting shirts, a reward for services they'd been providing the captain. The captain then ruined the gesture by adding, "And to show you what a just man I am I'll make sure you get your mop." Again, the grotesque smile. The mop appeared the next morning. The young seaman, Charles, brought it. "You can get a bucket when the deck's being scrubbed," he'd said.

Sarah returned to Jacob's side.

"I have to go on deck."

They squatted in a corner against the wall of the quarterdeck. Jacob wrapped his arms around her and his body shielded her from any wind. The sun was shining. Sarah tried to stare at it but had to look away. She wished she could swallow it and digest it when they had to return belowdeck. They had been at sea, they were told, for five and a half weeks. Other than the Royal Navy ship that stopped them weeks ago, they had not seen another vessel. The sea was empty, endless and, she thought, somehow arrogant. And cold, so cold. Yesterday, a seaman said they'd pretty much had fair sailing thus far. She thought him mad.

Returning below they heard the baby. She was in the arms of the man who'd fetched the knife. Sarah approached, Jacob behind her.

"She's gone. Her," the man said gesturing to the side with his head. "The mother, she's passed, and this one wants her breast."

Through the near darkness, Sarah felt all eyes on her. She no longer felt like the adult she'd been forced to become. She had no idea what to do.

At last the man still holding the baby asked:

"The mother there, bless her soul, would her breasts have anything for this one, even just this once?"

"We can try," said Sarah, without conviction. She took the baby and knelt next to the mother's body. With one hand she tried to pull the woman's blouse over her shoulder and far enough down to reveal her right breast. The blouse was too tight. Handing the infant to Jacob this time, she grabbed the blouse at the woman's waist and pulled upwards. To get it over the woman's shoulders and head, Sarah had to pull the woman toward her, her head against her chest, and away from the wall. The blouse off, Sarah gently placed the dead mother back against the bulwark.

Without her clothes, the woman appeared scrawny. It looked as if her breasts had not even begun producing any milk. Jacob knelt and handed Sarah the baby. Sarah placed its lips by the near breast. The baby's head jerked slightly as it pressed anew against the mother's skin. Short, anxious cries escaped her mouth. Sarah moved her to the other breast. Clearly the baby smelled no milk.

"What's going on here?" It was the young seaman, Charles. "Whose baby is this?" His eyes came to rest on the half-naked woman. "How long's she been like that, unconscious-like?"

"Not long," said Sarah. "But she's dead."

The young man looked at Sarah. His gaze was kindly.

"We can't have babies onboard, miss. Captain's orders."

"If only you could spare a little sugar, the tiniest amount. Sugar and water. We wouldn't bother you." Sarah was almost pleading.

Charles took his time before answering.

"Miss, I know this from past voyages. Listen because the captain will tell you the same thing. Even if this little thing's mother were alive and had enough milk for an orphanage she could not keep the baby."

"Why on earth not?" Sarah was shocked by the boy's words. They meant the baby in her arms would be killed.

"Look, miss. I think all of you have figured out that to pay for your passage you became the property of the captain and that you're going to be sold to the highest bidder in New York. A woman with a baby has no value. A motherless child has even less."

The boy hoped for understanding in Sarah's eyes. There was none. Slowly he stepped in front of her and reached for the infant. The child had gone quiet. Sarah did not resist as the baby was taken from her arms.

Charles disappeared up the companionway.

CHAPTER 7

Paperwork

NO ONE spoke of the baby for days, except a man named Rodriguez. He had been ill since not long after the ship sailed from France. For two days he had lain almost motionless. Jacob had seen other passengers bending over Rodriguez to determine whether he was breathing. He was, apparently. This morning he awoke and tried to stand but was too weak. He sank back to the deck.

"Where is my Antoinette?" he asked. When no one answered he repeated her name, more loudly. "Antoinette. My Antoinette." His hand hovered over the space to his left. At last a big man with curly black hair explained that she died the day before. The big man searched for words. Another man came forward.

"She bore you a daughter, sir."

Rodriguez tried to speak but no words came out.

The young man looked away, as if hoping to get permission to tell the awful truth. The baby had been dropped overboard the day before, within minutes of her mother's death, and at the same time as the refuse from that day's sailing. "I saw it, sir, with my own eyes."

Rodriguez closed his eyes.

Two days later, the captain said he wanted to see the man. Two seaman decided the easiest way was to carry him.

"I see you have not been well," said the captain when Rodriguez had been let down on a chair. "I am told you have just lost your wife."

"And my daughter," Rodriguez mumbled.

"A tragedy, sir," said the captain. "Of that there is no doubt."

The captain spoke no more while slowly passing his hands through documents arrayed before him on his desk. At last he chose one.

Speaking to one of the sailors who'd carried Rodriguez to the cabin, the captain said:

"Here, take this paper, pen and ink to this poor man."

When the document lay before Rodriguez, the captain continued.

"We must alter our arrangement, sir. While a personal tragedy of the worst order, the loss of your wife affects me as well." The captain paused, as if concentrating on making the muscles of his face reflect the gravity and sorrow of the moment.

"You and your wife signed a contract at the beginning of this voyage, by which I agreed to provide you transport and feed you until we arrived at our destination. Once arrived, I was entitled by the contract you signed to sell you and your wife as indentured laborers to the highest bidder. Sadly, for me, I can now seek to gain only from the sale of your contract. As much as it pains me, I must inform you that you must now absorb the debt willingly incurred by your departed."

Pushing on the left arm of the chair, Rodriguez attempted to rise. The chair began to tip over. In an instant the two seamen had righted it and Rodriguez slid back into the seat. His voice had barely returned and mouth rot denied whatever articulation might once have been possible. "No… can't ever pay."

"But you must," said the captain, softly. "It is the law. I feel for you, sir, and I promise that once we land I will do my utmost to obtain the best terms for you, an indentureship that is less than the whole term of your wife's."

Before the sick man could speak, the captain stood and looked down at him.

"My men will assist you below. You must eat and regain your health. The voyage will be over soon. The worst is over."

Rodriguez made his mark.

Eight days later, left alone to lean against the starboard bulwark in the waist after having been assisted up to the deck for fresh air, Rodriguez timed his move perfectly. He clutched a belaying pin as the port side rose high in the great morning swell. Just before roll reached its apex Rodriguez rode gravity and thrust himself up onto the rail, chest down, before kicking his right leg over the side. As skinny as it was, the leg was enough to propel him overboard as the ship paused before righting itself.

His disappearance was not noted for 45 minutes when the passengers were told to go back below. Ten minutes after that the captain cursed at the news.

The Yorkton carried mostly wine and French-manufactured furnishings fit for a nobleman, which the captain had bought in exchange for the coffee, sugar, cocoa, coconuts and snuff he'd brought from Saint-Domingue. His profit from the French goods would be more than decent, guaranteed in fact because much of it was custom ordered for the personal use of two wealthy New York merchants vying with one another for British respectability. However, his profit from the passengers might prove too little to support the investments he was hoping to make after arriving in New York.

As a shipowner he'd done well. Someday, he thought, when he was either rich enough or simply so old that the cold sea air never left his bones, he would hire someone to captain his vessel. For now, though, he trusted only himself. He kept his ear to the ground in as many ports as he could and sought out foreign skippers to keep him up to date on ports where customs officers were easily bought, and ports where navies, especially the Royal Navy, weren't overly zealous about interfering with trade. The British allowed only British-manufactured products to be sold in the colonies. He wasn't supposed to be taking on cargo in the great port of Bordeaux. But he always did. The French didn't care where their profits came from, although they were as bad as the British about insisting their own colonies in the Americas buy only French products. Their greed did little but spawn smugglers in the New World, among them Canadiens from New France, British colonists at Albany, and countless others up and down the eastern seaboard. He had a God-given talent for finding the lowest price for any good or service that might have a buyer.

The captain had hidden compartments built in his lower decks especially for illegal merchandise. He could also recite from memory the longitude and latitude of the many locations where he could offload the illegal portions of his cargo unseen long before dropping anchor at the ports of New York, Boston, Philadelphia or Charles Town. The goods would be rowed ashore on behalf of local businessmen who would arrange to have them transported to their destinations overland without a ha'penny of duty being paid to the King.

Now he wanted to expand, buying small shares in the outgoing cargos of ships sailing to the Caribbean. Soon, he thought, he'd have rum, brandy, women and status for a lifetime.

"Bring that woman to my cabin. And her brother, too." Having lost two bodies who would have brought him profit in New York, and knowing he'd probably lose at least another soul to disease or madness before arriving, he saw the girl and her brother as his last hope of making enough on this voyage to start investing now.

...

Sarah, especially, had spent a lot of time in the captain's quarters. It was there that she was asked to demonstrate her skills at what she soon realized were largely manufactured tasks. She never questioned them. However the captain treated her, verbally or silently, he bore an air of treachery, especially when attempting a smile. Furthermore, on deck, she'd witnessed what she now considered to be his true nature, a capriciousness that was more changeable than the seas he sailed on. In the cabin, the captain's iron-fisted rule was exercised on himself, a check on his true nature, as if he knew it and feared it.

"You both have exceeded my expectations," announced the captain, bidding them to sit at the end of his desk, while he stood at the other end, taking little footsteps to choreograph his words of gratitude. While he had no intention of divulging even a hint of his motives he wanted desperately to win their confidence and ultimately assist in his plans upon arrival in New York.

"It is impossible to make anyone comfortable on a ship such as this. Our first purpose is to ensure that the cargo is impervious to distress."

How he liked to put on airs, thought Sarah.

"However, in recognition of the work you have done for me, I in turn have done what I could. You both stand before me, like my men, clothed in canvas, not the summer rags you came onboard with. I have permitted you to eat the same rations as my men. Maybe because you are Jewish, you decline my ale, or perhaps you simply have not developed a taste for it. I don't know much about you people. But I can assure you that it is ale that gets a man on deck when a storm threatens to stand the ship on its beam-ends."

Jacob was tempted to add that it is ale that gets a man dead. Three weeks out of Bordeaux, a lithe blond-haired Russian sailor attempted a British jig on a yard arm 40 feet above the deck. Minutes later blood ran from his skull through the grating of a hatch cover.

"Jacob," the captain said, "you have shown yourself to be a capable young man. You are not afraid of work. You're good with your hands as well as your mind. I could make a seaman out of you but that would limit a man of your learning. To be frank, that would limit the profit I can make from you. Whoever buys your contract will make a bargain at any price. If a merchant does not choose you, despite your demonstrated knowledge in business, perhaps an artisan will see a future for you, a jeweler, an engraver perhaps."

During the voyage Jacob and Sarah had been charged with entering English bills of lading into a book and providing their sums. When that posed no difficulty for either, the captain tasked them with repeating the exercise for goods he'd acquired in Bordeaux. Though written in French, he wanted them entered in English.

None of the documents seemed to pose a problem to either. Over the punishingly long weeks he placed other documents before them at the end of his desk. Both Sarah and her brother were grateful they had tasks to pass their time.

What struck the captain about Sarah was that she possessed business and language skills identical to her brother's.

"You intrigue me, girl," the captain said one day. "The women I know, and certainly the women I've encountered in the New World, serve no purpose when it comes to business. If they are not comely, it strikes me they serve little or no purpose at all.

Sarah was acquainted with Catholic girls and some

Huguenots in Bordeaux. She knew that their education, for those few well off enough to get any, seemed designed only to attract husbands or please their god. Jewish families educated their daughters just as they did their sons.

Sarah and Jacob soon learned that some of the tasks were legitimate ship's business that would ordinarily be done by the captain or his cargo master or sailing master, while others were meant to verify their stated ability with languages. The captain had them copy old business documents such as certificates for duties on goods, or more nautical documents such as journal observations of longitude, latitude, course, distance, winds and weather, or merchants' letters with descriptions of currencies and weights. Some were papers from a New York firm engaged in the West Indies and northern European trade in commodities such as sugar, coffee, cocoa, and logwood. At the end of the day the captain would gather the documents and carefully place them in a leather-covered box.

While Sarah and Jacob worked, the documents all too often dissolved into images of their father. They would remember him suddenly appearing before them as they sat at the table doing tasks almost identical to the ones they were doing on the ship. He would tell them to hurry but not let a careless error cost them, and not just him, a franc. They liked the way he made his business their business. It made up for him being an obsessive stickler for the details of commerce.

"Young lady," the captain would say when Sarah's hand ceased writing for minutes on end. "Despite the vastness of this ocean I can tell you where this ship is. Where, pray tell, are you?"

She would lie. "I was looking for the right word in English." The truth was a question she couldn't answer. Was her father alive? Had he been found bludgeoned on the docks that night, his blood washed away by the rain at the moment she and Jacob were heaved aboard this ship?

Several documents held her undivided attention. These

she would slide carefully toward Jacob's pile. The first was an oath of ownership taken by their captain that the brig Yorkton, taken from the French in 1744 is now his property. That night, belowdecks, she whispered to Jacob:

"Is he mad? He dares trade in a French port with a French ship he took only three years ago."

Though more than willing to think the captain mad, Jacob offered a plausible excuse, that when under French ownership the ship never sailed out of Bordeaux. There was little distinctive about her to arouse any curiosity. She was a brig, like hundreds of other merchant ships.

The second document that aroused their interest bore a reference to deeds relating to land on the Susquehanna River, wherever that was, or islands in that river. Since they'd never heard of it they assumed it was a river in the New World. The deeds had been issued in England, by someone of rank. What did this have to do with the captain? There were other papers mentioning deeds.

Another document, which the captain allowed them to split up, seemed to have nothing to do with the captain's affairs. He wanted them to translate into English an address book written in French and alphabetized by city. It was entitled "*Livre de la Correspondence Générale*."

Had these documents, the deeds and the business correspondence of French firms, been stolen? Jacob and Sarah agreed the captain had the face of a man who would do such a thing. The more they knew him the more they found it impossible to believe he had nothing to do with their own kidnapping. What seemed likely was that he had counted on more passengers and at time of sailing had decided to make up for the shortfall by whatever means were at hand.

One morning, as a short-lived gale released its hold on the ship, the captain called them to his cabin as usual, except instead of simply pointing to two piles of documents for them to attend to he said he had some news.

"We expect to sight the shores of the New World before nightfall and possibly reach New York the following day. In the meantime, I have one more document to be copied by each of you."

Jacob was the first to look at it.

"Sharon O'Grady indenture, 1743

"Indenture, 1743 January 28, Co. Cork, Ireland., Indenture of Sharon O'Grady of Youghal, Co. Cork, to Capt. Noel Todd, master of the ship Fearless Union for a term of four years upon arrival in Boston, dated January 28, 1743. Indenture to be void if payment for passage is made within 15 days of arrival."

The captain wanted them to copy the contract.

"It will replace the standard contracts each of you signed at the beginning of our voyage. What I want you to do is change the dates, then fill in your own name and provenance and destination. Likewise you will substitute my name for the gallant Captain Todd. However, you will leave the term blank."

The captain stood behind them, pointing to the words requiring change or omission. Jacob and Sarah raised their eyes and stared hard at him.

"Why, you ask? Because I want to make the best arrangement possible for myself and, of course, for you. The last sentence, the business about making payment for your passage within 15 days, well that appears in all the indentures. I would like you to not copy that for your new contracts. You both are capable young people. Perhaps your father has contacts in the New World that could facilitate such a payment within 15 days. But such a person would certainly not be in a position to do for you what I can. If I may speak frankly, I wish to protect myself and leave myself free to obtain the best arrangement possible, as I said. I do not want to be pressured by that time-limited clause."

An odd choice of words, thought Sarah as the captain

paused to walk the length of the desk and settle into his chair.

"I'm sure you will agree I have invested a great deal of effort on your behalf in the recent weeks, gaining knowledge about your skills that, knowing men of position in the New World, I can put to profitable use. A word from me will open a world of possibilities for you both. Are we agreed?"

Jacob and Sarah looked at him in silence. They could not fathom what he might be up to, or what they would be agreeing to.

"I must know if you are with me in this," the captain finally said. "If I have to use the original contracts I would be forced to treat you like the other passengers. You would be kept aboard ship while I advertised your arrival. We would wait for potential buyers to come aboard and decide whether they wish to make an offer for you at the usual terms. What I would prefer to do, for your benefit as well as mine, is to not advertise you but instead proceed directly to making arrangements with a great merchant of the city, someone with whom I've been doing business for many a year. He has money because, better than most men, he can see the potential in things."

The captain left them with that thought and went on deck.

. . .

With the narrows that led to New York in sight, the ship passed a long spit of land a young seaman said was called Sandy Hook. "*Sant Hoek*," a Dutch-accented seaman corrected, only to be reminded that the Dutch had lost Manhattan to the British. "And that for the second time," the young seamen said triumphantly. "And you won't get it back." Jacob and his sister stood on deck next to them, on the starboard side, taking in the considerable breadth of the bay and its islands and the rivers that stretched above it. "Must be a good three leagues wide," said the Dutch seaman.

"A porpoise! There!" cried the Englishman. "Off the port side." Jacob and Sarah then spotted several more leaping above the water.

For a moment, life seemed normal, a young person's adventure. But it wasn't long before dread, excitement and relief that they'd survived the hellish crossing were fighting for attention in their guts. At first the emotions protected them from the bitter, late December cold. Finally Jacob averted his eyes from the approaching land mass and nodded to his sister, telling her that he now agreed they had nothing to gain by not complying with the captain's request that they draw up and sign new indentures for themselves, omitting the option of voiding the contract if their passage was paid within 15 days of docking. They knocked on the door to the captain's cabin.

CHAPTER 8

Task For Two

AFTER the ship dropped anchor in the East River, near the Great Dock at the southern tip of the island of Manhattan, the captain dictated a notice to Jacob. It was a notice to be posted in several locations along the waterfront on Water and Great Queen streets, from the Great Dock up to the eastern end of Wall Street. It advertised the sale of contracts for seven men newly arrived on the Yorkton.

Just imported, aboard the Yorkton, Captain Marcellus Flemming, Master, from England, A number of healthy French Servants and Immigrants, amongst whom are the following, viz., watch-maker, labourer, taylor, shoemaker, caulker, cabinet-makers, farmer. Enquire of the Captain onboard the vessel, off the Great Dock, or Blackthorn's Inn on Broad Street

Absent from the list were the skills of Jacob and Sarah.

In the days that followed, the captain spent most of his time ashore. Several times he passed the better part of a day receiving well-dressed men from the city. On the fifth day he informed Sarah that the contracts of all passengers had been purchased.

"I fear I may have been too generous with my prices." There he was again, thought Sarah, feigning decency. "Too bad about... What was his name? Rodriguez and his woman." He didn't mention the baby.

"With regard to your fate and that of your brother, I expect an invitation shortly from the man I believe will be interested in your services. I will mention your brother as well, but there is no guarantee your contracts will be purchased together."

Sarah had never considered that she and Jacob might be forced apart.

"As for the moment," the captain continued before she could truly contemplate the unthinkable, that of being truly alone in the world, "I have some correspondence I would like to dictate. Do you possess what might be termed artistic talent? For example, if you could draw or paint, I would suspect you could produce a fair copy of another's script, could you not?"

"My brother is the one with a sure hand for what he sees," Sarah answered.

"Well then, perhaps this is a task for two, a task of two parts. You will assist me with the first because words come to your tongue easily. However, your brother should attend so he will understand the importance of this chore."

Sarah left the cabin to fetch her brother, who she found standing near the bow under a bright winter sun, transfixed by the activity along the New York shore. The Yorkton was only one of, by Jacob's fastidious count, 61 ships at anchor or arriving and leaving, not to mention the scores of small craft transporting men and goods to and from shore.

"You're shivering," Sarah said when she reached him.

"I shiver below as well. More bearable with the view."

"The captain wants us. Warm your hands. I think he means for you to write prettily."

She spoke to him in English, which she had done more and more often in the final stages of the voyage. Jacob thought it a good thing.

"Practical," he said, "considering where fate has catapulted us so ingloriously. Achieving fluency can only help us." Sarah had already achieved fluency. Her oral gift was a true as Jacob's gift for drawing what he saw.

As they entered the cabin, the captain was standing at the stern end of his desk. Usually he would be seated, writing in his log, or sifting through papers, anything but acknowledging a visitor's presence. He always made them wait. Today was different. He faced them as they entered.

"Come, come, be seated," he said, extending his right hand toward the other end of the table.

"I'll get straight to the matter at hand. My New York colleague and I possess deeds for land in the southern part of the province of Pennsylvania, which was in third part owned by the estimable John Penn, son of William Penn, for whom the colony is named. The land was granted to his father by none other than King Charles II himself.

"Sadly, not much more than a year before we sailed from Bordeaux, John Penn passed away in the great port of Bristol, the city in which he was raised before venturing to the New World to tend to his newly acquired lands. Bristol is in England. Perhaps you've heard of it, considering your father's line of endeavor?"

"Yes," Jacob answered. He and Sarah had often encountered seamen from Bristol and heard tales of the most profitable trade of all, the one the city's shipowners carried on with the British Colonies, the West Indies, Ireland, Lisbon and France itself, all deftly routed to avoid the preventives, whose job it was to ensure the British Customs House got its due. The city's merchants grew fat. Their father once told them Bristol was as important to England as Bordeaux was to France.

"Yes, yes," said the captain, "of course you know of

Bristol. I am proud to say that the late Mr. Penn and I had a long and fruitful business relationship. He dealt in linens. He was indeed a friend.

"During our very last meeting, Mr. Penn granted a patent to myself and my New York colleague to a parcel of land in the colony. He had often spoken of his intention to do so. On my recent voyage to Bristol, prior to my arriving in Bordeaux, Mr. Penn's former secretary presented me with the statement of patent, as per his late employer's instructions. It was only after we set sail from Bordeaux that I found the time from my many burdensome responsibilities to examine the document."

He looked down to his desk and carefully picked up several sheets of paper.

"This is that document."

The captain sat down before continuing.

"It was with dismay that I noticed the document was incomplete. Perhaps Mr. Penn's health prevented him from entering the precise location of the land. I know only from his own mouth that the land amounts to some 100 square miles and is located in the very southern reaches of the province of Pennsylvania. Obviously, a document so incomplete holds no force in law."

"Furthermore," he said after a moment's reflection, "it is unsigned."

Jacob and Sarah waited.

"You can render me an enormous service, for which you'll eventually be recompensed, by completing this letter of patent.

"Sarah, you will recall similar letters among those I've asked you to copy during the voyage. By having you translate some of them, I wished to see if you truly understood them. You did. So now I want you to rewrite Mr. Penn's document inserting some details about the location of the land in question. I will provide that for you. The conclusion of the letter lacks a few of the customary niceties and formalities one would expect. You will provide them. Clear?"

Sarah nodded and the captain, treating the document as if it were made of gold leaf, slid the letter toward her. It was out of her reach. She got up and went halfway down the table to pick it up.

"Once you've done that to my satisfaction, it will be your brother's turn to put his talents to use. Jacob, you will rewrite this letter in its entirety, taking great pain to imitate the penmanship of its author. As for his signature, I have two examples. These date from the earlier years of my friendship with Mr. Penn."

A day later, the document was done. The captain pronounced himself impressed by Jacob's graceful hand. The land in question was now described as being to the west of the Susquehanna River and part of the land granted to the Penn family by the Walking Treaty of 1737. He provided other geographic particulars purportedly from a survey but, to Sarah, parts were suspiciously vague, particularly an expression stating "and extending 27 miles south of the foot of the creek." No creek was named.

That evening, the captain permitted Sarah and Jacob to dine with him. He toasted their invaluable assistance. However he never revealed any hint of how he planned to use the forged document. Sarah later told her brother she doubted the so-called Mr. Penn had ever written a word of the document, or if he had, it was never meant to be anything but a draft copy of a letter conceived for another purpose. He had probably dictated it to his secretary. Jacob agreed.

"Our captain is as at home on land as he is at sea."

"That's why I did something you may not approve of, Jacob."

Headstrong, impetuous, rash. How many times had he used those words to describe his sister's actions?

"What might I not improve of, dear sister?"

"I kept the copy, the letter you worked from."

"Why on earth... What if the captain looks for it?"

"Why would he? He's got the final document. Remember how pleased he was to have it in his hands."

"Why would you risk getting caught with it?"

"I'm not sure, Jacob. But something tells me it might someday buy us hope."

Late that night, they heard the captain order his boat to take him ashore for the night. He had told Sarah and Jacob that now that their work for him was completed to his satisfaction, he would apply for the earliest possible meeting with his principal business partner in the New World, Zachariah Croman.

"His wealth gives him the power to do what he wants, a state that I too aspire to," he had said before leaving. "And that day, my children, is near at hand. By my own endeavors on sea and land I have mightily enhanced my fortunes as any man of ability can. However, I possess an acumen that is particularly prized by Mr. Croman, which explains why he wishes to work as a team. I will put in my best word for you tomorrow by informing him of your assistance to me. Your fate is now in his hands. I pass the torch."

Sarah did all she could not to laugh at his words. His posturing belonged on stage.

"Did you hear that, Jacob, he passed the torch?" Sarah blurted it out the instant the captain climbed down to the small boat.

Jacob pushed her back into the cabin whose door had remained open when the captain let himself out.

"Not so loud!"

"That foul man kidnapped us, Jacob, and threw us in a stinking hole, and every day since he has lied to us and used us to his ends. Yet there he is letting his chest swell at the thought of the goodness he has bestowed upon us. I know where I'd like to pass his torch..."

Jacob, as fretful as his sister about what the coming days would bring, broke into laughter.

"I mean it, Jacob!" Sarah was beside herself. When Jacob said nothing, she started to laugh as well, about the absurdity, but not the danger it portended.

CHAPTER 9

The Rapes

May 19, 1751

HATRED entered Sarah's world like raindrops gliding down a window pane. In time she noticed them, the cold pool they formed where her heart had been.

Over the past year, Zachariah Croman had come again and again to the counting house on Hanover Square to see her, the only woman he had ever employed at the firm. At first he said he was just making sure she was "settling in nicely," as if he'd obtained commodious and comfortable lodgings for her, forgetting that he'd purchased her like a slave from a kidnapper. He lodged her with an old cooper, Aiden McDougall, and his wife in a wide, squat house on Duke Street, which ran into Hanover Square from the south. She slept on straw in the workshop on the main floor of the house. It smelled of oak and smoke. The cooper sold all his casks to Croman. Locally made casks were in huge demand because the cost of ones imported from England amounted to robbery. The cooper could not refuse to take in the girl from Bordeaux.

On those nights when Croman came for her at the counting house, his routine never varied. It was a short walk from his principal office and his trading company's primary warehouse on Queen Street, the biggest and newest structure to buttress the city's growing reputation as the major center of commerce in all of Britain's colonies.

The counting house's double front doors would be opened upon his arrival. A small boy watched the street through a small rectangular window to the left of the doors. He was told to never take his eyes off the street. It was his job to open the door for important people and those who presented trade cards. Job-seekers and itinerants drunk enough to dare ask for a handout were turned away. The boy was not good at saying no and was often beaten for it. He had been told by one of the little errand boys upstairs that merchants needed double doors because they carried their wealth in their bellies. They liked to joke that a single door would deny Mr. Croman, Esq., entry to his very own buildings.

Once inside the door, Croman grabbed the bell that sat on a clerk's stool by the door. It was brass and almost as large as a ship's bell. It was one of the little doorman's duties to polish it daily, in the early morning before the clerk-in-charge rang it to announce "Commence work" or rang it repeatedly if chatter had been detected in the upstairs storerooms or among the precisely aligned desks for bookkeepers like Sarah.

The magnanimity Croman felt when ringing the bell to signal an early end to the day's work for the 17 bookkeepers, stock keepers and errand boys who catalogued his enterprise came from the fact that it was meant to inflate his presence in their eyes. In reality, his chest did not swell as he supposed it would when he held his head high. All that appeared to swell as he arched his back was his belly.

No one asked why they were being released early. It was not the first time. "Thank you, sir," some said. Croman did not acknowledge them. His eyes were already on Sarah, in the gloom at the desk in the far corner of the room. The eyes told her to stay put.

Two years before, when the businessman first set eyes on Sarah, he turned to the captain of the Yorkton, who had arrived with Sarah and Jacob in tow.

"Last night you extolled her abilities, Flemming, and," gesturing toward Jacob, "those of the young man." He motioned for Sarah and Jacob to occupy the high-backed chairs in front of his grand desk.

Taking the captain's left arm, Croman led him slowly to the back of the large room, beyond a tall oak bookcase whose shelves were stocked with wooden document boxes labeled by country. He released the captain's arm when they reached the back of the room, dominated by a waist-high globe that stood beside a long table topped with glass. Under the spotless glass were sea charts.

"I can only take your word for her skills, Flemming, but I can state already that she is utterly comely." He had been speaking in a private whisper, but he now laughed openly. Sarah and Jacob shifted in their chairs 30 feet away, half turning their heads toward the laughter. The captain flashed his flat smile.

"I will take her on, Flemming, even at the larcenous price you insisted upon last night. I'll have someone acquaint her with the warehouses on the waterfront, then get her started as a bookkeeper here on Hanover Square until she gets used to her new home. I also want her to get to know everyone in the room, who is good, who is cheating, who is stealing from me. I will then see what else she is capable of taking on, whether her aptitude for learning goes as far as loyalty to the firm."

"You will not be disappointed, Zachariah."

"Your plan for how she may be of ultimate service to us intrigued me," Croman continued. "I've given it much thought and have decided that we shall sit down shortly to set the matter afoot. Once again, my dear captain, you are proving to be a worthy partner.

"There is one concern that leaves me somewhat less than at my ease, Flemming. If we are to proceed with the matter of the deeds, Sarah's silence will be imperative. I will need something to hold over her."

"What about the boy?" the captain asked finally. He was pleased with the price he got for Sarah's contract.

"No matter how resourceful he may be, I have no immediate need of him, not even at the going rate. He and his sister must separate. Find another buyer."

"The girl won't be happy."

"She'll learn. It's time she grew up. She doesn't need her brother for that." Croman glanced at the front of his office. The boy and the girl were seated side by side and their heads were huddled together in urgent conversation. "Just make sure your buyer for the boy keeps him in New York, just in case we need him some day. He may prove to be the guarantee of his sister's cooperation."

"As you wish, Zachariah," said the captain, delighted to see his partner still shared his gift for the big picture. The seventh, 13th or even 21st step from now.

They returned to the front of the room. Croman eased his bulk behind his desk while the captain whispered in Jacob's ear.

"There are some details I need to work out with you in private."

As Jacob rose from his chair, Croman ignored him and continued to address himself to Sarah. The girl turned toward Jacob and raised her left hand to Croman, bidding him to be silent. Croman's face flushed red.

"Jacob, where are you going? You're not leaving me are you?"

"No, no, my dear," Croman said, answering for her brother, summoning sudden avuncular charm to defuse the girl's concerns. "The captain informed me just now that there are forms he neglected to have Jacob fill out yesterday."

"I won't be long," Jacob had said. They did not set eyes on each other for two years.

. . .

The first time Croman raped Sarah, he waited until he was sure everyone had left the building, and until he had heard the nightly announcement by the little doorman, "Closing, sir." She stood in his presence, as she had learned to do. He then sat on her stool, his elbow resting casually on the sloping desk top, and attempted to chat. "Is the light sufficient, my dear?" "Do you esteem our record keeping?"

Besides the gross horror that was to follow, Sarah always remembered absurd little details of that evening, the fact that Croman had worn a brown silk waistcoat instead of the linen one, his standard work attire. She also recalled him casually undoing the waistcoat buttons as he approached her. Like a vice, his goat-hair wig served to exaggerate the fraudulence of his smile. It was not a conversation, and she never remembered him speaking any other words. His belly held her firm against the wall as he loosened his breeches. She had no memory of the half-block she must have walked to get home to the cooper's.

The following morning, it was the cooper's wife who roused her from sleep.

"Here, dear," the woman said, handing her a plain petticoat. "Yours has somehow become torn." Nothing more was said of the incident, by the kind cooper's wife or the grotesque man who owned Sarah.

On the three subsequent visits, Croman wore his linen waistcoat. He seldom said a word while he had his way with her against the same wall. The belly that pinned her grew to the size of a nightmare.

After the second assault, Sarah caused a commotion in the usually all-but silent room, where the only noise came from the scratching of pens. She turned her desk to face the room instead of the wall. Her supervisor ordered her to return the desk to its original position. Sarah refused to do so, and refused to explain her gesture. The supervisor took the matter to the office manager, who took it to the owner. Croman grunted. “It is of no account,” he said. “Let her have her way.”

CHAPTER 10

Late-Night Reunion

SARAH was awakened by rapid tapping on a window at one end of the workshop. The cooper's quarters were at the other end of the building, on the second floor. She had no idea of the hour. It must have been very late because it was August and the sun set late. It was dark and unusually quiet.

It was her job to sweep the workshop before retiring. She had not done it this night. She worried about stepping on nails or discarded hoop ends. If she cut herself it would be her fault. Neglecting responsibilities was once unthinkable to Sarah. Now, lots of things didn't matter.

She made it unscathed to the window. Through it she saw the immense face of Noah, her only friend in New York. He held a lantern, as all black men were required to do after nightfall. That had been the law since 1741, the year of the Negro Plot. Noah, like most of the city's black population, second in size only to Charleston, South Carolina, knew there had been no conspiracy to burn the city and kill the white man. An Irish girl, an indentured servant, had made up the story to escape charges of theft. Yet 100 slaves had been found guilty at trial and hanged, exiled or burned at the stake.

Sarah dressed quickly and slid out the door.

"Your brother," said Noah. "I know where he is."

Sarah was speechless as she stared at Noah's bushy gray eyebrows, so thick she sometimes wondered what they would look like if she brushed them.

"Come," Noah said, pointing to the far end of Duke Street. They made their way across the cobblestones until they came to an alleyway at the end. With Noah leading, they turned right and crept along the alley, turning left at the next street. Alley gangs were everywhere in New York and Noah looked nervously up and down the street. Besides that danger, though he was a free black, he did not want to run into the night watch, especially in the company of a white girl. At last he waved Sarah forward. A block later they arrived at Broad Street and turned right. In the August heat, the stench of the open sewer that ran down the middle of the street was enough to chase away anyone with evil intentions. They stayed close to the houses. At Beaver Street they turned right. A few doors down, a hanging sign read, "Henry Fitler, Esq. Engraver".

As Noah raised his fist to knock, Sarah stopped him.

"You will wake everyone!"

"Mr. Fitler is absent, as is his wife. They are in Boston."

"How could you know that, Noah?"

"Because Jacob told me," he said, giving her a wink.

Sarah grabbed his shirtsleeve. Her mouth was open but no words came out.

Noah smiled and knocked once.

A minute passed but he did not knock again. At last he heard the sound of a latch being lifted on the other side.

As the door started to open, Noah slipped behind Sarah and pushed her through the door with his body to get them off the street as quickly as possible. They heard a thud and looked down. Noah raised his lantern. On the floor was Jacob, caught by surprise and bowled over by his sister and Noah.

Before he could get to his feet Sarah threw herself down on top of him, encircling him with her arms and holding on as tightly as she had aboard the Yorkton in the face of a nascent gale.

Noah doused the lantern and waited.

"I am fine, Sarah," said Jacob for the third or fourth time as they lay on the floor, Sarah alternately touching his face, then his arms and hands to make sure he was real.

"My owner looks mean but he is kind. He has taught me much. I am truly grateful to him. I am decently fed and warm even on the coldest winter night. I can ask for nothing else."

"Except your freedom!" said Sarah.

"At the moment, dear sister, I am better in servitude with a full stomach. My master says I am suited to this work, to engraving. He says I have the eye to become a master, too. Maybe then I'll have my own business."

Jacob was not only alive, but alive inside and out. Sarah beamed.

"Show me what it is you do, oh happy slave brother of mine."

Jacob led them into the atelier, dominated by a screw-press made of wood whose once-dark stain betrayed years of use. He explained that when the screw was tightened it caused a flat board to be forced down against the framed type set up on another board below. "In between the two," Jacob said, "is the sheet of paper you want to ink." He showed them cabinets of different-sized blocks and wooden letters that were all reversed.

He left his favorite tools to last, the etching tools and the burin, a steel bar with a sharp point and wooden handle.

"You push outward, away from you, guiding the

instrument with your thumb and forefinger, like this. The palm does the pushing." Noah noticed how deftly Jacob's hands demonstrated the tool's use. "You create thin furrows in the plate's surface, this is where the ink will go, in the furrows.

"What I love the most is the beginning process, etching. I do the basic design this way," Jacob said, "using tools like these." One by one he picked up and laid down etching needles, scrapers, burnishers, shading tools and varnish brushes. "When I've learned my trade," Jacob said, "I wish more than anything to paint a scene, then copy it to copper and print copies for all my friends."

"You're blushing," teased Sarah. "And I don't think you've ever in your life spoken in one go so many words or uttered them so quickly." Jacob's calling, thought Sarah, was not in business. Hers was.

Jacob would be released from his contract in December, when he hoped to continue working with the master but do so for a wage. They had already discussed it. The aging master wanted to expand his business and a young man like Jacob could help.

Sarah's contract would also end in December. Waiting was out of the question, and had been for a long time. The decision to flee was made the morning after Croman raped her for the second time. But just deserting him wouldn't be enough. She had to find a way of getting even with that vile monster.

In the coming days, before the master engraver returned from Boston, Jacob managed to close the atelier a little bit early on two evenings. He would hurry to Hanover Square in hopes of seeing Sarah as she left for home. When he did, on both occasions, he took her to a tavern because he would not be welcome at Sarah's lodgings at the cooper's. Noah had suggested the tavern. It was on the waterfront. He said Sarah knew it.

"Why would my sister be familiar with a tavern?" Jacob had asked.

"Her pig of a boss started her out working at his warehouse on Queen. He sent her on errands to other traders up and down the street. That's where we met, Sarah and I. "

"I'd seen her around. She stood out in a man's world. One day I saw her sitting on the road, crying. I picked her up and told her sitting there would get her run over. I'll never forget what she said: 'Good.'"

Jacob suddenly understood the horror his sister had alluded to when they met at the engraver's.

"I took her to a tavern. She was starving. We shared a beer," said Noah.

Noah met them outside the same tavern, the Pig's Friend. It was small and already crowded. With Noah leading, they pushed their way through to a table in a corner of the room. Noah returned to the barrel-supported planks that served as a bar and ordered ale.

When he returned, Sarah was talking straight into Jacob's right ear, cupping it with her hands so he could hear her.

When Noah's bulk thudded onto the third chair, Jacob pulled away from his sister and stared hard at her.

"He might kill you," he said.

"I can run circles around all that lard," Sarah answered. Jacob could see the hate in her eyes.

The night Noah reunited them at the engraver's, despite Sarah's evident joy and relief in finding him alive, Jacob had sensed a change in her. After he'd confessed his dream and Sarah stopped grinning at his unusual enthusiasm, Jacob demanded to know everything that had happened to her since they were separated.

They didn't have much time because Sarah had to return to the cooper's before he locked up for the night. However she managed to summon the courage to finally stop describing her job and to give Jacob an idea of how Croman was using her.

Jacob had looked at Noah. Noah nodded slightly, confirming the unthinkable.

"We have to do something. This can't happen again, ever." He was pacing the workshop. His hand knocked a hammer to the floor. He ignored it.

"Jacob. Jacob!" Sarah had to raise her voice to make him hear her. "I have a plan. We will discuss it later."

Noah was already standing by the door. He lit his lantern. "Come, Sarah, I will take you home."

After giving her brother a long hug, Sarah followed Noah out the door.

For some time later that night, Jacob didn't move. He remained standing by the door. He felt a huge sadness impale his throat. Sarah grown up, he thought. At home, in Bordeaux, they'd often agreed that passing into adulthood was not a good thing. Growing up meant growing bent, like their father, or growing suddenly close to death, like their mother, who was still a young woman when she died. It meant facing things you had no idea how to handle.

Now, at the tavern, his eyes burning from the smoke, Jacob tried to decide whether his sister had been driven mad or whether the plan she hissed into his ear a moment ago might actually work. For much of the voyage on the Yorkton, the endless copying, translation and dictation numbed his mind and let him forget his body which had never stopped aching from the cold and damp. It was Sarah who suddenly saw through the captain's feigned disinterest in the documents relating to land deeds. His make-work project was a scheme to make himself rich, and his merchant friend even more so. Why otherwise would the captain have on his own worked out possibilities for making the documents appear legitimate? He was simply testing the ingenuity of his young prisoners.

While he thought, Sarah had been bending Noah's ear. He was smiling. He clenched his hammer fist and pretended to pound the table, pulling up short at the last second. Sarah's eyes then met Jacob's. He'd come back from his thoughts. Yes, he nodded, though he still needed to learn how she was planning to pull off her scheme against one of the most powerful men in this city of more than 11,000 people.

CHAPTER 11

Revenge

"MISS Da Silva!" Croman bellowed. "My office now!"

The floor was deserted. Croman had rung the bell and his staff sped by him and out the door. But he didn't corner Sarah as he usually did. After a minute, she thought she was meant to leave, too.

When he called her from his office at the other end of the floor, she froze. When she regained her breath she began to mouth her vow: "Never again. Never again." From under a stack of account books she pulled out a leather-bound volume. Making sure she wasn't being watched, she quickly flipped back groups of pages until her fingers felt an object. Without looking, her fingers found the knife and clasped the handle. She withdrew it with her left hand. With her right she reached under her petticoat and pushed her wool stockings below her knee. She then placed the knife against her calf, letting her petticoat and skirt drop over it.

Croman bellowed a second time, this time using her

first name, as he did whenever they were alone. He once tried to look her in the eye and say the name with fatherly affection. The result was patently false, like the captain's smile. Sarah was already halfway down the row of desks that led to the office. Some of her long black curls had escaped from her cap and bounced with each determined stride. She pursed her lips. Jacob was right. She would have to measure her words whatever Croman demanded of her. Perhaps he had found an error in her accounts. As she walked, the knife, a gift from Noah, shifted further down her leg. She prayed it wouldn't fall noisily to the floor as she arrived at Croman's office.

"You must be exhausted from this long day. Please seat yourself," he said graciously. Sarah had seen this side of Croman only once, the day she and Jacob were presented to him for the first time by the captain. He was gracious towards them because the captain had told him the children had advanced skills that might be of value to him in the future.

Croman sat behind a massive ornate desk, procured in England on his order by the captain from Thomas Chippendale himself. Wealthy Londoners coveted the cabinet-maker's designs. For his desks he used mahogany from the Caribbean islands, a wood that was polished until it turned a deep reddish brown. Chippendale's wealthy London patrons often placed the masterfully embellished desks in country house libraries. Croman's estate, unlike English nobility, was his office on Great Queen Street, a pearl shell's toss from the river. He had a handsome residence near the west side of Manhattan, by Bowling Green on Broadway, but, unwed, he socialized only when business was in the air.

"I am too busy for niceties," he would say, energetically sipping his Madeira and brandy, when his bulldog style of doing business was challenged by the high-born English and pretenders who governed New York. Behind his back they might ridicule him but not to his face. They were too in awe of the ever-increasing number of ships entering and leaving New York's harbor. The city had become the undisputed capital of commerce among all the colonies. It had an energy of its own. Croman's Chippendale desk sat in the epicenter of Manhattan's money machine.

Sarah waited for Croman to speak. She was exhausted.

Since revealing her plan to Jacob and Noah to rid her life of Croman once and for all, and have her indentureship declared null and void, she had scarcely slept. That was three days ago. The three of them had sat in the rain on the wharf facing the tavern. The rain provided relief from the relentless heat of the past week. It also assured them of privacy.

Croman finally spoke.

"I shall be voyaging to Philadelphia at week's end. Before leaving I want you to review certain documents, ones you prepared for Captain Flemming concerning land titles in the province of Pennsylvania."

He passed them towards Sarah. The desk was so large she had to get to her feet to reach them. Awkwardly, she grabbed the edge of the desk and pulled herself up, propelling herself with only her left leg, leaving the right, and the knife, as undisturbed as she could.

"To my eye," said Croman, "all seems in order. However, you have the advantage of having seen the incomplete originals, the ones the much-mourned Mr. Penn valiantly attempted to complete on the eve of his passing. Captain Flemming tells me you and your brother… how is he acclimating to the New World? I meant to ask after him some time ago."

Sarah nodded and Croman took that as a sign she had no desire to waste his time by replying to his question.

"As I was saying, the captain tells me you and your brother provided superlative service in restoring the written intentions of the late Mr. Penn. I wish you to verify that nothing is amiss. As you are aware, this is a document of legal import and will eventually support the transfer of a considerable moneys with regard to these properties."

"You are selling land in Pennsylvania, sir?"

"The particulars beyond the wording of the document are not really your affair, Miss Da Silva. You are undoubtedly blessed, as the captain said, with a quick intelligence but I truly doubt it would be sufficient for you to comprehend the complexities of the transactions I intend to generate."

Sarah expected to be ordered to start reviewing the documents. Instead, Croman's condescending claim to complexities beyond her reach stirred him to hint at the secrets of his mercantile mastery.

"A man can achieve wealth in this New World the instant he grasps the truth that, here, the law has barely fledged. It is flux. It varies from county to county, let alone province to province. And ignorance of it abounds everywhere. There are but a few lawyers, and most of them are self-taught and engaged in little more than drawing up conveyances or collecting debts. To a man of perception, making a fortune here, compared to England, is child's play. You make the law work for you, as I will with these deeds. So, Miss Da Silva, read."

As she did, she became aware that Croman had put aside his other papers and slid down in his chair. He leaned to one side, his elbow on the armrest, watching her.

She was afraid to finish. When at last she shoved the documents forward, Croman placed them in a leather folder.

"What is your verdict, Sarah?"

Her heart stopped.

He righted himself in the chair.

"They are…" Sarah began, then paused. "They are what you wish them to be. I am sure they will serve your purposes."

"Excellent!" Croman beamed at her like a proud father. "This evening marks a transformation in my fortune and yours. We will drink to that."

His half-full glass and the bottle of fortified Madeira were already at arm's reach on the desk. Croman rose and retrieved a second glass from a cabinet by the window overlooking the East River flowing by at ebb tide. Fidgety ships' lanterns pierced the darkness.

Sarah reached for the glass with her left hand. Her right hung by her side, ready.

Croman began to suggest that despite her being a woman he could foresee possibilities for advancement in the firm.

"You're certainly no longer a child, Sarah. Larger matters are within your grasp."

He rose and edged his way around the desk, to Sarah's side. He sat on it, to her left, close enough to reach forward with his glass and nudge her glass in a toast.

"Our futures."

He savored the last gulp and simultaneously, with his other hand, seized her left forearm. Again she froze.

"I do believe, Sarah, that it is time to say thank you."

As he pulled her arm toward him, pulling her from the chair, she thrust the knife into the bicep of the arm that held her. He bellowed in surprise and anger as she spun away, upsetting the chair. Clutching his wounded arm, he started forward but stumbled on the chair. Sarah seized the opportunity, dropping all her weight onto his good arm and pushing the blade against his throat.

"How dare you!"

She pushed harder. Blood trickled from his fat neck as Croman cried out again. Whether it was disbelief or pain, Sarah didn't know. Nor did she care. She had the advantage, not just because of the knife she held so tightly her knuckles were bloodless, but because Croman's immense belly prevented him from sitting himself up unsupported. His right arm was useless and his left bore her entire weight.

"Our business is not concluded… sir!" The word "sir" came out as a hiss, the warning of a deadly snake. His eyes were fixed to hers, paralyzed. She dragged the knife lightly along another inch of fat.

"Pretend all you want, you are not a gentleman despite your wealth. You are not even a man. You are a pig. But you are the worst of pigs. Have you been to the tavern across the street? I think not. It's called the Pig's Friend, but you would not find a welcome there, especially after I tell them what you've done to me."

Sarah slowly eased herself to her feet. Croman tried to roll onto his left side but Sarah kicked him hard in the shins.

"Don't move or I'll open your throat like a spigot. It would be a shame if your blood stained this handsome desk. Maybe I'd use your Madeira bottle to decant it."

This wasn't Sarah's plan. Her hatred had taken over. Jacob and Noah had warned her to control it. She needed a clear mind to pull off her scheme. The plan called for her to use the knife to force him to liberate her once and for all by writing at the bottom of her contract:

"Indenture to be void if payment for passage is made within 15 days of arrival." That made the indenture a standard contract. He would then be compelled to write:

"Indenture voided by Zachariah Croman on the 27th of September, 1751, with gratitude to Miss Sarah Da Silva for all services rendered."

Watching Croman closely, Sarah used the knife to tear off a long strip of cloth from her under-petticoat. Quickly, she used it to tie Croman's ankles together, using a knot she had seen a seaman use on the Yorkton.

Holding the knife to his neck again, she demanded to know where her contract was. Finding it, she placed pen and ink on the floor beside Croman, and dictated. As he wrote, he breathed heavily as he struggled to keep his bulk balanced on the floor above his left arm as he wrote with the wounded right arm.

Sarah inspected the document. She was a free woman. She waited for the ink to dry. She didn't want a single letter blotted and blurred.

"Let me up. Please."

Sarah ignored the request. Croman was now sweating.

"We have another piece of business to conclude. Two pieces of business, in fact. First," said Sarah, passing down another piece of paper, placing it within Croman's reach, "write the following:

"To whom it may concern, I, Zachariah Croman, merchant, of the city of New York in the Province of New York, solemnly swear to the fact of having commanded Captain Marcellus Flemming, of the brig Yorkton, to take by force if necessary, young persons of French nationality in the port of Bordeaux, France, of sound body sufficient to the performance of the tasks required of indentured servants in this city. Furthermore, I declare that it has been made known to me that two such persons, named Jacob and Sarah Da Silva, of Bordeaux, France were brought to this colony against their will in the year 1748. Desirous of acting according to the law, I have released the above mentioned girl from her indentureship. That of her brother Jacob was sold to a local engraver, by the name of Henry Fitler, of Broad Street. This impropriety should be brought to his immediate intention."

Part Two of the plan was now complete. Armed with this letter, not only could she pursue Jacob's freedom, she could hold their crime over the heads of both Croman and the captain. By itself, it would not be regarded as a serious offense. Kidnapping of people to be indentured was not uncommon. But Sarah sensed it might turn out to be worth its weight in gold should Croman refuse to comply with the Part Three of her plan.

The effort to write the longer letter left Croman moaning. Sarah was deaf to it.

"Now we have arrived at the final item of business. Listen carefully. Do not interrupt, and know that my demands are beyond discussion."

Croman was breathing heavily.

"You will acknowledge in writing that on at least six occasions you violated me in your very offices, threatening to throw me out of the lodgings you provided under my illegal indentureship if I spoke a word of the atrocities you have inflicted upon me.

"Secondly, you will immediately, that is before you go to Philadelphia, find proper lodgings for me. These will be private lodgings, which will remain at your expense forever. You will testify that this does not reflect generosity on your part but a God-fearing man's desire to right the vile wrongs you have committed.

"Thirdly, you will rent warehouse space for me here on Great Queen Street or Water Street and stock it with cloth, wines and other merchandise for me to sell, the anticipated profits from them being enough to establish myself as a trader. Once I have turned a profit with those goods and you have helped me restock my warehouse, I will release you of further responsibility to my enterprise.

"So," Sarah summarized, "three things: your confession, my lodgings, and my warehouse stocked.

"Lastly, while you compose the document I have just requested, I will be seated at your desk, in your very chair, drawing up an inventory of the documents and deeds you clearly plan to put forward as having been written by the late and esteemed Mr. Penn of Bristol, documents I know to be false."

"Leave them be, I beg you." Croman's face was beet red. "We have done nothing illegal."

"Ah, but you will." Though she looked as small as a child seated behind the grand mahogany desk, her voice brimmed with the confidence of being free again.

"And when you do sell these deeds, both myself and my

brother, and even your dear captain Flemming if necessary, can testify to the unlikelihood that they were ever yours to sell. Furthermore, even if we do not learn that you have tried to sell them, my brother and I shall not hesitate to take this evidence of your intentions to the authorities should you ever, in anyway, attempt to do us harm or interfere with our affairs, whatever they may prove to be.

"For good measure, I am taking Mr. Penn's incomplete originals upon which these false documents were based. They will serve as absolute proof of your fraudulent intentions should the need arise."

When Sarah had at last verified Croman's confession and promises, which assured a living for her on top of the freedom she had gained only an hour earlier, she placed all the documents in Croman's handsome leather folder, the one in which he'd stored the Penn documents.

Croman's neck had stopped bleeding. Sarah used the inside of his red coat and some Madeira from his glass to wash away the blood. She then prodded him with her foot to make him heave himself to his knees.

"Sit up," she said. The hiss and tone of command had vanished. She spoke as if it was just another day of business. He was now powerless. When he complied, she gently placed his wounded arm in the sleeve of his coat. When she placed the coat over the left arm, she guided him to his feet. He cried out as his right arm pressed hard on the desktop for leverage. She then made him shuffle to his chair, where he sat almost gratefully.

"Unbind my ankles. Please."

"I don't think so," said Sarah. "Once you've caught your breath, I think you might manage to undo the knot. I know your belly prevents you from seeing it but it's a simple slip knot. I'm sure you will have it undone by morning. I trust so," she said, waving the letter folder, "because you have many affairs to attend to on my behalf. I will arrange to have someone call on you in the late afternoon for written confirmation of my new lodgings, my warehouse and delivery of merchandise."

As if strolling in a park, Sarah walked to the other end of the counting house to her desk in the corner. She retrieved her cape and headed toward the door. As she was about to open it, she stopped and turned. The stool was two steps away. She reached over and grabbed the big brass bell with two hands. She lifted it above her head and loudly rang it four times. The old urge to slam the door had vanished in the reverberations of the bell.

CHAPTER 12

Done Deal

AT 3 O'CLOCK the next afternoon, Noah knocked on the door at the Croman company. The boy peering back through the window shook his head. He would not open the door for this stranger. Noah smiled at him, and while staring the boy straight in the eye slowly pounded twice on the door with his rock-hard fist. The boy's mouth opened in alarm. Noah continued to smile. The door opened an inch.

"I am not allowed to let you in," the boy said, almost whispering. Though further fright was not necessary, Noah pitched his voice even lower and said: "Tell Mr. Zachariah Croman that Miss Sarah Da Silva's assistant is downstairs awaiting certain important documents." The boy hurried away.

Sarah had been waiting at the other side of Hanover Square, the small, triangular retail center of the city. Today it was crowded as New Yorkers streamed in and out of shops selling every imaginable imported product at prices only the people of means could afford. It seemed only natural that counting houses occupied the same square. Sarah had worked there for almost three years but never shopped there. That day would come, she told herself.

Despite the passersby, Sarah had a clear view of Noah banging on the door. She knew that for once a bold black man in New York would not be denied by a powerful white man. She now owned the air Zachariah Croman, Esq. breathed and she knew Croman knew it.

Ten minutes later, Noah was walking toward her at the southwest end of the square, envelope in hand. As he neared her, he lowered his head, let his shoulders droop and stared at the ground. Obsequiously, his hands extended the envelope toward Sarah. Any of the few hundred people on the square would think he was one of the city's thousands of slaves doing his mistress's bidding. They would not have been able to see the quiver of his lips as he fought to contain his smile.

Not waiting to even peek inside the envelope, Sarah whooped with joy as Noah rose to his full height. His eyes shone as he returned Sarah's tight hug. Participating in the humbling of a man like Croman was a victory for him as well.

They walked quickly out of the square southeast down to the foot of Old Slip. At the foot of almost every street extending to the river there was a market. Noah was a man of the waterfront, like most blacks, free and owned. He drew no attention here. They sat on a crate next to a vegetable stall. Sarah read the documents aloud, but just loud enough so Noah could hear. As she read, she realized that hearing the words with her own ears made them more real than hearing them just inside her head. Her voice declared her freedom from servitude. Her voice broadcast Croman's confessed guilt. Joyously, she read the confession a second time in a much louder voice. She was careful not to read the signature aloud.

"You did it, Sarah," said Noah. "It seems Goliath has

more to fear than David in this world."

If only she could have shared this moment with Jacob. She had gone to the engraver's shop that morning but was told her brother would be needed until late in the evening.

She now read the details of the warehouse she was to occupy. It was on a street she'd never been on, Maiden Lane. Noah said the street rose from Fly Market Slip.

"It's a good place to be. The slips and wharves south of there can't handle all the boats bringing cargo in and out. Ships can wait for days before being unloaded. The docks will have to grow to the north. In time, you should have good hunting here."

The document contained a list of the merchandise Croman had placed in the warehouse. It was from his own warehouses and already paid for. Finally, there was a letter of credit for 150 Spanish dollars.

"Will that be enough?" Sarah asked.

"Let's just say in my entire life that much money has never touched my fingers at any one time, if ever, but I guess that's not saying much. You're the one who loves figures. Let's say you won't be putting on a satin dress in the morning but with 150 bucks you'll be able to feed me and Jacob for many a year to come."

"It would be my pleasure," Sarah laughed. "Why do you call them bucks?"

"Because that's what one buckskin is worth. A dollar."

The envelope contained a second, smaller one. In it were two keys. She slipped out another piece of paper from the main envelope. It was a deed to the warehouse. Sarah had asked Croman only for a deed to a house, thinking he'd be more likely to agree to the smaller property. As for the warehouse, she made him consent to pay only the rent. Instead he'd signed over ownership to the warehouse.

But what about the house? Was Croman betraying the agreement?

Both anger and anxiety crippled her mood. She wanted

to barge into Croman's office again.

"Give me the knife, Noah." She had returned it to him before he went to Croman's office to pick up the documents that afternoon.

Noah looked at her for so long she finally exclaimed, "What?"

"We're going for a walk. Tide's coming in. Enjoy the salt air."

They walked one block down to Water Street and turned north. Maiden Lane was only a few streets away but Water Street was submerged in its usual chaos. Carters cursed longshoremen who in turn cursed the drunken brawlers they were heaving off the street. No one heard the crack of a coachman's whip as a driver tried to make way for a wealthy merchant's carriage. Had anyone heard it they would have paid no attention. So unlike France, Sarah thought. There no one dared interfere with a nobleman's carriage.

When they finally made their way through to Maiden Lane they found the house immediately. A small, old two-story stone house, it was located closer to Water Street than Queen Street, which crossed Maiden Lane to the northwest. It looked pleasant enough. But she was now more confused than ever.

"First I think I have a house, then I get a deed to only a warehouse. So where's the warehouse?"

"All maidens like mysteries," Noah replied with his usual patience, which she adored. It would never be one of her qualities.

She followed him a short distance back down toward Water Street and the slip. Suddenly to their left was an alleyway running at right angles to the house. They had not even noticed it when they arrived in search of the house. The alley came to an abrupt end 50 feet further north, where a brick wall marked the back of a property that must front on the next street.

They took a few steps into the alley. On their left was a coach gate with a giant padlock in the middle of the two tall doors.

"Give me they keys," Noah said.

He took the larger of the two. Opening the padlock was a struggle.

"Rust," said Noah. At least they now knew the smaller key must be the one for the house and, more importantly, that the warehouse and the house were adjoining and on the same property described in the deed.

A moment later they stood inside a high-ceilinged room with stone walls. To the left was shelving that ran almost the entire height of the wall. In the middle was a waist-high object covered with a tarpaulin. Sarah lifted the edge. Boxes, several of them, different sizes. Using his knife, Noah opened two of them. One contained soaps, the other linens. Croman had made good on the agreement.

"Come, Noah. I must see the house."

The house was nicer than the one she and Jacob grew up in. The fireplaces on the first and second floor were bigger and the walls thicker. That must be because of the horrible cold of winter in New York, thought Sarah. There were two large rooms on the first floor, each with a paned window looking out onto Maiden Lane. One side would be her storefront, the other her office, where she could keep more stock within easy reach. Upstairs would be living quarters and kitchen. She wondered about removing the wall that separated the two rooms so both sides could benefit from the fireplace at night. She and Jacob could live together easily there.

As they stepped out onto the cobbled street, Noah reminded her he had a few things to attend to along the route they'd come, on Water Street.

"Why don't you wait for me in the tavern at the corner? I have a few coins. You can buy an ale, maybe something to eat. I won't be long. I know you have some things to pick up on Duke Street."

The tavern sign read The Homeless Mule. It was barely half full and not half as loud as the Pig's Friend.

"Ale and bread." The barmaid had approached Sarah's table a few minutes after she sat down near the door. She hadn't asked what Sarah wanted. She just glared, as if daring Sarah to inconvenience her.

An hour later, slouched in her chair, absent-mindedly clutching the last crust of bread, Sarah watched through the open door as men walked slowly by in the late afternoon sun, stepping aside at the last minute to let a rumbling cart pass. Mostly her eyes rested beyond the street, on the ships anchored in the river. In Bordeaux, the sight of ships once excited her. Here they were floating dread.

Sarah now wanted nothing more than sleep. Because she still carried the envelopes that enabled a new life for her and her brother, she dared not fall asleep. Taverns here were like those in France. Drunk patrons, or sleeping ones, seldom went home with what they brought in. Cut-purses thrived in New York. The number of drinking places was so out of proportion to the population they didn't worry much about getting caught from time to time. At worst they'd be dragged into the street where they'd get a beating, during which everyone from the tavern would participate. When their bruises healed they sought out another establishment where they weren't known. To help keep her eyes open, Sarah started singing to herself. It was an old French tune. No one objected.

Noah returned as promised. They walked up to Queen Street and followed it down to Hanover Square and her old lodgings just below on Duke Street.

Sarah did not tell Mrs. McDougall all her news, only that she was free of Mr. Croman. The woman squeezed both of Sarah's hands acknowledging the extraordinary news. She then broke away and retrieved a cape, a few petticoats and stockings belonging to Sarah.

"They smell of oak," Sarah said.

"As does my very breath," answered Mrs. McDougall, smiling at Sarah. "Do you want the mattress? It's near time to change the straw but it will do you for now."

Noah put Sarah's clothes under one arm and picked up one end of the hemp mattress cover. Sarah took the other. No sooner had they turned into Burgher's Path, which connected Duke to Queen Street, than Sarah wondered aloud,

"Why did I come this way?" She had previously said she wanted to wait outside the engraver's on Broad Street until she could talk to Jacob. Instead she was heading back to the warehouse.

Noah answered for her.

"You are in a hurry to become what your father is."

Sarah pulled up and looked into Noah's face for a moment before amending his statement. "Or was."

"You don't know that," Noah said.

CHAPTER 13

Separate Dreams

"NO? What do you mean 'no'?" Sarah's knees began to buckle. She slid down to the floor of the engraver's atelier, almost knocking over a tray of assorted gravers. Never in her life had she heard such insanity. Her beloved brother, the most important person left in her world, had just rejected freedom.

"Jacob. Jacob. Jacob, for you, for me, for us!" Sarah couldn't finish the thought.

"Sarah, you're not hearing me. Please. I beg you. Sister, understand. We have a future. You've just told me yours. I have mine, as an engraver. Do you know what that means? Soon I'll be able to put up my own shingle. I'll be an artisan.

"Mr. Fitler has too much business. Did you ever hear father say that, 'Too much business'? This will be soon, Sarah. Because I'm indentured and not a child, I don't have to serve the seven years an apprentice does. I'll be free at the end of the year. I can stay with Mr. Fitler or go on my own. He even intimated that he might refer people to me.

He says I'm already a good engraver.

"Think of it, Sarah. We'd each have shops of our own."

Sarah felt cheated, even though she understood why Jacob was so excited. As she had walked to Broad Street, the city's major commercial street, from her new house on Maiden Lane that Sunday morning, Sarah was still trying to digest her change in fortune. Though she had awoken in a house with no furnishings, not even a stool to sit on, and not a scrap of food in the larder, her mind filled with something that had long been absent: possibilities. They all included Jacob. It had always been that way.

"I can't do this without you, Jacob. I'm exhausted. I've hated for so long I feel empty most of the time. I'm not the girl I was in France."

"Of course you are, Sarah."

Almost angrily, Sarah cut him off. Had he seen so little of her since they were indentured that he didn't understand what she had gone through?

"Jacob, I've been violated over and over. I put a knife to a man's throat. I threatened to kill him. And I extorted retribution. Is that the sister you know?"

Jacob could think of no reply. She had walked in the door excited. And until this moment, he had been, too. After Sarah turned toward the window, Jacob sat down before his work table. He fidgeted with a graver.

"Let's go for a walk," Sarah said, as if she'd snapped her fingers and reclaimed her old self. "I want to see where the rich people live. Maybe we can be like them some day." She laughed but Jacob sensed she was serious.

The noonday sun was cooler than usual for late August as they headed up Broad Street. When they came to the City Hall at the intersection of Wall Street they turned left towards Broadway and the grand Trinity Church she had heard of. They were soon enveloped in a calm that the overcrowded east side of town never knew. Many of the imposing stone houses were fronted by rows of trees.

Sarah stopped to watch a young woman being transported in an Italian chaise by two men. How much profit would the fabric of her dress bring? Had she bought it in a shop on Hanover Square? Did the rich only shop there or could they be drawn to her future store on Maiden Lane? She had so much to learn about the city. She knew the streets on the east side like the back of her hand, even places a lady shouldn't know about. She knew people who lived day to day with a few words of English for begging and little else. Rich merchants did business on Queen and Water Streets but she didn't know them, or more importantly, their wives, the clients she wanted to pursue someday.

Jacob was just happy to be walking with his sister down a handsome thoroughfare. He was unaware how much they stood out from the gentlemen and red-coated officers with ladies on their arms. Sarah was aware. It wasn't envy, not in the slightest. It was the observant, calculating mind of a she-merchant.

When they reached the park at Bowling Green they sat down on the grass. No one else did so, probably, Sarah thought, because their clothes were too fine. Even the maids and coachmen had finer clothes. Finally she saw a man dressed no better than she and Jacob. He was heading back up Broadway, crying out "Tea water! Tea water! Come out and get your tea water!" Though the city sat between two rivers, the water was too brackish to drink. Ale was better. Fresh water, to drink and to make the fine tea the rich bought on Hanover Square, had to be bought from the men who threaded their way through the city, often blocking traffic, with carts bearing huge casks of water drawn from the springs that fed the Collect Pond northeast of the city.

"Come," said Jacob after a quarter of an hour, passed mostly in comfortable silence. Especially on a Sunday afternoon, the little green was an oasis to both of them. He reached down and took Sarah's hand, pulling her to her feet. Continuing south, he led her across the street. Before them was Fort George, where the city began when the Dutch owned Manhattan.

Jacob remembered the young British seaman on the Yorkton as they approached the harbor, lording it over the old Dutch sailor. "You lost it, twice," he had said, referring to Manhattan. Now Jacob could make out ships approaching the narrows, the mirror image of his memory of that cold December day on the Yorkton. Since their kidnapping almost two years before, it had been the first moment he felt hope of any kind. As they gazed beyond the battery, Jacob searched in vain for porpoises.

Sarah turned around to face the city and the two rivers, the North River to her left and the familiar East River to her right. There were ships as far as the eye could see. From a distance, she didn't feel dread. She even imagined one carrying cargo for her, for her and Jacob and no one else. The daydream was hazy and momentary but it left a seed of something she couldn't name in her mind.

Instead of walking down to the water they decided to head back to the engraver's. Rather than retrace their steps up Broadway they decided to explore. Before Bowling Green they turned right on a much smaller street. Despite the early hour, several women were slowly pacing back and forth eyeing soldiers and the few gentlemen who passed by. Later Sarah learned the street was known as Petticoat Lane, a lucrative stroll for prostitutes.

At Broad Street they turned left and soon spotted Mr. Fitler's sign. Sarah felt her good mood evaporating as she parted ways with Jacob. She was continuing home without knowing whether Jacob would be by her side on Maiden Lane.

When she had risen from her mattress that morning, she was eager to trample the odds that a young she-merchant had little chance of succeeding in a world of wealthy men. The city teemed with them, British aristocrats who had been awarded endless tracts of land to develop at their leisure, merchants who had discovered standing in society could be bought, and the original old Dutch families who needed neither land, money nor status.

This morning she had a future but now she was far from certain. As she made her way home, instead of noticing the handsome stone dwellings that housed merchants and well-off artisans she saw only ramshackle tenements, gin mills and brothels, and the rickety store fronts of shoemakers, seamstresses and laundrywomen. On Queen Street the voices coming from the public houses were already getting loud. In the late afternoon there was laughter. By evening there'd be fighting words.

As Sarah turned the key to her empty house, she thought of Noah. This was his world, a man who made his living from the docks, a man who had survived the brutality of the job and the competition from men who would kill to get to the head of the line in the early morning when jobs were handed out.

As she crossed Wall Street she paused and looked to her right. At the end of Wall Street, a slave market stood at the edge of the East River. It was known as Meal Market, the only market allowed to sell corn, grain or meal. Under its sharply pitched roof there was room for 50 men, women and children to stand on display for buyers. The city collected a tax on each head sold.

Noah was a free black, unlike most of the 2,000 blacks in the city. He'd told Sarah his family once had its own land under the Dutch but in the wake of a slave revolt the English had long ago denied blacks the right to own.

"We can't even stand in the street in groups of more than three," he'd told her. Whenever tension between slaves and their owners rose, Noah would make himself scarce. He had never told Sarah where he hid out. He said only that free was a word that angry white men don't understand.

As she closed the door behind her and looked at the two empty rooms on the first floor she decided to spend the first of her money. She would put it into Noah's hands to arrange for tables and chests for merchandise. For now, she wanted nothing for herself apart from wood, plates, utensils, a pot, a frying pan, and a kettle to suspend from the lug pole in the fire place on the second floor. She remembered the day she became responsible for the cooking after her mother died.

By the time Sarah got upstairs, she was remembering conversations she'd heard on the docks when running messages for Croman. People talked freely because she was a girl. She'd learned everything had a price. Croman blackmailed more than one importer of goods from the West Indies or England. The importer would have to give him first choice of everything, at a price he stipulated, or Croman would make sure they had no buyers, starting with him.

She and Noah needed to have a long talk.

CHAPTER 14

Taking Inventory

MORNING had barely broken when Sarah went around to the alley beside her house. Her bookkeeper's hands wrestled with the key to the heavy padlock that secured her warehouse. She left the tall half-crescent doors open to the breeze coming from the northeast off the river. The moment had come to discover the contents of the chests and casks and crates Croman had given her to start her business.

She had hoped they included fabric because her father sometimes traded in fabric. Though she'd never worn clothes made of anything other than linen, and once a shift of Indian cotton that had become damaged in shipment to her father, she knew fabrics well enough to sell them. She knew about fibers and weaves, colors and patterns, although she knew she needed to learn what women here thought was fashionable.

When she opened the first case she found no fabrics, only what looked like masonry tools, trowels, chisels, levels and gavels. Another chest contained pots and other cooking utensils. Sarah lifted some of them out and spread them on the floor. She wondered what they were worth on the New York market. Though her days in New York had been filled with figures while keeping Croman's books, she never had money of her own. Indentured, her owner provided everything he decided she required. On the second floor of Hanover Square she had handled silver and gold specie and paper money, but never spent any.

Suddenly, Sarah realized who her first customer would be: herself. She placed cast iron pots and a frying pan, as well as an iron spit and a spit basket inside a big baking kettle. Using two hands she attempted to drag it to the door. It was far too heavy. She removed everything from inside the kettle and tried again. The kettle budged, then scraped noisily across the stone floor. Forgetting to close the big doors behind her, she hauled the kettle to the house and got it through the door. She decided to leave it there so she wouldn't scratch the hardwood floor. Another chore for Noah. Returning to the warehouse she gathered the smaller items, which she managed to get to the kitchen. She was starting to feel the house was really hers.

When she got back to the warehouse, she found its doors closed. She didn't recall closing them. She hauled hard on the vertical wooden handle of the right-hand door. Noah blocked the way, hands on his hips.

"Trusting soul, aren't you?"

"My favorite burglar," she cried. "There's not that much in here now but someday there will be. I don't know how I'm going to manage to move it. The heaviest thing I ever carried in Bordeaux was a case of wine, and that's something Jacob and I would do together. For really heavy things, like furniture, my father would hire boys off the street, and if it was really heavy we'd leave it downstairs."

Noah quickly wedged open the other containers. Only one contained more kitchen items, including andirons, which she needed, but one piece was a luxury item, one that Sarah had seen before but never in someone's home. It was a spit jack, a mechanized rod used for turning meat over a fire. It was powered by cranking a handle, activating a series of weights that turned the rod.

"I'd wager you'd have some ready customers not too far from here," Noah said. "In the summer you often see a whole bunch of dandies and their ladies get together outside one of those fine homes by the water and roast turtles. At least once a week. They'll love this machine."

A larger container revealed great quantities of leather products, including shoes.

"I wouldn't have bought this load," said Noah. "Everything from England sells for a hundred times as much here as in London. We've got leather and we've got harness makers who can make anything out of it, belts, holsters, money purses, trunks, hoses. And we've got shoemakers. The British don't want us making our own things but only the rich can afford what they make in England and ship here. No, Croman didn't do you a favor unloading this on you."

Only one of the chests contained fabric. Sarah wanted to move it immediately into the room that would become her storefront. "Let's get some of this to the house, a bit of everything," said Sarah."

Immediately, Noah held up his hand.

"You've got some thinking and deciding to do first, about all this," he said, pivoting and waving his arm around the entire warehouse.

"Let's lock up and go talk," said Noah, as if he'd read her mind from last evening, when she returned home realizing she had no idea how to start out as either a storekeeper or a merchant. You owe me an ale from a few days ago."

"And a hunk of bread," said Sarah, keeping her books balanced.

CHAPTER 15

Two French Girls

New York City,
March 1, 1752

WINTER was nearly over. It had been kinder than the first three, when Sarah thought she would never be warm again. The snow, what there was of it this winter, had long gone. The air was fresh and the city had not yet wrapped itself in the stifling stench of summer when the drainage channels that ran down the center of streets became clogged with the festering sludge of refuse and human waste. The putrid streets alone were enough to make an ambitious merchant think twice about uprooting himself from Philadelphia or Boston to stake a claim in the fastest-growing commercial force in all the colonies. As a visiting Quaker businessman once put it:

"It is frightful hard to determine whether the greatest part of the malodorousness of the city is due to problems of sanitation and lack of water, or those of rank corruption."

The talk with Noah had borne fruit. While no

businessman, he had worked the docks all his life, since he was little more than a boy, and the docks were the lifeblood of the city. "A man hears things," he would say when Sarah pressed him to find out how he knew this or that. He had become a true friend since the day he found her crying in the street, but she often felt she knew little about him. She knew he shared a rickety wooden apartment in a yard between two buildings on Queen and Water streets with several other Negroes. She also knew he vanished from the city at times. He never explained why, or where he went exactly. She knew only that it was north, out of the city.

The first advice Noah gave Sarah about selling contents of the new warehouse was to not think like a storekeeper, although that was what the city's she-merchants usually were. Some occasionally inherited a warehouse but few ran them. Trading was a man's business.

At Noah's instigation a gangly, pock-marked man with a German accent knocked on her door not long after the talk. He introduced himself as Manfred Bauer.

"*Fräulein* Da Silva," he said. "I am always looking for new suppliers, ones who, how shall I put it, yes, ones who haven't learned to confuse greed with good business." Despite his accent and syntax, Sarah noticed, his English was fluent. "You will excuse me for my bluntness but my business depends on making many small sales rather than highly profitable single sales. I travel through the countryside selling directly to farmers and hunters who have no nearby towns where they can shop. I keep my prices low. Sometimes my customers have no money so we barter for goods I know I can sell elsewhere. Sometimes they pay me with a meal and a mattress and hay for my horse. It all works out in the end."

"What brings you to my door?" Sarah asked.

"I am told you have leather to sell."

Noah had talked to him.

"Yes, that I do. Come. My warehouse is at the side."

In her excitement about the opportunity to make her first sale, she got to the big warehouse door and realized she'd left the key in the house. Out of the German's sight, she ran up the stairs like a child on the trail of freshly baked bread. She'd stored the key under her mattress.

Manfred Bauer took every scrap of leather in the warehouse, including the shoes. "You can't have too much leather, *fräulein*." He also took the remaining kettles, pots and pans. "Even in hard times," he said, "people have to cook." He also uncovered two axes and several blacksmith's hammers Sarah had forgotten about. He spotted a chest Sarah and Noah had shoved toward the door. It contained small items. Sarah had decided to keep it for herself. She thought she might try to sell both at her house, which is where almost all shopkeepers conducted business, and by going through the streets, shop by shop. Even if she made no sales she would learn what price merchants paid for the things the chest contained, like soap, candles, dyed yarn and cloth.

When the German's cart pulled away, Sarah turned back and took stock of her warehouse. All that remained were a few of the linens and masonry tools. In her hands was enough money to restock her warehouse, in part at least.

In the coming weeks, Sarah walked every street of the city, entering every door bearing a sign of business. When their owners saw she wasn't there to buy goods or services, some literally turned their backs on her, complaining they were too busy to talk to a girl. For the most part, though, Sarah discovered that most were barely eking out a living and the merest hint of reduced costs found a sympathetic ear. Sarah realized as well that she had an advantage over male suppliers. The women, the seamstresses, laundry ladies, soap-makers, identified with the pretty young woman who stood before them. They once looked like her, and they knew the poor girl would look like them in a few years, if she survived at all.

On her walks, Sarah discovered that the suffocating

congestion and noise of the east side of the city made it feel huge. In fact it wasn't. She calculated that, without stops, she could walk every street and alley in city proper in just over an hour. The chaotic city was manageable, she thought. She'd either make a name for herself or make a nuisance of herself trying.

With the money from the first sale, Sarah had managed to cobble together several small deals to buy goods from minor merchants with parlor-sized warehouses. Rather than pay a carter, whose rates were established by the city, she carried most of it on her back, making multiple trips. One morning, her head bent under her load, she bumped into Noah. After she explained what she was doing, Noah told her to give him the load and sent her back to the seller to take on another charge. By noon, the two of them had deposited her week's purchases in her own warehouse.

At moments like that, a restocked warehouse, a first sale, Sarah's mood soared. She felt she was back to her old self, and she cherished that. It seemed like a miracle. Was it even possible, she'd wonder. It meant not everything died inside her on that rainy night in Bordeaux, or in the upstairs workroom on Hanover Square, being raped by the most hideous human being she'd ever known.

However, the buoyant mood was now enduring for shorter and shorter periods of time. She'd hit the streets again in search of business. The smell seemed twice as foul, more of the people she shouldered her way by seemed destitute and their harried faces less friendly. Sales brought in a pittance and she feared for her future more often than not.

It was not something she could talk to Noah about because he regarded a precarious existence as simple reality. You do your best to survive but you don't ever presume to control your fate. Only Jacob knew how to steer her straight again without dismantling her dreams. But she had rarely seen him in the past two months.

Jacob was now a free man, a paid man, but it seemed

to Sarah that whenever she visited the engraver's in the evening he was still working, both to help Mr. Fitler meet his surplus of orders and to put away money for his own shop. One evening she met Jacob on Beaver Street. He was in such a deep conversation with a young man the two would advance only a few steps then stop to better talk, then set off again. She caught up to them easily.

Jacob introduced his young friend as a recently apprenticed silversmith. "He has much to teach me," Jacob said, leaving Sarah utterly confused. Jacob didn't think he'd ever seen his sister speechless, then he realized it had been so long since they'd had a real talk that he had not mentioned his latest plan.

"Peter, this is my sister, Sarah." He was not much older than Jacob, Sarah thought, but he had the air of a man who had a place in the world. "I have shown Peter some of my etchings and he said…"

"Allow me," Peter interrupted, "or you will seem boastful." To Sarah he said, "Your brother possesses an extraordinary eye. I feel he could design or copy anything."

Sarah could feel the excitement the two young men shared.

"I have only recently put up my own shingle," said Peter, "but already I am unable to resist the idea that with your brother's skills and mine we could make our mark."

"Not immediately, Sarah," Jacob hurried to add. He hadn't forgotten how upset she was when he wasn't prepared to say he would set up shop in her house at the end of his contract. "Nothing is in stone."

They were on their way to a new coffee house on Wall Street.

"Coffee," Peter had said grandly, "what an ingenious way of disguising our foul water."

When they arrived, Sarah peeked inside. It looked as if it was intended for gentlemen and merchants. Sarah declined to join them, lying to Jacob for the first time in her life.

"I've arranged to meet Noah at the Homeless Mule." As she walked down Wall Street toward the river she felt something familiar but foreign. She felt a chill overtake her.

It was only late that night as she lay awake on her mattress, listening to the tide-like rise and fall of inebriated eruptions from the street, that she realized the chill was identical to the abandonment she felt when her mother died, a sense of abandonment that echoed in the darkness of the Yorkton's hold that first night at sea when her father ceased to be in her life.

The following evening, Sarah did in fact go to the Homeless Mule. After dipping her bread into a bowl of thick soup, her eye fell on a woman seated alone against the back wall. She was not young and looked frail. She lowered her lips to the ale the proprietor had just placed on her table. Was it too heavy for her to lift? Sarah watched her discreetly and ate.

When she finished, she walked over to the woman's table.

"May I join you?"

The woman looked up. Sarah first noticed the sunken eyes, then the fine nose.

"I have nothing to share," said the woman.

"I need nothing," Sarah replied, noticing a slight accent.

"Sit, if you wish," said the woman. Sarah could barely hear her small voice. The tavern was already getting loud as men streamed in from their jobs on the docks.

"Are you French?" Sarah asked in French.

The woman's eyes brightened for a moment.

"Yes, from La Rochelle."

"I'm from Bordeaux."

Both were port cities, La Rochelle being right on the ocean about 35 leagues by sea north of Bordeaux.

"Do you need something to nourish you?" Sarah asked.

The frail young woman protested with surprising vehemence. Sarah saw the pride.

"What do you do here?"

"I'm a seamstress. I sew for ladies. At least I once did."

"What is your name?"

"Geneviève."

Sarah ordered an ale and bread. When it arrived she shoved the bread to the middle of the little table.

Geneviève's story came out in pieces, as if well-intentioned short phrases had come to her tongue and no further, only to be forgotten about for moments on end. Geneviève seemed unused to talking to people. Then, unexpectedly, the thought would escape her mouth. Because of the time that had elapsed since her last statement, Sarah wasn't always sure whether it had been meant to complement something she'd said earlier or whether she was introducing something new. Between particles of explanation, Geneviève's mind seemed to get lost looking back in time, like someone going to the attic to find an old waistcoat but ending up sifting through articles from their youth.

"Here, Geneviève, eat." When the seamstress had turned inward again, Sarah used hand signals to order another bowl of soup. She didn't think that Geneviève was crazy. She was simply too hungry to think. Sarah had known that feeling on the ship when, even during moments of violent seasickness, the gruel she needed was so repulsive that in her delirium she wished to starve to death. She had already been too weak to put two thoughts together. While the winds on deck screeched and the sea nearly stood the Yorkton on end, she remembered having a thought that was crystal clear but linked to no previous thought: "if only this one thought vanished from my mind there would be nothing. I would be dead, and free."

Geneviève ate.

"I was born in Martinique. My parents were Huguenots.

I'm not sure what that even means. I have no church. I am damned. New York is the door to my damnation."

Sarah could tell the woman had received some education. Perhaps she had come from a merchant family with some money.

"The story I was told was that the king hated Huguenots. He decided to expel them from France because they would not convert to Catholicism. My parents were sent across the sea. Few people survived, yet there were soon more than 1,000 of us there on the island. All of us who were expelled from France were sent as *engagés*.

"My mother taught me to sew and I began to work for the wife of a plantation owner. I was still a little girl. The mistress said my little fingers created miniature flowers that made my dresses unique. No one could copy them. That's what my mother told me."

Sarah, the she-merchant with few prospects, was dying to ask one question, but forced herself to let Geneviève's story run its fractured course.

"It was a beautiful island, more beautiful than France, but my mother said the plantations were dying. Even though the king sent us there he then decided he wanted all of us to leave Martinique. My mother said the plantation owners were Huguenots also, like we were, but the King's decrees made it impossible for them to make a profit anymore. Many of us started to flee to the nearby British islands and the colonies here. My mother said the Catholics lined up to buy the plantations for next to nothing."

Geneviève said her mother wanted to go back to France. She wanted to die there, where her family had lived for generations. Her father didn't want to go back but was willing to because her mother was ill.

"The plantation owner and his wife announced one day they were going to South Carolina," Geneviève said. "They might be able to once again run a plantation. At least that's what they'd been told. While preparing their belongings to leave, the owner's wife returned two dresses to me and gave a bag of Spanish dollars to my father. She told him we would no longer be welcome in France because we were Huguenots, just as we were no longer welcome in Martinique.

"The owner's wife had given my father enough money to buy our passage to France. My father told me this once we were aboard ship. He said that while onboard, if anyone asks, and especially when we get to France, we must lie. We must say we were on the island before it became overridden with exiled Huguenots. We must say that we are good Catholics and we are returning to France because your mother is ill.

"And that's what we did," said Geneviève, staring into the empty soup bowl.

Sarah wasted no time. She didn't ask whether Geneviève's mother had survived. She didn't ask how Geneviève came to New York.

"I have some cloth in my warehouse. Would you like to look at it and tell me if you think you could ever use it for your customers? I could make you a good price. Between two French girls."

Geneviève smiled for the first time. It was a small smile, expressed mostly with the eyes.

"May I bring some fabric to your shop tomorrow?"

CHAPTER 16

French For Sale

THE following morning Sarah found the dressmaker's shop on Bridge Street, two houses west of Broad near where it ran into Queen. She carried two bolts of cloth from the warehouse goods Croman had originally left her. One was a light brown, the other a forest green. To Sarah's eye, the cloth was well made, but selling dresses to someone as far down the social ladder as she was wouldn't return much profit. Her opinion didn't count.

From the street, Sarah couldn't see Geneviève through the window. Once Sarah had entered, she found the dressmaker's small frame seated before a large table facing the window, absorbing every last bit of morning light. Geneviève appeared to be cutting out a sleeve for a dress, which was spread horizontally on the table. Sensing Sarah's presence, Geneviève carefully placed her shears in what looked like the lid of a hat box, alongside brass pins and needles of varying sizes and a collection of thimbles. Next to it was a box of threads. An iron sat on a counter at the back of the room.

The smallness of the shop surprised Sarah. Everyone said the city had never been more prosperous and that meant the rich wanted more than ever to dress the part. She remembered looking in the widows of milliners' shops on Hanover Square and on Broad Street. The items for sale seemed countless, not just fabric but baby and children's clothes, hats, dolls, needles, thread, laces, ribbons and hair pieces.

This time, Geneviève greeted Sarah with a full smile and launched into a wave of excited French. Being able to speak her own language again was like suddenly encountering a long-lost sister. Sarah, too, felt a warmth between them that defied the fact they'd only met the night before.

"I'm sure you are wondering how I can make a living in such a hole in the wall," Geneviève said, somehow reading Sarah's mind. "As you can see, I cannot even offer you a place to sit."

Geneviève then ushered Sarah to the large table and she reached for the bolts of cloth in Sarah's arms. Together they placed them on the table. With practiced hand and eye, Geneviève quickly appraised them.

"A countess would shake her head no, but a merchant's wife? I am sure I can put these to use, Sarah."

The night before in the tavern Sarah had told her she would part with the fabric for the tiniest of profits.

"Shall we sit together and talk of other possibilities?" Sarah nodded but, to Geneviève's amusement, rescanned the room for a chair.

"Come."

The dressmaker led Sarah through a back door to a second room, about the same size if not a bit smaller. There was no window. It was clearly a fitting room. Against the front wall, by the door, was a partition that could be used if a lady required privacy for her fitting. Against the wall to the left was a stepladder to reach materials stored on high shelves, and a bench underneath. On the facing wall, to Sarah's right, was a large mirror with candle holders on either side. At the back there was a door that led to another room. To the right of the door were square shutters that blocked the back room from view. It opened, Geneviève explained, to the kitchen, which would provide heat in winter to the fitting room. Geneviève slept in the kitchen. She rented the two rooms upstairs.

They sat together on the bench, seeing themselves in the mirror opposite.

"I work slowly," Geneviève explained, "because I have no help. But that has ceased to be the major problem it was when I landed here and first put my services on offer."

She explained that when she was young, in La Rochelle, she worked in a large atelier with six other seamstresses under a mistress.

"Sometimes gentlemen would come to speak to the mistress and pretend to watch us work. Their perfumes would cling to everything and nauseate me for days. Some of the girls said these men would sometimes tell the mistress to have this seamstress or that one conveyed to a chateau. Days later the same girl might be brought back and left at the door to resume her work. If it happened to a young girl she wouldn't say much but she mightn't look you in the eye. If the mistress wasn't watching, the other ones, the older girls, would show off a trinket the lord had bestowed on her for her service. A priest even came in from time to time to request a girl to recut a dress for a lady supposedly too ill to leave her home. We would never get to the lady's home. We would always be told to stop at the church vestry. On parting, the priest never closed our hands over coin or a bauble. He would say, 'You can't spend or sell a blessing such as the one I've bestowed upon you.'"

She told Sarah tailors would come in and tell the mistress what the girls were doing wrong.

"The men were the artists, the mistress would say,

while we were nothing but stitchers. That's why she paid us almost nothing. But we still had to be on our best behavior if a great lady came in to have a gown prepared. Often it was the mother who dictated what the daughter wanted."

As Sarah listened to the bitterness in Geneviève's voice when she talked about men, she wondered if her new business partner would also find herself capable of holding a knife to a fat man's neck. At times, Sarah was haunted by the awareness that she could. Other times, the knowledge made her feel taller, stronger. Her father or mother would have been horrified if they'd seen her with the fat man that night. What would they think of their little girl?

"Now, my dear," said Geneviève, "you have heard my story, just as I heard yours last night. We are two French girls stranded in a very strange land. But I find that this is a very different land. At home we had no options, ever. We had no money and no way of making money. Our lot was our lot. Here, however, I suspect that's not quite the case."

While listening to her, Sarah was about to protest that her France was not nearly so bleak. She loved working for her father. Though they had little money each new shipment of goods, coming in or going out, meant possibilities. Her father's eyes reflected them. He wanted his children to know that the next deal he made might mean expanding the business and having good food on the table year long. The children felt they helped him play his cards. They were all in it together. In France, Sarah never felt the bleakness Geneviève talked about. That was foreign to her nature until she was dragged aboard the Yorkton. It was full-blown by the time Croman's belly pinned her to the wall. Now her nature was an unknown. Her moods were fickle. Some days the sun shone. Other days it rained and the wind blew cold.

"How do you survive?" Sarah finally asked, rising from the bench to walk about the room. She stopped in front of the mirror and looked at Geneviève's image as she asked, "Do you make more than shifts and dresses for the wives of poor men?

"In fact, I do," Geneviève answered. Sarah turned to face her. Geneviève paused, her eyes suddenly assessing Sarah's, as if deciding whether it would be wise to reveal a secret.

"England is so often at war with France, and we are so often afraid the French in Canada will invade us, I at first tried to hide the fact I was French by birth. I still have an accent but everyone here has one of some kind. I began to realize first of all that no one really cared because we're all from somewhere else. Then, while fitting a dress for a young woman, I realized from her conversation with the friend who had accompanied her that a British gentleman, wholly loyal to His Majesty, was prey to having a soft spot for French women. And, here's the important part with regard to us, an English gentleman was also prey to having, shall I say, a hard spot for the way French woman appear in French clothing. Remember, Sarah, the mothers of these English gentlemen are not here in New York to disapprove. While all the chatter may be about the latest men's and women's styles in London, men will be men, and French women will always be French."

Last night, this little woman found full sentences painful. Had it been simple hunger, or general distrust, or the intimidation women feel in a smoky room full of half-drunk men? This morning she commanded rapt attention as easily as a needle pierces cotton.

Sarah, too, was feeling French again.

"When that woman returned for her final fitting," Geneviève said, "I addressed her in French. It was just as I suspected. Haltingly, she replied in French. She was not French. No, no. Not by any means. But she wanted to be, or pretend to be at least. I could tell. And, I learned in no time at all, that there was a young monsieur who had captured her heart. She wanted to capture his. You know the story."

Actually, Sarah didn't. Her young life had been so busy

in Bordeaux with business, and taking care of her father and the household after her mother's passing, she'd never had time to idly gaze at boys and wonder. Her family never had time or money to socialize. She was a young girl with a head for the puzzles of business and happy to be no more than that.

"It turns out the girl could carry on a polite conversation in French. It had been part of her education. It saddened her she had so little occasion to speak the language, so I prolonged the fitting a little in order to encourage her French."

The result, said Geneviève, was another dress order.

"She'd just bought one and now she wanted another, but not cut the same way. She wanted a French dress and asked me about the latest Paris fashions. I lied a little and said I was not abreast of the very latest styles. The truth is I'm entirely out of touch. Nevertheless, I assured her I could come up with something that would arrest the attention of the beau she'd mentioned. She was so excited. The choice of fabric would be up to me, just like the design."

Geneviève said she made more money with that one sale than she'd made in seven months.

"And as for the design, all I really did was make it less English. She told her mother the design was French influenced. That's how she put it, French influenced, a crime far less serious in her mother's eyes. The next thing I know, a friend of her mother wants one. She, too, knows a phrase or two in French.

"And this is where, should you be interested, you come in, *ma chère*."

Geneviève's idea was simple. Instead of having certain regular customers come to her shop, she would offer them the convenience of going to their homes.

"Between the two of us, Sarah, we could carry a good number of fabric samples with us. We needn't carry bolts. For this kind of customer I stand to make enough money to be able to afford to cut samples from bolts. I would cut them in a way that would leave them still usable for trims and the like at a later time.

"Once there, at their home, I would present you as a teacher recently arrived from France. I would say that while you're getting settled I was employing you to assist me from time to time. The details are of no consequence. The important thing is that during the discussion with the customer about her new dress I would often confer with you, giving us a chance to prattle on in French.

"As silly as this must sound to you right now, I can all but guarantee I personally know of several well-bred woman in New York who are bored out of their minds and would delight in spending their husband's money. I even foresee some of them inviting their young lady friends to attend the fittings.

"Furthermore, to show you how I've thought this out, I think it not at all impossible to see you engaged to teach French, to them and their daughters, should they have any."

Sarah could only say yes. The idea seemed brilliant on its own, not to mention that she desperately needed money. The stock that now sat in her warehouse was the only thing that separated her from poverty. She had reached the point where she could not afford to buy any more.

"You are pretty, Sarah, which is of great value to our scheme. They will be easily charmed, and more importantly, so will their mothers, who are the ones in a position to loosen purse strings. However, you will need a much nicer dress. Is that the best you've got?"

The dress betrayed the warehouse work she did, the dirty taverns she ate in, and the cobblestones she sat on when the summer heat made scouring the city on foot for business a Herculean task.

When Sarah didn't answer, Geneviève said she'd have a new one ready for her in two days.

CHAPTER 17

Scottish Justice

SARAH was still thinking in French after bidding Geneviève goodbye. The thought of another potential source of income inspired her. She had barely walked half a block up Queen Street when another idea overtook her thoughts. Why hadn't she thought of it before? It was at least worth a try.

She turned left at Hanover Square and walked by the familiar shops, turning left again on Duke. Her heart beat faster as she spotted her first home, the cooper's atelier.

The cooper's wife immediately showed her in, clearly happy to see her looking well.

"I'd like to propose something to Mr. McDougall if he can spare a moment. It's an idea for business and it has to do with Mr. Croman."

The mere mention of Croman's name alarmed Mrs. McDougall.

"Don't worry, please. It's just an idea. Your husband will probably say no out of hand, but I'll not know until I ask."

It was at least five minutes before she returned with her husband. Sarah suspected she had been reminding him of what Croman had done.

"So, Sarah," he said, "you come to me as a person of business."

"And as a woman who will always feel gratitude toward you and your wife."

"Out with it then," he said, giving full vent to his Scottish accent. "Your idea, lass."

Sarah explained how Croman had given her a house and a warehouse on one hand but on the other, she had recently learned, he had apparently instructed merchants under his control to not let her buy from their warehouses or even talk about investing a little money in an order from overseas. More and more, Sarah said, she had to rely on the city's Jewish merchants, who seemed more independent of Croman's influence.

McDougall nodded. He knew as well as anyone how Croman worked.

"I'd be nigh on becoming rich if it weren't for Croman's monopoly on cask making."

"It is true that I am in need of money," Sarah said, "but I'd happily have to fast a day if I knew I was hurting that man. The crux of my idea, Mr. McDougall, is this. My warehouse doors are almost never open because I have almost no business. Furthermore, it is located almost out of view on the side of my house, in what looks at first glance like an alleyway between my house and the house beside me. There are no passersby."

McDougall was clearly listening, she realized.

"Since no one knows I exist I imagined having one product to sell in my warehouse, a product I would be absolutely discreet about, made known to the right ears only by a second party."

"Spit it out, girl."

"I would like you to provide me with a few casks at a

time, somehow disguised as a load of something else, in a wagon I hope to provide, not from a licensed carter. At first, I would carry your casks on consignment. I would sell them at their just price, far above what Croman forces you to accept. I would take only the smallest of profits. The rest would be yours."

"How would you alert buyers without alerting Croman's boys?"

"On the docks I've seen over and over again that trade is expanding so fast that it is impossible to meet the demand for casks. All kinds of casks. And I have listened to merchants who are desperate to be able to ship their cargos. If we could secretly get the casks to my warehouse I know I can eventually find discreet customers who will be thankful just to have access to them. I repeat, sir, we would have to start small."

When she finished, McDougall laughed.

"I've made a fool of myself," thought Sarah.

"What does a lass like you get fed as a child to turn you into such a wily practitioner of business?"

"Business is all I've ever known," Sarah answered.

"Well, Sarah, we do indeed share an opinion of Croman. And he takes money out of our purses, yours like mine. But unlike you, I do not worry about where my next meal is coming from. A Scotsman most certainly does not turn away money, but he's more greedy about seeing justice meted out to those who do him and his family harm. I would happily see to it that some insecurely fixed casks fall off the next load I deliver to Croman's minions. I'd have already been paid for those by Croman, so they would be free to you to get you started as a supplier of casks."

Sarah told him she would first have to arrange for access to a wagon, but she already had an idea for that. McDougall told her he would immediately begin work on designing an illegible cooper's stamp to put on the barrels he'd make for her.

"We can't have Croman's lads discovering you selling my own casks."

He stated the price he would accept for his "new line of casks". It was actually higher than the price Croman had driven down. That way, there be a small profit for Sarah as she helped McDougall find more buyers. He hoped the greater volume would restore his profits to the days before Croman muscled his way to a monopoly.

They shook hands on the arrangement. He said Sarah should make sure her people arrive on a day when the street has already been busy with Croman's carters taking away casks.

"They're usually gone just before noon. Keep your eyes open but you should be good to start at noon. You will not arouse anyone's curiosity."

Mrs. McDougall hugged Sarah.

"This time it seems you are parting with something more valuable than a mattress."

CHAPTER 18

Childhood Ends

September 13, 1752

"DEAR Sarah, you are indeed part of the family now."

Patricia Van Huisen was 19, not many years younger than her French tutor. She was blond-haired. Her locks were thick and curly. Sarah found them not just pretty but luxurious. However Patricia confessed she wished her hair was black. "More French" was how she put it. She made a joke of it but Sarah realized that Patricia was one of those people who are never happy with what they have, and Patricia had everything Sarah could ever imagine. Patricia was willowy and graceful in her every movement, and her eyes were so blue they ought to be copied as a background for the family crest.

Patricia was the only daughter of Clara and Johannes Van Huisen. Her mother was English born. Her father's family had settled New York when it was still known to the world as New Amsterdam. He began planning the mansion before he started courting Clara. His first instinct was to employ Dutch architecture and construct it with a gambrel roof. For the most part, he thought of himself as a British subject, and proud to be one for he had prospered. However, unlike some of the original families, he still could speak Dutch fluently and was doggedly proud of his ancestry. Most of all, he simply liked the symmetry of a two-sided roof with two slopes on each side, the upper slope positioned at a shallow angle and the lower one at a steep one.

Not long after he began courting Clara, the idea of a Dutch-styled mansion was put in a mahogany drawer and never spoken of again. Clara had been raised in London. As a child, the dollhouse of her imagination was always Georgian, and so it would be now, she told Johannes. She also intimated that she was not speaking of a townhouse style of Georgian construction but of something more along the lines of a British country house.

"Already," she said after her future husband agreed to the anglicizing of his future home, "I see the pilasters in the grand foyer." For a moment he feared she would request towering columns on the outside to frame a grand entrance door. He was not going to hand her such a suggestion.

Patricia told Sarah that her father sat on the Provincial Assembly of New York, and had for many years. He owned a great deal of land north of the city, along the North River, as well as some closer, above the Trinity Church Farm west of Broadway. She said he also leased numerous properties in the Dock and the East wards, which provided the bulk of his immediate income.

"Mama says he is the city's cleverest speculator."

From the moment her French student mentioned property, Sarah's mind chiseled into her memory trying to unearth details of the land fraud Croman and the captain had cooked up. After several months of lessons, Patricia introduced Sarah to her father. Sarah had come that afternoon in the company of Geneviève, who was by then making her fourth dress for the girl. Today would be the final fitting.

Geneviève's plan to enact a French invasion of Patricia's world had proved highly profitable. When Patricia first asked her mother to dismiss the middle-aged tutor she had hired for her, her mother refused outright, thinking her daughter simply wanted to lighten the burden of education that would make her a marriageable lady someday. Then Patricia explained that her new teacher would be the dressmaker she already knew.

"I cannot and will not accompany you to that fetid part of town for both fittings and French lessons. Good heavens, girl, why spend our days in Gomorrah when we have the joy of this home? Have your French seamstress attend to your betterment here."

When Geneviève arrived that first day with Sarah in tow, carrying the bolts of cloth, it was her mother who ushered them into the salon. Sarah wore the new dress made for her by her friend. She felt she'd never looked more presentable. Beyond the niceties, Patricia's mother said nothing and left the room soon after.

"She likes you, Sarah," said Patricia, almost gushing.

Having the company of two women from France convinced Patricia more than ever that mastery of French would eventually distinguish her from the other attractive girls entering society. She soon announced to her mother that Sarah would take over the instruction, leaving Geneviève free to concentrate on her trade. Within weeks, Patricia doubled the frequency of Sarah's visits and whenever possible contrived clothing-related excuses to request Geneviève's presence to enhance their conversations.

Geneviève was as pleased with the development as much as Sarah. She had already made four dresses for Patricia as well as undergarments. Soon she would be able to afford to purchase the satins and silks she needed to make the gowns Patricia imagined and reap a vastly higher profit. Thinking of Patricia's eyes, Geneviève already knew the colors she would recommend: ivory, sand, blue-grey and, maybe, pink.

After the first meeting with Sarah and Geneviève together, Patricia had dropped any pretense of treating them as tradespeople. They were her French companions, proving, thought Sarah, that rich people can be as lonely as poor ones.

Patricia and her mother no longer went to Geneviève's shop. Patricia's mother liked the new arrangement. She spoke of how utterly overwhelmed she was planning for receptions she would host or preparing for other society events, let alone the time required to redecorate the house. Once one room was redone, another would rankle her finely honed English esthetics.

By chance, a few weeks after the French invasion, Patricia's father appeared unexpectedly in the salon. He embraced his "dear, dear daughter". Later, Geneviève said she had never seen Patricia's mother do that. Perhaps, she suggested, family warmth was a Dutch thing.

Mr. Van Huisen confessed he had forgotten the French his ancestors had once been required to know to conduct trade in the Nieuw Amsterdam. Sarah switched immediately into English, which she sprinkled with a few phrases of Dutch she'd learned on the Bordeaux waterfront. The broad-shouldered Dutchman laughed. Sarah had already won over "the city's cleverest speculator".

Sarah walked Geneviève to her shop before continuing home. The coins for the French lessons were starting to add up. As she walked, the small but reliable income left Sarah feeling relieved enough to enjoy the freshness of the early autumn air. When she arrived at Maiden Lane she went down the alley to open her warehouse. The first things her eyes fell on were barrels.

The first barrels the cooper made available under their arrangement to get back at Croman had been purchased by the man who Sarah had hired to pick up the casks that accidentally fell from the shipment destined for Croman. It was the German country merchant Sarah had met through Noah. To avoid suspicion, the cooper dictated that only four casks would make their way to Sarah's warehouse.

It turned out that was all the German merchant could handle when he arrived at the warehouse and announced his intention to purchase them. To save room in his wagon, he immediately filled them with goods he'd bought earlier in the day to take back to the country.

The deal Sarah had made with him was that she would forego her small profit in exchange for the service he provided in retrieving the "missing" casks and delivering them to her. On subsequent visits he would pay full price like any other customer. He returned two weeks later saying he had buyers for more casks. By that time, the cooper had arranged for 16 casks to arrive at Sarah's door. Eight of them had been transported by the German and Sarah happily gave him the discount to take care of his unofficial carting fees. Two new merchants had inquired about buying casks from her.

She would have no difficulty making sales as time went on. Her biggest worry was that her customers would mention the new source for casks to the wrong people, Croman's warehouse workers and goons. Noah had told her Croman forced some competing merchants to pay him to ensure their cargoes were delivered safely.

Because so many merchants had turned their backs on her when she sought to make modest purchases in the past, she had made it a point of getting on greeting terms with a couple of the Jewish merchants down toward Dock Street. At first, like all the established merchants, they were cautious, and especially suspicious of her sex and her youth.

Sarah had learned that establishing a relationship was a necessary first step before proposing business. Often she made it look as if she was just passing by. There were plenty of reasons for her to walk those streets that were the engine that drove the city's economy. By mid-summer she felt one of them had started to take a liking to her, appreciating both her smiling perseverance and her looks. He was far from young but he was far more agile on his feet than her father at about the same age.

"I am Asser Pietersen," he said. His family had come to the new world from Amsterdam under the old regime. Sarah introduced herself in Dutch. He nodded and switched to Yiddish. When she explained that she was the daughter of a Bordeaux merchant, Asser's interest increased. "Perhaps we will find a way to do business someday. Maybe we have connections in common."

Sarah didn't want to press her good fortune, explaining she had to be on her way. Though she had nothing to offer at the time, nothing to sell, no money to buy, she knew what her new acquaintance meant by connections. Jews had the advantage over many merchants by the very fact that they had been forced to stay on the move and settle in many lands. They had learned to invest in many countries to make their wealth less vulnerable than it would be in a single location. Because it was a boon to conducting international business, many, like her, spoke several languages: Hebrew, Yiddish, German, Spanish, Portuguese, Dutch, and whatever other language that could lead to doing business. Shared language and family ties underpinned a network very different from the one open to British merchants.

That first meeting with the Jewish merchant was several weeks ago. As Sarah closed the door to her warehouse, she found herself thinking of Asser and the fact she now had casks to sell.

After depositing the warehouse keys safely under her mattress, Sarah went out again. She would walk down Queen Street until it became Dock Street in the hopes of spotting Asser.

It was her lucky day. She didn't know if his office was at the warehouse where she first met him or not, but it didn't matter. There he was gesticulating with both hands as he spoke intensely to a young man. She waited at a distance until he was through, then approached him with a big smile.

He seemed pleased to see her, a break in his busy day, she thought. Soon she found herself telling Asser a little more of her own story, the kidnapping and that her father was a Jewish merchant in Bordeaux.

"You didn't tell me you're Jewish, but I knew from the moment you first addressed me last month."

He did not make a big thing out of it. He didn't smile. He didn't hug her. Yet she felt her brother was suddenly no longer her only family. She didn't tell Asser that her father rarely went to synagogue, although they kept a Jewish home.

Sarah went on to tell him that her father used to trade occasionally with someone in the West Indies, in Hispaniola. She didn't remember his name. "Do you have business in Bordeaux?"

"Ï have a cousin in the Antilles who does do business in Bordeaux. I'll make enquiries. Thank you. Any contact is good."

"Mr. Pietersen." A man with a gold waistcoat interrupted them. "Good day to you, sir. May I call on you tomorrow afternoon? I will have some news for you about a ship bound for Africa."

The man was an agent, Asser said, before turning his attention back to Sarah.

"So, you are all alone here?"

He listened while she told him about Jacob, explaining that although he was now an engraver he had grown up as she had. Their whole world was business.

"There's a synagogue in Mill Street. Did you know that? Perhaps you brother would like to attend."

"I intend to see him this evening. I will tell him."

Thinking this was as good a time as any, she asked if he was in need of casks.

"Not today but I surely will at some point."

"I can get them at a price much fairer than what is usually charged on these docks," Sarah explained without explaining how. She knew Asser would know of the artificially fixed price and the pressure many merchants were under to buy from Croman's people.

"When that day arrives, do you think it possible that I could provide casks in exchange for inventory for my warehouse?"

"There are infinite ways of doing business," he said. "I'm sure your suggestion numbers among them."

By the time Sarah got to the engraver's on Broad Street 15 minutes later, she suddenly felt exhausted. She had been French all morning, then Jewish for much of the afternoon. She had been a language tutor and she had been a businesswoman. How many cobblestones had her feet traversed since getting out of bed? She would be home soon. She'd come only to hold her brother and make sure he was fine. Of late he always was.

As soon as Jacob came to the door, greeting her with his biggest smile since their youth in France, he took Sarah by the hand and stepped into the street with her.

"Come. I have something to show you."

"I'm exhausted Jacob. Could we sit here and catch up?"

He laughed. "No, we can't. It's not far."

They walked up Broad Street and turned left on Beaver Street for one block. Jacob took her by her shoulders and turned her to the right onto narrow New Street. He guided her forward past the first door on the right, then turned her to face the opposite side of the street. He released her shoulders and stood beside her, facing the same way. He waited.

Finally Sarah saw it, a handsomely lettered sign above a door: Longsmith & Da Silva, engravers of fine silver and copper.

"Jacob, you are a free man." Sarah said the last two

words softly and slowly. She turned to look into Jacob's glistening eyes. "We have survived the nightmare, each of us in our own way."

As Sarah embraced her brother, she felt both excitement about the future the two of them would now determine entirely on their own, and a vague melancholy that her beloved brother was now a man, an independent one, working on his own, living on his own, deciding on his own. As adolescents in Bordeaux, they were inseparable. They had one goal, their father's success, one that would be passed on to them someday. Another life could not be imagined. Now the man she clung to was also a man apart. Childhood was over. The pain and fear of the past three years had made that clear, but she'd never formulated the thought before.

Jacob made no attempt to add to his sister's words. He was speechless. Finally, he shoved his tongue into his left cheek to sabotage the grin that had frozen on his face as he stared across the street at the sign, his sign. He then took Sarah's arm and they walked back to the corner and turned right. In a moment they were at Bowling Green. Like the first time, they sat on the grass and talked.

CHAPTER 19

Pope Day Profiteering

November 5, 1753

THE evening had been cold. The glowing embers in the fireplace offered only an illusion of warmth. Sarah had gone to bed wearing three shifts and had bundled her feet in a homespun dress. She pictured her feet like the pedestal of a statue. Sarah often thought she would never become accustomed to New York winters. Her last thought before falling asleep was sensible: "For God's sake remember to unwrap the dress before trying to stand up in the morning."

The ship rocked and twisted. From behind her closed eyes she saw light. The night always black. She opened an eye. A lantern hung from the companionway. It swung angrily, each extreme of the pendulum illuminating an expanse of the ceiling before the light swept downwards, soaring over bodies huddled against the horror of certain drowning. A sudden corkscrewing of the ship caused the lantern's side-to-side motion to stop. For a second, the lantern hung motionless the way gravity intended it to. Then, following the ship's dive into a trough, the lantern's base crashed hard into the ceiling. The lantern's glass shattered. Then darkness. A scream. "Fire!" Sarah floated over her dream and saw flames igniting the dress wrapped about her feet. As her body floated back down to the deck, she watched indifferently as the flames reached higher. "Warmth. At last," she thought. Then, footless, her body toppled on top of the others. In panic she tried to wriggle herself away from them, using only her upper body. Suddenly the ship stopped moving. She stopped her frantic wriggling. Light streamed down through the companionway, brighter and brighter. Morning had arrived. The sea was calm. Not one of the bodies around her even twitched. She could hear no breathing. She was alone in the hold. Then she saw she had feet again. They were bare. Shielding her eyes, she climbed to the deck. The sails hung limply. The crew had disappeared. She was alone. The ship was hers. She climbed to the quarterdeck and grasped the helm the way she'd seen the seamen do. She used all her strength to spin the wheel to port. Nothing happened. She spun it to starboard. Again nothing. She felt powerless. The sea had ceased to move. It was as flat as the sky. Because the ship sat still, she felt she was standing on dry land, surrounded by water. For an absurd instant, she also felt she may have been standing on the sky, upside down, and that there was no land. Because the sun felt good, she didn't care where her dream had taken her.

When Sarah got up to prepare porridge, she was filled with an extraordinary sense of gratitude, but to whom? To what. She had no idea, but there were worse ways to start a new day. She felt it was going to be an important one. Something of significance would occur.

Before leaving to do her waterfront rounds, which she did regularly in the hope of finding business, overhearing useful gossip, or running into Noah, she went around to the back and entered her warehouse. She'd looked in the day before. This morning its contents might have something to do with the mysterious gratitude the dream bequeathed her.

The trade in Mr. McDougall's casks, despite the fact she gave most of the profit to him, had been a godsend, not only because of the money it put in her purse but because having them for sale opened doors. They were her lifeline.

To her, seeing the casks stacked in her warehouse was like seeing a cask floating in the sea like a buoy, unsinkable. She and the cooper still kept the cask numbers small to avoid causing suspicion but along with the money she got from tutoring the rich speculator's daughter her income was such that she'd managed to increase her inventory to the point where it was close to half full. The German had become a regular customer, for casks and much of what else she'd bought for resale. She'd also been established long enough that people were dropping buy to see her goods. Being located almost right on top of the Fly Market at the bottom of the street meant that a lot of people now saw the large sign Jacob and Peter had made for her. Noah had joined the two young men to help them mount it on the stone wall of her house: Da Silva Wholesale & Retail. It was 12 feet in length.

As she started walking down to Water Street to do her rounds, Sarah felt a surge of pride as she took in the sign. Her father would be proud of her, or would have been, she thought. In an instant, her eyes were stinging. If only she knew what tense to use when his face floated before her eyes.

It was low tide and the shoreline of the East River stunk of the sea itself and refuse from ship and shore. Having lived her entire life by the water, the smell was comforting. Her morning routine seldom varied. She would walk by the newer warehouses, homes and little offices on Water Street, reclaimed from the river not so many years before by the draining of swamps and little inlets and covering them with landfill obtained during their construction. Eventually she would continue south to Dock Street to see

Asser Pietersen to share a few moments in Yiddish and, as always inquire about news of her father. Some days he was too busy to talk about the weather or even business, but he always had time to answer her question.

"We will know some day," he would promise. "Perhaps the very next sail entering the bay…" He always let the sentence trail off. Sarah would always nod optimistically and thank him for his concern. "Adie," she would often say, good luck, as she gave him a little wave goodbye.

When she found Asser at his office, she remarked how quiet the docks seemed. "Not much business to be had today."

Asser laughed, but not unkindly, at her ignorance.

"Perhaps like me you have no desire to strut about drunkenly condemning a religion that at the moment has no effect whatsoever on my life."

Sarah didn't get the hint.

"It's Pope Day," Asser said. "A holiday."

Sarah remembered. She'd never witnessed the procession because she had not been allowed to go out at night during the three years she was the fat merchant's servant and slave. However, on her errands for him one day she had come across a copy of The Gazette, the city's first newspaper. The paper proposed new anti-papist verses that could be sung on Pope Night, the colonial version of England's Guy Fawkes Day. In England they celebrated the capture of the converted Catholic who had plotted to burn down the House of Lords as part of a conspiracy to assassinate King James I and restore a Catholic monarch to the throne. Here in New York, Sarah read, drummers led the way as the Pope Day effigies, "hideously and humorously contrived", were carried about the city on a bier at night. The Devil stood behind the Pope, paying his compliments to him with a three-pronged pitchfork. The third effigy on the bier, Sarah read, was the young pretender to the throne, standing before the Pope, waiting his commands.

Sarah's father had told her about the Catholic Church's persecution of the Jews in Portugal and Spain, and Asser had told her about the persecution spreading to the Jews who'd fled to Brazil, some of whom ended up being dumped in Nieuw Amsterdam, for a price, by the captain of the French ship that transported them. At first the settlement's governor, Peter Stuyvesant, wanted no part of the Jews, but was finally ordered to accept them by his boss, the Dutch West India Company, which had several Jews on its board.

"We're not loved, Sarah, but we do well here," Asser said.

"Do they hurt the Catholics here?" Sarah asked.

"They've broken some windows over the years," Asser said, "but it is my understanding, not being British nor feeling any particular loyalty to them, that the celebration here only pays lip service to the Crown."

Asser was the most interesting person Sarah had met in the New World, not just because like her father he was a Jewish merchant but because he seemed worldly. He knew things.

"I think the authorities," continued Asser, "are likely aware of the shallowness of our loyalty toward the King, but they tolerate the celebration and debauchery because it goes down in their reports to His Majesty as subjects standing up like their brethren in England to praise the monarchy.

"And they know it lets off steam," Asser said. "They're nervous right now about the mood of the city. People feel threatened, yet the Assembly does nothing to silence the French in Canada once and for all.

"More pressing, there's constant whispering that a certain mercantile cartel is conspiring to cause the value of the penny to be devalued. Since the Assembly fixes the price of a loaf of bread, more pennies would be needed to buy that loaf. Members of that unofficial cartel not only make the flour, they pay the wages of many a worker. As you know, they're paid in pennies. If this all comes to pass, the workers will see fewer of them."

Asser paused.

"Don't be alarmed, Sarah. It is my nature to see backroom deals. I am a businessman, am I not?"

Sarah laughed with him. She was now a businesswoman, but, as yet at least, her mind didn't work that way.

"So the Pope Day celebration is a protest?"

"Of sorts," Asser replied. "The authorities, unless they are more dull-witted than generally thought, know the pretender on the bier has come to mean not a pretender to the throne of England but the aristocracy, of whom we have too many representatives here in New York. As you surely know, the big merchants and the aristos run this colony arm in arm. When the cheers ring out tonight as the pretender bursts into flame, the people will have a local authority or two in mind. The people can't storm into the Assembly to complain. They would be considered troublemakers or traitors. But at least a night of fireworks and firewater dulls their resentment."

Sarah knew nothing about who ran the city, only that a lot of people were rich while a lot more were desperately poor. She saw both every day. Jacob would be all right because he had become an artisan. She wasn't sure how to measure her status.

Tonight, she decided, she would celebrate having simply survived in New York. The effigy of the devil on the bier tonight will have a name. Sarah didn't know any politician's name but she knew the devil: Zachariah Croman.

He had earned her hatred for a lifetime. Sarah doubted she had ever hated anyone in France. If she had, it was a passing annoyance compared to what she felt for the fat man. Though she wanted to throttle him, there wasn't a day when she didn't hope she would never set eyes on him, and she seldom did. But she often heard people speak of him, on the streets by the East River, by shopkeepers she sought to supply. Jacob told her Croman's name could be heard at the Wall Street café he and Peter now frequented, fascinated to have a bird's-eye view of earnest young men and arrogant dandies with money to invest in shares of cargo or the insuring of ships, or how to win back clients in the West Indies who were abandoning high-quality New York flour for cheap Pennsylvania flour.

"If I were wealthy," Jacob once said, "I'd soon be even wealthier by acting on what I hear at this café."

"Such as?" Sarah enjoyed playing him along because it made her happy to see him dreaming.

"Such as, my dear sister, investing in a unimaginably large quantity of flour, to be transported by ships owned by several different men, and dumped on the market in the islands, Barbados, Jamaica, the Leeward Islands. I have learned that they give over every speck of land to the growing of sugar cane. They must import everything else. The scheme, and Peter here is my witness, should it come to fruition, would suffocate the export trade of the Pennsylvania mills.

"And here," Jacob said, putting his arm around Peter's shoulders, "is where we ride the coattails of entrepreneurial genius and make our fortune." Sarah could only imagine what stories Jacob would spin if he were drunk, which he never was. "Once the Pennsylvania markets were all but shuttered, we would start increasing the price of flour in the islands. At that point our profits would know no limits. We, the astute gentlemen of business who gather in the convivial atmosphere of our café on Wall Street, would have a monopoly."

Peter never mentioned Croman in connection with flour, but Noah had a short time ago. She and Noah were sitting on a crate under a hot sun on Water Street. Sarah had simply asked if Noah had been finding work. He answered that he'd spent two days loading barrels of flour, stamped with Croman's mark, onto a brig that plies only the Indies run. Sidestepping Britain's Molasses Act, which tried to force the colonies to buy more expensive British-made molasses, the brig would return with smuggled molasses for New York's distilleries. Croman had one, Noah said. It helped keep him fat because there was not only a huge local market for rum. New York now exported rum to England. It was the only locally manufactured product His Majesty would accept. "His royal subjects must be a thirsty lot," said Noah.

Like Asser, Noah knew things. Sarah wasn't surprised by what Asser knew. He was educated, worldly. But she never ceased to be amazed at what Noah knew. His sources were different. As the docks thrive, so did New York. Dock workers knew things. So did slaves. They eavesdropped on their owners and they talked among themselves. Many of them worked on the docks and few didn't know Noah. Over the years he'd become an institution to anyone who'd care to remember the face of a black man doing a white man's bidding on a wharf.

. . .

From Asser's, Sarah headed west to the Van Huisen home. She was sure Patricia wanted what she referred to as "a French afternoon" today, but now that she knew today was a holiday she wasn't certain.

The maid who answered the door said the family had gone to the country for a few days. Because she knew Sarah, she divulged that they'd gone to Greenwich Village to the north of the city.

"Far from any rowdiness that might occur tonight."

Sarah was no stranger to rowdiness. Seamen and longshoreman made a second career of it in Bordeaux as they do here. But she had always been smart enough to keep her distance. She fully intended to do so tonight, although she acknowledged a building excitement. She had survived. She and Jacob were free. Jacob had a profession and she had a future. All that deserved celebration. Pope

Day would be her stage.

Though the leaves on Broadway's many trees had fallen, the street remained stately in Sarah's eyes. Patricia had said there were now more than 13,000 people in New York. As she stood on the wide street and gazed at the handsome homes she thought the air seemed fresher there compared to the east side of town, where almost all those 13,000 people lived.

She turned east to New Street and Jacob's atelier.

"Fear not," he said. "Peter will be joining us tonight, willingly or otherwise."

The next stop on her way back to her dockside stomping grounds was Geneviève's little shop. Sarah let herself in and found her friend in the back room, napping.

"Will you join Jacob and I tonight at the Mule? I feel like celebrating."

Geneviève, looking more frail than usual, appeared to feel little inclination to get out of bed.

"There should be enough people squeezed into that little room that we'll be toasty warm no matter how late we stay."

After giving herself another moment to wake up fully, Geneviève nodded her agreement.

"I'll be grateful for the company, Sarah. I'm too slight of frame to force my way to the little bar on my own."

They agreed to meet at Sarah's house, a holler away from the tavern.

Now to do the impossible, thought Sarah: Find Noah. Because it was a holiday there was little reason to think she'd find him on a wharf. Of the thousands of people in New York, he was the kindest. She wanted him at their table tonight.

As she passed through Hanover Square, she realized she was famished. She'd had milk and bread after rising but had simply forgotten to stop somewhere for dinner. At the Old Slip market below the square she bought roasted oysters and set off up Water Street toward Maiden Lane. Not far ahead she saw men milling about a warehouse. A few wore check shirts, fearnought jackets and Monmouth caps. Sailors. As she got nearer, she realized it was one of Croman's warehouses, situated conveniently across from a ship chandler's shop. He probably owned that as well, she thought.

When she came abreast of the warehouse she heard orders being barked from down the wharf. Crates and casks were being unloaded from a single-sail boat while another, smaller boat sat about 30 feet from the end of the wharf, its small crew using the oars to keep the boat from being carried down to the bay by the outgoing tide. Standing in the bow was a small man in a blue cloak. When a gust of wind momentarily lifted the cloak, Sarah saw the man was wearing a deep yellow waistcoat. Why would he stand precariously in the bow when he could wait seated on the front thwart? Impatience?

Hungry, Sarah decided to sit by the side of the street, opposite the warehouse, and eat her oysters while watching the men work. It turned out the offloading was nearly complete. Within 15 minutes of her arrival the last of the cargo was being deposited in the warehouse while the long oars of the single-sail boat were pushing it away from the wharf. As it did so the oarsmen of the small ship's boat began making for the wharf. The first combined thrust of the oars toward the shore sent the little man sprawling backwards between the first pair of sailors. No sooner had the boat tied up than a large man began to approach it. Sarah had glimpsed him from the corner of her eye as he exited the warehouse.

The absurd silhouette was Croman's. He approached the little man with the yellow waistcoat. They shook hands but the little man was clearly upset. Sarah couldn't make out the words but she saw Croman spread his arms with his palms facing upwards. Since it was Croman, Sarah knew the gesture was not one of supplication. A knife to his throat was the only way to make him beg. Croman must be telling the little man that he had no choice about something. The two men walked up the wharf and disappeared into the office in the front of the warehouse.

As Sarah reached for the last oyster a large man appeared from nowhere and silently squatted beside her. Noah.

"It seems the whale has made another enemy," Noah said before Sarah could swallow the last of her supper and greet him.

"What was going on down there? Were you working? It's a holiday, isn't it?"

"It is," answered Noah, "and because it is I've got a few unexpected pennies in my pocket."

Moving almost in unison, they got to their feet and began walking slowly toward Maiden Lane. Noah explained that in the morning Croman had arranged for a small group of longshoremen to stand by despite it being Pope Day. He promised a bonus if he found work for them.

"I heard about it only because I know the skiff owner Croman hired this morning to visit a few of the most recent arrivals in port. Each ship's cargo, or at least part of it, was in Croman's name. From what my friend understood, the message he was told to have passed on to each ship's captain was that Croman was in a position to see to the unloading of their cargos but it would be at a price since laborers were scarce on a holiday. He knew they'd be anxious to offload so they could take on outbound cargo and make sail quickly."

"Why was the little man in the blue cloak so angry?"

"It turns out," said Noah, "that our fat friend demanded a king's ransom for the service he'd provided. When the little fellow, the ship's owner, refused to pay, Croman mentioned as calmly as you like that he had the power to make sure no one in New York would be available to load his ship with outbound cargo. I heard him say it myself."

At the house, Sarah offered Noah cider and a bowl of raisins. As he supped, she told him about her plan for the evening, a celebration not of the thwarting of the Catholic plot against the King of England but of the kindnesses that had made it possible for her to escape certain destitution on a foreign shore. She didn't mention anyone by name, or mention the specific kindnesses.

Noah agreed to join them at the Homeless Mule. The early evening was growing chilly. They sat by the fire and waited for Geneviève.

CHAPTER 20

Fire

SARAH could only stare in wonderment at Noah. Geneviève had just arrived and the two women greeted each other warmly in French.

"Bonsoir, Geneviève," Noah said.

"You speak French?"

"Some," said Noah.

Sarah thought she knew him well by now but he always had a surprise or two to remind her that no one knew him well. Sarah had already noticed that he pronounced the dressmaker's name correctly. Geneviève cringed inside when people addressed her as Jenny Veeve.

Sarah could see that Noah wasn't about to offer an explanation. Perhaps, she thought, he'd picked it up on the docks. About a quarter of the longshoremen in the city were sailors who decided that the back-breaking work and irregular employment was preferable to the brutality of life at sea.

"But most of all," Noah had told her, "seamen decide

that a world without women is fit for only priests and madmen."

Revelers packed the street. Geneviève tripped over one of them before they'd gotten half a block from the house. The man was unconscious. Noah slapped his face lightly hoping to revive him. If left on the street he was sure to be trampled by a horse or run over by cart wheels. At best, he'd wake up without boots. But the man was out cold. Sarah bent over to help Noah drag him to the side of the street but Noah didn't need any help.

When they stepped into the tavern they saw that Jacob and Peter had already secured a corner table. Sarah had meant to ask him to get there early to do just that but had forgotten.

Sarah sat on a bench beside Jacob, putting her arm around his shoulders. Geneviève squeezed in next to her. Out of room on the bench, Noah took the chair facing them. As Noah adjusted his chair, Peter looked at Jacob questioningly but Jacob never saw the glance as he toasted to "All our good friends under one roof."

That launched a series of toasts, the first from Sarah whose joy-filled awakening that morning led her to bring them all together under the guise of marking Pope Day, which meant nothing to them, except possibly Peter, who had grown up here and had English parents.

"In gratitude to all who helped my brother and I survive freedom."

"An odd concept," said Peter. "Surviving freedom. You make it sound like something onerous."

"You're in a cage," said Sarah. "You have no money. You have no friends. You know of no place on earth that would offer you shelter or sustenance even if you were free to go there. Remove the cage. What have you got?"

"*Toujours rien*," said Geneviève. "Still nothing."

Sarah gave Geneviève's shoulder a light squeeze. They understood each other perfectly.

"Well, it's still preferable to being caged," Peter said.

"I suppose so," said Sarah, giving Peter a polite smile before taking another small sip of ale. Conversation petered out for a moment. Restarting it was daunting in the tavern when other voices refused to give way for minutes on end. It was like waiting for the tide to go on the ebb.

Sarah saw her chance and said in her loudest voice:

"I'm so proud of you, Jacob."

Jacob smiled broadly and kissed his sister on the forehead.

"You're an artisan now, a professional."

"A poor one, sister, but that will change. Peter and I have big plans."

After a moment, he added:

"But we have worked no harder than you, Sarah. You've overcome more than both of us put together. And look at you now."

Sarah had not grown accustomed to seeing her brother so infrequently. The affection behind his words told her she needn't worry.

"To Sarah," said Peter, although he knew nothing of what Jacob was referring to when he said she'd gone through more than they had. Though he was recognized by fellow engravers as a master despite his youth, apprenticing for the required minimum of seven years was not a boy's idea of happiness. However, Peter had worked hard at letting pride in achievement negate a youth spent working long hours and sleeping in the cold corner of his master's atelier. He even agreed to another two years of apprenticeship in order to have food and lodging while advancing his skill to that of a master engraver. When he was released from his apprenticeship, his parents sang his praises but they didn't offer to take him back under their roof. He wasn't overly upset. They had long ago become strangers to him. He knocked on their door because of a vague notion that it was the proper thing for a son to do.

Jacob was speaking English. His time in New York had removed any trace of an accent, yet his words now bore a hint of his French origins. Geneviève noticed. "He's thinking in French," she thought. "He's speaking with his heart."

"You're my little sister," Jacob said, "who came here with only the clothes she wore. And you have a house made of stone, a store and a warehouse. There's nothing between me and survival but a sheet of copper that I have learned to master. Because I love it, it's not so hard. But you, you have to put your sweet face forward in a man's world, a far from honest one at that."

"And," said Geneviève, "we have a foot in the door of a wealthy family on Broadway. Who knows where that will lead? Maybe even down State Street. I hear it's even more fashionable."

Eventually the ale loosened Noah's tongue. He was in the middle of a story about how he learned French. It was like pulling teeth, thought Jacob, but Sarah didn't mind. She knew Noah's rhythms. He was chained to the bulwark of a leaking Antilles-bound ship when a gale overtook them less than a day's journey from their destination. Noah stopped talking when he noticed the room growing silent table by table. Most eyes had turned toward the door. An old man seated near the entrance pushed himself to his feet and pulled the door open. The sound of panic flooded into the tavern, growing louder as the message spread up and down the street.

"Fire! Fire!"

It took a long time for the small tavern to empty. Even when most had made their way out the door, it was clear that people on the narrow street were still forming an almost impenetrable wave of bodies, all pushing north toward Maiden Lane. Fire brought everyone into the streets at any time but the numbers were already swollen by Pope Day revelers.

When Peter and Sarah stood, Geneviève stayed where

she was, at the table. Her tiny frame would be crushed in an instant. Suddenly, Peter hurried toward the door. "The fire must be close. I can smell it," he announced as he leaned out. A moment later he hurled himself into the crowd. The last thing his friends heard was, "I don't want to miss this."

Sarah could see that Noah was agitated, although his body was motionless as he stood next to her with his eyes fixed on the street. When the crowd finally started to thin, he pulled Sarah aside. He cupped his big hands and placed them against her ear. The pitch of his voice was so low she had no trouble making out his puzzling words over the sound from the street. "I can't stay here."

"I want to go, too," she said, puzzled.

"I mean I have to leave the city right now."

The puzzlement on Sarah's face dissolved into alarm.

"Do you know something about the fire?"

"No, no," he said, taking her shoulders and looking into her eyes to reassure her. "Nothing like that."

He left his hands on her shoulders. After a moment, she placed her hands around as much of his wrists as she could.

"Fire is the last word a black man wants to hear in this city. Every time there's a fire someone runs through the streets yelling that the Negroes are rioting again. All someone has to do is say they saw a black man running from the scene."

"But you were here with us all evening."

"That won't save my skin in the street."

With that, Noah bolted from the tavern, turning the opposite way, against the flow of the crowd. Sarah got to the street in time to see him suddenly stop running. He turned slowly and looked up Water Street. Was he looking for her or looking for anyone who might be coming after him. Almost casually, he turned on his heel and sauntered down what Sarah thought was probably Old Slip, the river just a few yards away.

Jacob was waiting for her at the tavern door.

"Let's find out what all the excitement is about," he said, taking her arm. Before Sarah could tell him she was afraid for Noah, they arrived at the corner of Maiden Lane.

"No! No! No!"

The instant Jacob heard her he thought of the terrified wailing aboard the Yorkton when a gale convinced them all they were about to drown in a black, frigid sea. Jacob grabbed her from behind as she started to bolt to the other side of the street, her side of the street.

CHAPTER 21

More Fire

MEN had already formed a bucket line from the river just below the Fly Market.

While a bull of a man with an axe quickly broke the large black padlock that secured the tall warehouse doors, two others had scaled ladders placed where the flat warehouse roof met the pitched roof of the house. For now, the flames were breaking through the middle or the warehouse roof. The two men poured the first buckets on the roof adjacent to the house, then took their positions on the roof itself. Four men, after handing up their buckets, remained on the ladders to complete the line. Sarah watched breathlessly as the men on the roof hurled the contents of the buckets toward the center of the roof.

Jacob still stood on the other side of the street, now holding Sarah close to him in a hug. Shock had paralyzed Sarah's mind. As he'd done on the ship, Jacob used observation and logic as a wall against his feelings. He'd already determined that the men on the roof knew what they were doing. They were saving the house. He also took in how quickly men exhausted themselves hoisting heavy bucks. From what he could make out in flame-brightened light on the street before him, and in the torch light that reached the river, there were 41 men battling to save Sarah's house.

"Do not move from this corner, Sarah. Promise me."

She looked at him steadily but said nothing. Her eyes followed him as he turned and dashed toward the river. Half an hour later she spotted him a hundred feet away, above the market. He was tirelessly passing buckets to the man ahead of him. As rested men replaced the weary, Jacob moved up the line.

"Eleven o'clock. The fire is contained." The night watch was more confident than Sarah. The bucket line had stopped. The men who comprised it stood wearily on the street. One man stayed on the edge of the warehouse roof, while others entered in search of smoldering cinders. Sarah ran down Maiden Lane until she found Jacob.

"Come, Jacob. I need to see with my own eyes."

Jacob put down his bucket and led the way to the alleyway and the warehouse. He physically pushed his way through the wall of men at the gates, calling out, "Owner. Owner. Kindly make way."

All was black. All was lost. Small objects were unidentifiable. Larger ones left traces, a barrel hoop here, the tongs of a hoe there, and axe blades. They had been her last purchase, made from a small merchant who rented a tiny warehouse space not far away. She bought all two dozen, thinking her German friend would have no trouble selling them on his rounds among farmers and hamlets. The fabrics she'd meant to take to Geneviève weren't even worth looking for.

Tears rolled down Sarah's face.

"It's the smoke," she said when Jacob reached out to comfort her.

"Come. We must inspect the house," Jacob said. She led the way around the corner to the entrance.

Sarah retrieved two candles from the table in the storefront. Nothing seemed damaged. The smell of smoke was more intense on the second floor. Sarah collapsed on her mattress.

"What am I to live on?" Her voice was small. It was a declaration of dismay more than a question. Jacob did not attempt an answer.

While outside he'd seen that the roof on the warehouse side had been blackened by the rain of soot. Now he stood on a chair passing his hand along the edge of the ceiling where it ran along the wall of the warehouse. It was cool. He pounded his fist against the ceiling but detected no weakness.

"You can't stay here tonight, Sarah."

"I want to."

"The smell is worse here. You'd blacken your lungs. Besides, you can't risk building a fire to cook. We must wait for a day or two. You can stay with me."

Jacob sat on the mattress beside her. She leaned into him, head against head. At last Sarah stood. She reached down to offer Jacob a hand up. Maybe the gesture was nothing, Jacob thought, but Sarah was taking charge again.

No sooner had they set out for the atelier on New Street than Sarah remembered Geneviève. They stepped into the Homeless Mule. It was almost full again but there was no sign of their friend.

Peter was waiting for them when they arrived. He quickly poured two mugs of cider and offered Sarah a cloak to warm herself. Jacob sat her on his mattress and pulled one of the room's two chairs close to her.

Peter remained standing as he listened to their account of the damage.

"Why did you leave us?" Jacob asked.

"When I got to Maiden Lane and saw where the fire

was I turned back and tried to find you. The crowd was impossible. Besotted, for the most part, intent only on witnessing a spectacle. I know as a fact they greatly delayed the men and women who tried to do what they were supposed to do: bring their buckets from home. When I finally got to the corner there was no sign of you. I was about to return to the Mule when a voice cried out that there was a second fire. They ran up to Queen then and I followed. Someone said, 'Maybe it's the niggers again.'"

By the time they'd reached the Old Slip, Peter said, flames could be seen to their right, somewhere near Hanover Square.

"The flames rose much higher than they did at your warehouse. When we got near we couldn't make out the house right away because the fire engine was in front."

"Why was their no fire engine at Maiden Lane?"

Peter said he didn't know.

"There are only two in the city."

"You would have still lost just about everything," Jacob said, "even if the engine had been sitting outside when the fire broke out. All they can do is try to stop fire from spreading to other buildings."

Sarah's eyes dulled. Her mind needed sleep.

"Sarah, Sarah," Peter said gently. She turned her head just enough to see his face. "Who lodged you while you served out your indenture?"

"A cooper. On Duke Street. Why?"

"The place is no more."

When the news finally sunk in, Sarah asked:

"And the cooper, Mr. McDougall, and his wife?"

"I fear I can't say. I don't know them."

Sarah was on her feet and halfway down the stairs before stopping to tell Jacob what she was doing.

Looking up the stairs at him, she yelled, "This is no coincidence!"

She called to Peter, asking if she could borrow his cloak. It was now well past midnight on a November night.

"I must know if Mr. McDougall is safe."

Duke Street was barely three blocks away. Moments after arriving at the blackened, smoldering shell of what had been her first home in the New World Sarah spotted the old cooper and his wife seated on the opposite side of the street, the same vantage point she had had when watching her own dreams get sucked up in flames. Neighbors had offered them blankets and capes. The cooper stared across the street unseeing.

Sarah made her way through the crowd, tense with fear that another fire would breakout in the city. When she reached the cooper and his wife, she kneeled and took Mrs. McDougall's face in her hands.

"We've lost everything, Sarah. Everything." As she spoke those words, she clasped her hands over Sarah's.

They remained motionless for a moment before Sarah spoke.

"As have I. Everything. This very night."

The cooper stirred himself at those words.

"Fire?"

"Yes. At least I still have my home, where you must come and stay. Only the warehouse burned, with all your casks."

"Are there other fires?" He let the question hang.

"I think not," said Jacob. "We appear to be the sole victims tonight."

"You mean targets," the cooper said with vehemence.

His words echoed Sarah's reaction the instant Peter told her the location of the second fire.

"Croman," Sarah said.

"Croman," repeated the cooper.

CHAPTER 22

Friends

AS THE four of them made their way to Maiden Lane and Water Street they heard the night watch call "3 o'clock and all is well". He repeated, "All fires have been extinguished. All is well." The cooper had not said a word since he had struggled to his feet on Duke Street to properly thank Sarah for the offer to stay at her home until he and his wife could get back on their feet. In his heart he didn't believe they ever would. He'd spent 33 years crafting the most important tool of international trade, casks of all sizes and descriptions. His atelier and home was beyond repair, most of his tools probably unusable.

At Sarah's door, McDougall stopped Sarah, who had her key in hand.

"May I?"

She led him around the corner to the alleyway and what was left of her warehouse. Every seventh house was required to light a torch after dark. Sarah's was one of them. She took it to light the way to the alley off Maiden Lane and the warehouse. At the warehouse door, she handed the torch to the cooper. Despite the flames and having been splintered by axes, the tall doors still hung from their hinges. Sarah grabbed the edge of one of them and pulled it partially open. The cooper's torch betrayed a dark swath of soot on her dress.

She was the first to step in. Though it was already soiled, Sarah raised her dress a few inches and waded through the debris. She picked up a curved barrel stave and faced the cooper. She dropped it and picked up an intact hoop that hours before had firmly embraced staves. The cooper found a bolt of patterned fabric. Somehow a hand's-width portion of one end escaped the flames. The torch illuminated pockets of the dark room. The pile of ash lay over the remains of what were once sturdy beams and boards. To Sarah they were like bodies covered in black cloth, like the barely breathing lumps that lay around her by night aboard the ship. She remembered often wondering whether they were alive or dead. Morning would tell.

"Mr. McDougall?" Sarah spoke softly. The cooper stood motionless, seemingly looking at the back wall. A flickering of the torch's flame revealed blue-gray eyes that were looking inward.

"Mr. McDougall?" He turned, facing her as she waited by the door.

"Girl," the old man said in his gentle Scottish brogue, "you may call me Aiden. This night, I think, two fires have forged a family. We should speak as such."

Back in the house, by the unlit fireplace, they drank cider. They sat in near total silence. Was it shock and fatigue, wondered Jacob, or was everyone afraid to speak the name of the man who boasted of being the lord of the docks, the rapist, the thief, the extortionist and, if he'd had his way tonight on Duke Street, the murderer.

Determined to get past the despair in the room, Jacob asked Aiden if he had money to buy new tools.

"As Sarah told you, you are both welcome to stay here as long as necessary. Without your tools you can't start rebuilding your future."

"We have a little money. What of it there is is stored under the floor near the fireplace. I fear the heat may have melted the coins."

"If the flames didn't reach them directly," said Jacob, "it is possible they survived. I am an engraver by training but I am learning the art of silversmithing from my partner. I may be wrong but I have reason to hope your coins will be safe."

For the first time since arriving, the Scotsman seemed alert. Jacob could see the power in his wrists and forearms as he clasped his pewter mug.

"If only that turns out to be the case," Aiden said.

"You could work downstairs if you use the two rooms, could you not?" said his wife, Arlene.

Aiden didn't answer her question. He was focused on Jacob's suggestion he might not be without a penny to his name. He was calculating.

"If that money is usable, yes, I can replace some of my tools. But more important, I'm thinking now, is that until I can re-establish my own cooperage, I should be able to assign some of my orders to other coopers. They would keep the King's share of the profits but I could save again."

"Would that be enough?" asked Arlene.

"Remember, lass, I own half a warehouse of oak. I could offer them a more than fair price on fine oak, guaranteed clear of sap, for the staves and headings. Is there more cider, Sarah?"

After a throat-full of the new cider, he looked at his wife. There was both affection and hope in his eyes, Sarah thought.

"And, my dear, as you very well know, I am owed some tidy sums by buyers of my casks. Sarah is the only one I allow to sell on consignment."

Sarah wondered whether one of his debtors was Croman. He was infamous for delaying payment to workers, then disputing what they claimed he owed.

Aiden did not name him. There would be no point in speaking Croman's name until they had at least an inkling of an idea about how to make him pay for all but ruining their lives. Each of them hated Croman, and had for a long time. There was nothing to be gained that night from listing his sins. They had to focus now on simply surviving.

Sarah squatted beside her brother's chair. He put his arm around her. Again he had been the one to stand above tragedy and try to point the way to hope. Thanks to him, Aiden was eager for the new day. Sarah prayed he would find his money under the rubble. As for herself, she saw herself eking out an existence on the pennies she might continue to earn for teaching a rich girl French. Patricia's enthusiasm could disappear like last year's fashions.

Cold November rain fell on Aiden and Jacob later as they used sticks and a broken brick to clear away the rubble near the spot Aiden hid his money. Dawn had scarcely broken. They set out early because Aiden was impatient to find out whether he was a pauper. He dismissed the offer of a bowl of corn mush and quickly downed a tankard of ale. Jacob was also anxious to return to New Street, both to do his day's work but also to pick Peter's mind about the double arson.

They were in luck. They smashed through the small piece of flooring, the loose end of a broad plank giving way quickly. Prying it up, tthey not only found the sack of coins but mixed with it was a small amount of paper currency, a fact Aiden had not mentioned last night. To disguise the sack, he had placed a thin, flat rectangular piece of stone on top of it. If a burglar had pulled up the loose floorboard he would have seen only what looked like rock-strewn earth.

Quickly, Aiden separated the paper money and ran his fingers through the coins. Jacob performed the same exercise, inspecting the coins with an engraver's eye. The only damage he noticed was the curse of the province, coins whose edges had been filed off for copper and silver to use in counterfeit coins. And, after hefting several, Peter was sure there were a good number of those as well.

It was said that half the money in use in the New World was counterfeit. After a silver-engraving lesson one night, Peter had even joked that Jacob would soon have the skill to become a master coiner, or clipper, as counterfeiters were called in the sentencing notices posted in front of City Hall, which housed the city's jail on Wall Street.

Once, while running an errand for Mr. Fitler, his master, he stopped to watch a man being punished for coining. He was tied to the back of a horse-drawn cart. The sentence stipulated that a portion of each ear was to be cut off, to mark him permanently for what he was, a counterfeiter. He was then condemned to be paraded at the cart's tail to six different locations, going counterclockwise around the city, for public viewing while he suffered three strokes of the lash at each stop. The final three were administered at the starting point, City Hall.

"A right unlucky one he is," said a bystander. Jacob eavesdropped on the man's conversation with two others. He learned that counterfeiters were rarely caught and even then, rarely convicted. Who was to say who created the false coins they were caught passing. The only way they could be convicted was either being caught with tools for forging or being squealed on by a counterfeiter trying to make a deal.

Peter thought no more of coining until now.

Aiden was beaming, holding the heavy sack high in triumph.

"I'll not only rise from the ashes, Jacob. I'll exact retribution on that blubber-bound soul."

Jacob clapped Aiden on the shoulder in solidarity, then whispered in his ear. "Half the town would know who you mean by that description. I think it wise to let Croman think he has gotten away with his deed and that he has ruined us, that we are too weak to retaliate."

As they parted, Aiden said, "Young man, you are as clever as that sister of yours."

When Aiden let himself in and stepped through into the kitchen on the second floor, Sarah embraced him even before Arlene could reach him. Holding the sack out to them, Aiden had no need of words.

"This rain can't dampen my spirits," Aiden said, "but my bones are aching with the cold. I think we can make a fire. The rain has surely drowned the last burning embers. We're safe."

"When you were a young man, my husband, you never took notice of cold."

"Age only means I need you by my side more than ever. Come here." He wrapped his arms around Arlene and held on as if he were never going to let go.

Once the fire had taken hold, Sarah went out to the Fly Market at the bottom of the street. With Aiden's success that morning, she didn't tremble at the idea of parting with money to buy a leg of lamb, potatoes and squash. They would dine well that afternoon.

CHAPTER 23

Something To Chew On

A MONTH later the meal celebrating hope for the McDougalls had become the last one Sarah remembered enjoying. Jacob, worried for his sister, had taken to visiting her every evening. He was ready to wager the meal was the last time she'd even eaten. Sarah was growing increasingly sullen.

When visiting a few weeks ago, Jacob saw that Sarah had at least gotten out that day. He had found her cloak on a chest by the front door.

Geneviève had arrived in the early afternoon. She talked Sarah into joining her at Patricia's to provide a French lesson and assist in a fitting of what Geneviève hoped would be a highly profitable gown. When her friend first broached the subject, Sarah had immediately said no. The two women sat in silence for a long time, Sarah on her mattress, her friend on a stool drawn up close to the bed. Geneviève knew how few resources Sarah had left. There was no need to remind her. Sarah had spent almost her entire life keeping track of money, her father's, then hers. Now there was nothing to keep track of. Finally Sarah spoke, not emotionally but just as a simple statement of fact.

"Hanging would be too good for him. The guillotine would be a kindness. Do they draw and quarter the evil in this country?"

At first Geneviève thought the question rhetorical, then realized it might not be. She simply shook her head.

Sarah stood suddenly. There were tears in her eyes.

In the first sign of determination she'd demonstrated in days, Sarah crossed the room and opened a small trunk. She pulled out a fresh shift and petticoat. Geneviève barely had time to react before Sarah was adjusting her cloak and walking toward the stairs. Sarah didn't say a word until they were about to turn onto Broadway within sight of their client's grand house. "How well do you know Patricia's father?" Sarah asked.

"How well can someone like me know a man like that?"

"You know what I mean."

"Patricia often speaks of him. She thinks her father should be governor. She says her father can't wait for Governor Clinton to finally leave. Patricia once told me the King of England would be no less autocratic as governor than Clinton. He says the people of England would not let him get away with it there and the governor should damn well understand the people here won't tolerate it either. Mr. Van Huisen has made a career out of fighting him in the Assembly, but the governor doesn't give two hoots about what the people want."

"I didn't think rich people thought those kinds of things," said Sarah.

"Remember, he's Dutch and his family has been here since long before the English came. Patricia says the Dutch didn't serve any king. They worked for some big Dutch trading company that owned Manhattan and the people were free to say what they pleased about it.

"Anyway, Patricia once said the governor hates her father, and that if he hadn't already made arrangements to return to England he would probably find some excuse to arrest him."

"Isn't her father afraid?" Sarah asked.

"Apparently not in the slightest. Every time the governor dismisses the Assembly the people re-elect more people who detest him. He can't do much about it, she says."

When they arrived at Van Huisen house, Patricia wanted to begin with French conversation practice.

"The fitting can wait. I need stimulation and fittings are so tedious."

Sarah seized the opportunity and, politely, suggested she try to express her understanding of politics. Patricia immediately uttered the standard rote answer. "Politics is not a matter for women's minds."

"But your father has been elected to the Assembly many times, has he not?"

"Oh yes, for as long as I can remember."

"Then why don't you tell me about your father?"

"That's different. I would be pleased to," she said, launching into a stilted and dutiful résumé of her father's principles and achievements. Sarah stopped her now and then to summarize what Patricia had been saying. Sarah's purpose was not to make sure she had understood correctly but to rephrase Patricia's points in a more French way. Patricia understood the process and was quick to embrace the niceties of the language. Sarah's nodded approval when Patricia resumed the story of her father made her more naturally loquacious. Censoring herself less, she betrayed having a point of view about politics in the city.

Sarah was improvising. She didn't know what she wanted to learn from the young woman on the love seat opposite her, hands meeting primly in her lap, her back straight as a maypole. But besides desperately wanting to tell Patricia that French is best expressed with gesticulating hands, she wanted to unearth any information about the workings of her father's world that might help her strike back at the one man in the world she hated with weapons he understood better than a knife point.

"Speculating on land must be terribly exciting," Sarah said, steering the conversation home.

Patricia paused for a moment before a light went on.

"Oh yes, I recall telling you that Mama thinks he is the cleverest speculator on all Manhattan Island, not just the city."

"How does it work?" Sarah asked.

"Well, you might start by buying properties that are already built upon in the hope they will become more valuable in time. And of course you get to charge whatever rent you want. It's like making your own money," Patricia added, laughing. "I suppose if I desperately wanted to spend more than I was supposed to be spending on clothing, Papa could increase a rent, just enough, for example, to pay for the gown Geneviève is making in the next room.

"Since there are so many new people arriving daily in the city there's scarcely room for them to live. There's always someone willing to pay more. But Papa says the key to real estate is having your ear to the ground."

Sarah didn't understand the expression "ear to the ground".

"Listen, and find out things before other people do. I even have an example. Papa has big hopes for this project."

New York was already the flour milling center of the colonies. Patricia said one of the city's biggest refineries was considering building another one right by the East River. Her father learned of it when one of the investors in the present mill mentioned it in passing at a café. He was hesitant to take a chance on the profitability of a new refinery.

"Redundant," the investor said. "Very likely redundant."

Patricia's said her father nevertheless bought the property in question, just north of the present docks.

"That's one thing he and the governor fight about. The aristocrats come here and give immense tracts of land to each other for this little favor or that. Our richest merchants also get to share the same pie for next to nothing. But my father is the smartest man in the world. He finds the land that will bring the biggest return later on, while aristocrats behave as they do in England, judging status by the size of one's estates, not revenue. Papa said those of our very own merchants who want to emulate them are equally short-sighted."

Each year, she said, she saw there were more and more merchant ships arriving in port but there was no place for them to offload. They had to wait interminably, or pay someone off.

Returning to her point about her father's current project, Patricia said:

"Selling land for that second refinery would be profitable in itself, but by keeping his ear to the ground my father also knew that the West Indies now needed our flour. Apparently they now use every square foot of land for their sugar plantations. There is none left for growing grain.

"The refinery's owners of course know that the flour market is about to explode but they don't yet know my father owns the land that will allow them to build the refinery right on the port and from there run their own exporting business.

"My father wants not just to sell the land at a very handsome price but to own a share in the new trade to the Indies. If the refinery owners won't grant him that share he will set the price for the land beyond even their means and let them know another refinery will surely accede to his request."

Sarah was impressed by her student. Patricia didn't have

any of Sarah's experience in business, nor had she received the slightest encouragement to even think about it, yet she had pieced together a great deal over the years from merely eavesdropping on her father's drawing room conversations with colleagues, or listening to his simplified explanations of some success or failure in business or in the Assembly.

Geneviève sent word through a maid that Patricia could begin the fitting at her pleasure. Patricia rose and Sarah followed, her mind racing to conceive of a situation where she could ensnare the fat merchant as cleverly as Patricia's father could. The only tool she had was knowledge of Croman's worthless land deeds. She hoped an occasion would arise whereby Patricia would again present her to her father. If having your ear to the ground meant listening to everyone, rich and poor, he might stoop to listen to a merchant's daughter from Bordeaux, especially if Patricia told her father they were now becoming fast friends.

After the fitting, the maid handed Sarah a small bag of coins for her services. Geneviève would be paid when the gown was done.

Patricia stood under the portico and thanked her teacher.

"I so enjoyed our conversation," said Sarah. "I would consider it an honor to be permitted to continue to sit with you in the future at no charge."

"I'll hear of no such thing," said Patricia. "Father allots me discretionary money for my betterment. What I pay you is less than what he allows me to spend each year on ribbons and other 'unnecessaries,' as he puts it. I am sure you can make good use of it.

After a pregnant pause, Patricia went on:

"I often find the days long in this big house. There are only servants to talk to and we never discuss things of any interest. Feel free from now on, Sarah, to send word if you feel like chatting, even in English."

As the women left Broadway and turned east, Sarah

asked Geneviève if she had other rich clients.

"No. Not one. I dream that when Patricia appears at some grand ball wearing my gown she will have occasion to tell a jealous woman where she had it made."

Sarah put her arm around her as they squeezed through a crowd greatly amused at the site of a burly woman madly hurling a man's clothes and belongings onto the street. A gaunt man took a step toward her and she pounded both palms into his naked chest, causing him to stumble backwards, almost tripping. She whipped around and pointed at a cart driver, unable to proceed because of the crowd.

"You, you on the cart!" she screamed. "Run your filthy wheels over this infested testimony to a heartless man's conniving ways.

"Make way," she yelled, arms flailing as she plunged into the bystanders, making a path for the cart.

When the cart began to move forward, the gaunt man slipped in behind, getting to his knees to gather up a pair of leather breeches, a shirt and shoes. Sarah had not noticed he had been shoeless as well as shirtless. His smell probably still hung over the burley woman's bed.

When Sarah got home, the McDougalls were out. Sarah lay down, at first relieved by the sudden quiet. But she was soon as depressed as she'd been before Geneviève dragged her out. She would soon be out of money. She had no control over how and when Croman would pay for his crimes. It was foolish to put her hopes on a chance meeting with Patricia's father and the even lesser possibility that he would partner with her in bringing Croman to his knees.

Sarah slipped back inside herself. Nothing she could think of doing, had she the energy, would make any difference. As the weeks passed, Sarah left her house only for the few minutes it took to walk down to the Fly Market. It was so close that from her window she could hear the vendors hawking their produce, meat and sundry utensils.

There was little to occupy her in the house. The McDougalls had moved out weeks ago to share the cramped quarters of another cooper who was thrilled to go into business with a man of McDougall's connections and God-given talent. For that's what it was, talent. All coopers had their tools, adzes and irons, bits and vices, augers and gimlets, but casks were built by eye. There were no standard measurements. That was why coopers were the most respected of craftsmen. Shaping a barrel was hard enough but it was also one thing to craft a sturdy barrel for dry contents and quite another for wet. Not a drop of rum, it was said, ever escaped a McDougall cask, not even in a shipwreck. A McDougall barrel would always come in on the next tide, as right as rain.

Sarah would take to her bed at any time of day. Often the sun had gone down by the time she woke up, as it had today. Before she opened her eyes she sensed a presence in the room. It was Jacob, seated on the stool looking at her, as he now did almost every evening.

On the evenings when he talked her into getting up so they could talk facing each other across the table he would hope to see progress but more often than not he found her morose. Sometimes when he watched her sleep he thought she was trying to leave this world. Not die, just wake up somewhere else where her story would not begin with kidnapping and rape.

"I don't know whether it will lead to anything," Jacob said, "but I have news."

Sarah sat up but didn't get up. Jacob sighed and rose to get her some ale. At least he would make sure she had sustenance.

"Noah has sent word."

"Where is he?" Sarah asked.

"Somewhere in or near New Harlem. I think you'd have to take the Post Road to get near there. I'm not sure."

"Or go by boat," Sarah said, suddenly remembering

Noah running in the opposite direction of the fire, then abruptly turning down a street that would take him to the river where boatmen could be hired or ferries taken."

"Is that where he hides, in New Harlem?"

"I don't know, although it would be a good place, according to Peter."

"What does Peter say?"

Jacob hesitated.

"I'm not sure Peter understands your friendship with Noah. At first he assumed he was a slave. Even after I told him he wasn't, and that Noah had shown himself to be a friend to you, he said you shouldn't trust him too far."

"What right does he have to express an opinion about Noah? Does Peter's family have slaves?"

Jacob looked at his sister, pleased. She was on the verge of being angry. That was a good sign.

Jacob chose his words carefully, not just because he was in business with Peter but because he liked him.

"Peter almost never mentions his family. He feels no affection for them and they don't reach out to him. They may have had a slave or two. It seems like everyone in this city who's not poor does. But Peter was very young when he was sent away from home to apprentice. He wouldn't remember. However it seems that over the years his master found time to instruct him on how the world works."

Jacob decided to pour an ale for himself. While he did, Sarah rose and sat at the table by the small fire. The New Year had begun fresh and sunny, but not overly cold.

"Peter said everyone had a right to worry about a slave revolt when fires started breaking out. He said there have been several rebellions. The last one was more than 20 years ago but every white man remembers it as if were yesterday.

"I asked him how it started. All Peter knew was that over several days fires had broken out in different parts of the city. I asked if they got the slaves who set the fires.

He said his master told him the authorities never found out who actually started the fires but they killed a horrible number of people, about 100, he said, burned at the stake, hung, deported. Even a poor white girl."

"So Noah knew what he was doing," Sarah said.

"I would have done the same thing," Jacob said. He added that while it looks like everyone sort of gets along, the fear is still there.

"After the uprising, even if it wasn't one, who knows, they passed a law making it illegal for more than three Negros to gather together on the street."

"Do they enforce it?"

"I don't know. There are so many Negros here you see them together all the time, at least down here on the docks. Peter said that's what the whites are worried about. There are so many black men here that in a few years they might make up almost half the population. If they rebelled, who could stop them? Peter says they have reason to be afraid. People at the Assembly are saying we should stop importing slaves and instead import indentured white men."

"Is Peter afraid of Noah?" Sarah asked.

"He might be."

Like Jacob, Sarah knew little about the city's history. Most people were from somewhere else and thought of little else but surviving. Noah, thought Sarah, might be the wisest survivor of all.

"What news do you bring, Jacob?"

"It's not much but I thought you would be happy to know that Noah is alright. He sent word to a man who shares his room off Queen Street. I've been going there from time to time looking for him."

Interrupting his own account, Jacob suddenly asked:

"My lord, those stairs at the back! Do you remember them? Three of the steps have now broken completely. To get past them you have to grab a rope they've slung alongside the stairs and hoist yourself up to the next good step like a sailor hauling himself up and around to get to the crow's nest. And there's no light if no one's home."

Jacob didn't notice the little smile Sarah's lips betrayed as he described his landlubber's ascent of the back stairs at Noah's.

"Yet again, you've risked your life for me, brother."

Jacob laughed, then leaned closer to Sarah, conspiratorially.

"Noah's message to you was that he knows what damage the fire did and that arson was the only explanation. There was no mention of revenge, Noah's friend said, but he said Noah wanted Sarah to not give up hope. There were ways, maybe not exactly legal, to obtain goods to resell. He said it was important not to rebuild the warehouse yet. Croman's men would be watching for that as a sign you were back in business and would eventually burn it down again. He didn't say when he was returning to the city."

Sarah offered Jacob bread.

CHAPTER 24

Forging A Future

WHEN Sarah handed him the bread that evening, Jacob felt his little sister had returned to this world. He fervently hoped he'd seen the end of her moroseness and sudden mood changes during which she'd spoken harshly not only with him but her friend Geneviève. Jacob knew as well as anyone that sisters and brothers always squabble but Geneviève was a saint. She had remained devoted to Sarah, letting her share in her gown-making profits. When Sarah refused charity, Geneviève told her in no uncertain terms that it was Sarah's growing friendship with Patricia that kept the door open for Geneviève as well.

"If she threw one of her earrings down the street she would hit another seamstress. She doesn't need me. She needs you, Sarah." Geneviève had a way when speaking French of making every point seem irrefutable.

Jacob held his tongue on one matter, though he was sorely tempted to speak after seeing Sarah's reaction to Noah's message, the part of about resorting to steps "not quite legal" to obtain merchandise to sell. There had been no reaction. She hadn't batted an eye. Upright Sarah, as honest a soul as Jacob had ever known. In fact, he suspected he governed his life by the same rules mostly because he was sure she would descend on him with a lecture he wouldn't want to hear twice if he stepped onto the wrong side of integrity. Jacob remained at the table that evening until he himself needed sleep.

After the fire it had become clear to him as well as Sarah that they were living in a dangerous world, filled with people more powerful than they could ever dream of becoming. They always got their way, those people. Jacob knew that apart from revenue generated by Geneviève's prodding of Sarah, his sister's future was growing bleak. Noah had yet to return and explain the allusion he'd made in his message.

As Jacob climbed the stairs to the kitchen, having called out a greeting to Sarah as he entered the house, he was still rehearsing the announcement he wanted to make.

He sat down at the table and Sarah did likewise, sitting to his right. Jacob drew a folded cloth from his coat pocket and placed it on the table. He then removed his coat and placed it on the chair to his left.

"What is that?" Sarah asked when he unrolled the cloth.

"Shavings," said Jacob. "From coins." He reached back to his coat and took out a small purse. He emptied it on the table in front of Sarah. Coins from some of the money in common use in the colonies to make up for the shortage of the King's coin: Spanish pieces of eight, Portuguese moidores, German and Dutch thalers.

"Those shavings come from these coins. Get enough and you can sell it as bullion. I've been practicing." She looked at them briefly, then at her brother. Her eyes were interested but neutral. She said nothing.

"Look at the coins, Sarah. Closely."

She did, for several minutes, picking up each one in

turn and examining it from every angle.

"If I hadn't seen those shavings, I wouldn't have suspected these coins were anything but worn by usage."

"Good! That's what I was hoping you'd say."

Same old Jacob, Sarah thought. Meticulous in everything, and proud of it.

"Peter told me he'd read in the Gazette that Governor Clinton says half the money in circulation in the province of New York is counterfeit. The governor says counterfeiting should be made a treasonous act, but Peter says he's just saying what the representative of the King is supposed to say. Peter says even prominent people counterfeit money."

Jacob said most counterfeiters never get caught and that depending on what colony you're in it's not even illegal to counterfeit the money of another jurisdiction.

"They do it everywhere, not just here. You can't counterfeit English coins in England but you can in Ireland, for example. Or France. A lot of those coins end up here.

"Peter says that counterfeiting is all England's fault. They force us to buy goods manufactured in England by not allowing us to manufacture them here, and they mark up the price to 100 times more than someone in London would pay for the same thing. All our English money goes back to England to pay for what we import. Peter says it's not just poor people who counterfeit money. Who knows, maybe even the government does it when they want money but don't dare raise taxes anymore."

"Has my brother become a counterfeiter?"

"No, Sarah. At least not yet." He smiled in the face of Sarah's still non-committal look.

Getting serious again, Jacob said:

"We're going to have to do something. Maybe not right now but we should be prepared. Peter is teaching me to work with metals, not just silver. It's too good an opportunity to waste. I won't be with him forever. I'm hoping I'll learn enough to make my own coins. I'm not saying I'd do it. I just want to know I could if I had to."

"What if you get caught?"

"My chances would be better than most. You know me. If I do something I do it right. And I'd hide away alone somewhere to do it, not at the shop.

Jacob said Peter showed him some counterfeit coins he'd come across. He was interested as an engraver.

"Most coiners have no skill at all, and some are clearly illiterate. They can't even spell the value of some coins. I saw one that spelled 'twenty' as 'twenny'. And if someone accepting the coin is illiterate they'd never know the coin was valueless."

After several minutes of silence spent clearing the table and stoking the fire, Sarah gave what, in effect, was her approval to Jacob's proposal.

"Someday I'd like to stuff the fat man like a French goose, pinch his nose and make him swallow a sack of counterfeit coppers."

As Jacob walked home he realized that his sister had changed. Only now did it dawn on him that he had as well. The sack of coins and the cloth-wrapped shavings were the proof. The quiet life of a master engraver no longer seemed to be his future.

PART II

CHAPTER 25

Please, Steal My Ship

Quebec City, New France
April 1, 1753

MICHEL Rousseau. Antoine Cloutier.

Young merchant captain. Balding merchant trader.

Nephew. Uncle.

And sparring partners, verbally, for the most part. Antoine, a quick-witted and fundamentally gentle man, had a weakness, like some men do for wine or women. He liked to fight, to scrap. An old acquaintance once suggested Antoine's penchant derived from the fact he wasn't an imposing figure. Antoine dismissed the idea but to himself conceded that he did feel bigger when he sat down 10 minutes later, chest expanding to suck in air, heart pounding, and sore fists eager to raise a tankard with his opponent, who, more often than not nowadays, was his nephew.

The arrival of spring meant *le fleuve*, the St. Lawrence River, the silver-and-white mottled highway to the world, was free of ice. Any day now sails would populate the horizon, piloted ships working their way around the Île d'Orléans, which sat in the middle of the river like a smushed dumpling in a bowl of soup.

The ships would be carrying fine French furniture for the colony's administrators and wealthiest merchants, fabrics for their wives so they could replicate the latest French fashions, correspondence for the religious orders urging their local order to do everything in its power to usurp control of the colony, alcohol for trade with the Indians who hunted most of the furs the colony's existence depended on, and, for everybody else, tools, muskets, knives, pots and pans and, perhaps, playing cards.

Of desperate interest to the governor and intendant, one of the ships would be carrying specie, although it would represent only a fraction of the money they had all but begged France for to maintain the colony's growth over the coming year. Also unknown as yet was whether the colony's men, be they habitants or nobles, would get their fondest wish: a ship or two carrying women, a commodity as scarce as peace in recent years.

The vagaries of peace were what Antoine and Michel were now discussing, ensconced in a tavern on rue St. Paul. Outside, the sun shone, but little of it reached the narrow cobbled street because of the three-story stone buildings rising on each side. The tavern was located in Lower Town, the narrow strand of land that sat more than 200 feet below the invincible fortress that crowned Cap Diamant. When Michel was young, returning from his first voyage and seeing the Lower Town from a distance for the first time from the bow of a ship, he thought the massive granite promontory, whose surface sparkled in the sun like armor, was a giant, and the Lower Town the giant's feet, cooling in the waters of the great river. Now he lived there. The river was only a few blocks south of the tavern and Michel's room was less than a block away.

Because Michel was sailing to France in a few days,

there was no end to the agenda the men had planned the night before. They needed to discuss the details of the voyage, agents to contact in Europe, new trade possibilities to explore while there, ports of call in the second leg of the trip, the Antilles, and finally the voyage home. But the main item on the agenda was one that Antoine was hesitant to broach. It smacked of treason. Would his head-strong "son" understand?

The hold had already been loaded with dried fish, staves, lumber and furs, the products that had entirely financed the colony for most of its existence. France no longer wanted all the fur the colony could send. Antoine had been shaking his finger for years warning that the trade's days were numbered. Michel, a minority-owner of their ship, the Fabienne, had toasted his uncle the previous night, at this very table, upon learning that Antoine had managed once again to get the furs without paying the 25 percent sales tax France had imposed.

The cargo aboard the Fabienne was bound for La Rochelle, then Bordeaux, France. Michel had made the trip many times, both as a boy barely strong enough to raise a slop bucket high enough to dump its contents overboard, and now as a man of 26, broad shouldered and wiry.

Though the two had planned on discussing other matters first, the drinking had accelerated that morning when Michel wove an intricate curse in which he blasphemed every symbol of the Catholic Church he could bring to mind to sum up his frustration with trade restrictions. Both Antoine and the boy he had raised as his own son shared the view of every merchant in the city. Trade with France benefitted only France.

From the inception of the fur trade, French outposts were frequently as close as many furs ever got to Montreal, the center of the trade. With the connivance of the now outlawed *coureurs de bois*, Montreal merchants, and even a governor of Montreal, furs were often routed south to Albany in the Province of New York where British colonists were happy to pay a handsome price. For the Indians, not having to go all the way to Montreal shortened their journey.

What Michel wanted to know this morning was how merchant ships could make similar detours, and profits. In French ports, Michel always felt like a smuggler when the King's customs officers boarded. The feeling persevered until a tedious verification of the ship's manifest suggested he wasn't. Some said the customs officers prolonged the inspection to give ship masters time to make a wise decision when determining the amount of money to slip into their hands. Michel was still learning how to navigate the ritual. It was different in every port.

While Antoine could drive a bargain as hard as any merchant, he was judicious in the corners he cut. He had profited greatly over the years and lived in a handsome fieldstone house in Upper Town, set well back from a wide street. He was loath to risk his standing any more than he had to.

Some nights were too quiet for his taste. He had admitted as much to Michel. His wife had passed away years before and not long afterwards Michel moved out, deciding he needed to be a crow's nest hail from the harbor and the Fabienne, and just a few blocks from the ship chandlers, his crew and their families, and, especially before and immediately after voyages, brothels and taverns.

Antoine came to Lower Town most days to oversee the running of his two warehouse stores but more often than not he was unable to escape the feeling he was merely marking time, but for what?

Antoine had intended to raise the matter at the end of their meeting today but his opening tirade about trade restrictions and stagnating profits convinced him to order more wine and table the concerns that were slowly overrunning his dreams. They were taking on the weight of premonitions. He wanted Michel to tell him he was crazy, that the future would take care of him as it always had.

When the wine was set before them, Antoine made a simple statement.

"Things have been quiet since the last time England and France did battle, dragging us into it."

Michel was eager to get to sea. After a long, slow winter of reminiscing, he wanted action.

"That was during King George's war," Antoine continued, oblivious to Michel's restlessness at the table, pretending to never find a comfortable position. "It ended in 1748, accomplishing nothing whatsoever. Early in the war the governor of Massachusetts captured our fortress at Louisbourg, on Cape Breton Island in Nova Scotia."

"I know where it is," Michel interrupted. "I've sailed by it."

"The point is," said Antoine, "the English and their New Englanders went to all that trouble to lay siege to the fort and finally take it only to see it returned to us by the treaty that ended the war three years later. The only thing that changed, Michel, and this is what always happens where there's war, merchants like us had more money than we did before the first shots were fired.

Michel waited.

"There's another war going on, Michel, and I've got a bad feeling about it."

"Since when is the prospect of more money something to dampen your spirits? Who's fighting?"

"They call it Father Le Loutre's War. The British and New Englanders are brazenly trying to steal all of Nova Scotia from the Acadians and Catholic Mi'kmaq. These lands belong to them by treaty."

Michel had gotten to know local Indians well as a boy. His first love was a teenage Huron woman. Intermarriage was encouraged because there were too few white women to increase the population. However, a Recollet priest warned Michel that if he decided to marry her he must make sure he was the one to wear the pants in the family.

"Indian women are given too much power in their world," the priest said. "Theirs is a matriarchal society. That is not right, according to God." Though still an adolescent himself, Michel had already been to sea many times. That's where his destiny lay, he decided when the priest departed. After his next voyage for his uncle, Michel simply neglected to try to find the woman on his return.

"I only learned about the war last month," Antoine continued. "No one's been paying much heed, but I've been thinking about it, and I'm worried."

"A battle in Acadia is no threat to us, uncle."

"True but what worries me is the principle of the thing. Whether we are the ones in need of reinforcement, or whether it's our Acadian colony in peril, France never gets troops here when we need them. I even heard, and more than once, that, miracle of miracles, our noble King had even sent a fleet of ships of war to save Louisbourg. They had plenty of time to make the crossing but somehow their captains spent so much time being rowed from ship to ship to discuss the pending fleet action amongst themselves that they failed to leave France in time to make the crossing and engage the British. You'd think they didn't want to."

Now Antoine was wound up. A fistfight behind the tavern wouldn't be enough to change the subject.

"How often have we begged France not just for troops but for settlers? The British colonies outnumber us 10 to 1 but we've been here longer. And now I hear that in clear violation of a treaty 13 British transport ships suddenly appeared in Halifax harbor. On those ships were thousands of settlers. Overnight they had a city with one of the world's greatest harbors and a Protestant population larger than the entire Mi'kmaq population."

Lowering his voice to a treasonous whisper, Antoine asked:

"Can you imagine France solving our problems that

simply?"

He said that together the Acadians and Indian militia were striking back where they could, even at Halifax itself, but thousands of their own people were now fleeing to Prince Edward Island and Cape Breton.

"One of our Jesuits who had gone to live with the Indians on the peninsula 18 years ago returned last month. A messenger preceded him and he was taken directly to the governor and bishop at the Chateau St. Louis. They didn't even let him report his return at the Jesuit residence. As usual, no one told us anything. Then a few days ago that I learned that a troop ship will be arriving this summer from France."

"We're getting ready?" Michel asked.

"But for what?" Antoine asked. "That's what I'd like to know. Maybe the troop ship means nothing. Maybe they're just replacing soldiers who've decided not to settle here. But my dreams tell me there's more."

"You should talk to an Indian about your dreams, uncle."

"Why would I do that?"

"They're not afraid of them."

When no words followed, Michel stopped staring into Antoine's eyes and sat up straight, pulling his long chestnut hair into a pony tail, which he secured with a strip of cloth. He always did that when he was about to leave for the docks to see to his ship, their ship.

"If I were a betting man," Antoine began.

"Which you are," said Michel.

"If I were to wager on the future of bourbon lilies in the New World... This is not me talking, it's what my dreams keep saying... I'd say there isn't much of one. Think about it, Michel. If the British can assemble a fleet just as quick as you please and create a strategic port city in the time it takes us to unload a cargo of molasses on a hot day, I'd say they're in it for the long run. As for our Beloved Louis

XV, I don't believe he has ever kept anything he's won in war. He makes a habit of giving our hard-won spoils back to our enemies, the Louisbourg fortress being the closest example and the Austrian Netherlands being another. I'm told he does so out of a sense of chivalry. His defense is that he is the King of France and not a shopkeeper. I can but imagine how he regards the tedium of keeping our shop here in the New World."

It was now almost 11 o'clock in the morning. Madame Lalonde's salon-sized tavern was beginning to fill up.

"Let us continue outside," Michel said. "Because you've been talking so much I had nothing much else to do but drink. I need to clear my head."

The docks were just minutes away. Antoine quickly noted that three other ships were being readied for their first voyage of the season, and judging by the suddenly urgent orders being shouted and the tense acknowledgements that came back from a group of at least a dozen dock workers, another ship was ready to be slipped from dry dock back into the harbor.

The frosty spring morning made every sound carry and also worked wonders for Michel's spinning head. His uncle's convoluted attempt to explain his recent dreams without sounding treasonous, to Michel's mind, could have been expressed in a single sentence.

"You think New France is doomed and you want to get out."

As they walked slowly to the end of the pier where the Fabienne was moored, Antoine put his arm around Michel's shoulder.

"I see that I no longer need to go to an Indian to interpret my dreams. For a man who drank too fast this morning, you see clearly."

Michel smiled.

"You know I'm impatient with blabber. I'd rather take one of your punches than pretend to listen to your mercantile philosophizing."

Antoine released his arm and punched Michel hard in the shoulder.

Though Michel feigned disdain for long-winded discussions he had received several years of Jesuit instruction. It made him adept at pulling an ill-conceived argument out of a broadside. If it meant a punch in the arm, he didn't mind.

"Why don't you come with me, uncle? I'm a better listener when land is out of sight. You haven't been to sea since I was a boy."

"You were all but a boy when I made you captain, Michel, and I'm not sure you've grown up much since."

"Indeed I hope not," said Michel, laughing.

"No, I won't join you this time."

"Will the time come when you want to leave for good?"

"I think not, Michel. I can't imagine living anywhere else, even if the English should overrun us. This is my country whatever pompous fool claims to rule it. But what I want is enough money to live out my days in comfort. My house in Upper Town would satisfy a minor noble. My little garden in back is my Sunday joy. Mass and manure."

"Again you have lost me, uncle."

"Then I will express myself in terms that even a merchant captain will understand. I want you to steal my ship."

CHAPTER 26

The Secret Army

New York City,
April 11, 1754

NOAH returned to New York almost two months after the fires destroyed Sarah's warehouse and Aiden McDougall's cooperage. The first things he noticed when he entered Sarah's were how drawn her face had become and the two large casks sitting in one of her first-floor rooms, the one below the kitchen that she first planned to use as a storefront for her warehouse.

"They're mine to sell," Sarah said, "except this time there's no share of the profit to pay. They were a gift of gratitude from Aiden McDougall. He and Arlene stayed here briefly after they lost everything."

She added that she wished she could find a buyer.

"If it weren't for Jacob and Geneviève I wouldn't even have enough money to eat. No one ever comes here now looking to buy. They see the warehouse in cinders and don't bother knocking on my door.

"Anyway, I'm gratified that Aiden is getting back on his feet. Word is out that his barrels are available. Aiden's wife says a few of his former clients have tracked him down at the cooperage he's sharing. That's good. I liked him. I was happy when Arlene said he beamed like a little boy when one of the buyers said he knew it was a McDougall cask the moment he laid eyes on it down on the docks."

As Sarah talked of the McDougalls' happy recovery, Noah noted a sudden shine in her eyes. Jacob had told him Sarah always looked at the world that way before the kidnapping. The shine had gone.

As Noah sat motionless atop one of the casks he focused unblinkingly on her eyes while listening, Sarah had the feeling Noah was, as usual, filing away each and every piece of information about the docks, who bought from whom, at what price, who went broke, who was suddenly flush, and who supposedly fled the city in the middle of the night.

"I'll spread the word about these," he said, tapping the cask he sat on with his knuckles. "But we'll have to do better than that."

Sarah invited Noah upstairs for some cider Jacob had brought over the night he was so eager to tell her about his newest hobby, learning how to make his own coins. Jacob hadn't mentioned it on his recent visits, so Sarah was unsure whether he intended to add criminal to his talents or rest satisfied with having scratched his permanently inquisitive itch. One day she found herself reflecting that Papa would die, if he hadn't already, just thinking that one of his children was doing something illegal. She now realized the hungrier and more hopeless she got, the less she cared about how she or other people survived. Only rich people blamed the hungry for being hungry. France and the New World weren't so different.

Noah remained silent as he drank his cider. Sarah was used to his ways and felt comfort at his return. He was a survivor, a ferocious one, she thought when trying to imagine all that he'd gone through in his life. When he was with her she hoped some of it would rub off on her and that she would wake up the next morning clutching fate firmly in her own two hands.

Noah had continued to tell her not to think of rebuilding the warehouse. It was important that the fat merchant think he ruined her.

"I want him to forget you exist," Noah had said.

"When I was away," he said, "I thought about all the people I'd done little favors for over the years."

"Where did you go?" Sarah interrupted. "Some days I wish I had a hiding place."

"Hear me out. Maybe I'll tell you later," Noah said.

Sarah nodded.

"The list of people I've done little things for is long because I am getting old. And these people rarely leave the city. For the most part they are slaves. Some are inside slaves but most are rented out to do dock work for whichever merchant trader needs them at the moment. They know all the warehouses and the men who supervise them. And so do I."

Noah stood and reached into the pantry a few feet away. He turned toward Sarah and opened his big fist. She took some of the raisins.

"As for the white men who are so afraid of us because they think we all want to murder them or burn down their houses, they're right. I don't know a black man, slave or freedman, who isn't angry. Their mothers are angry and their brothers and sisters are angry. But they're not stupid. They know that if one slave gives a rich white man the eye we're all in danger. Revenge is sweet only for the smart man."

He popped a few raisins in his mouth and savored them.

"And you, Sarah, are the smartest person I know. In case you didn't know," Noah said, smiling, "Jacob says the same thing."

Noah's plan to inflict revenge on Zachariah Croman was beautifully simple.

"I've already been talking to my men, my army."

Sarah laughed.

"You laugh, but I think you should call me 'General' from now on, or at least until the end of our campaign."

Noah said that he'd already enlisted more than 20 men and hoped to make that number grow.

"I'm moving very slowly on purpose. What I told them to do was this: Whenever they found themselves working directly or indirectly for the trading house of Zachariah Croman, I wanted them to see to it that accidents happen, or small amounts of cargo simply go missing. Not enough to arouse much suspicion. The convenient thing about slaves being assigned temporarily to work for one merchant, then another is that the men working for Croman's people when one theft or accident occurs are not the same men working for him when another occurs three weeks later.

"Some of the cargo may find its way to me," said Noah. "Some will simply find its way to the bottom of the river."

Because he was calling in favors, he said he wouldn't have to compensate any one at the outset.

"We can start doing that in a small way when we, and I mean mostly you, start selling the goods miraculously laid at our door."

To be safe, Noah said, several other small storekeepers could easily be enlisted to take in some of their new-found inventory.

"And if some of the goods turn out to be ripe for selling in the countryside, we both know a certain German with a horse and wagon who would be happy to take evidence of your skullduggery off your hands."

Noah had never said so many words at a single sitting in all the time she'd known him. He'd clearly done a lot of thinking wherever it was that he'd gone to hide.

"I salute you, my general," she said after letting his plan

digest. "When do we start?"

He said they'd probably find a target within the next couple of weeks. Several ships were already in port waiting for an available dock for unloading cargoes that likely belong in part to Croman.

"If some of my people get assigned to work them we're on our way. But there's nothing for you to do until we've got some merchandise in hand, and any money we make from selling it will go mostly to paying the troops. After that, if you've got the patience, Sarah, I think you should be content with getting other people to take the goods off your hands for a small price and let them do the selling. That way, if Croman eventually decides to try adding two and two it's far less likely it will add up to you.

"My people won't be doing this to get rich. That's something they know they'll never be. They'll mostly be doing it to offload a bit of anger. That does a soul good, and that would do you good, too."

Sarah passed in front of Noah to get to the chest where she kept her money. There was almost none left. Peering into the tin box marked buttons and thread, she picked out a handful of coins.

"Shall we sup and drink to quiet revenge?"

Sarah held out the coins.

"No, I don't want money. That's yours and there's not much of it by the look of things. Keep it."

"Look at the coins, Noah. Look carefully."

Noah noticed the usual assortment of foreign coins mixed in with a few English shillings and coppers. Pieces of eight, thalers, moidores.

"So?"

"They're all shaved or counterfeit."

"All I can see is that they look old. Worn down."

"Jacob brought them to me a long time ago. Like you I didn't spot any fake ones. Then he took some coins from his other pocket, real ones. He showed me the differences.

He said the fake ones were good but he could do even better someday."

"You're not telling me that our Jacob has gone to the other side…"

"No." Sarah laughed at Noah's surprise. She had been shocked when Jacob first told her about his hobby, and he hadn't mentioned it since. However she often thought about it. In the end, it wasn't so hard to rationalize. People all around her in the often squalid and cramped east side of the city were doing what they needed to try to survive. She and Noah had just justified stealing in the name of revenge against an evil man. Not for a second did she find the idea immoral. And the coins she was now retrieving from Noah's outstretched hand, there was nothing immoral about them either. As Noah says, survival is war.

Once on the street, Sarah started to walk toward the Homeless Mule.

"I have a better idea," Noah said, leading her down Maiden Lane by the market and on to the river. He pointed to a little boat with a single sail.

"Before coming to see you today I'd returned to my hiding place. I borrow this boat to get there, like I did the night of the fire. If there's no wind you can keep warm rowing."

"Yes, General."

"We're going to a tavern well north of the city. In the village of New Harlem. I'll feel safer about using your coins there. Afterwards I'll show you my hideout. If you want to you can spend the night there or I can take you back. The only people who know I stay there are friends. It won't seem that way to you because it's in the woods, but we're safer there than at your place. We could return in no time on the morning tide. You won't have to row."

"Thank you, General."

CHAPTER 27

New Ship, New Name

Quebec City, New France
April 14, 1754

WHEN his uncle, walking behind him on the pier, told him to steal his ship, Michel turned so quickly to face him that he stumbled. Only grabbing his uncle by the throat with his left had saved him from falling into the still ice-cold water. The two men then stood motionless face to face. Michel searched for a sign his uncle was playing with him. He found none. His eyes then darted up and down the pier in search of potential eavesdroppers.

"You could be burned at the stake for such madness!"

With an upward nod of his head, his uncle motioned Michel to continue down the pier to the Fabienne.

"My ship. My very own ship," Michel said, standing by the gangplank. "Will I be hung for this, dear uncle?" His eyes scanned the ship, then fixed on his uncle, standing next to him like a proud father.

"Come aboard, uncle." Michel led him aft to his cabin.

Most of his crew was at work loading cargo and provisions. Michel noted they were also making enough noise to remove any concern about being overheard. It was the same every spring. The sailors acted like boys being let out to play for the first time since the bitter winter cold had vanished. They pushed and shoved and taunted each other, and sang. By late summer the same men would be cursing their labor.

Seated on opposite sides of the chart table, Antoine, facing the stern windows, squinted from the sun as he outlined his plan.

"You are right, Michel. We can't make real money as long as we confine ourselves to the trade that France permits. I've been a relatively good citizen for far too long."

"I'm glad you said 'relatively good,'" said Michel. For as long as Michel had been old enough to figure out such things, his uncle had raised his glass to His Majesty while arranging to sidestep France by buying and selling with English smugglers wherever he found them. Neither king had revenue agents in the wilds. English smugglers, he found, were kindred spirits.

"We must cease flying French colors, Michel, unless it serves our purpose from time to time. I wasn't joking when I said I fear for our empire in the New World. Bad dreams? Perhaps, but since I have but one life to live I intend to, should I prove to be in error, err on the side of wealth, mine and yours, not our Majesty's. That requires that we trade wherever there is good business to be had, on land as we have been doing, and at sea. That is why I want you to steal this ship. To avoid the risk of both of us spending the rest of our days playing piquet with the keeper of His Excellency the Governor's prison, or being deported to France, I must cut off my right arm."

Michel frowned.

"And you, Michel, are my right arm."

"That would make me a thief, a pirate, a wanted man, a

traitor, a homeless man. Is there anything else?"

"That sounds accurate enough," said his uncle.

"So far I'd say I'd be better off running to Father Daniau and begging him for immediate damnation."

"No, worry not, Michel. When you fail to return in the fall I'll report you as being lost at sea. As for now, your first task as citizen of the world will be to rename the Fabienne. What would you think of the Chameleon? Appropriate, don't you think?"

He could see Michel was warming to the idea. The frown had gone.

"Obviously," his uncle continued, "you can't do it here in port. Everyone would know about it in less time than it takes to genuflect to the King's treasury. No, wait until after you're near the Gulf. Find a sheltered bay where you can apply the new name. Chameleon is almost the same length as Fabienne. Just one letter shorter. That will make it relatively simple to remove any signs that the name has been changed. Once you scrape off the last letter in Fabienne pray for a spell of foul weather to give the new name a properly weathered look."

Michel stood and squinted out the stern windows. The harbor sparkled. As well as anyone, he knew how quickly the forever battling currents of the great river could put his uncle's plan in action. Buying more time, and without saying a word to his uncle, he lowered his head to avoid the beams and walked out of the cabin.

On deck he watched his men prepare the Fab—the Chameleon for its maiden voyage of the year. The sudden thud of a cask landing too hard in the hold and the curse that followed from a hand below deck made Michel realize he would also be stealing his crew from their homeland. Most had been born in New France. The more he thought about his uncle's plan, the more questions he had.

As he regained the cabin, his uncle's eyes betrayed excitement. He knew Michel was digesting his absurd proposal and he wasn't going to let him waver.

Still needing to buy time to think, Michel raised his hand to stop his uncle from launching into another flight of lunacy.

"Jean-Jacques!"

He had to bellow the name twice before a seaman appeared at the cabin door.

"Sir?"

"Do we have wine and brandy aboard yet?""

"My personal supply, you mean?" the seaman asked, piqued.

"That will do nicely," Michel said. "I've yet to have had mine hauled aboard.

The seaman's face fell.

"I'll have it replaced before we sail if you're back with it before I finish my rosary." The seaman hadn't noticed there were no beads in his hands. Antoine resumed as soon as they were alone again.

"This ship is now yours, Michel. You own it all. I've already drawn up the papers. A transfer of property from guardian to son. It will be legal here in New France. But, as I said, you've got to disappear for a time. You must arrange to have papers forged somewhere that state another provenance for this ship, your ship. The papers must list you as sole owner. Have them say you purchased it from an agent in La Rochelle many years ago. I have a name for you. The man died seven or eight years ago. No one will question the sale."

Noticing again that his careful planning appeared to have won over Michel, Antoine felt it was safe to express what he thought of as a minor uncertainty.

"Not having done this before I'm not sure what would be the safest port to seek the forgery."

When a bottle sat between them, Antoine casually mentioned he had a British merchantman flag at his house in the Upper Town. "Remind me to have it brought down to you tomorrow."

"How on earth did you get that?" asked Michel, savoring the brandy. How many times had he sat back and listened to his uncle's tales?

"A soldier who owed me money," his uncle said. "About nine or 10 years ago. Our militia and some Abenaki were harassing villages in Massachusetts, somewhere around Pemaquid. At some point a merchant schooner had broken up on the Muscongus Bay coast. We found a handful of men at the shore trying to scavenge what they could. They must have been rowing back and forth to the wreckage when we attacked the village.

After they saw our uniforms they rowed like possessed men into the bay and out of musket range. It was then that my indebted soldier friend noticed some rigging that had washed up on shore. My flag was attached to it. After they set fire to the village some of our boys found and slaughtered a fine Pemaquid pig. My friend wrapped it respectfully in the flag, where it stayed until they bivouacked later that day."

Canons sounded from the fort high above Michel and Antoine. Ships were finally arriving from France.

"That's your next step, Michel, to sail to France as you always do and sell our cargo. Then find someone to doctor your papers. Your new life will begin then. I wish I could join you."

"Why don't you?"

"Because I must stay in Quebec and subtly construct the tragic tale of my son and ship being swallowed by the sea or captured by pirates. The more time passes, the more the story will become common knowledge. I will continue to invest in other ships. In time, if you ever settle, you can send for me perhaps. If that is not convenient, be assured I will accept any money you might choose to send me."

"With the greatest pleasure, uncle."

"But remember. Never sign your real name. Our

connection has been severed."

"What shall I call myself?"

"Why not something like Michel d'Antan? Michel of Yesteryear."

"Somehow appropriate," Michel replied, enjoying the whimsy his uncle clearly relished employing to further his deceit. Their deceit. Their treasonous deceit. Even staring down the pointed barrels of a firing squad, Michel thought, his uncle's eyes would still find an excuse to sparkle.

Michel d'Antan walked his uncle down the gangway and along the pier to the street.

"I'll send a man with you to pick up the flag. On his way back he can find a replacement for the bottle of brandy we drank."

Despite the sunshine, there was still a chill in the air. Neither Antoine nor Michel noticed.

CHAPTER 28

The Hideaway

NOAH hauled hard on the oars to direct the boat away from the shore so they could catch the full force of the East River current. By sheer luck, his timing of the tide had been good and with the added help of a small sail they were soon beyond the city's newest shipyard to their left and the last of the merchant vessels at anchor to their right. Far behind them, the stench of the city. In the years since she'd been in New York, Sarah could remember escaping the smell only when visiting her French student at the big, tree-fronted house on Broadway. Even then there were days when a contrary wind brought the fetor with her.

"Where does the river go?" Sarah asked.

"It's not really a river," Noah said. "It's a strait. If my arms would let me I could row to the ocean. I'd just keep to the other side, the Long Island side, and we'd end up in the Sound and before we knew it we'd be on our way to visit King George himself. Since I hear he's too busy to receive us today we're going to branch off up the Harlem River and stop at the village of New Harlem. Our little boat here may not be elegant but she saves us more than a half-day's march from your place."

Noah was a different man today, Sarah thought. Maybe he just liked being away from the city where he lived with the fear of being kidnapped into slavery. It had happened once before, long before Sarah and Jacob had arrived after themselves having been kidnapped into another kind of slavery as indentured workers. When Sarah first met Noah, the night he found her crying in the street, he said he was a freedman by birth. He didn't tell her until much later that his grandparents had been slaves when the Dutch ruled the island of Manhattan but had been eventually freed and given a small amount of land to work.

With the breeze and current doing most of the work Noah let Sarah ask her questions. All she knew about her new home was that it first belonged to the Dutch, and there were still lots of Dutch in New York. Some of the richest families were still Dutch. Then the English took the city only to be forced to give it back for a year or two. Finally the English conquered for good.

"My parents spoke some Dutch. I still know a few words."

"Did they treat you better than the English?"

"My parents said they didn't care much what color you were as long as you were their kind of Christians, by that I mean Calvinists. The church said its mission was to educate everyone as Christians and baptize us. Apparently they never seemed to manage to convert the Indians. They found that humiliating. So they were happy when, miracle of miracles, Negros proved to them we could do an honest day's work and live a Christian life. In return, we got freedom and land. When you're a slave that's a good deal. Not only do you get freedom, you get a way to feed yourself and keep warm in the winter.

"They offered the same deal to indentured whites. Some of them had years and years left to serve on their contracts, eight, nine, who knows how long they were owned. However there was a catch that applied to only Negroes. Someone decided that the children of freed Negro Christians would be automatically born back into slavery. My parents never understood whether there was some Calvinist reasoning… that's what the Dutch church-goers are, Calvinist, Reform Calvinists. Anyway, as I was saying, my parents never figured out whether the Hollander's god decided our kids should be slaves again or whether the West Indian Company decided that.

"My parents told me The Hollanders didn't practice slavery in the Netherlands but they didn't have a law about it for the colonies, for or against. So no one really ever knew what was legal. Their company, which ran the colony here before the British came, thought only about money and had their own rules about slavery. As I said, for the most part the Dutch didn't care what color you were as long as you showed up at church, their church. The English never did quite see things that way.

"In the end," Noah said, "time passed. My grandparents passed on and so did some of the Dutchmen running things. Others simply left the colony. When my grandparents died, my own parents just kept working the land as they always had, and somehow no one seemed to remember that they shouldn't be free. My father always told me to act like I was legally a freedman and people would start to believe I was.

"It worked while I was in New Harlem, but I sometimes used to go to New York to work on the docks until one night when some guys beat me unconscious down by Coenties Slip. I woke up in chains on a ship bound for the Indies."

Noah said a French privateer captured the ship somewhere around the Turks Islands. Because of her father, Sarah knew about several of the islands in the Antilles but she hadn't heard of Bermuda. It was British. She knew mainly the French islands. Noah told her that he and several other men were taken on the French ship to

Saint-Domingue and sold as slaves to a plantation owner.

"I was there for two years until Maroons burned down the plantation. It was their leader, a man named François Mackandal, who ordered the raid. I met him in the mountains a few days later. I'll never forget him. He had a mission and you could see he could be fierce about it, but he was a smart man, and kind. I told him I wanted to go back where I came from because I was free there.

"Not long after he assigned somebody to help me get off the island. He gave me fancy clothes stolen from the whites and told me just what my father did. There were lots of freedmen in Cap-Français, which was about a day's journey from the plantation I'd been sent to when I arrived. Many of the freedmen had never been freed, but their fine clothes made them look as if they were. So I acted like I was a freedman until I found a ship that would take me away if I worked as crew."

As Noah guided the boat into the left channel to pass between Buchanan's Island and Manhattan Island, Sarah switched to French. Noah replied in kind.

"You have an accent," Sarah said.

"I learned your language in Saint-Domingue."

When she'd first heard him speak French to Geneviève the time they'd met at her house on Pope Day he'd said too little for her to notice the accent. She hadn't connected his knowing French with his time as a slave in Saint-Domingue. She'd always sensed Noah had not told her the whole story about that time. Except for today, free on the water, he never said much more than necessary.

Conversation lapsed. When Noah looked behind him to make sure his course was true, he said the current was even stronger than before they'd entered the narrower channel.

"The water's not nearly as deep here. We're getting a free ride," he said, dipping the left oar into the water to make a slight steering adjustment.

After they'd passed the northern end of Buchanan's Island they fell silent as several more miles of alternating swampland, forested hills and farms drifted by on the Manhattan side. When another island loomed in the river, Noah finally broke the silence.

"That's Blackwell Island. It means we're getting close. We're entering the Harlem River."

The waterway wasn't nearly as wide as the East River and the proximity of land on both sides caused Sarah's sense of serenity to be overtaken by her natural curiosity.

"I smell food," Noah said.

"I don't."

"Then I'm just plain hungry." The Harlem River was sluggish compared to the fast-moving East River and Noah had to row hard. The breeze was too light to fill the little sail.

"We'll eat as soon as we get to the village. There's a tavern that was once run by a black woman. She was a slave but she was doing it for so long that everyone thought she owned it, but she didn't really. She just worked there. That's what I mean about impressions giving people an idea of what they think is true. After a while, they just go on believing it forever. They don't think about it anymore. Act like you're free, just as my father said."

Noah was now hugging the shore. When he started working his way into a small inlet he announced they had arrived at the village of New Harlem. Minutes later he had tied up the boat, near the ferry that crossed the Harlem River. They walked off the wharf onto the Great Way, the village's northernmost street. She followed Noah down another street. As they came within sight of the tavern Noah had spoken of, he returned to the account of his life as a freedman, which started there in New Harlem.

"The problem is I don't have any proof that I'm a freedman. Here, everyone thinks I am, but when the English took over they said every freedman had to carry a pass. I sometimes think I should stay here. A lot safer, I reckon. I've kept paying the land tax on my folks' little farm here, but I don't have any kind of paper saying it's mine."

As they stepped into the spacious old tavern it took a moment for their eyes to adjust to the darkness. Sarah had noticed the tavern had a thatched roof. That and the lack of light inside made Sarah feel she'd stepped into an all-purpose refuge. A window at the far end admitted the afternoon light. On a table below the window were flowers. Sarah knew the Dutch loved their flowers.

Noah had walked straight to the bar and greeted a small, square-shouldered man wearing a large apron. Sarah stood watching. The warm welcome Noah got made her understand why he felt his free-status was not in danger in New Harlem. When he returned there was a smile on his face.

"Why don't you stay here?" Sarah asked, smiling at his smile.

"As small as it is, I can't work the farm alone. I'm not even sure I want to."

"Can't help you there, Noah," Sarah said. "I've never been on a farm. In France, I never left Bordeaux. My whole world was the city by the port, my father's account books and ships' cargoes."

Noah laughed.

"I just pictured you chopping firewood. I think we'd freeze ourselves to death come winter."

"I'm stronger than I look!"

"That may be but your muscle is up here," he said, pointing at his head.

Two plates of venison stew suddenly appeared before them, accompanied by Dutch gin for Noah and hard cider for Sarah. There were few patrons. As the stocky tavern-keeper returned to the kitchen his boots thudded on the plank flooring.

"*Eet smakelijk!*" Noah said, digging into the stew.

"I assume that means bon appétit?"

"See, you already speak Dutch."

Their meal done, they returned to the main road and followed it inland briefly before taking an old Indian path that veered northwest.

"The farm is to the south. I wanted to show you something else first," Noah said.

Sarah noticed that he almost whispered his words. It occurred to her that it might be out of respect for the forest she was now discovering, that the sounds of birds and rustling leaves should not be interrupted.

They soon came to a stream, then a clearing. Noah pointed ahead, to the right. A mill, a large one, two-stories high, built next to the stream. There was little water in the stream and the mill's huge wheel was still.

"This," Noah said in a normal voice now that he stood in the clearing, "is my hideout."

He took Sarah's hand to help her up the small hill leading to the steps to the second floor of the house that adjoined the mill. Once inside, the smell of the forest came with them. On one side of the room Sarah marveled at the mechanism that drove the great wheel. On the other was a large hearth. A bed, a table by the window, and a single chair completed the furnishings.

"Hideaways aren't designed for guests. I'll bring up a fat log to sit on."

He did just that. It had already been sawed.

"This is a good place for contemplating plans," he said. "Such as driving the fat merchant crazy."

CHAPTER 29

Bonjour, La Mer

Gulf of St. Lawrence, New France
April 22, 1754

THE Fabienne dropped anchor at a small bay just east of the port of Matane, first discovered by traders from their destination, La Rochelle, well over a hundred years before. Michel d'Antan hoped no one was watching from shore. When he raised anchor a few hours later, it was the Chameleon that dipped its bow into the ever-widening St. Lawrence River. By the time its blue waters emptied into the Gulf it would be more than 60 miles shore to shore.

As the ship rounded the tip of the Gaspé Peninsula and altered course to the southeast, Michel arrived at the pitching bow with an already half-spilled tankard of brandy. More than bidding adieu to land, he was greeting the ocean head on. In reality, it was more of a staring match than a greeting. He would always conduct this private ceremony regardless of weather. On occasion the winds slapped him around and roaring waves salted his spirits. He never minded. Nor did he mind that the ocean winds always made him the first to blink. That was the way it should be when man pitted himself against the sea.

As he left New France behind, the sun shone. He was happy.

In the coming days he would sail past Newfoundland and the Grand Banks and then veer north again until he found a favorable westerly wind just above the 50th parallel to carry him to France. In the North Atlantic, currents pulled east. On return journeys, Michel often sailed as far south as the 43rd parallel to take advantage of currents pulling his ship westward. If the weather remained fair, this outward voyage promised to be routine. However, Michel had promised himself one thing would be different. He wouldn't grumble at the exorbitant duties La Rochelle's revenue agents would demand for the privilege of risking life and vessel to bring a cargo across the North Atlantic. It was a small cargo anyway. New France always had trouble filling holds for the France-bound portion of journeys.

As the weeks rolled by, Michel tried to work out how and where he should sell the much more valuable cargo of manufactured goods he would be taking on in France. He was tempted to sail directly to the American colonies where he hoped to learn the tricks of avoiding British revenue cutters and selling his cargo at what would seem like bargain rates to New Yorkers and Bostonians used to paying a king's ransom for any article from Europe.

Finally, he told himself no. He would follow his uncle's instructions. France forbade its colonies from trading with nations other than France, forcing them to buy only goods manufactured in France. The rules were clear, but his uncle liked a challenge. In fact, after seeing examples of the dance his uncle did to obtain and sell goods on the side, Michel thought him a mastermind. Michel remembered him once boasting, "I think I could have taught that devious Cardinal Richelieu a thing or two about sleight of hand, even in his prime, may somebody bless his soul." More than a century had passed since Richelieu's death but, as Antoine never hesitated to point out, "The obsession the King's chief minister had with the glory of France made it the miserable state it is today."

One morning in late May as the Chameleon sat becalmed for a second straight day not far from the Bay of Biscay and the great French ports, Michel finally decided that when the time came to turn backsides to France, his bow will be pointing to the Indies.

As he rode out the calm, he took note of how uneventful the voyage had been so far. He had shoved the excitement of carrying out his uncle's mad scheme to one side of his brain. It was one of those league-at-a-time journeys in unknown waters. For now he had to captain his vessel just as he had done on so many other voyages. His thoughts returned to the routines beloved by men in dangerous jobs. He remembered Day One, when once again, he had said the quickest of prayers of thanks just after raising anchor at Quebec City and reading the owner's instructions for the voyage. His uncle had once again not followed the practice of most merchant shipowners, and all French navy vessels, requiring their captains to find a priest to accompany the voyage in order to in turn provide any needed solace and instruction to the crew. All but four of the 27 men who sailed with him last year had returned. They were starting to become a veteran crew, one that required little commanding, by their captain or their God. Two were married to local Indians, one a young Huron woman and the other an Odawan. Whatever their other charms may have been, neither of their husbands were ever heard again to exercise their daily right to prayer aboard ship.

Rules like those, and so many others, made Michel realize for the hundredth time that life in the colonies never did square up with the men who wrote rules in France. Now that it wasn't frivolous to daydream of someday adopting a new home port in a more prosperous colony, and, hopefully, one with a much more inviting male to female ratio, Michel was more convinced than ever that those born in the New World had more in common with him than their always bickering home countries.

He now had much more to think about than before, and the time had presented itself. It had been a peaceful voyage so far. Other than fishing boats off the Grand Banks many weeks before, Michel's log had recorded the sighting of only two ships, and those only in the past week, one a similarly sized brigantine slightly to the north of them, heading west under a British flag, and the other a much larger northbound ship, an East Indiaman, with more guns than he had crew. It was flying Swedish colors, probably returning to Gothenburg with a cargo full of Chinese tea, much of which would undoubtedly be smuggled later into England at prices cheaper than tea from England's own East India Company.

Despite his youth, Michel had worked every post on the ship, starting at the bottom, as a ship's boy. When his uncle finally made Michel captain, Antoine's first love remained the sea and sailing it. But in recent years his uncle had convinced him there was a game to be played that, if you had the mind for it, could be more complicated than navigating a ship and far more satisfying. It was mostly a game for agents to play among buyers and sellers on dry land. But, as uncle Antoine would say as they sat passing away the winter hours in the comfort in his grand fieldstone house, a smart captain can make deals of his own.

"Not only do agents always have an ear reserved for proposals, but so do individual merchants desperate for this reason or that to turn a quick profit with little investment. So, my boy, stand tall in port," his uncle would say, "like a beacon of hope for merchants on the edge, the ones denied the big prize because their purses aren't quite full enough. They're often the ones who have no choice but find a way to undercut the fat and prosperous. You need to keep your wits about you, of course, but remember that you have what they all need, a means of transport. The more desperate they are, the higher your price. So, in port, look successful and you need not buy your own drinks or want for conversation."

Michel had learned to listen closely to what his uncle chose to share with him over the years. He had spent his own youth aboard ship and knew more ports intimately than Michel might ever know. He was also adept at cajoling custom's officers.

"The thing to remember," his uncle would say, "is that they are poor men, and fearful men. Somebody higher up has already shouted at them or threatened them by the time they come aboard your ship. They have to collect at least some duty, but the amount depends on you, on how much money you put in their other pocket. The cargo deck is so dark it's easy for them to miss things. Who knows, you might make a friend for life."

Though he was standing directly under the foremast, Michel was so lost in thought he hadn't heard the first flap of sail nor the quartermaster's call from the helm that followed almost instantly. "West with some north in it, sir." Ideally it would drop the Chameleon in front of La Rochelle like a well-struck billiard shot with just the right amount of side spin. By dusk, they were in the Bay of Biscay and, as if choreographed, a French frigate appeared in the distance on the larboard side at exactly the moment Michel had confirmed the crow's nest sighting of the finger-like Île de Ré that pointed the way to the mouth of the ancient French port just to the south. Soon a French pilot would guide the ship past the medieval forts of La Chaîne on the port side and Saint Nicholas to starboard, and find an anchorage in the always crowded harbor that was second only to Bordeaux.

The revenue inspector had come aboard with the pilot. He allowed Michel to see his ship safely secured along a dock before beginning his tedious examination of the ship's manifest. The old man was clearly both tired and in foul humor. Michel determined the latter was entirely due to the former and wasn't entirely surprised when the inspector chose to leave the cargo as it was instead of ordering it to be endlessly shifted so he could see what lay below last-loaded items. As the inspector demanded the pilot's hand to ease his struggle up the companionway to the main deck, Michel touched his shoulder and said softly:

"You've clearly had a long day, monsieur. I can't imagine at this late hour that more work awaits you. Perhaps you could lead me to a good inn where I might have the pleasure of buying you whatever you feel will lighten your load, so to speak." With practiced skill, the inspector wasted no time snatching the coins from Michel's hand. "I don't want company," he grunted, stepping on deck.

Michel's crew was free to start unloading the cargo from New France. Unbeknownst to them, it would be the last time they would do so. They didn't yet know they were now homeless. He knew they had questions since the moment he slipped into a sheltered harbor near Matane and had them change the ship's name. At the time, Michel took a perverse pleasure in how his always gossiping crew made a meal of the name change. He didn't dare tell them the reason at the time. He might have had a mutiny on his hands and he couldn't blame them.

Michel was thinking of telling them as they neared land, figuring his crew would have no choice but to sail on to port. Now he wished he had. Those who wanted to jump ship in La Rochelle could have. Some may have even been from there originally. More Frenchmen set off from La Rochelle to settle in New France than from any other port.

He could replace the departing crew members. He was planning on sailing down to Bordeaux to hire more men anyway. He wanted more English speakers, and there were plenty to be found along the docks of the Crescent City. But he also feared that if he let crew members leave in La Rochelle they might mention the name change and arouse official curiosity. Michel still didn't have papers stating he was the legal owner of the Chameleon. That forgery was on his agenda for Bordeaux.

As darkness fell over the city, Michel gave his crew leave to go ashore as soon as the cargo was unloaded. Tomorrow he would arrange for a new one. It had already been set up by Antoine through his regular agent and friend, a man named Ladouceur, who was undoubtedly expecting to be notified of the arrival of a ship called the Fabienne.

Michel had already concocted a story to explain away the name change to him. He would make it exotic, he decided. He would joke that his dear uncle was getting dotty. In his cups one cold winter day his uncle met with an Indian soothsayer. In return for illegal firewater, the Indian said he'd had a vision in which a French maiden named Fabienne fell from her horse in the clouds into the sea below and drowned.

"Even the next day," Michel would say, "when my uncle was sober, he insisted I have the name changed before we reached the open sea in the spring. I obeyed."

CHAPTER 30

The Other Side Of The Coin

New York City,
May 18, 1754

CURIOSITY got the better of Sarah. Noah had warned her to stay away from Croman's main wharves for a month while his army was sporadically sabotaging the loading and unloading of ships belonging to Croman and other merchants. The plan was to accidentally damage casks and crates, or carelessly let a pallet of sacks slip into the harbor. Among the tactics Noah had discussed with his band of dockworkers was one whereby a fight would break out close to the boat being loaded or unloaded. The commotion at the far end of the wharf would make it a relatively simple matter to pass along a sack or hog's head to a carter waiting in the street.

Noah also offered a reward to any men who could manage to delay unloading a newly arrived Croman ship by rowing to the foot of the wharf at night. While the guard, as he invariably did to fight boredom, stood at the Water

Street end to watch passersby, the longshoreman would climb onto the wharf and crawl to the weights Customs officers had brought to assess duty on imported cargoes. When the moment was right, he would let them slip into the water, saving the heaviest weights for last because it would be almost impossible to avoid a splash. Even if he noticed, before the watchmen could run the length of the wharf the saboteur would have rowed into the darkness and safety.

Croman's wharves were now the largest on the East River. They could berth some of the larger vessels on either side. The warehouse at their foot on Water Street had been recently expanded by the expedient of buying out the merchant next door. Croman had offices on Hanover Square but most days he could be found at newly built ones on Water Street itself.

His portly profile alone was enough to make him stand out in any crowd. What caught Sarah's eye the instant she peered down a wharf was the lamé vest he wore over a white linen shirt. Affecting to work as hard as the longshoremen, he had removed his red, knee-length coat. Mostly, he strutted up and down, pointing emphatically at this and that. Over the din of the waterfront, Sarah could not pick out his voice but it was obvious he was issuing impatient orders.

If Sarah were spotted near the wharves around the time the sabotage was going on, the risk was too great that Croman would conclude she was somehow involved. It could only be assumed that the thugs who'd set fire to her warehouse on his behalf knew her by sight.

As Noah outlined his plan at the old mill in New Harlem, he didn't have to tell Sarah that Croman was a man to be feared. He warned her that none of the goods his people stole from Croman must end up in her possession.

"My men can get rid of some of it and I'll make sure you get a small share," he'd told her. "The other goods will have to be stored elsewhere."

He suggested Jacob and Peter's engraving shop and the tiny yard behind Geneviève's. Geneviève agreed immediately, though it meant that whoever carted the load would have to traipse through her little shop and enter the yard through the kitchen at the back. Makeshift one-story rooming houses on the street behind blocked outside access to the yard. Geneviève didn't complain when the buildings were erected, occupying a lot where the original house had been heavily damaged by fire. Being hemmed in made her feel secure. Sometimes, looking at the yard from the kitchen window, she fantasized that it was a little courtyard, a little like those she'd seen behind the homes of the wealthy in France.

When Sarah arrived at New Street to tell her brother about Noah's idea, he wasn't home. When Sarah pressed Peter as to Jacob's whereabouts, he reluctantly said that Jacob had gone to City Hall to watch a court proceeding.

"Some poor fellow charged with counterfeiting. Jacob absolutely insisted that I allow him to go."

Peter invited Sarah to enter. Seated on a stool in the workshop, she asked Peter if she could store some goods there. Though she liked Peter, there was always something about him that made her hesitant to say too much about anything personal. Rather than mention Noah's scheme, she reminded him that she still had not found the money she needed to repair the warehouse. She had little room left in the house proper where she already had merchandise stored. The truth was that she now did, thanks mostly to Geneviève and the French lessons, have the money, but Noah said a rebuilt warehouse would be an open invitation to Croman's arsonists.

"It would be only temporary, until I can find a buyer."

Immediately, she knew Peter wasn't keen on the idea. He lived on the second floor, where he also had his office. He was very particular in his dress and manners, as if still trying to please the British parents who no longer spoke to him.

"The only storage space is down here," he said, his hand indicating the side wall where he kept cartons of paper of varying weights, sheets of metals, lacquers, paints and inks. "Your brother beds down in front of them. If you take away his sleeping space, we could move our supplies further into the room and stack your goods against the wall. The width is, I believe, 18 feet, but the ceiling is high."

He could see Sarah calculating what she could get into such a storage space.

"I don't see where else you could store your goods that wouldn't be in our way while we worked."

Sarah could see that he was probably right, although she'd couldn't remember whether there were any possibilities upstairs, perhaps even an attic. Since he was not forthcoming with other ideas, she asked Peter to pass on that she hoped Jacob could visit her that night.

"Speaking of visits," Peter said, stopping in mid-sentence. He suddenly seemed uncomfortable. Sarah assumed he might be feeling guilty about not helping out with her need for storage space. He resumed, awkwardly. "What I meant to ask, Sarah, was whether I could visit you sometime on Maiden Lane." Anticipating a refusal, he quickly added, "or go to the Mule some evening, you and I?" He started to speak again but nervously rejected another possibility he'd rehearsed, that of sitting with her at the wharf at the bottom of the street.

Sarah searched his face, finally saying in a matter-of-fact manner, "Perhaps, Peter. Now is not the time."

Peter ignored how neutral Sarah's voice was when giving him his answer. His foot was in the door. Sarah turned to the door before seeing the blush appear on his cheeks.

Leaving the atelier, she walked north on New Street. She had decided to heed Noah's advice and avoid the docks. Her plan was to walk up to Wall Street and follow it east toward the river and walk up to Maiden Lane. Suddenly the skies opened and she was drenched with rain. She tried to shelter herself under the doorway of an old Dutch-built house made of red brick. It was there that a behemoth tackled her to the ground. He was in a fury. As his body weight knocked the air out of her lungs, he bellowed something. She did not understand, but she knew it was German. Lightning flashed seconds after a roar of thunder. He looked to the skies in the same instant that a broad-shouldered woman flung open the house door and struck him with an andiron.

"I hope he's dead this time," she said, letting the andiron drop to the ground and adjusting the apron that somehow managed to cover her girth. "He grabbed me once," she said. "At my age I should have been flattered but I pushed a radish I was eating into his eye."

Her English was perfect but the rhythm of her words was Dutch. Seeing the confusion in Sarah's face she added, "Returning from Marcktvelt Street," using the old name for "Marketfield Street." She grabbed the giant's belt and one leg and hauled him off Sarah. Sarah was astonished at her strength. "Come, girl," she said, offering Sarah a hand to help her get to her feet. "Lucky for you I cleaned the grate today." She picked up the andiron and disappeared into the house.

...

Jacob had never been to a trial before, in France or here in New York. Everyone seemed bored, except the accused, whose expression floated from hung-over to defiant and back. Jacob had learned of the trial in the New York Gazette but had forgotten the details of the case except that it involved forged bills.

Just over a year ago, about the time Jacob first began testing his artistic hand at engraving partial imitations of paper currency, he read about the trial of an infamous counterfeiter whose story had been reprinted in newspapers throughout the colonies. Learning that several of his collaborators, the men who distributed the forged money he printed, had turned King's evidence, which apparently was the only way the authorities could convict anyone. It was not illegal to possess counterfeit notes nor spend them if you believe them to be legitimate. Short of nabbing a counterfeiter with plate and press, the only way of putting him behind bars was to have someone testify they had knowledge that the accused was manufacturing and using false currency.

Upon hearing that one of his men had betrayed him, the counterfeiter turned himself in and, along with the informer, was convicted. Moments after being locked into the pillory outside the court his head was branded with the letter R for "incorrigible rogue" and portions of his ears were cropped off. The man who had informed on him then replaced him in the pillory. Once the forger had had the satisfaction of watching the informer punished, he grabbed a sword and broke away from his captives.

As Jacob recalled, what made the case memorable was that the counterfeiter returned to town a few days later to mock the authorities by voluntarily turning himself in for the second time, and once again heavy chains were not enough to keep him in jail. In the process, according to the newspapers, the counterfeiter had earned great public support, not only for his daring but for doing what everyone wanted to do: make money.

The man being arraigned today before the New York Supreme Court of Judicature on counterfeiting charges had first been nabbed in New Haven, Connecticut. He promptly escaped and fled the jurisdiction, finally being apprehended in Dutchess County, New York, near the Connecticut border, according to the report in the New York Gazette, which went on to mention a fact everyone knew, that New York was floundering "in counterfeit Bills in imitation of the true Bills of the Publick Credit".

After trying unsuccessfully to bribe his captors with fake cash, the man Jacob was now observing from the back corner of the courtroom had been sent to New York to stand trial because New York's penalties were far more strict than Connecticut's, where authorities went out of their way to avoid the expense of keeping prisoners in jail for long. Connecticut was well aware that New York had previously resorted to the cheapest solution of all, hanging, provided the culprit had been found to have forged New York currency.

Since his arrival in New York, the prisoner had been chained in the city's jail, located in the basement of City Hall at the corner of Wall and Broad streets. The court room was directly above the little jail. Jacob wondered whether the prisoner, from his cell below, had been able to hear the footsteps of the men about to try him. Coming from France, Jacob had a paralyzing fear of any judicial system. It existed for rich men. Everyone said so, even though there'd be stories of aristocrats occasionally suffering the king's displeasure in the Bastille in Paris.

Jacob had only once seen a newspaper, left at his father's by a wealthy wine exporter. It was called the Mercure de France. Most of the articles were about music and plays, of which he knew nothing, and the latest fashions, of which he knew even less. His father said Cardinal Richelieu once wrote many of the articles, and even now its editor owed his job to the King. Perhaps, Jacob thought then, the stories about aristocrats going to the dungeon were just stories people made up because they liked the idea. The one thing he did know for certain was that once the judicial system swallowed you up, you knew exactly what the rest of your life would be like.

For a fleeting moment the chilling thoughts about life in prison made Jacob consider the possibility that he was a fool for trying to recreate paper money. He had gotten bored with clipping coins. Engraving, engraving anything, was where his talent lay. He had comforted himself with the thought that he was just like a great musician deciding to learn a new instrument.

After the entrance of the chief justice of the Supreme Court had been announced, little seemed to be happening.

The grand jury had already returned its indictment. The defendant now faced the jury of 12 men, pled not guilty and placed himself on God and country. Jacob had not noticed the well-dressed young man, probably seven or eight years older than he was, standing beside him. The man whispered that "placing oneself on God and country" simply meant the defendant's countrymen would decide his fate, not the formidable-looking judge whose face seemed too big for his wig.

"Arnold," said Jacob, smiling as he took the man's hand. With his finger, Arnold, whom Jacob had gotten to know at the café almost next door, frequented by investors and speculators, motioned Jacob to be silent as the judge began to speak:

"I am of course well aware that it is standard procedure for felony trials to begin the day after the indictment has been returned, but I have been informed of exigent circumstances which dictate that this case be heard immediately."

At that, an inebriated Cockney-accented voice from the other side of the room proclaimed, "They's afraid he'll break jail again. Convict'm quick, they will." A soldier who'd been standing by the door immediately tried to push his way through the small crowd, awkwardly clinging to his musket. Unable to determine the source of the outburst he happily returned to his station. Jacob thought he looked relieved to have avoided having to wrestle the spirited offender out of the room.

Five men then quickly testified for the prosecution, including the man who'd found the defendant at the farm near the Connecticut border.

"I knew I had the right man because I'd seen him arraigned in Hartford, and his countenance never left my mind during the month and a half I tracked him down after his escape. I was hired by some prominent men in the community to find him, and I did, though it took me more than a month to do it."

The prosecutor added that the defendant, first collared in New Haven, had been found guilty in Hartford and that upon his final apprehension had tried to bribe the witness.

"Two thousand pounds is what he offered me," the witness stated. "In fake money," he added after a theatrical pause, raising his voice. "That's not moral."

Laughter told the court that the public didn't quite agree with the pontification. Jacob felt like joining in but clamped his teeth shut at the last moment. He glanced to his left and saw that Arnold was amused as well.

Three of the prosecution's next witnesses were men who had not been involved in the Hartford trial but had testified against the same defendant four years earlier in New York. They had testified that he had offered them "a discount so astonishing on several hundred pounds worth of New Jersey paper that it sorely tempted a good man's resolve. Only a forger would do that," they'd said.

The defendant called them liars and claimed they were trying to get back at him for pointing a gun at them when they failed to pay their gambling debts.

"Besides," the defendant added, "no one's ever seen me with ink on my hands." That time, the jury acquitted him for lack of proof that he forged money or knowingly spent any.

The fourth witness this day had testified at the more recent trial in Hartford. He prefaced his testimony by saying the authorities in Connecticut had declined to pay his way to New York.

"I wish the court to know that I am here because honesty is its own reward."

Before the witness could say another word the defendant exchanged his hung-over look for the defiant one and proclaimed:

"Honesty be damned. That man crossed the Sound to New York only because he has a mistress here."

Even the chief justice smiled before nodding to the

witness to continue.

"I never saw his printing press with my own eyes but I personally saw paper notes hanging from a line behind a shack he keeps outside Hartford. There they were, all that money drying in the air. The country thereabouts is infrequently travelled but I was not the only one to see the defendant's laundry on the line."

Finally, the prosecutor called the farmer who offered the defendant shelter up north in Dutchess County.

When the prosecutor asked him if the defendant had paid him in return for hiding him, the farmer answered yes.

"How much did he offer you?"

"The defendant told me it was £100."

"Don't you recall? You took it. Was the money real?"

"Can't say, sir. Can't read."

With no more witnesses to testify for the King, the defendant was offered the opportunity to speak or have someone testify on his behalf.

"In a better world than this, I would call upon my friends, but I can't. You're lookin' at them," he said, indicating the prosecution's witnesses. "They were my friends. Don't know anyone else hereabouts in New York."

The court adjourned for half an hour and when it re-opened the jury announced its verdict: guilty. The defendant had already turned his back on them.

The judge passed sentence, ruling that "the prisoner at the bar be taken to the place from whence he came and thence to the place of execution and there to be hanged by the neck till he be dead."

The chief justice ordered that the execution be carried out the following day, between 10 a.m. and 2 p.m. The prisoner would be taken by cart to a triangular field less than half a mile north of the jail. The field was known as The Common. It began where Broadway ended. A rope would be thrown over a tree and placed around the forger's neck. Jacob had been to The Common, on a walk with Sarah. They'd laughed a lot that afternoon.

A hissing sound came from the general area where the Cockney had offered his opinion of the trial earlier on. Not everyone disagreed with the verdict. Several people clapped.

Arnold, still at Jacob's side, look amused. "Will you be attending?"

Jacob couldn't take his eyes off the condemned man, the man who evidently had learned to etch copper plates. When he was escorted out of the court and back to his basement cell, Jacob turned to Arnold.

"No," he said. "Absolutely not."

"Then shall we try to find a table at the café?"

Any other time Jacob would have gladly accepted the chance to accompany his rich friend. Wealth seemed less mysterious when they shared coffee and talked.

"I have someone I must see. My sister, actually."

He parted company with Arnold in front of the café and walked east to Maiden Lane. He hoped he would find Sarah home.

CHAPTER 31

The Deed Is Done

La Rochelle, France
June 3, 1754

MICHEL's impatience soared. Twice it had got the better of him as he sat in his cabin. Standing abruptly with the intention of charging on deck to see what the problem was he cracked his head on a beam. The second time had been so severe he took to his bed for an hour.

The hold had sat empty for a day and a half ago. His men were happy to rest while a new dockside argument threatened to prolong the delay in bringing the outgoing cargo alongside for loading,

Michel uncorked a bottle of wine and invited his first officer to join him in his cabin. Jean-Luc Delaville was more than a first mate. He was a childhood friend who outdid Michel in daring for mischief-making on the often snow-covered streets of Quebec City, on days so cold that older children were dispatched to run errands while parents stayed by a hearth. Their favorite prank was to take skins of water mixed with ale to prevent quick freezing and climb the never-ending steps to Upper Town. Once they caught their breath, which hung about them in clouds, they would make their way to the Séminaire de Québec and pour the liquid on entranceway steps. In fear that they might have been spotted, they usually hurried straight home without waiting to see a religious literally fall for their prank.

Michel attended the Jesuit College until his uncle decided that a life at sea would be more educational for his adopted son, and more profitable for him. Jean-Luc was orphaned at the age of three and was also given an education by the church, thus providing both boys with targets for their pranks.

Since Jean-Luc was without family, the idea of leaving Canada behind for good required only one glass of wine to accept, at least in principle.

"A share of your profits, Michel? All this will be hard for many of our men. You will have to let them work for a share of future profits, like pirates, which, of course, we are not. Are we?"

Like his uncle, Michel's friend was faster than him at seeing financial opportunity. Michel agreed completely. Money… what better first argument to make to his crew. Since they wouldn't be paid until the end of the voyage, this offer would cost him nothing while he worked out the logistics of somehow translating his uncle's dream into reality.

"I agree with you, Jean-Luc. Consider it done."

Pouring them each another glass, Michel continued:

"As for your last point, there are two things that could turn us into pirates. The first would be if I am unable to find a rascal in Bordeaux with the skill to forge me a letter of ownership of the Chameleon, or that he provides one that makes a harbor master erupt in tears of laughter. Either eventuality would put me in possession of a stolen ship, and make me and all who sail in her pirates.

"The second possibility that could make pirates of us is that I might not be able to find an agent in New York or Boston to find me buyers for my cargo and sponsors for my subsequent voyages. I know not a soul in either city. My uncle knew people inland, in both New York and Maine, maybe elsewhere, English traders and smugglers, and Indians, of course, but he never traded or smuggled by sea."

Michel added that he'd been thinking a lot about that final barrier to becoming a rich trader.

"I can't just sail into New York, sell my cargo and pay my men. I can't sail into New York until I can find a buyer. I'll have to anchor outside the harbor and make my way ashore on my own. I'm hoping to find a sailor here in France who not only speaks English but who also has sailed to the British colonies."

Jean-Luc smiled at his life-long friend.

"It is truly a relief that the announcement you made to me 10 minutes ago was not a spur of the moment thought. You are subject to those, you know."

"Well, Jean-Luc, you know my uncle well. He's the clever one of the family. A schemer and proud of it. This was all his idea."

"I'm doubly relieved," said Jean-Luc. "I trust him. Now let's get back to the crew, your immediate problem. Not counting either you or me, there are 24 onboard.

"To the best of my knowledge, there are three to four of them who hail from La Rochelle. There might be more. I would suggest we call them in first. They might be willing to let you pay them off right now here in their home port. But regardless of their response, you should tell them only something safe, something that can't come back and haunt us if they pass it on to the crew that's staying, or worse, are overheard by the wrong person in some tavern in port."

"I've thought of that," Michel said. "Just this morning after deciding to let you in on the news. First I will say this ship has a new owner, which is true. Second, I'll add that I will be meeting with them later in Bordeaux, which in a twisted way is true also. I will cite the change in ownership as the reason for having changed her name.

"I will then prattle on gravely about having just received a message from my uncle via a ship that left home in our wake. The messaged stated that his plans have changed. We're no longer going to be sailing the standard triangle that brings us back to Canada for the winter. I will tell them I can't say how long we'll be at sea.

"I will then add something about how the news deeply concerns me as it must them. You know, about us all having family and friends in Canada and so on. What do you think, Jean-Luc?"

"I would say you have just betrayed yourself as every bit the schemer your uncle is. I don't see any holes in your plan. However, it is important that no one goes ashore here in La Rochelle until we are all set to weigh anchor. There's bound to be someone here who knows your uncle and his ship. If someone repeats the story you've just told it could raise curiosity if not questions. As it is, customs inspectors will be onboard assessing the cargo we'll be taking on shortly. Let's hope they don't ask for your papers, Michel. If they do…" He paused. "As you put it to me earlier, this plan of your uncle's has put you on the verge of becoming a pirate."

Michel suddenly wished he'd spoken to his friend much earlier in the voyage rather than let the potential pitfalls of his uncle's plan lay siege to most of his waking moments.

When Jean-Luc returned half an hour later, he was accompanied by five seamen. He was right that four came from La Rochelle but there was a fifth who said he had a wife there.

"I sort of ran off and left her, sir. On those cold nights back home I really miss her. Didn't think I would. My sister, she's in Toulon, sir. She says my wife moved to La Rochelle not long after. If what the first mate says is true, sir, I'd like to get my pay and look for my woman."

"Of course what the first mate says is true," Michel said, glaring at the seaman.

"Just a figure of speech, sir."

"And what of you other men? What would you prefer to do? It's entirely up to you."

Three of the four Rochellois opted to quit the ship. Of the five seamen Jean-Luc brought to the cabin, only one elected to stay aboard. That left 19 other crew members who would have to be told about the change in plans. However, Michel needed them to load the ship first. Once the ship was loaded, this time to near capacity, the goods would be worth a lot more than those he came with.

A week later the cargo was aboard and stowed. Once the preparations were all but done he summoned the seamen who had decided to quit the ship. As he watched them debark Michel gave the order to weigh anchor. He told his helmsman to follow the coast down to Bordeaux. Once under sail, Michel called for the bosun.

"I assume you've heard that there has been a change in plans."

"Nothing official, sir, but the men have been talking."

"Well, it's true. I myself only learned of it when we arrived at La Rochelle. Since a number of our crew were originally from here I gave them the option of leaving then and there. I need the rest of you to get me to Bordeaux to take on more cargo and meet with the new owner. You can pass this news on to your men and tell them that they will be given an opportunity to collect their partial pay and leave the ship in Bordeaux. I'm sure they will eventually find a ship in need of experienced crew for a voyage to Quebec City.

"In the meantime, pass on what I've said and let me know before we reach Bordeaux how many wish to part company. Tell them if they have any questions they can speak to the first officer."

A day and a half later they were sailing up the Gironde estuary, the largest in Europe. Michel was still nervous about finding someone to forge the ownership papers, but he found himself putting the worry aside as they made their way past the tranquil beauty of the vineyards, marshes, cliffs and islands that made up the Gironde. Today it was all drenched in an unusually warm June sun. Michel couldn't help comparing it with the different kind of shoreline he was now saying goodbye to forever, the wild beauty of the St. Lawrence River and the majestic Cap Diamant that had pointed his way home so many times both as a boy and a man.

When they arrived at the harbor the Chameleon was obliged to drop anchor. The port appeared to be choking in ships large and small. A pilot came aboard and informed Michel that a frigate had run aground and before she could be towed back into the channel she capsized.

"Every available small craft is there now," the aging pilot said. "They're trying to both rescue the crew and whatever cargo has floated clear of the ship. One of the small boats also capsized trying to get a cask aboard. I knew that would happen. They weren't seamen. Maybe they were the owners. You'll be here for a while, captain, I assure you."

Michel signed to Jean-Luc to follow him to his cabin.

"Maybe," said Michel, "this confusion is to my advantage."

"How so, my friend?"

"I would rather face a broadside from a British man-of-war than get caught passing myself off as the captain of a ship that has no verifiable ownership or provenance. We were lucky in La Rochelle.

"It's a gamble, but if I win I will be the soul of serenity upon my return. Here is what I propose, Jean-Luc. It may take hours before we can get to a berth. I wish to put the Chameleon under your command while I am rowed ashore.

I know Bordeaux quite well. If we have a crew from here, you can assign them to convey me ashore. I may want their company for protection."

"This is all getting very mysterious."

"Yes, it could turn out that way but my hope is that a few *livres* in the right hands will get me the paper I need in time to return aboard to welcome the inspector. With that paper in my hand I won't have a worry in the world."

Fifteen minutes later the pilot stood by the rail looking puzzled as the captain expertly descended to the ship's boat below. Before he'd seated himself, an oar had pushed the boat away from the Chameleon. Michel told the oarsmen to go as far as they could toward the center of the port before tying up along the quay. With more than a few bellowed threats to other craft, the Chameleon's boat managed to tie up along the Richelieu Quay on the left bank of the Garonne River. Michel's uncle had told him to make his way to the Rue Sainte-Catherine and the Rue des Trois Conils at the Place Saint-Projet, which he would recognize by its fountain. At the corner, Trois Conils became Rue de la Merci. He was to follow it one block and turn left.

"Knock on the second door to your left," Antoine had told him. "A matronly woman will in all likelihood answer the door. Tell her you wish to see the public scribe to write a letter for you, and add that the matter is urgent. Be prepared to pay her a small sum."

Instead of a stout woman, the door was answered by a boy of no more than seven or eight. He didn't utter a word after Michel presented his request. He merely turned and disappeared into a room at the end of a narrow hall. Moments later, a man appeared, his shoulders almost too wide to navigate the hallway without turning a little sideways.

"*Bonjour, monsieur.* How urgent?"

"Pressing, very," Michel answered, lifting a purse from his coat pocket. The man did not introduce himself.

Michel told his seamen to wait outside.

The room at the end of the hall was surprisingly bright. It must have faced onto an alleyway or yard. A long table stretched below the window. On it were several piles of neatly stacked paper, pens and pots of ink. Despite the neatness of those items, the surface was ink-stained and gritty with blotting sand.

Michel handed the man the paper identifying Antoine as the owner of the Fabienne, a 110-foot, 91-ton brigantine built in Saint-Malo. It would now be the Chameleon, also built in Saint-Malo, Michel d'Antan, proprietor.

Less than an hour later, the boat clunked against the Chameleon's side. Michel had noticed on the way back that order was being restored to the channel. The return trip took half the time it had taken to get to the heart of the city. As he stepped on deck he was relieved to see the pilot still aboard, seated on the deck smoking a pipe and talking to the bosun. He rose when Michel approached.

"She'll be hugging a pier before sundown."

Michel had barely settled behind his desk when he heard the anchor being raised and bare feet padding quickly along the deck above. Intentionally, he hadn't relieved Jean-Luc of command, which also meant he was too busy on deck to raise a glass with him. Michel resisted the temptation, deciding to wait until they'd docked.

Once they had, Michel stood beside Jean-Luc.

"Care to relinquish command?"

"If you insist," he said, smiling.

"My cabin. Now. That's an order," Michel replied, grinning back.

The next morning, Michel sent his first officer ashore to find replacement crew members, including as many native English speakers as possible. Jean-Luc understood why he had to remain vague about the Chameleon's future destinations. If all went well, within the next three months she would be sailing under a British flag.

As casks of Bordeaux wine were raised aboard two days later and lowered into every last remaining space in the hold, Michel chatted with the customs officer, showing him the manifest that had been verified in La Rochelle. After Michel paid the duty owing on the wine, he asked the officer, "Will that be all?"

"Yes, I bid you good sailing," he answered, turning toward the dock. Michel was disappointed. He ached to show him his paper of ownership.

The following afternoon, Michel ordered "weigh anchor". The topsail was unfurled and a new voyage began. As always, those two commands made Michel feel free. He was his own man. Now, as he was about to set sail for Saint-Domingue, he felt weightless. He was not only his own man but his own man with his own ship, officially. The deed had been done. The deceit had gone unquestioned. Even better, his crew, now numbering 31, had not keel-hauled him, or worse.

CHAPTER 32

Setting The Bait

New York
June 28, 1754

AS JACOB descended Maiden Lane he could make out a large black man at Sarah's door. It had to be Noah. Jacob was glad to see him. On one hand he seemed so aloof from everything, while on the other he seemed to know everything that was going on in New York. Jacob had learned to trust Noah's advice as had Sarah.

Sometimes he thought Noah had become some sort of father in Sarah's eyes, father and protector. Jacob missed his father but thought that it must be different for a man. He was proud of his much-in-demand skill as an engraver. He felt independent. On the other hand, while Sarah was independent of mind, in fact more so than he was, she was somehow always in need emotionally. She didn't speak of their father often. It was too difficult even knowing how to refer to him: dead or alive. If he had been attacked as violently as they'd been kidnapped, he was likely dead. He was not a strong man.

She still dreamed a French ship would appear in port and take a letter to France but she knew that was not going to happen. Months ago Asser, her agent-merchant friend, had put a letter she'd written to her father in the hands of a ship's captain about to leave for Jamaica. Asser had actually placed Sarah's letter inside one of his own, addressed to a Jewish agent he did business with in Kingston, Jamaica. He asked him to forward Sarah's letter to Bordeaux. He never heard back.

Sarah was also surprised to see Noah. When she heard his knock at the door she thought it was Jacob. The two of them had barely climbed the stairs to the upstairs kitchen when Jacob knocked and let himself in. As he took the stairs two at a time, he'd already started talking excitedly.

"So relieved, sister, to find you at home. My mind feels like it's been drowned by two waves crashing on it simultaneously from opposite directions. An impossibility, but there you have it."

"Have you not been home?" Sarah asked.

"No. I've lived life and death today."

"What on earth are you talking about? Are you OK?" Sarah was alarmed. Noah stared hard at Jacob.

"Forgive me, Sarah. I'm fine. I'm perfectly fine, except I want to make us a thousand pounds, even more. I know now I can do it, but I just found out I don't want to hang."

Sarah was relieved when Jacob laughed.

He laid his shoulder pouch on the table and sat down. With great ceremony he reached in and slowly pulled out a flat object wrapped in cloth. It was a small sheet of copper.

"Look closely," he said, standing up and inviting Sarah and Noah to sit at the table.

As they did, Jacob pulled another plate from the shoulder pouch.

"The first one," Jacob explained, "is for printing a North Carolina six-pound note. And the other one is a

Maryland four-dollar bill." Jacob let them try to make sense of the reverse images etched onto the plates. After a minute, he said,

"They're mine. I made them." He then put paper versions of the two notes on the table.

"I've seen as much forged money in my time as real money," said Noah. "Is that money real?"

"It is. I've never printed any money, although I've studied it and practiced drawing it until I can almost do it from memory. I've done four other notes as well. Over time I've acquired the typefaces I'd need, the inks, the papers. They're basically the same ones I use every day." He recovered the plates and returned them to his shoulder pouch.

"That's why I was in court today," Jacob added.

"Jacob!" Sarah sprung to her feet and grabbed his shoulders.

"No, no, no," Jacob said, taking her hands and gently sitting her down again. "I was observing the trial of a man accused of counterfeiting money. I read about it in The Gazette. The man is famous throughout the colonies." Jacob explained that he was convicted only because his supposed collaborators and friends turned King's evidence. "I felt sorry for him."

Noah smiled.

"What I learned is that it's not even illegal to spend counterfeit money if you don't know it's been forged, and it's not even illegal to make it if it's the currency of another jurisdiction and if you don't intend on spending it. This is what the King needed the informants for, to say that the prisoner had given them the false money knowing full well that they knew he'd forged it."

"Didn't that make them as guilty as he was?" asked Sarah.

"The prisoner said he even paid them to spend it but they all said the money they accepted had been for an old gambling debt. Said they never used the counterfeit money. The prisoner was the famous Sullivan character. He's the only one the Crown wanted to hang."

Sarah almost choked when she repeated the word "hang".

"Yes, tomorrow at The Common." Jacob looked at both Sarah and Noah. "And before you ask, no, I'm not going. Can't even bare to think about it. Remember our walk there? If I witnessed the hanging I'd never want to go back."

Noah lifted his chair closer to the table, then leaned forward, his face now only a couple of feet from Jacob's.

"Would Peter turn you in if you started forging at the shop?"

Since the question was directed at Jacob, Sarah waited for him to answer. When he hesitated she said,

"I think he might. I don't know why I think that. He just always seems to be saying only half what he thinks. You know him much better."

"Peter's my friend," Jacob finally said.

"And the men who got a man condemned to death today were once his friends," Noah said.

"Noah's right," said Sarah. "It's too dangerous."

"You're right," Jacob conceded. "That's why I came here, besides wanting to show you my 'paintings'. That's how I think of them."

Jacob looked Sarah in the eye.

"We've got to do something. Time's going by and your situation isn't getting any better. I came here because I've got the beginning of an idea. Tell me if I'm mad."

Before he had a chance to launch his plan, Sarah announced that she and Noah hadn't been standing still.

"Some days I'm just plain hungry. Other days I'm hungry for a bit of revenge."

Jacob looked at his sister, then nodded. They knew each

other as well as any two people could.

"You first," she said.

Jacob was glad Noah was there. He was part of his plan, if he agreed.

"In a perfect world," Jacob said, "I'd be able to make the fake money at our atelier, but you're right that Peter is an unknown. We do the same work. He's a good engraver, a very good one. We both are. But I sometimes think he feels my work is better. Maybe it's just the way the English can look at you, at people like us. I could be wrong. He's always been good to me."

"Do you know his parents?" asked Sarah.

"No. The way he tells it, nor does he, not really. He feels they abandoned him."

"Were they rich?"

Jacob shrugged his shoulders.

"He had a tutor when he was small, before he started apprenticing. That's all I know. Maybe they encountered some kind of misfortune later.

"Anyway," Jacob repeated, "I agree with you that it would be unsafe to approach him about any of this, at least right now. That means I need a place to work."

The expression suddenly shared by Sarah and Noah told Jacob they weren't sure they really wanted to hear the other shoe drop.

"My first thought," he began, looking at the floor and trying to contain the enthusiasm that new ideas always engendered in him, "was that I could help you repair the warehouse and print there. All we really need is a new roof and to scrub the soot off the walls. It wouldn't be perfect because printing can be noisy. Your neighbors know you're not a printer. They'd wonder. But if we're careful, if we keep the doors closed, this place might be ideal. No house abuts the warehouse. The walls are stone. As for drying the new notes, why not right here by the hearth?"

Neither Noah nor Sarah said anything. His excitement

getting the better of him, Jacob continued.

"We could eventually move the press elsewhere, or stop forging altogether. The thing is we would have made enough money to set you up as a wholesaler and merchant, with money to stock enough to supply a large clientele. Maybe in time you could even invest in ships."

Sarah beamed at her brother. Upon hearing such a plan, only she would understand that Jacob never once thought of making a farthing for himself. He had visions of his sister being happy and secure, even rich someday. It would likely never happen, but for the moment she was happy to relive the childhood joy of accepting fantasies as imminent reality.

"Dear Jacob, your plan is a grand one, and I thank you with all my heart, but the time is not right."

Jacob's face looked more confused than crestfallen.

Noah began explaining the plan he and Sarah had worked out to sabotage the fat man and drive him so mad he'd have a heart attack.

"But," Noah said, holding up his index finger and looking straight into Jacob's eyes, "the fat man will certainly figure out that we're behind it or at least part of it. And men like that step on men and women who get in their way. We must not repair the warehouse at this time. If we did, I am sure the fat man will send men to burn it down again. I don't even want Sarah going anywhere near the docks. We want him to think Sarah is just scraping by, which she is, and that she is nothing more than a girl who begs work from a seamstress."

"I see," said Jacob. His eyes betrayed the concern he now felt for his sister's safety and the power of the giant bear she was now poking. Suddenly, his get-rich plan seemed no more than a child's invention.

"That's why I went looking for you at the atelier today," Sarah said. "To find storage space. When Peter said there wasn't really much, I told him to send you here. I was thinking you could move in with me so we could take advantage of Peter's space. There's almost no space left here in the house to store anything apart from this kitchen. It wouldn't be forever."

Jacob said he'd be glad to move in.

"I could use the company, Jacob. And I miss you. You're always so hard to find, you're at the atelier, or you're out visiting customers, or at the café you love so much."

"Speaking of which," interrupted Jacob. "The café. The fat man goes there now and then. He even bade me good evening one night. Don't worry, Sarah. He has no idea who I am. He only saw me the once, when we first arrived, when he bought your indentureship but not mine."

"What kind of café is this?" Noah asked.

Sarah explained by repeating what Jacob and Peter had told her when they first started spending evenings there.

"They go there to eavesdrop. And," Sarah added, smiling, "pretend that they, too, are investors and speculators."

Jacob said they'd made a few friends there as well, including the wealthy young man who watched the forger's trial with him.

"I'm hoping it will pay off some day, if only we had the funds to take advantage of an opportunity."

Sarah and Noah both sat up straight in their chairs.

"Jacob," said Sarah, "do you remember those deeds we forged on the ship?"

"Yes, for land somewhere in southern Pennsylvania."

"Do you think if the fat man decides to sell that land he might make its availability known at the café?"

"It's as good a place as any," said Jacob. "At times it seems there are more speculations than men there."

"I'm only thinking out loud here, so just hear me out. It occurs to me that if we had the cash we, I mean you, could let it be known that you were looking for land to buy and resell in Pennsylvania. How well do you know your friend from the trial?"

"Arnold?"

"Yes."

"Well enough to know that we enjoy each other's company. Why?"

Sarah paused before posing her next question. She knew she could be reckless, and after being admonished by Noah for hanging around the docks while his men pilfered, she didn't want to risk his distrust.

"Are he and the fat man competitors?"

"Not really. Arnold comes from wealth. I think he simply enjoys speculating."

"Would the fat man take him seriously if he expressed interest in property Croman claimed to have for sale?"

"Absolutely. Arnold has the breeding men like Croman try to obtain by wealth alone. What on earth are you planning?"

"Would your friend Arnold enjoy what I think the English call 'a little sport' at the expense of the fat man?"

"I'm guessing," answered Jacob, "but I would imagine he finds the fat man's appearance and manners repulsive. Arnold even seemed amused today when the forger was condemned to hanging. While I was horrified, he was smiling and asked if I would join him at the execution. As you say, it was as if he saw it as a chance to have a little sport."

Sarah asked Jacob to broach the subject the next time he saw Arnold. "Be vague about it. Just say you've heard there's a wealthy merchant who might try to sell land he doesn't own. See how he responds."

Jacob agreed, again delighting in seeing Sarah's other side at work.

"But go no further than that. Once Arnold has shown a little curiosity, I might have an element to add to our plan to expose Croman. It would be on a much bigger stage than what your café has to offer."

Sarah was smiling ear to ear. The two men found it infectious.

They decided to go to the tavern before calling it a night. They first toasted Sarah's deviousness. Noah then returned to Jacob's scheme to literally make money. He was careful not to use words like "counterfeit" or "forge".

"There's place at the mill in New Harlem for your machine. We'd have to measure but on the second floor there's a room that was meant for some kind of storage, maybe provisions in the days when the village got attacked now and then by Indians."

Jacob jumped on the idea. Noah was suggesting that his plan to rescue Sarah by manufacturing money mightn't be dead after all.

"Do you have a press?" Noah asked, almost whispering the question in Jacob's ear.

Jacob shook his head no, but said he thought he could get one cheaply. A few days before he had seen a notice in the newspaper that there was a press available from the estate of an engraver who'd just died. The notice stated that he'd had no family and that the administrator of the will wished to expedite the sale of the man's property to cover his debts and the cost of burial.

"Then it seems," said Noah, "that only one problem remains. A big one. How do we transport a press from here to New Harlem, and then through the woods from the village to the mill? We don't want anyone to even suspect we have a press. As you said, Jacob, the whole city's talking about forging right now. If we transported a press to New Harlem we might as well be transporting gallows."

CHAPTER 33

Hidden Talents

Latitude 36° N, southeast of Norfolk, Va.
Aug. 27, 1754

IT HAD been a week since Captain d'Antan ordered the British colors raised. With that gesture, made on a breathtakingly clear day when his lookout could assure him the ocean belonged to him and him alone, he officially became a smuggler and enemy of the French.

As the flag rose, the crew on deck and up on the yards seemed frozen in time as they stared upwards. When the colors began flapping in the wind they looked toward their captain as he clapped his first mate on the shoulder, the two men smiling.

The sugar, indigo and coffee that filled the hold of the Chameleon was not going to a French port. That meant that it would not comply with the French mercantile policy known as the Exclusive. To ensure that France alone always profited, it stipulated that Saint-Domingue's raw products had to be exported to French ports in French ships.

Likewise, all manufactured goods consumed by colonists had to be ones imported from France. Saint-Domingue might be the richest colony in the Caribbean, far richer than any colony owned by Spain, but its merchants were handcuffed precisely like those in New France and the British colonies, which had their own version of France's Exclusive policy to deal with, Britain's Navigation Act.

Michel was not only free as owner and captain of his own ship. He was determined to conduct trade with anyone who would pay the price. Just as his uncle once traded and drank with New York traders near Albany, he'd raise a glass with any man.

A few weeks ago, as the Chameleon sailed out of the harbor of the Saint-Domingue capital of Cap-Français, a city known as the Paris of the Antilles, he turned to windward and bellowed a fine curse in the name of the king, Louis XV. The trailing gulls paid no attention.

It had not been the first time Michel had done business in Saint-Domingue. When he stepped ashore wearing an unadorned, tan-colored tricorn, beige coat and a white cravat so loose against the Saint-Domingue heat that it looked like a topsail on a windless day, his feet took him unhesitatingly to the door of his uncle's long-time agent, Origène Deschamps.

Outside his door, a slave swept dust that didn't exist. Before he could knock on the door, it was opened by a serious-looking man in a butler's uniform. He took Michel's hat and led him to a curtain that Michel remembered separated the foyer from the sitting room. With his uncle, Michel had once been inside the Chateau St. Louis, where the governor of New France lived. He was a marquis, a minor title but a real nobleman nonetheless. Curtains didn't separate rooms in the chateau.

There were people of noble rank in Cap-Français as well, many more in fact than in Québec City. There were also many more pretenders in the bustling Saint-Domingue capital. Slaves outnumbered whites 15 to one. Whites competed to prove their wealth by being accompanied by more slaves than they could possibly find work for. Most of the whites, the "petits blancs", the merchants, bureaucrats, lawyers and tradesmen, were frequently heard saying they were just passing through. Few truly wanted to stay under the Antilles sun or put up with the rainy seasons. Although many had their own slaves, they hated the truly wealthy for their ostentation.

Origène Deschamps, a skinny man in his 50s, with a small but nevertheless incongruous pot belly, knew all about pretension. He didn't hide it from Michel because his uncle knew him when he was simply Monsieur Deschamps, bookkeeper and haggler extraordinaire. With his first modest successes buying and selling at the waterfront, Origène decided to embellish his ancestry, or at least the ancestry of his father, an indentured servant brought to Saint-Domingue as a boy.

Unlike most white indentured workers, or *engagés*, as they were known there, he survived the sun because he was not sent to work in the fields. Eventually he bought his freedom and married. His wife bore him only one child, a son, Origène. The boy's father loved to tell the boy he had a tiny claim to fame. According to the story, the boy's grandfather, Jérémie Deschamps, was once mistakenly named by the British to govern Tortuga, the infamous pirate island off the coast of Saint-Domingue. It was then settled by both English and French. No sooner had Deschamps been named governor than he sent up the French flag and claimed the mountainous island for France. He beat off several British attempts to reclaim the island.

Origène's father didn't know where his gallant father was buried.

"The brethren of the coast probably ended his days," he said. That was good enough for young Origène. He was later to claim during social occasions that his grandfather was a viscount, appointed by the King himself.

About five minutes after Michel arrived, two slave women parted the curtains, revealing surprisingly handsome French furnishings. Yet another slave handed Origène a cane to help him rise graciously from a lavishly upholstered, high-backed Baroque armchair. Michel suspected that those five minutes had been spent retrieving his finest clothes. Michel could not imagine anyone would sweat out such a humid day dressed for royalty. During the wait outside the curtains, Michel had been unable to resist the temptation to use his cravat to wipe his brow.

"My warmest greetings, young Michel," said Deschamps.

"It's indeed warm enough, thank you," replied Michel. "It's good of you to see me. I'd been hoping to see you by chance on the docks when I arrived."

"It's much more comfortable here, don't you agree?" With that he showed off the creole he'd learned as a boy and ordered refreshments.

While waiting, Michel surveyed the furnishings and complimented his host.

"I can't imagine there is anything you're in need of but I've come to tell you I've just dropped anchor in your fine harbor with some particularly fine pieces from Lyon… Paris, too, come to think of it. The rest of my cargo is the usual. I doubt you'll have trouble selling any of it, but as for the furniture, you might care to take advantage of your being my agent."

"Ah," said Deschamps. "Now I'm your agent, not Antoine's."

Michel bit his tongue to remind himself later of the stupid slip. There could be no hint that anything was out of the ordinary. The Chameleon's name change was going to be tricky enough to explain. Michel had simply forgotten to think of an explanation that would satisfy those familiar with the Fabienne.

"Practically speaking only," Michel hastened to add. "I

could live to make a thousand voyages and never come between you and my dear uncle."

They drank to Antoine's health, then the agent announced grandly that it had been his intention to do business with another captain that afternoon but "every one of those 82 ships now in port will have to wait for Antoine's son." Deschamps had no children. Michel wondered whether he wished he had the same arrangement Michel had with his uncle.

Deschamps excused himself briefly, leaving Michel to enjoy the large fan being waved by a young girl standing to the left of his chair. When he returned, he was dressed in clothes almost suitable for being rowed out to Michel's ship to examine the cargo. They entered the street followed by a middle-aged black man. Michel remembered him from a previous trip. He knew how to write and made a record of cargo items and values dictated by his master.

When they arrived at the dock, the harbor captain's representative was waiting. When they climbed aboard the Chameleon, Michel took the two men into his cabin. He offered them both chairs and stood while the harbor agent looked over the manifest before checking the cargo himself.

"Michel," Deschamps suddenly said, breaking the silence. "Did you manage to load the furnishings left to me by my uncle in Nantes?"

Michel couldn't resist smiling at the man's nerve. He had pulled the same stunt before in order to claim items as personal property, not subject to duty.

"They were waiting for me when I dropped anchor in Bordeaux. Not to worry. My men handled them as if they were loading the finest wine."

When the inspector left in the late afternoon, unloading began. Deschamps chose an ornate armoire for himself, paying Michel the amount he asked for minus what he would have paid in duty. That evening he sent three young slaves to the wharf to hoist it into a hand-pulled wagon.

Before they were ready to sail several weeks later, Michel let Jean-Luc convince him to let the crew have a day off to let loose in the capital.

"They won't be drinking and whoring with the authorities. No one will wonder what happened to the Fabienne."

Just more than 20 days later, his charts telling him he was as far north as Norfolk, Virginia, Michel watched a sailor begin his ascent to the crow's nest. Before he'd gotten 15 feet above the deck, Michel turned to Jean-Luc.

"I see what you mean. He's no sailor. Bring him to my cabin."

"I think you'll find his story interesting," his lieutenant said.

Twenty minutes later they realized the man represented potentially more value than their cargo.

His name was Nicholas Cadieux. He thanked them profusely for taking him on in Bordeaux. He said he'd been chased by the authorities halfway across France. Then, with pride, he said he was France's most wanted counterfeiter. He worked near a tiny village called Charolais. He said it was in central France. Neither Michel nor Jean-Luc had heard of it. Cadieux said it was important to work away from the big cities. He seemed eager to explain his profession.

Michel raised his hand to silence him.

"In not many days we will be making landfall. You will not be permitted to leave ship without being accompanied, even if I release the entire crew. Do you understand? If you do try, I'll turn you in myself. Now get back to work."

Cadieux turned to face Jean-Luc.

"Do you still want me to climb?"

"No, neither the captain nor I want you dead. Not yet anyway. We may have use for you."

CHAPTER 34

While The Merchant's Away

New York City

JUST after sunrise, Jacob locked up the mill and set out along an ancient Indian trail that wound its way through woods that kept the morning almost uncomfortably fresh until the trees gave way to brush and farm land about half a mile north of New Harlem. He was exhausted after six days of working his press from sunrise to sunset. His plan was to walk all the way to New York. He needed to stretch his legs and silence his mind.

In his shoulder pouch were bills of credit worth slightly more than £1,000. It was a rough calculation. Though he was not a businessman, Jacob had been in colonial America long enough to know that the value of money lived in men's minds, nowhere else. From listening to discussions among businessmen at the café on Wall Street, he knew that the value of a colonial pound varied from province to province. A pound in New York paper currency was worth about eight shillings sterling, but a pound in

New Jersey paper was worth seven shillings, a pound in Pennsylvania flat money about six. The real thing, a pound sterling in England, was worth 20 shillings. In the end, Jacob learned, a pound in America was as different from a pound in England as a cat and a dog, as an Englishman and a Frenchman.

It was so nonsensical to anyone who actually used money, and many didn't, that coins represented the only secure currency, and for everyone the most certain value was a Spanish dollar, the most common currency in the American colonies and in Europe. You could test its value. All you needed was a scale. You could at least measure their weight in silver, copper or gold. Was the situation the same in colonial countries everywhere?

In France he had never thought about the value of money. A *livre*, a pound, was a *livre*. Here, in America, the value of money was what businessmen said it was. In his study of paper money, Jacob had learned that only bills of credit, which is what paper money represented, from Maryland stated that they were redeemable for the value stated on the bill itself.

Merchants had told Jacob that the provincial assemblies printed money when needed to pay their bills. Massachusetts was the first to print money. It had no other way of paying the soldiers who'd fought in a failed attempt to capture Quebec City from the French. Even the government found dealing with the various issues of paper currency so complicated the province outlawed the use of paper money just a few years before, although they still had to honor the bills still in circulation. Jacob had not forged any Massachusetts bills.

More astonishing, he learned that from time to time wealthy merchants from different provinces would meet and declare that this currency and that currency were worth such and such. It was entirely arbitrary and always in the interest of merchants who imported and exported goods. If someone disputed the value set by the merchants, the courts almost always decided in favor of the merchants.

As for the real value of his £1,000, the precise amount didn't matter to Jacob. All that mattered was that he'd made good on the wish that he'd expressed to Sarah two months earlier. When he showed his sister and Noah the plates he'd made, it was his love for his sister that made him pull the figure of £1,000 out of the air. Jacob later admonished himself for his display of hubris about his engraving talent. Nevertheless, if it had taken him twice as long to print £1,000 he would have persevered gladly.

Jacob stopped at the tavern for ale and bread. Usually with Noah, he'd been to the tavern half a dozen times, frequently enough to have earned a nod of recognition when he entered. He hoped the breakfast would carry him all the way to Maiden Lane. He needn't have worried. When he returned to the street, a young man who had also been in the tavern was climbing up to the seat of a small wagon. Spotting Jacob he wished him good morning. Jacob's mood was so good he couldn't help but return the greeting with a smile. The man asked Jacob where he was headed.

"New York," Jacob said.

The driver said he wasn't going all the way to the city but he could shave a couple of hours off Jacob's journey if he wanted to accompany him.

"Haven't conversed with a soul for days," said the young man.

It was early afternoon when Jacob let himself into Sarah's house. He called out but there was no answer. As he climbed the stairs to the kitchen he suddenly felt weary from his trek. He sat for a moment at the table. When his gaze fell on the bed he rose as if his legs had a mind of their own and made for it.

Though he still lived at the atelier, he had an overwhelming sense of now being at home. As he lay on his sister's bed he could make out the sounds of the market at the bottom of Maiden Lane. He found them soothing, unlike the voice of a belligerent carter on Water Street that was soon silenced by an eruption of jeers and laughter.

He closed his eyes and thought about his press. It cost him less than he thought it would. He was prepared to pay up to £50, which would have left him close to penniless, but the administer of the will seemed to be in a sour mood and was interested only in getting rid of what remained of the engraver's property. Jacob offered £35. They settled on £38.

The previous evening he had met with Noah. They sat with their legs dangling off a wharf near Coenties Slip, where Noah had been working of late.

"Noah, I realized this morning I have no idea how to get the press to New Harlem. None. Would it survive a cart ride that distance? And even if it could, we can't have it delivered to the mill. We might as well hang a sign on it saying Forger's Press."

They discussed the logistics until the sun set behind them. Every idea fell apart after a moment's thought.

"We can't hire a cart in any case," Noah said, "because they're not allowed to work after dark, so they'd never be willing to go all the way to New Harlem. Even if they could, our destination would set off alarms, as you say."

Jacob asked Noah if he could bribe a carter to let him use the wagon for the day, returning it the next morning.

"Two problems with that. One, the city won't license a black man to be a carter, so no carter is going to lend me his cart for any amount of money. What we will have to do is hire a cart to get the press down to the river and take it the rest of the way by boat. We'll have to cover it up with canvas or something."

Jacob looked lost in thought, then suddenly shivered.

"I just had a vision, Noah. You know, a press is taller than a man if you include the big star wheel you use to turn the rollers. I saw the press sitting in a wagon on its way down to the river. Picture this, Noah. I am just another person in the street. Hundreds of us have stopped to watch the slow procession of the wagon. Men have removed their hats. What we are staring at in silence is not a press. It's a gallows, or a gibbet, covered by blankets, being hauled to the site of a hanging. Our hanging."

Noah's face was expressionless as he stared into Jacob's eyes.

"I'm being silly, I know," said Jacob, when he could no longer hold Noah's stare. "It's just that since the Sullivan trial people are seeing counterfeiters around every corner."

"Your vision is now mine, damn you," said Noah.

Both men became silent for several minutes, their eyes taking in the growing stillness of the harbor. Soon the scores of ships would light their lanterns.

"We take it apart," Noah said matter-of-factly.

"What?"

"Your press. We put it back together at the mill."

"I don't know why I never thought of that," Jacob said. "Problem solved."

"Do you know how to take it apart?" Noah asked.

Jacob said he was certain he could figure it out, adding that it would be a two-person job.

"I'm sure the administrator won't want us spending the whole day there."

"I'm good with my hands," Noah said. "If you show me how to take it apart I'll know how to help you set it up at the mill. It's good we both know. This may not be the only time we have to move the press."

Even with two sets of hands, it took more than an hour to dismantle the press, much of the time spent removing bolts and mortise and tenon joints that had been in place for decades. Jacob made notes on a sketch he'd made of the components. When he and Noah began carrying them out to the wagon, the carter offered no assistance.

"He thinks I'm your slave so his help isn't needed,"

Noah whispered to Jacob.

The ash side frames and oak press bed were the first to go in the cart, followed by the star wheel. Last were the upper and lower rollers. To protect them, they were wrapped separately, as was the press bed. Once a canvas was secured over the entire load, they set off, Jacob giving the carter the destination, a small wharf just north of Maiden Lane. Noah and Jacob walked behind the horse-drawn cart. The carter walked alongside, frequently cursing pedestrians and carts blocking his way or slowing him down.

When they arrived at the wharf and started to unload the press, they stopped in their tracks when a surly voice boomed:

"About time, Noah!"

Noah looked up and laughed.

"Who's that?" Jacob asked.

"None other than Commodore Barry himself."

Before Noah had a chance to explain the presence of this Dutch-accented bull of a man with a carpet's worth of unruly white hair, the Commodore's hammer fist grabbed Noah's.

"I am hoping we are embarking on another adventure, my friend. My soul has been at anchor so long barnacles are clinging to my daydreams."

Noah introduced the Commodore to Jacob.

"He's the only one among us young enough to have dreams. As for adventure, for our sakes I hope this is not one, but young Jacob has embarked on one of his own. I'll explain when we get underway."

"I brought a couple of otherwise useless *jongelingen* to help us."

Turning toward the boat he ordered:

"Boys, here, take this load aboard. Make as if you're carrying the girl of your dreams. Gentle, gentle. I'll be watching you!"

The boys did as they were told. Jacob was relieved. When he shook hands with the Commodore he was too numb to feel the crush of the Dutchman's fist.

"I've never seen a boat like this," Jacob said.

"There's no better boat than this for our purposes, lad. It's a Dutch-built boat, called a *boejer.* Her name's Citroen."

The Commodore ordered the boys to raise the headsail. Almost instantly the strange boat started to edge away from the wharf.

"See her bow and stern? They're rounded like a Friesland farm girl's behind. Current and wave will have a hard time altering our course," said the Commodore. He then pointed to what looked like wooden wings, standing upright amidships. "They're called leeboards, lad. If I lower them, depending on the current, they keep our course true, just as if you were foolish enough to paddle a canoe in the East River with all its currents and twirly-twirlies and tides. Best canal boat, river boat or coaster there ever was."

As they slowly made their way into the river, the boat swayed sickeningly, but after a few minutes the Commodore had the mainsail raised and soon found the channel the current had chosen for the day. They were New Harlem bound with a press Jacob hoped would reverse the evil that descended on him and Sarah in Bordeaux.

In what seemed like no time at all, they'd left the East River and were edging toward shore just north of the usual Harlem River entrance to the village. The Commodore barked a staccato series of commands and the two boys jumped to comply. Suddenly the Citroen was pointed precisely at a slipway. Despite his age, the Commodore jumped onto the right bank and ordered a boy to throw him a line. He pulled it over his left shoulder and began pulling the boat further into the narrow slip.

"Boys, with me!" he ordered, and they leapt to the left bank, taking a line with them. As soon as their feet landed in the marshy grass, they joined their Commodore in hauling. Within less than a minute the captain had secured the boat to a tree standing at the end of the slipway.

"OK, lads. Get your girlfriends ashore as gentle as you please."

The ship's stern now rested about a yard inland from the edge of the Harlem River. The Commodore hauled a six-foot-high piece of wood upright.

"Boys!"

They came running, each grabbing a side of the wood. The three of them edged it toward the water in the slipway. The Commodore then aligned it with a wooden bracket neither Jacob nor Noah had noticed. At the Commodore's command, the two boys stepped into the shallow water and began guiding the wooden panel above the slot on the right side and, keeping it hoisted level vertically, positioned it above an identical slot on the other side of the slip.

"In she goes," the Commodore said, and the boys let it slip into the slots. They'd dammed the slipway.

"Did I mention the shallow draft?" said the Commodore, grinning. "In winter or when I need to do repairs, we pump out the water and she sits pretty as you please on timbers. My very own dry dock."

Noah had been around the Dutch long enough to be aware of their mastery of eradicating swamps with landfill or turning them into canals or slipways. The very quay where they met the Commodore was the product of the same engineering. Now, when New York sold waterfront lots along the rivers to private citizens, it often required that they extend the island by filling in the river before they could build their home or place of business. The quay they'd been to that day fronted a vacant lot. The Commodore's boat was probably the first to ever tie up there.

The Commodore announced that his work was done. He took payment from Noah, who received it from Jacob before they set sail.

"You can use my boys to deliver your whatever it is."

It took two trips. On the last one, the boys carried the awkward press bed while Jacob and Noah shared the sacks containing wooden typefaces, inks and paper.

No sooner had the boys left the mill than Jacob started peppering Noah with questions about the Commodore.

"I'll tell you while we work," said Noah. If there was work to be done he always set to doing it. Chat could wait.

They started by unpacking the paper, inks and fonts, which they placed in a box hidden behind the mill's wheel mechanism. It was made of the same wood as the wheel and wouldn't stand out. In another hiding place on the second floor, under the floorboards, Jacob placed the plates for counterfeiting.

The basic reassembly of the copper-plate rolling press went faster than the disassembly, but Jacob knew it would probably take some time after Noah left to get the upper and lower rollers, one slightly smaller than the other, adjusted perfectly. When dismantling the press, he had been sharp-eyed enough to notice the layered shims of pasteboard and felt that had been used to adjust the rollers until they provided sufficient pressure to get a good print. He would have to experiment to get the shims placed exactly as they were. He could verify that only by printing test sheets in the coming days.

Once Noah and Jacob had attached the table, they lifted the frame erect. Darkness was starting to fall and Noah went upstairs, returning with two lamps. He also produced a bottle of rum, which Jacob saw only after Noah lit the lamps.

They sat down on a bench. Noah passed the bottle.

"The Commodore. Well, Jacob, the Commodore isn't a Commodore of anything, apart from being owner and captain of his boat, which is rarely in the water these days."

Jacob chuckled at the word "boat".

"Did you notice, Noah, how the Commodore looked

like his boat, round in front, even his face, and round behind and overall built to carry any load?"

"He's a good man," said Noah. "I suppose a man can be anything he wants in his mind, even a Commodore. Everybody around here knows the Commodore. His family goes back to the Dutch days. Everyone's forgotten his family wasn't originally Dutch."

The forest around the mill had gone silent. The stream that was originally supposed to turn under the big wheel had been nearly dry all summer. The mill had been abandoned for several years. Noah's bass voice was the only sound for probably miles around, thought Jacob.

"The Commodore's parents farmed around here, like mine did. He still lives on that farm. But his grandfather was a sailor, an Englishman. According to the Commodore, his grandfather was in the Royal Navy and deserted ship in the Dutch East Indies. Somewhere in the Indian Ocean is all I remember. The Commodore says his grandfather made it to Batavia and before he could wink at a pretty Indonesian girl he had signed aboard a Dutch merchantman. Years later he dropped anchor here. By then he could curse in Dutch with the best of them."

"The Commodore's name, Barry, it sounds English," said Jacob.

"It is. His grandfather's name was Barry Clark, enlisted in the navy as a boy. Whether it was just a coincidence or whether he was as eccentric as his grandson turned out to be, I don't know, but after endearing himself to the people of New Amsterdam by opening a public house he married a girl named de Klerck. Apparently that's the Dutch version of Clark. His little joke? Anyway, by the time they had children they were known as the de Klerck family. They gave the name Barry as a middle name to one of the boys and the name Clark as the middle name to the other son. They were determined that the English name would go on.

"Years later, along comes the Commodore. Now that they were under British rule, they named him Barry Clark de Klerck. Call him just Barry and you risk a bloody nose. He's Commodore Barry to everyone. Buy him some ale and he will tell you all the great battles his grandfather fought at sea. I think he just makes them up and just likes imagining himself with a fleet of his own. British or Dutch, I don't think it matters to him. When he plies the East River with a crew of New Harlem children, he thinks he's commanding a frigate, or, who knows, maybe even a man of war."

"I would love to listen to his stories," said Jacob.

"There's a good chance you'll see him again. He will be useful to us. If he suspects we're doing something on the sly against a rich Englishman he won't be able to resist helping us out. He loves his English name but he's as Dutch as they come. Besides, it would be another story for him to tell."

"What kind of things are you thinking about?"

"Not just the money but also goods we've taken from Croman. The Commodore has plenty of place to store things on his farm. I haven't talked to him about it but I'll have to soon. We've got goods stored all over the city and Sarah can't sell them as fast as my guys steal them. By the way, did Sarah tell you the fat merchant sailed for England in July?"

"No, I've hardly spoken to her this summer," Jacob said. "God, he's going to have a fit when he returns and counts the losses."

"That's why we're going to have to be really careful, really smart. Sarah has to keep low by approaching only small customers to sell her goods. She's got enough now that she's getting repeat orders. But most of the goods, it's my guys who sell them as payment for trying to cripple Croman. Most of them have never seen so much money and that's how I know they'll keep their mouths shut. For the future, what I'm thinking is that if we could get the Commodore to sail to New York some night, we could send him back with a full cargo. That boat of his holds a lot. With all that stored away here in New Harlem we'd have lots of insurance. If things get hot when Croman returns we can simply stop the sabotage for a while and live off what the Commodore is holding for us."

Noah left the following morning and Jacob set to work. It wasn't until he returned to Maiden Lane six days later and lay on his sister's bed reviewing what Noah had told him that he realized how big their revenge scheme had grown. It was no longer just he and Sarah. Noah had built a network of thieves, and Sarah had built a network of clients, from little shop owners to her seamstress friend and acquaintances of Patricia, the daughter of a prominent politician.

When Sarah came home she jumped on top of Jacob in joy and held on tight for at least a minute. When she finally let him get to his feet he could see the old Sarah had returned, the optimist, the one who enjoyed life and challenge. He worried that his accomplishment would seem anti-climactic.

"Sit," he told his sister.

He laid his leather shoulder pouch on the table before her.

"Close your eyes and open it. Tell me what you feel."

An hour later they were walking in The Common. The September night sky was clear and star-filled. It seemed like half the city was there enjoying the same thing. Jacob had forgotten that this was also the place where Sullivan, the counterfeiter, met his end. The realization made him stop.

"What's wrong?" Sarah asked.

When he told her she answered that after he'd first told her about the hanging, she walked to the park to see if she could feel the presence of death.

"I couldn't, Jacob. It's just a nice field. You're not that poor man. I know because you once tried to imitate an Irish accent. You were horrible at it."

She took his arm and they walked on. Sarah told him one of the items stolen from a Croman ship was a large shipment of fine cloth from London.

"I offered it all to Geneviève. It would set her up for life, but she couldn't come close to paying for it all. I sold her half and gave her terms she'll have no trouble meeting. All she needs to do is sell two or three dresses to fancy ladies and she'll be able to pay me for the lot. She is so happy, Jacob. I've started going with her to women recommended by Patricia to see if the fabrics tempt them. We have a grand time talking. She made me this, free."

She was pointing to the dress she'd changed into before setting out on their walk. Jacob had noticed it instantly. It was the finest dress Sarah had ever worn, by far. He didn't compliment her on it right away because that would beg questions and there were already too many questions, too many things happening, for him to take in all at once.

Sarah also said she saw Patricia at least once a week now.

"Geneviève told me she made my dress because I couldn't keep going into the homes of fine people dressed like a street urchin. She said it was bad for business, her business. It was so sweet of her."

Sarah said Patricia's French had progressed so much that she didn't have to formally teach anymore.

"We just talk. I learn about her world. She doesn't often inquire about mine. I like it that way."

As they left The Common to return home, Sarah asked:

"Where shall we keep all that money? What do we spend it on?"

From the mouth of his sister, it was the most innocent question Jacob had ever heard. It was as if they weren't stealing. Had any court ever justified avenging a crime, or being hungry?

"Yes, a good question, Sarah."

It was a question neither of them had ever had to deal

with in their lives.

CHAPTER 35

New York City

FOR the past week, Michel had been worrying about how to get himself to New York City without bringing his ship into the harbor. He wanted to find someone in the city to translate his ship's papers into English. He himself spoke only a few words of English, and with so few of his crew able to do so, he feared raising a custom inspector's suspicions.

He had already offered the English-speaking crew members a bonus to impersonate officers when the time came. One of them would be required to remain at his side at all times to help him answer any questions about his cargo or point of departure. He had also told Jean-Luc to ask every member of his crew whether they were familiar with the New Jersey coast. Two said they'd been to New York years before. One had been on the starboard watch at the time and never got a good look at the eight-mile-long slip of land close by on the port side. The other was below deck grabbing his four hours of sleep.

Then, while still 100 miles south of New York, a lookout reported a schooner closing in on them quickly from the north. Michel raised his glass and saw that she was under British colors. His heart skipped a beat as he looked skyward. No, he had not forgotten to order the British flag to be raised when out of sight of Saint-Domingue.

Ninety minutes later the schooner drew alongside as adroitly as could be.

"Where you be heading?" bellowed a man from the schooner's deck. Neither he nor his crew wore uniforms.

"New York," answered Michel.

"Then, sir, you've found yourself the best pilot there be. Permission to board, sir?"

"Granted."

Michel quickly turned to the young Englishman he'd asked to pretend he was first mate.

"Fast now, tell him the captain requests he bring his papers aboard. I'm going to my cabin now. Bring him there and stay."

Once installed in his cabin with the two other men, Michel made a show of examining the pilot's papers, understanding little because they were written in English. It didn't matter because pilot was *pilote* in French. Same word. He had no reason to think the man was other than what he pretended to be.

"Why, sir, do you approach me so far from port?" Michel asked, standing to retrieve a bottle of rum and glasses. He feared he wouldn't understand a word and would betray himself by displaying an expression of blank incomprehension. Damn, he thought, he should have assigned the young man to duties as some sort of captain's servant, and made him teach him English during the two legs of their journey from Bordeaux.

It turned out that the pilot was a man of few words, and the words he chose were direct and simple.

"New York is now the busiest port on this coast, sir.

Ships arrive by the hundreds. There are many pilots in the Sandy Hook area. I have to compete against them and I have to compete with the scum who pretend to be pilots."

"I see," said Michel. He said no more, forcing the pilot to fill the void.

"If you've examined recent charts of New York harbor and its approaches, sir, you know about the bar. Only an experienced pilot can get your ship beyond that and the shoals that abound between the bar and the southern point of Long Island. The channel by Sandy Hook is deep and perfectly suited for ships of far greater draft than yours, but peril lies beyond that point. I have been piloting for more than 30 years, and my father before me."

"How much?" Michel asked.

The pilot looked confused. Before Michel could signal his acting first mate, the young man had the presence to insert himself into the conversation.

"I believe the captain wishes to know your pilotage fee."

The pilot could have stipulated a price 10 times the amount he uttered after pensively stroking his chin for a minute. Michel would have paid it, without bargaining, which the pilot's delayed response was meant to suggest.

It was on the tip of Michel's tongue to say *d'accord* and thereby agree to the price. He took a breath and said, "Yes."

The pilot looked pleased and swallowed the rest of his rum.

Resuming his place at his desk, Michel motioned to the Englishman pretending to be his first mate to come near. Michel drew him closer and whispered:

"I want to say to him I have what may be an unusual request. Before proceeding to New York I wish to travel there without the Chameleon. Do you understand? I need a means of getting there and back. I am going to offer the pilot more rum and go back on deck for a moment. Pretend that I have perhaps a concern of some sort about, let's say, shifting cargo, that I must attend to. In the meantime, extend my apologies and make my request. Assure him I am prepared to make this worthwhile for him. Yes?"

The Englishman stood straight and answered smartly, "Yes, sir."

When Michel returned to his cabin 10 minutes later, he offered his apologies to the pilot.

The pretend first mate was smiling broadly. Clearly the pilot had accepted more than one additional glass of rum.

"Nothing," said the pilot, waving his glass before him, "could be simpler, sir. I can show you a safe anchorage at Sandy Hook where I might even be able to arrange to have a boat come to top up your provisions should that be necessary. You will then accompany me on the schooner when I am next hired to guide a ship home to port. I can assure you that you'll wait no more than a day."

Michel reached for the rum and poured them each a drink. The pilot drank it in a gulp and without the slightest sign of drunkenness made his way down the ship's ladder to his beautiful schooner. Once onboard he yelled up to the Chameleon.

"Follow me, sir, if you please!"

Three days later, the Chameleon far behind at anchor off the New Jersey coast near Sandy Hook, Michel climbed up from the schooner to the East River quay. New York's harbor seemed almost as congested as Bordeaux's, ships clearly at anchor waiting for a wharf or pier to become available. The comings and goings of small boats seemed chaotic, at least compared to Quebec City's harbor.

Quebec City had barely 7,000 people. New York City was well on its way to 13,000. To Michel's eyes, they all seemed to be on the docks at that very moment, all of them making noise of some kind or another. Unlike Bordeaux, there was no barrier that ran above the docks where the wealthy could promenade and find amusement in the sweating bodies of sailors and longshoremen below without ever having to brush near them. This was a city devoted to commerce alone.

He started walking north, above Coenties Quay. He didn't know where he was going but he thought the chance of finding rooms would be greater heading north. By the time he reached the Old Slip, Michel decided that Antoine would love it here. He promised himself that if he succeeded in living his life as an imposter he would one day bring his uncle to New York. They would talk in French all night long and laugh at life.

CHAPTER 36

Succor

THANKS to the windfall of the latest European fabrics from Sarah, Geneviève's business had tripled in a matter of months. It showed in her figure. She had gone from nearly emaciated to nearly shapely. She now had standing to ask storekeepers to show her their latest stock before it went to stores. Every two weeks she now made it a habit to walk the waterfront in search of deals or simply to bargain. As tiny as she was, she could bargain with the best.

As she had done for Sarah, she made herself two fine dresses. In the years she had spent in New York, she had never been invited to step out by a man. She accepted that she was no longer young enough to turn a head. But she had seen repeatedly that the right appearance said she wasn't in need of business. That alone brought her new customers, ones who could safely ignore the budget their husbands imposed.

She had started near Dock Street and was working her way north on Queen Street toward Maiden Lane when she almost stumbled on a body in the street. She had been lost in her own thoughts and hadn't noticed that pedestrians in front of her had been stepping around or over the body. She stopped and knelt. The man's right eye was swollen shut, his bloodied lips looked like mashed beets. Had he been on the other side of the street she would have walked by. She knew that prideless men resorted to their fists every day on the east side. The man was young, and were it not for the wounds, possibly handsome. What stopped Geneviève, though, was the sudden twitch of his lips. She leaned closer. He was saying something.

"*Au secours.*" Help.

She touched his shoulder. After a moment, the lips forced out the same faint sound. "*Au secours.*"

Geneviève peppered him with questions in French, his name, where he lived, was he with a friend when the beating happened, where could she have him taken? All she got was his first name and the word chameleon. "Michel Chameleon" could not be a name.

Still kneeling on the road beside Michel, Geneviève began calling for help. Almost immediately a well-dressed middle-aged man stopped and squatted beside her, inspecting the wounded man.

"Do you know him?" the man asked.

"Yes." Geneviève instinctively calculated that the well-off man kneeling beside her would be much more likely to help a young woman's friend than a stranger.

"Can you find a cart for me, sir? I must take him somewhere to be cared for."

"Madam, I can do better than that," he said. "My carriage is nearby, in the next alley." As worried as she was for the young man at her feet she couldn't help wondering if this gentleman would have responded so graciously had she been wearing the clothes she wore before Sarah's generosity. Maybe he just liked her accent.

Together with Geneviève, they got Michel to his feet.

"You, sir!" he called out to a man passing on the other side of the street. "Kindly assist us in getting this man to my carriage. Just around the corner ahead."

Geneviève could tell he was used to getting his way.

Because they were closer to Maiden Lane than Geneviève's place, they took Michel to Sarah's. The carriage driver got Michel to the street and, with Geneviève, to the door.

"I can manage now. Thank you," she said. She turned and thanked the gentleman as well. He touched his hat in response. Geneviève hoped he would offer a card but he immediately drove off. His wife may have made a good customer.

On hearing the carriage stop in front of her house, Sarah had come down from the kitchen. Geneviève had wedged the man between the doorframe and herself. When Sarah opened the door he tumbled in colliding with Sarah. With all her might, Geneviève held on to the man's shirt but she was not strong enough to keep him from sliding to the floor, where a moan escaped on contact.

"He's French!" Geneviève blurted out in response to the alarm that Sarah's entire posture expressed.

"Do you know him?"

"No. No. I tripped over him on the street. No one stopped because they thought he was mumbling, like a drunk. No one could understand him, but he was begging for help in French. I think he's badly hurt. We must help him."

Sarah fetched a spare straw mattress from the storage room and threw it on the floor in the adjacent room, the one that was supposed to have been her storefront office before the warehouse fire.

"*Aides moi,* Geneviève." Together, the two women dragged the man as gently as they could to the mattress. Once beside it, they each grabbed the man under an arm and lifted him onto the mattress. They couldn't manage to raise his hips and slide them onto the bed so they finally took a leg each, hoping neither had been broken during the fight. No sooner was he in place than Sarah hurried upstairs for a bowl of water and a cloth. Gently she began cleaning the blood from his face. Geneviève slid herself back against a wall, breathing heavily. Sarah smiled at her predicament.

"I was born to manipulate needle and thread," Geneviève answered, "by decree of the King no less."

"Well, my dear, I think our guest is in need of a seamstress."

"I have sewn sutures before, Sarah. In my own skin." She raised her dress and petticoat, Sarah could make out suture marks on Geneviève's right calf.

"A dog bit me. A French dog."

"Well," said Sarah, wiping away the last of the blood, "I hope this French dog doesn't come back to bite us."

CHAPTER 37

A New Partner

MICHEL slept through the rest of the afternoon. His mouth had been too swollen to eat even the tiniest morsel of the lentil stew Sarah and Geneviève had shared for their delayed mid-day meal. When he appeared to be sleeping soundly Sarah made her way through a labyrinth of alleyways and narrow passages to avoid the crowded main streets. She was relieved to find Jacob at the engraver's. Peter wasn't there.

"Are you being punished, made to work alone because of your week-long absence at Noah's?" The question was a teasing one.

"Deservedly so," answered Jacob, head bowed feigning remorse.

The £1,000 Jacob had brought to Sarah's had been buried that very night, after their walk in the Common, in a cheap tin box near the back of the burned-out warehouse. Jacob used a knife to excavate a shallow hole for the box, then stood and used his feet to drag, kick and push soot and pieces of charcoal over top. In the morning he made sure no boot traces led to the vicinity of their forged treasure.

They were both thrilled in the knowledge they were secure for the first time since being kidnapped from their home in France. They agreed that it was highly unlikely, considering the desperation they'd seen on their father's face during his last attempts to negotiate whatever deal he was after, that he had put away even a fraction of that sum after a lifetime of labor. A great deal of money exchanged hands at his shop but little of it was his to keep. The big merchants profited, as did the agents and ship's captains, but their father's fortune was never as predictable as the tides. His one gamble, an uninsured shipment of high-priced wine to Ireland, would have provided enough profit for him to start dealing at levels where profits could grow exponentially. It was not to be.

Jacob's first thought was to, at the very least, repair the warehouse "just to be ready to do business when the time is right." Sarah wouldn't hear of it.

Nothing, Sarah said with a firmness that closed the subject, would be done to restore the warehouse until she had brought the fat merchant to his knees. She would never feel secure until she had convinced him that attacking her would always cost him more than what he might cost her. She didn't know exactly how she would accomplish that but with the help of Noah and his network she was making better progress than she could have ever dreamed of. Some of Croman's men were now cooperating with Noah in return for good profit down the road. If he hadn't been such a bastard, Sarah wondered, would his own employees have been so quick to turn on him?

All she had to do at the moment, she told Jacob, was to await Croman's return from England. His reaction would be volcanic. He might expose his intentions.

There was the excitement of battle in Sarah's eyes. Jacob wished he could paint it, just as he had wished he could use paint to capture the innocence in those same eyes when she first asked what they were going to do with all that money.

On the way back to her house Sarah explained how a mysterious stranger came to occupy a mattress in her former office.

"When he fell asleep we searched his bag hoping to find out who he was or where he lived."

"And…"

"It wasn't a robbery because he had plenty of money, mostly French *livres.* But most intriguing is that it turns out he owns a ship or a boat of some kind. It's called Chameleon. When Geneviève heard him say that word in the street she thought it was his name. So all we know is that his name is Michel, he owns a vessel and he is French speaking."

After a pause, Sarah added,

"And he's rather handsome now that I got the blood off his face."

Jacob laughed with her. Sarah was indeed back to her old self. He also reminded himself that she was no longer a girl.

"Do you know where Noah is?" asked Sarah.

"Let's cut over to Water Street. I know where to leave word for him to come to the house."

Wherever it was Sarah had never been there. It turned out to be the tenement with the rickety stairs between Water and Queen streets. And to her delight, Noah was there, sleeping. Jacob left the room and said hello to an old man who had just sat down by the top of the stairs. They greeted each other by name.

"Ask Noah to come to Maiden Lane when he wakes up."

"He woke me from a heaven-sent sleep when he came home from the docks. I'd be happy to return the favor right now," said the man.

Jacob smiled. "No, no. When he wakes up will be fine."

"It's a wonder the city ever let someone build a house here," said Sarah, leaping over the last few stairs.

"I asked Noah about it once. He said the building on Queen Street, the back of which we're looking at now, was abandoned for many years. It was during that time that some poor people managed to sneak lumber through that passageway, the one we entered by, the one that separates the Queen Street building from the one next to it. They built themselves a tiny two-story shack between the two buildings in what must have been a yard. They're squatters. I have a feeling the city doesn't even know it's here and that the people who now own the commerce on the Water Street side never read their property title all the way through, and assumed the shack was always here. Something like that. Anyway, our friend doesn't pay rent. In turn, when his friends are in trouble he brings them here."

When Jacob and Sarah arrived at the house, Geneviève told them at the door that Michel was barely awake and clearly still in a lot of pain. "He managed to say he got beaten up by men calling him Frenchie but he has no idea why. He also said he has to get his ship."

"We'll leave him be for a while," Sarah sad. "Perhaps by evening he will be up to talking." Then to Geneviève she said, "You did well bringing him here. I can care for him now if you wish to leave."

Geneviève said she had to get home to do finishing touches to a gown for Patricia's mother.

"I'll be seeing her in two days. Do you want to join me?"

"Absolutely," answered Sarah. She wanted to visit the house on Broadway as often as possible in the hope of once again meeting Patricia's father. She still had no real plan but instinctively felt he would be the man to help put Croman in his place.

Noah arrived near 8 o'clock. Sarah had managed to get some cut-up food into Michel, who was now able to sit upright, though he said he'd find leaning against a wall less painful than sitting on a chair. Because that room was rarely used, Sarah sat on a crate. Jacob brought a stool from the kitchen and Noah opted for the floor, like Michel.

Because of the swelling, Michel's words were still muffled but he was clearly relaxed being among French-speaking rescuers. He decided to come clean and provide the complicated background to his story that took him from Nouvelle France to France, then Saint-Domingue and finally here, New York. Since Sarah, Jacob and Noah were up to their necks in deviousness themselves, they displayed not the slightest shock at Michel's subterfuge, which made it easier for Michel to make his urgent request:

"For me to get my cargo to port, and ultimately for me to make New York my home port I need this translated into English," he said, holding up the French version of his shipowner's title. "Only then can I somehow return to my ship, which is anchored in the lee of Sandy Hook, awaiting myself and a pilot to guide us in."

He added that he got to New York thanks to a Sandy Hook pilot who allowed him to board as a passenger while he brought in another vessel.

"That was yesterday. I was to get my business done and meet up with him today to return to my ship. Undoubtedly he has sailed back without me. Can't blame him for not sitting here and missing out on business. You see my predicament."

Jacob chuckled at the incredible coincidence.

"*Vous êtes bien tombé*," he said. "You couldn't have landed in a better place, among open-minded Frenchmen, one of whom has, let's say, certain duplication skills." At that, Noah smiled and Sarah laughed out loud.

"I will tend to your papers immediately," Jacob said. He examined Michel's document and said he would have to return to the atelier to avail himself of paper and ink. He would translate it there then return with some of the same ink for Michel's signature.

Loving the new adventure, Jacob all but dashed out the door.

"I suspect he'll run all the way to New Street," Sarah said.

While Jacob was gone, Michel described the words that led to the beating at the tavern.

"It was obvious to everyone that I was French. I couldn't even order a beer right in English. Then this man who smelled like a farm stood by my table and started saying something about France and something about Canada. Finally I understood he was asking if I was from France or Canada. The last thing I remember saying was the word Canada and something hitting the side of my head. After that I guess they all jumped me."

"Well they didn't rob you," Noah pointed out. "Something else riled them. I'm guessing they live farther north in the province of New York. The French have been coming down from Canada and burning their farms again lately. They're always long gone by the time the British get there, if they go at all. Too big a territory to protect."

Sarah asked Michel about his cargo. When Michel described it she immediately thought of just the person to be Michel's agent, her friend Asser Pietersen. He had the merchant connections needed to sell the cargo quickly and line up an outgoing one. In return for the new business, Sarah was sure he'd make some of the shipment available to her at cost. Thanks to her brother's work in New Harlem, she could afford to buy again. It was too late to seek out Asser that night but she would be waiting for him on Dock Street first thing in the morning.

The prospect of dealing with a well-connected and trusted agent in New York cheered Michel to no end. He couldn't smile but it showed in his eyes. Sarah felt they'd connected somehow.

Noah said he'd been talking again to Commodore Barry.

"The man needs money and adventure," he told Sarah. He said he took the liberty of asking the Commodore if he could see his way to finding safe storage for cargo he would be required to pick up in New York and transport to his farm in New Harlem.

Before going on, Noah closed his eyes and smiled at a memory.

"The Commodore's answer was a question," Noah said. "He turned sideways and looked down on me from the corner of his eye and said, 'By any chance, my friend Noah, would I be deceiving anybody while performing your request?' 'Of course,' I told him. The crazy old bugger would probably have refused otherwise."

Noah explained to Sarah that rather than transport and stash "mislaid merchandise" all over town in small quantities, the safest alternative was to transport everything to New Harlem.

"Up there, nobody questions the Commodore. He doesn't farm anymore but he has a boat and a wagon, and he pays young men and boys a pittance to convey things to the road where his wagon can handle the rest of the job. That's the only coin those boys ever see, so they know to keep the Commodore's comings and goings private.

"I could arrange to have him sail down and tie up at the new little quay just north of here like we did last time. Nobody seems to ever be there. I don't know why."

Sarah answered that Jacob's theory was that the property at the waterfront had been sold with water rights requiring that before building a home or commerce the owner was obliged to fill land a certain distance out into the river. Jacob thinks the owner did that, then built the wharf but for whatever reason hasn't started building.

"All the better," said Noah. "I can have all my men arrange to have their loot at the wharf on certain set days when the Commodore will be there. We'll keep record of everyone's share so they can collect when we eventually sell the goods they stole. I'll go up to see the Commodore tomorrow."

Noah and Sarah had been speaking a mixture of French and English, Noah's French being a bit rusty. Michel listened to every word with rapt attention. Maybe he could help these people as much as they were helping him. After all, he had a ship, an ocean-going merchantman.

Sarah said as much later that evening after Jacob returned with the translated ownership papers for Michel to sign. Since he'd been cold-cocked and never had the chance to throw a punch, his knuckles were unbruised. He even managed to sign with a flourish.

The final matter of immediate business was getting Michel back to his ship. Sarah said her agent friend, Asser, would definitely know somebody, especially since Michel would be docking at his wharf. Michel was so relieved he asked them if they could assist him to his feet so he could verify whether the boots that had landed all over his body had rendered him incapable of walking. Getting upright brought a cry from his lips, but once steadied he found he could take small steps without additional pain. Sarah and Jacob released him and he completed two tours of the small room on his own before getting their help to sit down again.

"I'll be fine on my own in a day or two," he announced. "No ribs broken."

As the evening wore on, everyone began to feel that the four of them had come together for a reason, that together bigger things were possible than those they'd imagined up until now. Michel was made to feel enough at home to enquire about Jacob's coy mention of "certain duplication skills." Someone else had already mentioned his profitable week in New Harlem.

Sarah, Jacob and Noah eyed each other briefly. One by one they gave a small nod of assent. Jacob explained he was an engraver by trade.

"And an artist," added Sarah.

Jacob explained that he first recreated paper currencies on copper as a challenge, admitting that "I seem to have been gifted with an eye for duplicating things." He went on to explain that the artistic pursuit had led to necessity because a "grotesque villain" was keeping his sister impoverished.

At that point Sarah explained how she and Jacob had come from France and the way the fat man had treated her. She didn't have to explain her desire for vengeance. Michel raised a hand to stop her from describing what was obviously a painful memory.

"I understand," Michel said. "Now perhaps I can return your kindness by offering a possible contribution that will assure your good fortune and give you the freedom to wage your battle in some degree of safety."

Though he had thought little of it at the time, when his first mate, Jean-Luc, brought the clumsy French seaman to his cabin, he now believed there was another man's talent to be explored and exploited.

"It was brought to my attention late in the voyage here from Saint-Domingue that aboard the Chameleon was France's greatest forger. He was wanted all over France and in utter desperation signed on to my ship in the hopes of fleeing the country. He is no good to me as a seaman. He has no skills I can use, but you people on the other hand…" He didn't finish the sentence.

After several minutes of silence, Jacob said he wanted to meet this man as soon as possible.

"We all do," added Sarah.

"Well then, my friends, find me transportation to my ship and return with me to Sandy Hook. You can talk to this man at length before we drop anchor back here at your friend's wharf. That way this forger won't have had a chance to flee into the city. He did not know I was bound for New York. When I took him on in Bordeaux I was flying French colors. I officially changed allegiance only after Saint-Domingue was well astern."

Noah rose.

"Captain, if I can speak for Jacob and Sarah, I can assure you that you'll have company on the voyage back to your ship. Your idea bears thinking about. I for one need some time."

Sarah then stood up.

"If our affair is about to include a merchant ship that can fly either English or French colors, and an infamous forger without a home, I believe I need some Dutch gin to clear my head."

"Since when do you drink Dutch gin, sister?"

"Geneviève and I sampled it one depressing rainy afternoon at the Homeless Hog. I'd never heard of it until we overheard a Dutchman order it many times over." Geneviève said she always wanted to try it because in France the genever gin was known as *genièvre* gin, almost like her name.

"Well I'd prefer to sit by the river and watch the ships," Noah said. "It will be a good sign if I can imagine Michel's ship being one of them. I do my best thinking by the water."

"And we won't be overheard," Jacob said.

On his knees, Michel made his way to his mattress. His eyes were already closed when his hosts shut the door behind them.

CHAPTER 38

More Partners

AS THEY sat down by the water's edge, on the quay between two small wharves about 100 feet north of the deserted marketplace, Sarah immediately threw out a question. As she spoke she was gazing across the river. Her voice seemed to float lightly over the water.

"Why are you two so interested in the forger on Michel's ship? You didn't say anything but I saw you exchange glances."

Noah was the first to answer.

"We talked about this when Jacob was at the mill. The mill is probably safe for printing for a while but there's still a risk. People wander the woods for all sorts of reasons. People getting away from the city, locals simply curious where the Indian paths lead, farmers doing some hunting, and, I guess, people who prefer trees to people."

Jacob chimed in. As he did Sarah shifted to face him, her brow furrowed.

"Noah gave me a lecture in New Harlem. He said he'd

be glad to spend the money that comes off my press but told me I have to stop being so full of myself for being able to engrave believable paper money. He said I should be shaking in my boots each time I hauled on the wheel to roll off another sheet. He said, and I remember his exact words, 'For now the birds are listening. Who will it be tomorrow? Someone's always listening. Someone's always watching in this world.'

"He basically said I should print out what I thought you needed to get on your feet for good. Then I should stop and sell the press."

Sarah turned to Noah.

"Thank you."

After the elation wore off about holding £1,000 in her small hands, Sarah's joy turned to worry each time Jacob talked about returning to the mill. If Jacob had considered himself a criminal, she would have felt more at ease. He would at least have adopted a criminal mentality and been more careful. But he didn't. He was a professional perfecting his trade on the one hand and caring for his only family on the other.

"The reason the captain's mention of a forger caught our attention," said Noah, "was that I told Jacob the safest way to be a forger was to do it in another province, or, better yet, another country. I knew a forger once. He told me you can make New York money in Connecticut and the authorities there don't care. But it's illegal to live in the province of New York and forge New York money. This forger was Irish. He said the Irish were good at making British money and they weren't breaking any laws. If they did it in England they'd hang."

Jacob said Noah's words hit home. He'd stop soon.

"In the meantime, we shouldn't put much of the money to use, to suddenly appear to have means."

"So where does the French forger fit in?" Sarah asked.

"That's what we should figure out now," said Noah.

"This could be a great opportunity."

Sarah didn't wait for the two men to devise a plan.

"I'll tell you what I'd like. I'd like Michel to take your press and this Frenchman and sail far, far away, to another country, preferably one of Michel's ports of call. The forger could forge to his heart's content using our plates and Michel could pick up the money on his next visits. We wouldn't have to worry about the forger keeping the money for himself because money from the colonies wouldn't be much use to him in a faraway country."

For the second time that evening, Jacob and Noah's eyes met, this time in astonishment. Sarah had grasped in an instant the answer they had been prepared to sit up all night searching for.

They returned to the house and woke up Michel. None of them would be able to sleep without knowing if Michel thought the idea workable. They needn't have worried.

"I'm sure he'll agree. He is a man without a country, without money, without friends. He can't afford to start over again. Why wouldn't he agree to your proposition?"

Michel then asked whether they all were about to become partners.

"We'll see after I talk to Asser in the morning," said Sarah, smiling at the prospect of building a business with these three men. For one of the few times since the kidnapping she was glad to be in New York.

The next morning Michel insisted on accompanying Sarah to see her agent friend.

"I need to make myself known," Michel said. "If your friend should ever entrust me with a cargo from the merchants he represents, he will first have to get my measure. I hope these bruises don't make me look like a pirate."

"I will tell him a version of the truth," said Sarah, "that you were attacked by a street gang and robbed. There are enough alley gangs in New York that Asser will believe us.

Besides, Michel, though your wounds have allowed you to utter but a few words, I find that you speak well."

"Jesuits," said Michel.

The walk was slow, and for Michel, grueling. On the way, Sarah stopped suddenly and told Michel to rest by leaning against the brick wall of a store. She entered the store, which sold everything from soap and candles to wigs, buttons, pewter plates and nails. Just as Michel was tempted to let himself slide down the wall to rest on the street, Sarah returned and handed him a simple walking stick made of crabapple wood. She also bought herself some vanilla.

She let Michel try out the cane. They stopped a block away where a crate sat in front of a building. "Let's sit a while and rest," she said. Michel nodded his agreement. Sarah wanted to know more about what Michel thought of Jacob and Noah's idea to turn the counterfeiting over to the French forger.

"He could make our money in a country like Saint-Domingue, could he not?"

Michel's one unbloodied eye met her earnest gaze. He could see in her expression that the idea she had tossed out was not a mere passing thought.

"If he knows what's good for him, he would entertain any suggestion I make," answered Michel. "I'll have to feel him out, but I suspect, Sarah, that this just might work."

Sarah gave him her arm to help him stand, then reluctantly released it as he put the unfamiliar walking stick to use.

As Sarah expected, Asser had arrived at his office early. He greeted her fondly and offered her a cup of a coffee he'd recently imported. As in London, coffee houses were the rage in the city. There was money to be made in the coffee trade. Michel declined the offer because of his swollen lip.

Asser said he was interested in the French cabinetry Michel could provide because the city's shops were inundated with fine English furnishings that no one could afford. Asser was bargaining already, Sarah thought. However when Asser was told that Michel's hold mostly contained molasses he clearly saw no need to bargain.

"New England cannot get enough molasses," Asser said. "The whole world is drinking rum these days and much of that comes from our distilleries."

Asser asked where the molasses came from. Michel looked at Sarah, who nodded.

"Saint-Domingue."

"Interesting," said Asser. The more suppliers he had, the better he could negotiate special prices. "And, like all the plantation islands, they need flour. Is that not true, captain?"

It was a rhetorical question. Sugar was so profitable, all arable land was given over to it. The islands couldn't produce the grain they needed to feed the workers.

"Should we end up doing business, captain, I could send you back with a hold full of flour. New York has long been the flour capital of the colonies but Pennsylvania is stealing our business with a cheaper flour. I need new customers for my flour producers here."

Because one of Asser's many languages was French, the two men had no trouble discussing tonnage and capacity. Michel explained that the Chameleon was anchored on the New Jersey shore near Sandy Hook for a small repair to the rudder that his own crew was attending to. If Asser had wharf space available, Michel said he could bring in his ship the day after tomorrow.

The two men shook hands.

As he stepped back onto Dock Street, Michel cursed the pain that the automatic smile produced. Sarah laughed at his discomfort. She was pleased for Michel but also pleased that she could finally offer Asser more than the odd crate or cask of merchandise. He knew he bought them just to help her out.

They made their way back toward the house slowly, Sarah telling Michel to stop whenever he needed to rest. He would have the rest of the day to let his body heal. The snail's pace invited conversation to fill in the time.

Michel forced himself to stop staring into Sarah's eyes. To appear casual, he returned his gaze to the East River and the ships.

"Does being on land make you restless?"

"I never know how to answer that question," Michel said. "I'm certainly not restless at this moment." His eyes briefly met Sarah's again before continuing.

"I love Quebec City. It's home. Yet I equally love having it at my back when I steer a course down the St. Lawrence River toward the sea. Maybe that's my first love. I'm beginning to realize I get more excited leaving than I do returning. No bureaucrats, no soldiers, no rules except setting a true course and outsmarting the elements."

"From what I saw I don't understand how anyone would want to be a seaman," Sarah replied.

"It's different for me, Sarah. The captain is God. Do you think you could ever look at me that way?"

"As God? Not a chance, captain."

"That attitude is exactly why we don't tolerate women onboard our ships."

"That's smart," Sarah said, laughing. "Any self-respecting woman would mutiny before you raised anchor."

"You've got insubordination in your blood, don't you," Michel said.

"No. I wouldn't have seemed that way if you'd known me in France. Here I have to survive on my own. It's a man's world and I feel very small here. I have to stand as tall as I can. I'm getting taller every day."

"Not exactly the definition of a shrinking violet," Michel said.

Sarah elbowed him in the ribs.

"Ouch!" The playful blow, as light as it was, stopped

Michel in his tracks. His whole torso still ached from the beating.

"Oh my God, I'm so sorry!" Sarah said, taking him in her arms.

After a moment, Michel replied:

"Now that wasn't too difficult, was it? You addressed me correctly, as God."

He gave her his arm for the rest of the walk home.

The house was empty when they arrived. Noah and Jacob had left even earlier than she and Michel had. They were heading to New Harlem in the little boat Noah always seemed to have access to. Noah needed to talk to the Commodore about turning his barn into their warehouse. Jacob had decided to profit from the rapid transportation to put his press to work again since it might not be his much longer. Jacob had left a note for Sarah to have delivered to Peter, explaining that he would be absent for a few days.

To Sarah's surprise there was a knock on the door just before sunset. The first face she saw when opening the door a crack was Noah's. Behind him the Commodore.

"Good news, Sarah," said Noah, suddenly noticing Michel sleeping in the front room. In a softer voice he said:

"The Commodore has joined us."

Sarah motioned them upstairs to the kitchen where they could speak normally.

The Commodore sat in a small chair by the table. Fearing the chair would collapse under the Commodore's weight, Sarah suggested he'd be more comfortable in another chair.

"Thank you, girl."

After he changed chairs, the Commodore sat beaming as Noah described the arrangement they'd made. Noah explained that work needed to be done in the barn to shield their future goods from the elements.

"Beyond that, we're set to go, Sarah. The Commodore says he can easily enlist some young men from New Harlem to get our merchandise to and from the barn. They will also accompany him as needed when he sails to New York to pick up our latest spoils."

The Commodore's obvious satisfaction with the deal grew even further when Noah said he drove a hard bargain.

"In fact," Noah said, "the Commodore's price was much steeper than I thought we should ever pay. But this arrangement is too perfect to pass up. What do you think, Sarah?"

Before she could answer, the Commodore finally spoke.

"Girl, you've fulfilled the dreams of an old adventurer. If only I had a tankard, I'd raise it to you."

Sarah rose and bowed to him, fetching ale a moment later.

"And," said Noah, "the Commodore has offered to take Michel back to his ship tomorrow if Michel will pay him the standard pilotage fee to guide him back into port. His crew of the moment will do their best to bring his boat home in our wake."

"My Citroen may not be sleek like those pretty schooners the pilots use, but I know these waters as well as they do. Do we have a deal, girl?"

"That we do, Commodore," said Sarah. "But first, I feel duty-bound to point out that I'm told there is a fine for posing as a pilot. I believe your boat will also be subject to seizure. It happened to an acquaintance of Noah's."

Noah confirmed what Sarah said.

The Commodore shrugged off Sarah's concern.

"If I get fined, you can pay it. And as for the Citroen, none of those schooner snobs would be caught dead manning her rudder."

CHAPTER 39

Forging A New Venture

THE instant the Chameleon was underway, with the Commodore fully enjoying his authority to lord over the young helmsman, Michel went to his cabin and called for Nicholas Cadieux, the French forger, to report to him.

"Considering your circumstance I can deal with you any way I see fit. You would agree?"

"Yes, sir."

Michel noticed, as he had on their first meeting, that Cadieux showed no signs of nerves as he sat before the man who could throw him in irons and hand him over to the authorities in any French port. He had evidently gotten out of tight spots before and felt he could do it again.

"I could throw you overboard and no one would be the wiser." Michel stared at Cadieux. Cadieux returned the look but there was no challenge in his eyes. "I thought I'd hired a much-needed seaman but it turns out that you are nothing of the kind. I then learn that you are a criminal wanted by authorities all over France. Since I do not command a naval vessel with naval discipline, I do not tolerate men I don't trust in my crew.

"I certainly don't trust you. However there is a way you can be of service to me. You would do well to consider acceptance of my proposition as an exchange for your life."

Onboard the Commodore's boat on his way to rejoin the Chameleon, Michel had an idea for completing the scheme suggested by his new partners. He would use the connections of his agent in Saint-Domingue, a longtime friend of Antoine's, to pay a small, needy plantation owner to set the forger up with a shelter of some kind, ideally far from any road. His belongings would include Jacob's press and plates, as well as paper and ink.

All the plantation owner would have to do would be to make sure the forger had provisions and occasionally other comforts, such as rum and women, and that the plantation slave watch include the forger's dwelling. He was not to be allowed to leave without being accompanied by a representative of Michel's agent in Cap-Français.

Michel doubted that he would be required to explain his purpose to the agent as long as there was profit in the picture. It wouldn't even require cash. Michel could offer the agent deep discounts on choice goods, ones the agent could sell for great gain, or keep for himself to enhance his "chateau" and further his pretension to nobility.

"Have you been to Saint-Domingue, Mr. Cadieux?"

Michel told the forger the plan: Cadieux would live in the countryside, not in Cap-Français. He would be provided with a copper plate rolling press, and plates to print from, in addition to paper and ink. Michel would collect the notes on his next visit. To enforce the arrangement, Michel informed him, he would have to sign a letter of indentureship. The arrangement would be perfectly legal.

He also told Cadieux that he would not have a chance to skim money for himself. The number of sheets of paper remaining in the original supply would tell Michel approximately how much money had been printed. The one thing Michel did not tell Cadieux was which currencies the plates represented. If Cadieux escaped while in New York that knowledge could raise questions about Michel.

Like Noah, Michel thought best on water. Not only did he figure out what to tell the forger, but it was also while being transported by the Commodore that the fear of being caught smuggling currency prompted a nearly full-blown idea for a unique hiding place aboard ship. More accurately, it would not be aboard, it would be under.

Michel pictured a small wing-like box that could be fitted near the bow below the waterline, far enough down that it would not be exposed when the ship carried no cargo. The forward end of the box would be narrow, like the front of a wedge. From the tapered front it would widen gradually to perhaps a width of five inches. As for its length, he would have to experiment with Jacob. They could have a model built to see how much money would fit inside a specific length of box. If it were well constructed and the notes were wrapped with oil cloth, the "wing" would work. The main concern was to keep the box narrow enough to avoid any loss of sailing speed.

While waiting for Cadieux to respond, Michel found his thoughts returning to the smuggling box. He was proud of the idea. Finally Cadieux spoke.

"So you would have me work as a slave?"

"No, you would be paid a modest sum for your work but you will not receive it until I terminate the endeavor. As I said, you will be provided with food, drink and shelter. Once I no longer have need for your services, you will be free to stay in Saint-Domingue or seek passage elsewhere. As for how long that will be, that will depend on the work you do. If you don't apply yourself, your stay under the sun that few Europeans can tolerate will be longer than you will likely find bearable. Apply yourself and you might be free sooner than you think."

The two men stared at each other for several minutes.

"I need an answer now, before you leave this cabin. Let me remind you that if you decline you will be in chains within minutes."

"Captain," Cadieux said, demonstrating more respect than when he'd first been brought to the cabin, "would it be of interest to you if I printed French livres in addition to the currencies you have in mind? I have the engraving plates. If so, I would need extra paper and perhaps different ink."

"Possibly," answered Michel.

"Then we have a deal," the forger said as if Michel had been negotiating with him instead of making him his possession.

"Good," Michel said, not returning Cadieux's smile. "You're dismissed."

If Cadieux did have plates, they were already in the hands of Michel's first officer. When telling Jean-Luc to bring the forger to his cabin, Michel also told him that once he'd seen to that he was to search through whatever kit the forger may have brought aboard in Bordeaux. Having possession of the plates would increase his leverage on the forger's loyalty.

After getting the results of Jean-Luc's search and learning that the plates had been found, Michel decided to join the Commodore on deck. The Chameleon was entering Upper New York Bay. Michel judged that he had thought of everything. Only one detail remained and as soon as he realized that the answer came to him.

"Who better to draw up a contract of indentureship than Sarah and Jacob?" He'd never seen one before. He was also eager to see what they thought of his idea for getting forged money by revenue officers.

"You're becoming a rogue, my boy!" The voice in Michel's head was his uncle's.

CHAPTER 40

Noah's Mission

THE fat merchant had returned. Before descending the rope ladder to the ship's boat, followed by Captain Marcellus Flemming, Zachariah Croman was witnessed in fine spirits, even clapping the first officer on the back at one point. He was not given to such gestures. An hour later, as he stood on one of his wharves, he was apoplectic. More than one clerk or stevedore secretly wished he'd die right then and there of rage. Croman had just been informed that he had become, in his absence, the target of a concerted effort to sabotage his business. Culprits unknown.

"But they are organized, sir," said his foreman. "It's like a revolt, sir, and it's spreading. Cargo disappears, winches are toppled, accidents happen every other day on this wharf or the others. Some merchants have refused to do more business with you, sir. They say our prices are unconscionable."

"How long has this been going on?" Croman thundered

as if the foreman was to blame personally.

"It started before you left, sir, but it was only after you sailed that it became so widespread that we suspected it was organized."

Croman turned to the captain, who by his own scheming and private deals with exporters abroad had acquired almost a quarter share in the fat man's empire.

"My home. Now."

Croman fumed as the carriage taking them across town encountered delay after delay. Other than cursing the driver, Croman said not a word until he and the captain had seated themselves in his study, as ostentatious as the rest of the house.

"It is time to sell our land in Pennsylvania. We must make up for these losses, and quickly."

"What is the rush?" replied the captain, dying for a glass of the fat man's fine brandy but not daring to suggest it.

"Before we left New York I invested heavily in no fewer than nine vessels, bound for Europe, Africa and the Indies. I don't yet know whether any of them have arrived back in New York, but I can tell you that six of them are not due to return for many months. My finances could not be more extended. I need revenue. I need money to fight whoever is behind this sabotage. I'll see them hanged!"

Captain Flemming noticed the fat man's face had again turned monstrously red, as it had on the wharf. He closed his eyes tight. When his lungs consented to finally take in air, the merchant growled one word:

"Brandy."

Retrieving a decanter from a table behind his desk, he repeated that the bastards would hang. The thought relaxed him.

"Marcellus, you and I must hasten to Philadelphia to make it known there are great tracts of fine land available for sale in the southerly reaches of the province."

"How can I, Zachariah? In a week's time they'll start

filling my hold with new cargo."

"The loading can be delayed easily enough," the merchant said. "In the meantime you and I will spread the word here in New York about our land in the principle cafés and taverns. There are speculators enough in this city to buy the entire continent."

Word of the fat merchant's return spread instantly. Noah's men didn't have to be told this was not the time to poke the bear. They would wait for instructions from Noah. As usual, Noah had left no word about where he was going or when he'd return. He had been gone for two weeks. In the meantime, the anti-Croman merchants had plenty of stolen goods to sell.

In the following days, Sarah made it known to the nine small merchants in her network that they would now have to wait a few days for delivery. Previously, Sarah kept Noah informed about what the various merchants wanted and he in turn arranged for carters to deliver the goods to the merchants as soon as they had been purloined and hidden somewhere in the city, usually not far from the docks. Some were actual warehouses, others private homes. Noah made special deals with two carters to guarantee their availability and their silence. The merchants were never told where the goods were coming from. Once deliveries had been made, Noah paid his thieves their share.

Now the system was different, safer for all and easier for Noah's thieves. Instead of them risking travel through the city transporting their goods to hiding places, small craft would be used to deliver them directly to the little quay north of Maiden Lane where the Commodore would tie up on preset days. No one paid attention to the countless small boats making their way up and down the waterfront. Many of the thefts could be now quickly dropped into a boat that suddenly appeared alongside the target warehouse or wharf. Sometimes Noah arranged for a boat to try to dock where it shouldn't just to create a commotion, leaving the thieves free to spirit away merchandise. Well before nightfall, the merchandise would be on its way to the Commodore's farm in New Harlem. The Commodore would also sail home with Sarah's latest list of orders to fill.

On the day Sarah finished notifying the last of the merchants about the new system, she arrived back at Maiden Lane to find Michel's now-undistorted face smiling at her from the street in front of her house. Definitely, she told herself. Yes, he was indeed handsome.

They kissed each other on each cheek in the French manner and exchanged a small hug before entering the house. Once seated at the table in the kitchen, Michel announced that he was in the Commodore's debt.

"He brought the Chameleon in as sweetly as if she were the lady of his life."

"I like him," Sarah said. "Like any good Dutchman he has an eye for profit but I don't see greed in that man. Maybe that's because he's so old. I don't know. I think he mostly wants a family, and someone who'll listen to the stories he makes up about his life at sea."

Michel said he understood full well what the fact of being a ship's captain did to a man's pride.

"Or even being the captain of a squash-nosed, fat-assed river boat. Thanks to you people, the Commodore's working on the water again and happy to be of value to someone. I scarcely know him, Sarah, in fact my English is so wanting I can barely understand him, but he's a man you can trust."

"While you're ashore, Michel, we are going to have to work on your English. New York is now your home port and you will have to talk to merchants and investors and harbor officers and maybe the Royal Navy while you're at sea someday."

In stilted English, Michel said:

"The pleasure of you, I mean the pleasure of seeing you again, made me *oublier*, made me forget, yes? Forget to tell you I have bad news. The *faux-monnayeur*, the counterfeiter, has escaped my ship. He went over the side last night in the dark."

The light went out of Sarah's eyes. Of all their schemes, the one that put her heart at ease was having found a way to make an honest man of her brother again. He would return to his career as an engraver of anything but currency.

"Jacob should be back any moment," she finally said. "And Noah, I hope. We all have to talk. Can you stay, Michel? I want you to be part of this."

"*Oui*, Sarah!"

"What?"

"Oh. Yes, Sarah. You make me feel like the Commodore, part of the family."

Sarah smiled at his embarrassment, but she liked the sentiment.

Encouraged, Michel went on.

"If I may say, it appears to me that you are the captain of this family."

"And don't you forget that," Sarah answered with mock sternness.

Sarah wrote a note for Jacob and placed it on the table telling him that she and Michel had gone to the Homeless Hog.

"Urgent you meet us there."

They had time to kill. She was guessing that Jacob would make the most of his time at the mill and wouldn't return until just before nightfall, leaving Noah just enough light to sail back safely.

After writing the note, Sarah excused herself and went to her room. Now was the moment, she told herself, although she had no precise idea of what she was expecting. She was now thinking of Michel every day. Earlier in the week she'd confessed as much to Geneviève. She also confessed that she'd never once worn makeup. Geneviève feigned astonishment but privately she thought that her friend was too pretty to need any.

"Then I will teach you," Geneviève said, returning her scissors to the hat box.

Half an hour later, Sarah knew how to use berry juice to enhance her lips and how to make a wash of orange and vanilla to perfume her face. There was no need for blush because despite the long periods of near starvation over the past two years, Sarah's complexion was still that of a healthy young woman.

"You also don't need to darken your eyebrows," Sarah. "They are already in fashion." When Sarah stared at her blankly, Geneviève explained that one of the latest fashions, even for blondes, was to darken eyebrows.

In her room, Sarah quickly applied a little of the berry juice and the orange-vanilla wash. The experience was so novel she felt self-conscious. She stayed in her room until she convinced herself she was being silly to feel that way.

After their long talk on the way home from Asser's, Sarah and Michel slipped into easy conversation.

"Tell me more about Quebec," Sarah said, sitting close to him at the table, close enough that Michel spoke softly in reply.

"As I told you, I loved it there. As long as my uncle and I could go about our business without having to deal with a bureaucrat, and administrator, a nobleman or, in short, and I ask your pardon in advance, a Frenchman, we were happy."

Sarah said that's how most people in New York felt about the British. Sarah was relieved that Michel had slid his chair closer to hers yet seemed happy talking about things other than his clearly reciprocated attraction to her. The perfume and makeup had not been a mistake. She felt more of a woman.

"The people seem poorer here," Michel continued, "but the merchants seem richer. My uncle and I, we did well but it was getting harder and harder before I left. My uncle sensed it. He said the future was shrinking. The King of

France is suffocating our empire here in America. More rules, more demands, but less and less money." Sarah was content to let him talk on.

The only people getting rich are the nobles the King sent to govern New France as a punishment. More often than not, the governors and intendants of Quebec and Montreal end up acting and living like kings. I just hope the British don't know how few soldiers we have, how little money we have for ships and arms."

"You'll have to stop saying 'we'," said Sarah. "You're a New Yorker now, an English-speaker." Tapping the table, she added, "This is your home."

"Let me try to say something in English," Michel said, smiling as if he'd found a sack of gold on the street. "You are to me beautiful."

Michel took Sarah's right hand with both of his. For a split second, Sarah flinched at his touch. Before he noticed, she squeezed his hand tightly.

"Never has grammar been more fractured." She didn't let go of his hand until they left to go to the tavern.

When Jacob and Noah stepped into the tiny tavern two hours later, they found Michel and Sarah discussing life in French.

To make room for them all, Sarah and Michel moved to another table, one located beside a long bench and offering more privacy.

"What's urgent, Sarah?" Jacob asked.

She quickly explained that the forger had escaped. There was no way of apprehending him, even if he remained in the city.

"Jacob," Sarah said, clasping her brother's right hand with both of hers, "you can't keep doing what you're doing. You just can't."

Jacob leaned over the table and, taking her head in his hands, kissed her gently on the forehead.

"I won't, Sarah. I promise. But what do we do?"

"I don't know either."

The four of them sat in silence. Finally Noah stood up.

"I need a little air." He strode out of the drinking house into the fresh October night air. When he returned he reversed his chair so he could sit with his chest as close as possible to the others. His expression was deadly serious as he looked first at Sarah, then at the two young men.

"This is what we are going to do. This is not a discussion. Do not interrupt me."

Noah looked down at his big hands for a minute, then spoke again.

"Jacob," he said, holding a finger up to Sarah's face indicating she was not to speak, "you and I are going to return tomorrow and go to work again, just as we've done for these past few days. But with a change. You are going to teach me how to place the paper, how to turn the roller wheel, and how to perfectly trim the result."

Everyone except Michel understood the words Noah wisely chose not to speak in the tavern. Then, looking at Jacob,

"I can't become an artist like you, but surely any man can finish the process. You will teach me, starting tomorrow."

Noah then turned to Michel, who was seated to his right. Michel had been leaning over the table trying to understand the words Noah was all but whispering in English.

"Michel, you will take me to Saint-Domingue on your next voyage. In your hold will be the machinery I've been talking about. I am going to replace the man who escaped."

Both Sarah and Jacob were shaking their heads violently.

"No!" Sarah said. Noah ignored her entirely.

"There are two conditions. Jacob or Sarah, you will write a letter of manumission, stating that I am a free black and resident of the British province of New York. You will use the following name as that of the person writing the letter, my former owner: Commodore Barry Clark de

Klerck, retired naval officer and landed gentry, of New Harlem in the Province of New York."

Noah gave the others a moment for the beginnings of his plan to sink in.

"With one exception," Noah continued, his voice still brooking no interruption, "we will follow the original plan and timing. I speak of the matters of provisions, shelter, and so on. As for the one exception…" He stopped and look briefly at each of the faces around the table.

"The exception is the following." His voice became conversational, the authority gone.

"I was once married. Jacob and Sarah, you know that. And you know that the marriage took place in Saint-Domingue where I had been wrongly sold as a slave. On a street not far from where we sit I was knocked out by two white men who put me in irons aboard their ship. I was not alone. Other black men were chained alongside me. Somewhere in the Indies we were sold to a French merchant captain, who in turn sailed to the capital, Cap-Français, and sold us to a plantation owner. It was there that I met my wife."

Noah explained that over time many slaves escaped and fled deep into the mountains. They were known as Maroons. The systematically attacked plantations, burned cane fields and freed slaves who reinforced them. Plantation owners feared them but managed to catch few. One night, while Noah's wife was at the plantation house, the Maroons attacked. Unable to rescue his wife in the chaos of flames, musket fire and clanging blades, Noah fled with the Maroons. Learning that he spoke English and was not from the island, nor recently arrived from Africa, the maroons taught him the ways of the island.

There were many free black men, they said, mostly in the city, and many escaped ones who passed themselves off there as free, having learned to dress as whites do and have a ready story to tell to explain the work they do in the capital. Eventually, Noah was shown where to get passage on a coastal boat that would take him to Cap-Français. Once there, it took Noah less than a week to join the crew of a merchant ship. A year later he had made his way back to New York.

"I have never forgotten my wife. I have no idea whether she even lives. The purpose of my plan is to find out if she does. It will be difficult for me to visit other plantations but I will eventually make contact with a Maroon. They will help me get news of her. If she is found, I will somehow arrange to free her with their help. I will hide her in the house your agent provides me for working the press."

Whether he found his wife or not, Noah said he wanted everyone to understand that she was the purpose of this journey. While efforts were being made to find her, he would justify his presence by operating the press "on behalf of some white men in the capital."

"You will have money to return with but not nearly what you hoped your Frenchman would have produced over a few years. Michel, you will rescue me on your first trip back to Cap-Français."

No one knew what to say. Sarah was the first to stand. The men followed her back to the house.

Jacob stirred the coals in the fireplace and added two small logs. It would soon take the chill out of the kitchen. Still not quite knowing what to say in response to Noah's bombshell, he tried being chatty.

"By the bye, while we were not gone long, Noah has already started his apprenticeship. With his strong arm pulling at the wheel we were able to almost work around the clock. It might seem anticlimactic at the present moment, but we produced about £3,400 in various notes. A prodigious output, if I may say so."

Even Noah grinned at that announcement.

"With what you produced the last time, it's all the more reason to feel no disappointment about the Frenchman's escape," said Sarah, maintaining her brother's levity. "We are well set."

It was Sarah now who turned her back on everyone to tend to the fire. She remained facing the fire while Michel started to speak, in English, his accent thicker than before. It dawned on her that it was emotion, the same as she felt, and the reason she'd turned her face away.

"Monsieur Noah, what you propose represents… It is a demonstration of bravery of a kind I have not experienced. A black man willingly returning to a land whose slaves are so many they cannot be counted. And even more noble, a man white or black walking into such peril for love… You have, Monsieur Noah, moved me deeply. If we all vote to go ahead with your plan, I will do so with great pride to be part of it. You can count on me in every regard."

Before Michel had finished, Sarah had moved to Noah's side. She comically pulled him to his feet and threw her arms around him, her eyes now so moist she could barely make out the details of the face of the giant in front of her.

"Back to the plan," said Jacob, giving everyone an easy out from the display of emotion. "It is essential that Noah master something else besides the proper trimming of the engraved notes. He must master the assembly of the press. When we first installed it at the mill, it was a two-man job. I'm not sure even I could do it alone. But, Noah, you will have to do just that in Saint-Domingue."

"Then we'd better get an early start tomorrow," said Noah. He thought of trying to express the gratitude he felt towards his friends but quickly decided it was one of the few things he was not brave enough to attempt.

Jacob then told Michel to feel free to start taking on cargo for his journey south. That would take a week or so, just enough time for Noah to learn what he needed to know and for them to get the Commodore to transport the press to the Chameleon.

Sarah took Noah's arm again. Turning to Michel, she said: "I want to sail with you and Noah. I insist."

CHAPTER 41

A Kiss

THE next morning, Sarah awoke in a state of panic.

Noah and Jacob had left for New Harlem and the mill. She thought about Jacob's last words to her, spoken at her bedside before she fell asleep:

"You hate ships. You hate the sea. You told me to pierce you through and through again with any sharp instrument at hand before allowing anyone to drag you aboard any vessel with more than one sail."

She remembered saying "Shush!"

From that recollection, the rest came back to her slowly. Jacob's warning had come at the start of the conversation, not the end. After she had dismissed his concerns, he'd said in astonishment:

"Sarah, sister, little sister, you just shushed me!"

"A woman can do that from time to time," Sarah replied, smiling.

"Damn," Jacob said, his head reeling. Only a woman could say that, not a girl. Then it dawned on him.

"You're in love with Michel!"

Sarah was now sitting upright on her bed. She looked at Jacob.

"I adore you, brother, my protector in all matters. But yes, I may have feelings for this canadien."

She let that sink in before continuing.

"However," she said, taking his hand, "I am willing to do the stupidest thing in my life, even risk it, in support of Noah. He has been good to me, and good to us at every turn since we were deposited in this place against our will. He did all that without even knowing us. Now, Jacob, we know him as a cherished friend. And now we know he would die for love."

Jacob looked at his sister in silence.

"Don't you dare laugh at me, Jacob. It's true."

"It's not a fairy tale." She almost added that Michel wasn't either, but she was too new to the feeling to dare speak of it even to herself.

"I look at all the things Noah does to get by, to eat, to stay a free man. He has stolen, and he has killed. But tonight I saw proof that doing all those things haven't made him dead inside. He doesn't have the heart of a bad man."

When Jacob again didn't say anything, Sarah thought she must be rambling. She decided to tell him what was really behind her words.

"Look at what we do, Jacob. We steal, we pursue revenge. Those are the kinds of things father said would empty our souls."

"You are right to speak of this, Sarah. But that's not at all what concerns me right now. The idea of you sailing anywhere will always frighten me but you can't sail to Saint-Domingue right now. We need you to be here in New York. Your heart is making you forget the careful plan we have to enact. If we're not careful we'll get caught by Croman."

Sarah was the go-between for their network of merchants and Noah's longshoremen. The merchants' orders went through her to the Commodore for shipping, and the stolen merchandise went through her to the Commodore for storage. In their new system, she was now the one who tracked the shares the thieves were owed.

"And," Jacob added, "I need you here to get Patricia's father on our side against Croman. He is the only important man we can approach about the land titles."

"But Noah..."

"Let Michel take care of setting Noah up in Saint-Domingue. When the time comes to bring him back home, that's when you should sail with Michel."

Sarah knew what her brother said last night was right. She didn't want to see Noah or Michel go, but they had to.

She got up and put bread on the table. There was a pint or so of ale remaining. She took the stairs two at a time and knelt by Michel, still sound asleep. She touched his hair lightly, then moved her palm to his cheek, the one that had been so badly bruised.

She called his name softly. On the second try, he twitched. On the third, without turning to look at her, he said, "Sarah?"

As soon as he sat down at the table Sarah told him why she couldn't sail with him. To her surprise, the first words out of his mouth were:

"I'm relieved to hear that."

Before Sarah could feel disappointed, he said he might be ashore a long time in Cap-Français arranging to get Noah and the press to a plantation.

"It might be very complicated, even dangerous."

He didn't feel comfortable leaving her alone aboard ship all that time and, furthermore, it was out of the question that she could come ashore on her own.

"When we rescue him, and hopefully this woman he loves, that's when you can come with me. He is your friend and he will be happy to see you there."

"Agreed," said Sarah. Jacob's words, and now Michel's, had restored order to her life.

Forgetting Sarah's insistence that he learn to speak English, Michel then proceeded to spend the entire time at breakfast in animated French, explaining what faced him when he set sail for Saint-Domingue within the next two weeks. He explained that the hurricane season in the West Indies had not yet fully passed, that once there he would be required to go ashore and convince a pretend nobleman that the black man in his company was a free man and that this pretend nobleman would, for a price, make Noah his responsibility, and that he would have to go to great trouble finding him safe accommodations on a nearby plantation for reasons that he, Michel, was not ready to explain.

"You would not be able to contribute to such a voyage," Michel said. "I would worry about you constantly."

Sarah stood and pulled his face toward hers. She kissed him long on the lips. It was the first kiss of her life. His hands closed on Sarah's shoulders. For a moment he stared at her in disbelief, then leaned back a few inches. He took in a deep breath and exhaled slowly. Sarah's kiss had somehow emptied his lungs. Gently, he explored her face with his lips, then suddenly pulled her hard against his chest and kissed her deeply. After their lips parted, they held each other in silence.

"I feel I've suddenly sighted land after an eternity at sea."

Still in his arms, Sarah laughed.

"It was clear to me that my fine captain has been sailing without a compass."

"Have you signed on then as my navigator?"

"Something like that."

Sarah walked Michel toward the Dock Street wharf where he would have to see to the loading of his outbound cargo and discuss financial arrangements with Asser. Perhaps he had found sponsors and could offer a share of the profits. This being Michel's initial dream upon leaving Quebec City, he couldn't separate his new energy from the feelings Sarah had awakened in him. He felt he owned the world.

Sarah left him at Coenties Slip, not far from his destination. He kissed her hand and she quickly retreated, still looking at him, before turning left to head to Geneviève's shop on Bridge Street just off Queen.

"I must see Patricia's father," Sarah said, without returning her friend's greeting at the door.

"What's come over you? You're flushed. And not in a disagreeable way, I'd wager."

CHAPTER 42

Countdown

IT was four days before the Commodore again eased the Citroen dockside. On board were Jacob and Noah. At their feet a disassembled press.

To accommodate them, the Commodore missed his regular day for picking up stolen goods for storage at the wharf north of Maiden Lane. Fortunately there wasn't as much merchandise to go back to New Harlem as usual. Since Sarah couldn't leave it on the wharf overnight she had to ask the men who delivered it by boat to carry most of it to her house. By way of apology she said she would give them her share of the profit for those particular goods but they refused. Sarah was always nice to them, and more important, honest. She always remembered to tally their shares and report them to Noah for payment.

One boat contained a cask too heavy to carry any distance. They said they could roll it on the street but Sarah said that might attract too much attention to the destination, her house. One of the men suggested leaving it in the boat and he volunteered to wait there with it until nightfall, then leave it in the darkness.

"Of late I've been staying at Noah's invisible house, a short walk away."

Sarah laughed. She knew that he meant the one between Water and Queen streets.

"I'm going to start calling it that as well, 'the invisible house'." To be safe, Sarah retrieved a canvas from the house to cover it up.

The Commodore tasked two of his three farm boys with taking the press to Sarah's and returning with the goods she'd been forced to store there.

Not long after the Commodore pulled away, announcing to his young sailors: "Home, me lads, that's our next port of call."

An hour later, the men arrived.

"I worked him hard," Jacob said, laughing, as he, Noah and Sarah stepped inside the house. He was referring to Noah's "instant apprenticeship."

"In order for Noah to perfect handling the paper and ink and the cutting out of the paper notes after printing I had to produce another £645. Noah destroyed a few at the beginning but none thereafter. I must say he has more patience than even I do."

"That was nothing," Noah said, "compared to the patience I'll need in Saint-Domingue."

"You'll manage," Sarah said. "I know you."

Jacob said they spent the final day slowly taking apart the press so Noah could fix the machine in his mind.

"I then asked Noah to do what I would not want to attempt myself. In fact, I'm sure I would not have been able to do it. He put the press back together all by himself. It took a long time to figure out the best order to proceed in but I think Noah could now do it in his sleep."

"I can tell you now, Jacob," said Noah, "that long before reassembling that press the only thing on my mind was sleep." He turned to Sarah and said it was almost sunrise before the press stood erect on the floor of the mill "with no unused parts lying about".

Noah had sunk to the floor and had to use his fingers to keep his eyes pried open to study Jacob's demonstration of how to load paper and ink a plate. He needed to do that now in order to test the press.

"Worked beautifully. It was too bad we then had to take it all apart again and wait for the Commodore's boys to carry it to the wharf. When they finally arrived Noah was sound asleep sitting up against a wall. Took us ages to wake him."

"Am I going to have to go through all that again in Saint-Domingue?" Noah asked.

"No," said Jacob. "Assembly only upon arrival. We're not going to bring it back. Just sneaking it into the country will be risk enough."

Sarah hid the new money in the usual place while the men ate stew she'd warmed up. When she returned to the house she called upstairs.

"The Pig? You must be thirsty."

"Right behind you," said Jacob.

At the tavern Sarah told them she'd made no progress with Patricia's father because he'd been in Boston.

"He is supposed to return by the end of the week," she told them.

Jacob said that was no problem because he still had to do the rounds of the cafés where investors, speculators and politicians congregated.

"I'll tell Peter it's all my treat. That way he might be less angry with me for all these absences from the atelier."

Sarah then told Noah that Michel expected to leave on Tuesday or Wednesday of the following week. Unless he stays aboard tonight we might see him back at the house. He can tell us whether he's ready to take the press onboard. He said he would make a special place for it, somewhere

where it wouldn't be spotted by an inspector. I think he's going to put the pieces of the press in different locations in the hold."

Michel didn't come to the house that evening, but to her surprise he showed up early the next morning. He was clearly happy to see "Monsieur Noah" had returned. He asked Jacob if they could hire a carter to take the press to the ship. It was Noah who answered:

"I have just the man." He would use one of the carters on his payroll.

Before Noah left to make arrangements, he sat down with Sarah to find out how much he owed his men for their "contributions". That was what they'd all taken to calling the stolen merchandise. Noah said he wanted to make sure everyone was paid before he left for Saint-Domingue. He said he would tell each and every one of them over the next few days that during his absence they were to arrange to get payment from Sarah.

"But," said Noah, "it can't be here. That would draw too much attention. Ask each of them to suggest a place to meet but don't let it be anywhere near Croman's offices. In fact, when I see them I'll talk to them about safe meeting places."

Though they all had different destinations, the three men left together. After spending most of the past few years all but alone, Sarah was getting used to the almost constant company. If something happened to Michel and Noah in Saint-Domingue that would all end. She shook the thought away by the time the men disappeared from view. She craved something soothing and uncomplicated. She decided to sit in silence in Geneviève's front room. When she was sad she liked to watch the nimble rhythm of Geneviève's small practiced fingers as she sewed dresses in the sunlight that streamed in through the window over her work table. Sarah wasn't sad today. Anything but. She needed the calm to make sure it was all real.

CHAPTER 43

The Rich Ally

DESPITE Jacob's offer, Peter remained distant all day. He was always civil and together they accomplished enough work to reduce by half the backlog caused by Jacob's absence. Shortly after 7 p.m. Peter announced:

"Jacob, I'm ready for coffee."

Peter's tone made Jacob wonder whether he was still pouting, not that he cared much at this hour. Even before starting work that morning Jacob was tired from the long days at the mill. Coffee and food mattered more.

They were on Wall Street minutes later. Jacob was hoping to find Arnold among the café's patrons, the well-off young man who stood next to him at the trial of the Irish counterfeiter, and the one who suggested it might be good sport to watch the hanging together the next day. He was a regular at the café and was always well informed about any matter Jacob or Peter inquired about. Jacob had been so busy in New Harlem, and then preparing Noah for the Saint-Domingue operation, that he felt out of touch.

He could not find Arnold's face in the nearly full café. It had been a spectacular late October day and evidently no one was in a hurry to get home to a warm hearth for the night. Within half an hour, Peter seemed to have forgiven him and conversation flowed easily. Whenever other voices were raised, though, they stopped and listened to see what they could learn.

This night it seemed that investment opportunities weren't the direct focus of the chatter. It was politics and the possibility of war.

Through its history New Yorkers had lived in fear of attacks from New France, even in the city. French raiding parties frequently attacked small communities near Albany. Montreal was a mere 300 miles to the north and within easy reach of the city by water. Peter said he remembered much talk in July when the French made George Washington surrender at a battle in the Allegheny Mountains in Pennsylvania. Now the skirmishes were moving into the Ohio Valley as France expanded its empire.

However, the atmosphere in the café was not fear. It was anticipation. War meant profits for merchants. In fact, Peter and Jacob clearly heard one of them say, "After all, chaps, we love war, don't we!" Even men at other tables, having overheard the remark, chanted "Hear, hear!" By themselves, imperial wars fought in Europe were bad. They hurt the import-export business. But if the British were forced to do some of the fighting in the colonies, that was another matter. Not that anyone would speak of it out loud in the café, it went without saying that some of those present had profited from trading with the French enemy as well as the British.

King George's War had ended just over six years earlier. Many of the men in the café had happily raised prices for all the merchandise they could to take advantage of a British army and navy in dire need of uniforms by the thousands, boots, food, transportation, accommodations and more. Merchants, carters, ale and gin houses, prostitutes and farmers were among those who bathed in the economic boom. There would also be privateers to invest in and arm. However, the war meant something different for the city's poor, probably a third of the population: steeply higher prices. The British army could afford the new price of bread. They couldn't.

After an hour Jacob suggested they try another café in the hope of gleaning current information about the kind of real estate speculators were interested in. Peter declined.

"If I hear anything useful, I'll let you know in the morning. By the way, I trust I will again have your services then?"

"You have my solemn word, Peter."

Jacob walked to the corner of Broadway and turned north past Trinity Church. On the west side of the street, between Crown and Little Prince streets, he entered the King's Arms for the first time. Immediately he felt out of place. He had been told it was a favorite of municipal and provincial officers, army officers and well-off merchants. There were curtained booths along the side of the barroom for private conversations. Though the main floor was crowded with men standing with glass in hand, Jacob doubted eavesdropping would be as productive here compared to the Wall Street coffee house. As he took in his surroundings, a voice behind him said, conversationally:

"And upstairs are spacious meeting rooms overlooking the magnificent North River. Committees of both the Assembly and Common Council find the comforts conducive to meetings."

Jacob spun around and found himself looking at Arnold, the very man he'd hoped to find on Wall Street.

"That second floor is also used for fine theater productions. I highly recommend them. It is good to see you again, Jacob."

"You make a habit of filling in my thoughts," said Jacob, shaking Arnold's hand.

Arnold led him to a newly vacated booth.

"Let us order food and beverage. My treat."

They spent the meal in mostly small talk. When the dishes were taken away, Jacob said:

"I would like to thank you for the meal but I don't even know your surname."

"Livstrom. I'm one of them."

"I'm impressed. I know the name."

"And well you should, Jacob. We're frightfully wealthy, unabashed peddlers of political interest, and owners of more land here and up the Hudson Valley than a hawk can patrol in a day." As Arnold had done on their first meeting, there was always a hint of a smile behind every word he spoke, as if he didn't care whether you found him sincere or not. If he was as rich as he said, thought Jacob, he could afford to not care.

After offering a few more details about his family, including the fact that they were the major rival to the equally influential De Lanceys, their son James being the acting governor at the moment of the Province of New York, and the fact that "the Livstroms differ greatly from practically everyone in this establishment in that we are not Anglican. We are Presbyterian to the core."

Jacob knew nothing of Christian churches, nor cared, but he did know that British nobles were all Church of England.

"What about you, Jacob. What brings you to this unlikely watering hole?"

Jacob decided to go straight to the point. He had nothing to lose. He felt certain Arnold would soon lose interest in him, although he did suspect that Arnold more than occasionally found his own kind tedious.

"For personal reasons, I must see an injustice punished, one committed by a certain merchant of this city. We have no legal recourse against him, at least not at the moment, but I believe we could have in time if events unroll as we suspect they might."

"Your cause," replied Arnold, "is apparently a noble one, but as to the rest of what you said I am totally in the dark."

Jacob explained the firsthand knowledge, and proof, he had of forged land deeds that the merchant in question will undoubtedly try to sell.

"He has suffered recent financial losses and we believe he will act soon to sell land he doesn't own. I read in the Gazette that one of his largest ships disappeared in a hurricane two months ago. That must have cost him dearly. But I want to make him pay, too. I want to lay a trap for him but I don't know how."

"How do you know the deeds are forged?"

Jacob looked him right in the eye and answered:

"Because I forged them."

Arnold was now clearly intrigued. He ordered a bottle of port.

Jacob explained the circumstances of the voyage from Bordeaux to New York and how he and his sister, whom he had not mentioned before, had been forced to reduce their terms of indenture by doing translation, correspondence and forgery for the captain, a business partner of the New York merchant in question. He explained in the most general terms the abuse the merchant inflicted on his sister, and how she in turn forced him to make restitution.

"We would have dropped the matter then and there but this merchant tried to guarantee our silence by burning our warehouse, making it almost impossible for my sister to survive."

"Jacob, you left out one important detail, the merchant's name."

"Zachariah Croman."

A smile spread across Arnold's face.

"I am acquainted with Croman. An altogether repellent creature. As a species, I don't generally care for merchants.

Let me tell you why."

Arnold went on to explain that the enormous wealth of the Livstroms came from their land holdings and the rents they charged tenants, although they also now owned businesses.

"However, merchants like Croman, and their representatives on council, are forever demanding that the royal province of New York fill its coffers by taxing our lands, and those of the English nobles who, like us, are also land barons on Manhattan Island. Our solution, we the land owners, is to tax imports and exports. The merchants won't hear of it. At the moment, Jacob, we are far wealthier than any merchant, but that will change. The commerce generated by the port of New York is growing faster than even the greatest merchant could have imagined."

This was all new to Jacob. He knew nothing of New York's great families, politics, councils, taxes and land barons. All he knew firsthand was the lot of a small merchant. In Arnold's mouth, all the rest sounded like a playground.

"Leave this matter with me," Jacob. "Believe it or not, while I can't even recite all our properties, we're always on the lookout for more, even though in this case there is no actual property to buy. I should enjoy laying a trap for a beast like Croman."

Jacob told him he frequented the café on Wall Street.

"Perhaps we could meet there if you come up with a plan," he suggested.

"I know the place. I prefer it," said Arnold. "It's so much more… it's so less Anglican."

Once outside Jacob looked down the street at Trinity Church, the gathering point and magnet for all men powerful, rich and loyal to the King and the Church of England. That evening, even while listening intently to Arnold's sardonic description of New York society, Jacob overheard more platitudes than he thought intelligent men could ever bring themselves to utter. Glad to be back in the fresh air, he was tempted to go to Sarah's to tell her about his extraordinary evening spent with a rich man. Finally he opted to spend the night at the atelier so he could get an early start the next morning on what remained of Peter's backlog or orders.

To Jacob's surprise, Peter wasn't at the atelier. He figured Peter may have returned to the café on Wall Street. He felt absolutely at home there.

In fact, Peter had not returned to the café. His feet took him along Wall Street, then up Water Street to Sarah's. He had not consciously intended to end up there, but he had been thinking of Sarah all evening, especially every time Jacob mentioned her name. He stood in front of her door for a full minute before knocking.

Sarah looked alarmed when she saw Peter's face.

"Has something happened to Jacob?"

"Thank God," Peter thought, relieved to realize the look on her face was concern for her brother and not discomfort at seeing him at the door. "No, no. Jacob is fine," he assured her.

When Sarah didn't immediately invite him in Peter felt his well-practiced gentleman's bearing begin to slouch as he searched for words.

"I found myself walking the streets and thinking of you, Sarah."

Despite the doubts she and Jacob now harbored about Peter, she still found him attractive, but the more she got to know him the more she knew he was not for her. His uncertainty now only added to that realization. It was as if he'd forgotten his mask.

"Would you like to stroll along the quay?"

"It's late, Peter," Sarah answered.

"It's important. Perhaps I can come in?"

Sarah hesitated then stepped back to allow him to enter.

They sat at the kitchen table.

"We've known each other for some time now, and there has been many a time when you invited me to be in your company with Jacob and your friends. When I think of those occasions, I realize I must have appeared as a man with little to say. I am sure Jacob has told you that is not the case."

Sarah was on the verge of interrupting and demanding that he speak his thoughts directly when Peter's words began to tumble out faster.

"I was often speechless because of you, Sarah. I admire you to that point, truly. My love for you leaves me mute in your presence."

At first, Sarah was stunned, but her memory was quickly flooded by the looks he'd given her in the past, the kind that would have been perceptible only if she were focused on him at the moment, which she rarely was.

"I'm… I'm flattered, Peter. I had no idea."

"Then I may have hope." Peter said it assertively, but it still came out as a question, a disguised plea.

"Peter, I've met someone. I haven't even talked to Jacob about it but I think he knows. It's Michel. We see each whenever we can."

Had Sarah blinked, she would not have seen the gentleman's mask redraw Peter's face. He did not look crestfallen in the slightest despite the British version of desperation that had tinged his voice and eyes moments earlier.

Peter rose and looked down at Sarah across the table.

"Clearly I have stumbled into delusion. Please forgive me. I doubt we shall encounter each other again."

With that he turned abruptly and quickly descended the stairs. Before Sarah could catch up with him, he had already let himself out the door.

Sarah watched him disappear down the street. This had been the second time Peter had tried to express his feelings for her. Both times, she realized, it felt painfully awkward for him. When she first learned from Jacob that Peter had been sent away by his parents at an early age and that they never made any effort to reconnect with him in all the years that had since passed, she felt a vague kinship with him. Even though it was irrational, the sense of abandonment she first felt when her mother died had continued to invade her soul and then retreat like changing tides.

She had just verbalized to Peter what she had not even dared to tell Jacob, that she was falling in love with Michel. She hadn't told him because her new-found happiness was often doing battle with the fear that pursuing her feelings for Michel would ultimately lead to more emptiness.

Sarah closed the door and went back upstairs. The encounter with Peter had shaken her. On the one hand, she knew she no longer felt the slightest attraction for Peter. On the other, she had been surprised to have felt an initial attraction to him when they first met.

Immediately after the first time Croman raped her, Sarah frequently flinched whenever a man stood close to her, even men with kind faces, or sometimes men who weren't even looking at her. Sarah had never made love to a man nor had she ever met a man her age who wanted to court her. She daydreamed about love from time to time, but her busy life working for her father precluded any possibility of a man discovering her. It was something she simply didn't spend a lot of time thinking about.

After the rape, she cried a lot. She had no girlfriends. Everyone she worked with was a man. The only woman she knew was the cooper's wife. She felt too much shame to tell her what had happened. After the second rape, she did. It was a relief to share what happened, but when Mrs. McDougall told her what had happened was the lot of most women, it didn't help. Would murdering those men be so satisfying that she'd willingly put her neck in the hangman's noose?

After each of the subsequent rapes Sarah added layers

of numbness. She still cried while lying on her straw mattress at the cooper's. The McDougalls slept upstairs and couldn't hear her. Sometimes the crying helped, but a solution never presented itself when the tears dried. It was as if she were now going through the motions of her life with only one lung to animate her.

It was far from the soul-cleansing murder that she once dreamed of but the humiliation of Croman reignited some of her taste for life. For the first time since Bordeaux she felt she had a modicum of control over her fate. Before enacting that revenge, she knew she would never have allowed herself to feel the slightest attraction to Peter. When she did feel that attraction, she felt somewhat human again. Was it that realization that wedged the door open for her profound attraction to Michel?

At that point images of Michel began floating around her every thought. When she came back to reality her eyes were still closed but she felt that her smile muscles were engaged. "I must look so silly," she thought, trying to look at herself in her mind's eye. Maybe something was changing after all, and it wasn't against her will.

By the time sleep finally took the upper hand the sun was up.

CHAPTER 44

Preparations

THE disassembled press was on a cart on its way to Dock Street, where it would be rowed out to the Chameleon. Michel was already there. When he arrived, Asser Pietersen motioned him to join him at water's edge a few feet south of his wharf.

"When you return this time I think it would be best if you unloaded at Sandy Hook and had your cargo brought to me by wagon," Asser said. "You were lucky to get by unscathed when you first arrived with cargo from France and the French West Indies. We'll be more careful next time. I'll try to arrange a contact for you at the Hook, someone to arrange for the wagons. Your boys will have to do all the unloading."

Michel filled Asser in on the dimensions of the pieces of the press. Asser said there'd be no difficulty hiding them from the eyes of French inspectors at Cap-Français.

"Getting the components to where you want to assemble them may not be so easy. You might want to get advice there. If it were me, once I found out my destination, I'd load it directly from the Chameleon onto a coastal boat. Everyone uses them because the roads through the mountains are almost impassable in places. Will you be bringing it back with you to New York?"

"No," Michel said, "but I'll be bringing back my friend."

"Then one of those coastal boats might be the safest escape. You can anchor your ship far out in the harbor and the boat will make the delivery there for a price. They all know the coast as well as a man can know anything. They'll work at night if you pay extra."

With that kind of advice, plus what his agent in Cap-Français will be able to tell him, Michel was starting to feel more confident that the dangerous mission had a chance of succeeding.

Michel signaled for two of his men to take him out to the ship. He found that the hold was already about half full. Jean-Luc took his eyes off the winch long enough to tell his captain that if he thought he could use them there were two local seamen who had offered to sign on that morning.

"They could be useful later, on our subsequent voyages," Michel said. "Don't think we really need them this time. What do you think?"

Jean-Luc reminded him the voyage to Saint-Domingue was relatively short. They wouldn't cost us much and we'd get a good look at how they handle themselves. If we don't take them now they might not be available when we get back. There's work everywhere here for seamen."

"Done," said Michel. "The time is good. I just gave permission for Richard Gauthier to leave the Chameleon today. He wants to make his way up to Canada to rejoin his family in Québec City. I understand him wanting to go home. I also need him to take some money to my uncle, the money from our last trip to France, and a little more. So come to think of it the timing is excellent. Now, Jean-

Luc, is the manifest in my cabin?"

"No, I have it here." Jean-Luc pulled it out of his coat pocket. "I've been cross-checking it with what's being brought aboard."

Much of their cargo was flour, corn, pork and beef. Most of the remaining load was lumber.

Noah showed up at the dock just past 4. He wanted to know if the press had arrived. With Asser's permission he hopped down into a boat transporting cargo to the Chameleon.

"I know you were going to hide it all over the ship but I want to make sure every piece is there," Noah said to Michel after climbing on deck.

"Be my guest, Monsieur Noah."

"Enough of that Monsieur business, *mon capitaine*, sir." Noah's deep voice made his words sound like an order.

Noah also wanted to check the storage of the ink, paper and plates.

"The paper has to be kept as dry as sand in an hourglass."

"It's in a well-made crate with oil cloth tied around it. I think it will arrive like new unless a late-season hurricane sends us to the bottom, in which case it probably won't matter."

Satisfied, Noah told Michel he was now going back to Sarah's place.

"If you want to make yourself comfortable by the bow, we could go back together in about an hour. My presence on deck makes the men work harder. I enjoy being a tyrant."

Jean-Luc, standing at the captain's side, smiled. His old friend was anything but a tyrant, yet his crew had never questioned their captain in all the years he'd sailed with him.

On the way back to Sarah's Michel stopped at the Old Slip market to buy oysters. While waiting for Michel, Noah was hailed by a man standing against a wall about 50 feet up William Street. He signaled for Noah to come.

"I overheard the fat merchant this morning, Noah. He just learned of more warehouse losses. He's convinced the young girl and you are behind the thefts. The man with him said the two of you have been followed many times but they have no evidence. The fat one said he'd bet his fortune you were guilty. Thought you should know."

Noah thanked him quickly.

For the first time since he announced he was going to look for his wife in Saint-Domingue no matter what the danger, he felt relieved that he would soon be leaving the city. The question now was how to protect Sarah. As soon as he caught up with Michel he told him about what he'd just heard.

Michel looked shaken.

"I don't know what to do. I have to sail. I have a contract with Pietersen. The Chameleon is almost fully loaded. Maybe I could leave some crew members to watch over her day and night."

Upset, Michel spoke rapidly. Because it was in French, it sounded almost like babbling to Noah's ear. But the worry was clear. Noah felt the same. He had warned Sarah about avoiding the waterfront and to never let a cart be seen near her house. He thought with the passage of time anyone watching them on the merchant's behalf would have given up. Perhaps they had. Now it might be just Croman flailing at any target he could think of. Either way, even if he didn't have a shred of evidence against either Sarah or him. Croman couldn't be trusted. He had more than enough henchmen to pummel any and all people he suspected.

Sarah looked puzzled by the relief Noah and Michel betrayed when they found her at home, safe and sound. Still holding the oysters he'd bought for Sarah, Michel started to explain. Noah interrupted and gave Sarah a word for word account of what he'd been told. Only then did he draw up a chair. Michel and Sarah joined him at the table.

Sarah suddenly had an image of fire raging in her warehouse and leaping to the roof of her house as she lay asleep upstairs. The last time the fat merchant's thugs had burned the warehouse she had not been home. Would they go for the house this time? Or would they drag her to an alley and slit her throat.

People died that way every few weeks in New York. The murderers were rarely found. As long as victims were poor, no one cared. She had heard that alley gangs had resorted to rowing their victims out into the river at night and dumping them overboard. On one occasion they cut off a man's head and then wrapped and boxed it. Drinking gin that night, one of the boys announced he had a great idea. In the morning he would ride the ferry to Brooklyn. He would lay the box with the head on the deck near the bow. Once on the other side of the river, he'd debark, find a tavern and enjoy himself until it was time to catch the same ferry back. On his way to New York he would casually check to see if the packaged head was still crisscrossing the river. When eventually apprehended by a night watchman on another matter, a robbery, he told a fellow accused that the head made the return trip at least five days in a row.

"Maybe the safest thing would be for Sarah to sail with us," Noah suggested after a long silence. "It would be like she disappeared. That might bring our sabotage operations to a standstill, but so what. I'll be returning eventually and we can start again if we have to."

Sarah wasn't sure if she was thinking clearly. The fear was logical. The idea of disappearing was logical. But was sailing away with Noah and Michel logical? Was the part of her that said yes to the latter the same part that last night wanted to sail with Michel because she loved him? Without venturing that idea, she said:

"The best way of making Croman think I'm not involved in any of this would be for me to disappear but to have thefts go on. But I don't know how we can pull that off."

Where in the hell was Jacob, analytical, cool-headed Jacob?

"When does the Commodore return, Sarah?"

"Tomorrow morning."

"Good, I'll talk to him," said Noah. "Maybe even go to New Harlem for a few days before we sail. Perhaps we could work something out between the Commodore and my men. I'm thinking, fewer robberies, fewer trips to and from New Harlem until we get back. But what would you tell your merchants, Sarah?"

"Let's not make any decisions right now," she said. "Don't go to the Commodore yet. This is all too much for me. I don't want to rush into anything, but with you going to Saint-Domingue in a few days with Michel, everything is a rush. I'll talk to Jacob first thing in the morning. I'm sure he'll be at the atelier. Can you meet back here tomorrow afternoon, Noah?"

"Anytime. If I'm not here I'll be home. Get me there."

As expected Jacob didn't make an appearance, so Sarah headed out to New Street the following morning. Out of habit she looked in on a couple of her merchants on the way. One of them placed a new order.

At the atelier Jacob greeted her as warmly as usual but was clearly hesitant to put aside his work at the moment.

"Go ahead. Step out a while," Peter said. "I can still smell the port you consumed last night." Peter merely nodded at Sarah. Jacob failed to notice the slight.

"I had a most interesting night," Jacob started to say before Sarah put her hand up to his face.

"Tales of your debauchery will have to wait, Jacob. Noah and Michel brought me alarming news yesterday. We are in danger, or at least I am. I need your advice. Everything's coming to a head with Noah leaving soon."

Jacob did indeed need to clear his head. He'd been hard at work for more than four hours but he would be hard-pressed to recite what he'd done. Because he and Sarah had done it so often, they turned down New Street to Beaver and right to Bowling Green where they sat on the chilly grass.

Sarah could see her brother's mind at work and didn't interrupt. She tried to sit still but it was a cold, grey morning. Winter was in the November air.

"Let's assume the worst. Croman's men will try to burn your house to finish what they started with the warehouse. Consequently, you must arrange to stay elsewhere. Can Geneviève take you in?"

"Absolutely."

"Good, see to that today, Sarah. Pack what you need from the house and take it to Geneviève's. If you need to make a second trip ask her to help you because you must also pack all the money we buried in the warehouse. Clean off all the soot and package it to look like anything but paper money. I would hate for one of Croman's men to trace you to Geneviève's."

"Anything else?"

"Yes. After you move your things and the money, make sure you see Noah tonight. Since we can't have you appearing at the house or being seen with Noah's men, we have to have a system for you to get your orders to the Commodore by messenger. Ask Noah if he knows a boy who can meet you at Geneviève's on the day the Commodore comes to town and use him to deliver the orders to him. Also inform the merchants that they'll have to meet the Commodore's boat and pick up their own orders for a while. I think that should work."

"That's good, Jacob. Noah said it was important that thefts continue even though I seem to have disappeared, and Noah, too."

Jacob then related his evening drinking at a tavern for the rich and powerful with a relation of one of New York's two richest families.

"Arnold was the one you met at the forger's trial?"

"One and the same. To cut to the quick, his class apparently hates merchants, at least ones like Croman who believe their greed qualifies them as being among New York's nobility. When I told Arnold about how we arrived on these shores and the price Croman made you pay..."

"Jacob, you didn't..."

"Sarah, I'd gone that far. I had to tell him everything if I were to get his full sympathy. While he is certainly supercilious at times, I saw that he also believes that injustice is wrong and, because he is who he is, educated the way he was, he has no compunction about confronting it. I told him about the deeds we forged under duress and while Arnold's words promised nothing I had the distinct impression that after hearing of the false deeds he was a man with a bit between his teeth. He would love to skewer Croman. It's a matter of waiting for Croman to make a move."

"Does that mean I don't need to try to enlist Patricia's father?"

"On the contrary. Arnold could expose Croman for a fraud and a cheat among other businessmen and investors, but Patricia's father sits on the Assembly and could embarrass Croman in the eyes of high society, the place the pig craves to be. Remember, Patricia's father comes from a long line of Dutch land barons. When it comes to merchants like Croman, the Livstroms and the Van Huisens think much alike. And, as Arnold might say, one of the best things the Van Huisens have going for them is that they are not Anglicans. They are Dutch Reform."

"What on earth do you mean?" Sarah asked, sensing that her brother was satirizing the class he'd so recently become acquainted with.

Jacob returned to his engraving. Sarah made straight for Geneviève's.

"Oh dear," cried the seamstress on hearing of the merchant's threats. "Of course, of course, you must stay with me. There is plenty of room for you and your things in my room upstairs. It's like two rooms in one. Somebody must have removed a wall between them at some point. Come, I'll show you."

Though money had ceased to be an immediate problem for Sarah, when calculating which of her belongings would fit in Geneviève's room she came to the conclusion that it would all fit for one simple reason. She possessed little in life.

When Sarah returned downstairs her friend was shutting her shop.

"Let's get this done," she told Sarah.

Sarah couldn't have put it better.

As Jacob had guessed, it took two trips, but neither were burdensome with four hands involved. Geneviève had become curious watching Sarah use a knife to pry two shallow boxes out of the soot in the warehouse, but Sarah dismissed them as top-quality engraving tools Jacob had purchased for the day when he would have his own business.

As they started walking back to Geneviève's place, Sarah realized she would have to go back for the evening to update both Noah and Michel. She would ask Jacob to escort her and suggest they gather at the tavern instead of the house. Michel would be sleeping at the house until he sailed, but Croman's gang didn't know him. At least her young captain was safe for now.

CHAPTER 45

The Plantation

ON THE Monday of the following week, the Commodore watched proudly as Noah and Michel stepped down from the dock above Sarah's into the Citroen. They could very easily have walked down to Dock Street and taken a ship's boat out to the Chameleon, but the Commodore insisted, claiming that he remained as moved as he was the first time he heard about Noah's noble journey. He was also overheard telling one of his boys that it didn't do any harm either to his reputation if seen by the whole harbor ferrying a ship's captain and his distinguished passenger.

Sarah and Jacob had said their farewells the night before, to Noah's great embarrassment. He asked them not to see him off the next day, then left to spend the night at the shack.

It was a beautiful morning by any New Yorker's standard, but even more beautiful from Michel's point of view. Both tide and wind favored an easy departure. "We'll be at sea in no time," he said, clapping Jean-Luc on the shoulder.

Michel showed Noah where he'd be quartered, a first mate's berth, both too narrow and too short for Noah's bulk.

As he did so he commented,

"That Commodore Barry fellow is quite the character."

"I think Sarah's adopting him," said Noah, "like she did the rest of us."

When they returned to deck, the Commodore was at the helm of the Chameleon with the Citroen in their wake.

Before they were abreast of Sandy Hook, the Commodore ordered the first mate to reduce sail, then signaled to the Citroen to come alongside. When the Citroen brushed the Chameleon amidships, he bid farewell to both Michel and Noah. His air was solemn and formal. With surprising agility, he stepped over the side and climbed down to his boat.

Michel immediately ordered the ship to resume its course. Half an hour later he had the flag dipped and raised twice in salute to the Citroen. In the distance, Michel was sure he could make out the rotund Commodore saluting him.

Noah could not separate the stew of apprehension and excitement that governed his moods during the first days of the voyage. Other than appearing on deck now and then to ask Jean-Luc or Michel where they were—Delaware, Virginia, Carolina, what beautiful names, he thought—he remained in his compartment until the fourth day.

"You never know what he's thinking," Michel mentioned to Jean-Luc. "Right now, if I were him, I'd be shitting."

The next time Noah came on deck he headed straight for Michel.

"How well do you know Saint-Domingue?" he asked, standing next to Michel, legs akimbo, hands at his waist, squinting into the morning sun, which he noticed was already a little warmer than in New York.

"Can't say I do. I've been only to Cap-Français, never beyond. I know the waterfront, where to unload, where to go if the ship needs careening. The only building I've been in is my agent's house. I've told you about him. Thinks he's nobility and that his place is a château. It's not. It's an ordinary house with the furnishings of a château, including slaves.

"Apart from that all I've done is stretch my legs after a long voyage. Place d'Armes to see soldiers sweat, the Cathedral for shade. Not much else. The food carts have more than enough for me, and I stock up on fruit at the big market. The crew probably knows more. I make a point of being back onboard when I let them go ashore to sample the hospitality."

After a prolonged silence, Michel asked Noah what it was like as a slave there.

"I was taken out of the city as soon as we were auctioned off. I remember being chained to three other men. I didn't know French then and they didn't speak French or English. They weren't the ones kidnapped in New York when I was. They probably just arrived from Africa and our new owner picked us for some reason. I remember swamps and mosquitoes, then lots of pine trees and climbing. I couldn't eat the shit they gave us on the voyage down and I thought I'd die before we got to the plantation. Then I remember stepping barefoot in the shit the mule in front of me left behind. Don't know why but I kept on walking after that and we finally got there."

Michel moved to the port side and stared out to sea, absent-mindedly holding onto a stay. Noah joined him. The ocean took his mind off the land and Saint-Domingue.

They talked about Sarah and Jacob and whether Noah thought they had much chance of getting rid of the fat merchant for good.

"We'll get old trying," Noah said.

After stopping to talk to Jean-Luc about having the

watch keep a sharp lookout for the Spanish or pirates off the Florida coast, Michel turned the subject back to Saint-Domingue. He wanted to know if Noah had any idea of how he was going to try to find his wife.

"Not sure. I can't imagine it would be safe for me to wander through plantations asking questions, or even trying to make my way into the mountains. That's where I found the Maroons who arranged to get me out of the country. I think this time I'll need to somehow get word to them about who I'm looking for. It's going to be hard because I don't know which plantation she worked on."

He then turned his eyes from the sea and looked at Michel.

"It's a long shot. I know that, Michel. A lot of time has passed and people don't live a long time there."

The Chameleon had been making good time but the next morning Michel said they we're headed into a gale. The sky was visibly darkening by the minute and even to a landlubber like Noah the ship was struggling to maintain its course. A moment later Jean-Luc bellowed orders for the reefing of sails Noah couldn't identify. If only his stevedores would respond as quickly. While men worked above him manhandling sails, others lashed down everything in sight on deck, anchors, the ship's boat, spare spars and yards. Michel's eyes darted calmly from sails, masts and yards to the deck, and back again in reverse order. There wasn't a single sign of worry on his face, only squinting when slapped by gusts of wind.

"What can I do?" Noah shouted in his ear.

"Nothing, my friend. To be honest, at this point, there's little I can do either. We've got lots of sea room so we should be able to ride this out. Just be thankful we left New York after hurricane season. Get caught in one of those and only a fool makes promises."

With his hand, Michel indicated that Noah should go below.

The gale lasted a day and a half. The wind and groaning of the Chameleon's timbers were so loud Noah couldn't think of Saint-Domingue. The fury of the storm was a blessing.

The galley fire had been lit again and the crew might know some sleep that day. Noah was famished, not that the ship offered anything that was worth putting both elbows onto the table and digging into with a vengeance. He was sore from the buffeting but in great need of moving about. He went on deck and greeted those whose names he now knew. To a man their response was weary and wet. They busied themselves getting the deck back in order, while a small contingent was going aloft to unfurl what Noah now understood to be the topsails.

"Good morning, Noah." It was Michel's voice. He was just returning from his cabin with a chart in hand. He must have been up all night like everyone else but he was clearly invigorated.

"Topsails only for the moment, Noah, while I figure out exactly what course to set. Last night's blow was more of a bully than I expected. I think at one point at first light our bow was trying to point toward New York. For most of the night, though, I had the feeling we were scudding nicely before the wind. Sometimes a wind can fling you forward in a direction you were already intending to go but the free ride can be over any minute if a stern wave decides to swallow you whole from behind."

"No damage?" asked Noah.

"None has been reported but if you've grown restless from lounging around all night while everyone else danced to the wind you might give old Gérard a hand pumping."

"We're leaking?"

"No. I don't think so. But storms have a way of infiltrating every stretched seam.

When Gérard saw Noah's frame, bent nearly double under the deck beams, he gazed up at him for a moment, then explained, "It's you. When I first heard you stumblin' about down here I thought you might be the priest coming to give me last rights."

Noah's bare feet stood in about six inches of water.

"This is nothing to worry about. And notice how it stinks. That should make you happy. Means it's not water freshly arrived from the sea. No harm in pumping it out anyway, captain says."

It was an old suction pump system. Men had to do all the work. And work they did. When Gérard caught his breath, he let the curse-accompanied rhythm of Noah's powerful pulling become his own.

Learning that food was still a few hours away, Noah went to what he called his cupboard and lay down, thankful for the chance to have used his muscles.

He was also thankful to be useful to Michel. Knowing it was none of his business, he'd kept a close watch on Michel since the moment he recognized the way he looked at Sarah. He relaxed when there were signs that the attraction was mutual, especially when Sarah insisted on joining Michel on this very voyage. Watching Michel's calm command in the face of a frightening gale, or at least frightening to a landsman, convinced him the man had character.

All that remained to be seen was whether the young captain could finagle his agent into setting up an illegal counterfeiting press, run by a man who looks like any of the hundreds of thousands of slaves that dominate the colony's population, and do it all under the King's protection.

The sunrise the next morning was not a New York sunrise. To start with, the unimpeded horizon made it huge. It insisted on being noticed. The hues of color that gave it its subtle beauty made it a woman in Noah's mind. The bold colors of sunsets represented men. These were new thoughts to him. When forced into slavery on Saint-Domingue he paid no attention to the rising and setting sun.

Noah spotted Michel aft of the mainmast and began heading toward him.

"Captain," Jean-Luc called from the far side of the ship. "I see them, the twin hills." He handed the glass to Michel. "Broad on the starboard bow."

"We've made decent time to be sure," Michel said to Noah. Then to Jean-Luc he ordered him to slowly come about to lay a course for the heart of the harbor entrance.

"The harbor at Cap-Français always makes me think of a hand poised to snatch a mango from a street cart, or even better a large jewel pinned to a countess's gown. Take the glass and look straight ahead. Do you see the two hills? For mariners, they serve as sign posts telling us we've arrived at the harbor. In a moment, you'll see the mouth of the port. Come to my cabin and look at the map."

As Michel had said, the harbor entrance was contained within a hand, a right hand with fingers curled on the east side, and a slightly crooked thumb on the west.

An hour later, as they sailed slowly within the grasp of the claw, a pilot pulled alongside in yet another small schooner. Michel had always coveted them, fast, open to any manner of handling for any given situation. Always responsive. They were too far offshore for the sun to be muddling his thoughts, yet an image of Sarah came to mind, then vanished the instant Jean-Luc presented him to the pilot.

Noah's mouth got drier as the Chameleon neared the quay. Sensing his friend's state of mind Michel began to point out the sights. From the moment their bow first faced the city, the eye was not drawn to the mountains behind the city and the forests between them. All eyes fell on what appeared to be uniformly red roofs of dwellings, glued to the soil in perfectly straight lines running north south and east west. In the sun, they became a blur. All that stood out was the main quay, straight ahead and, to the right, a formidable battery. Beyond was the Place d'Armes and finally the cathedral.

Noah and Michel could see a few paths and roads leading beyond the city, heading around some kind of plain that gave way to thicker vegetation and trees. Using the glass Noah could see the trees give way to brush as the mountains rose higher in the distance. They seemed so far away, yet he had once desperately clawed his way toward them in the company of the Maroons who had attacked his plantation, allowing him to escape. There had been a real possibility that he would die in those mountains at the Maroon encampment. They had little food.

He was so lost in the memory he failed to hear any of the routine commands that accompanied lines being expertly tossed ashore for tying up the ship to bollards.

To Michel's great surprise, a distinguished gentlemen waved to him from the quay. A boy held a sun umbrella above his head. Before calling up to Michel, he gently motioned the boy away so Michel could make out his face.

"Origène Deschamps," Michel said under his breath.

"Who's he?" Noah asked.

"In the name his Excellency, the King of France, Origène Deschamps is your protector, or, I hope he will be after I've spoken to him.

"Before I join him, Noah, could you place about £6,000 in a sack? It's in my cabin. There's a drawer built into the wall behind my desk, below the stern windows. You have to pry it open with a knife. There are no handles, on purpose."

Noah smiled and hurried away while Michel turned toward the quay.

"You were spotted by another merchantman," called Deschamps. "He says you nearly rammed him during the gale."

"Never saw him."

"All's well that ends well, I suppose. He said he saw no sign of you by dawn. Didn't know whether you survived or not. "

"I assure you I'm no ghost ship. Come aboard. Bring your friend the revenue officer and we'll save time going over the manifest together."

"Sounds reasonable, young sir." Deschamps turned to speak to the boy, who ran off toward the customs house less than 100 feet from the Chameleon's bowsprit.

"An officer will join us presently," said Deschamps. "Permission to board?"

"Granted."

Before turning to look for Noah, Michel glanced down at the side of the ship. Suddenly he spun around and bellowed to a seaman standing idle by the cargo hatches. "Charles-Yves! I do believe a gangplank will facilitate the boarding of the important gentleman you will see standing below in the hot sun."

"*Oui, mon capitaine. Vraiment désolé, mon capitaine.*"

"Got it." It was Noah, holding a bag in his left hand.

"Wait for me in the cabin," Michel said.

By the time the gangplank had been lowered and secured, the customs officer had joined Deschamps below. Both came up with a practiced stride.

Deschamps' greeting was effusive. Hands were grasped, cheeks were kissed. Torsos were hugged. Michel appreciated the slight bow and handshake offered by the customs official. Michel pointed the way to his cabin, happy to be getting out of the sun.

Noah half rose from a small table in the back corner of the cabin. Michel introduced him as Normand Moreau of Newfoundland, where ships of all nations had traded, fought and fished for centuries.

"Years ago," Michel announced, "returning from Bordeaux, I had rudder trouble off the Grand Banks. Another merchant towed me toward shore where local fishermen brought me to a safe harbor where I could do repairs. It was there that I met Monsieur Moreau, a man of more talents than I can count. He has been my assistant in many matters ever since."

Stepping behind his desk Michel retrieved a bottle of port which he placed on the desk in front of the two Frenchman. Noah provided the glasses. Michel dropped the ship's manifest on the desk between them.

"I'm sure you'd rather tend to that before I regale you with the reasons for which I'm grateful to my assistant."

The custom's officer read the manifest. He asked permission to go into the hold to do a cask count and do a perfunctory search for smuggled goods that might have value worthy of the Governor's attention.

Michel started to tell Deschamps what this special mission required. Deschamps immediately held up his hand.

"While we wait for the inspector, allow me to calculate the value of your cargo, basically nothing but flour and lumber by the looks of it."

"That's all there is, Origène," becoming informal now that the inspector was gone.

"When your uncle and I had anything sensitive to discuss we went to my office. It's a short walk from here, just a few blocks to Place de Clugny. The location is convenient for me, however I must inform you that the square is occasionally used for executions. I find them a good reminder to make everything count in life. People also meet their end a few blocks north of here, at Place Royal. What can I say other than bid you welcome to the many faces of Cap-Français, le Paris des Antilles."

Noah was dying to talk to Michel alone. Some 20 years before, funds were raised to build a place in New York City supposedly to get insane people off the street. If he judged by first appearances, Noah thought something about Origène would qualify him for that asylum-workhouse.

Michel and Origène quickly agreed on a price for the cargo. On this trip there was nothing of personal interest to the agent. Since his disappointment was perceptible,

Michel assured him that the time they were soon to spend in his office would prove somewhat more interesting.

The three men had time for another glass of port before the customs officer returned. Michel settled up with the inspector for the duties owed. The officer had dragged out his search of the hold merely to appear more efficient and important. Origène explained later as they walked to Place de Clugny, the boy shading his master as before with the umbrella. At the office, Deschamps told the boy to wait on the steps.

The office looked like an office would in France, Michel thought, not that he'd ever seen one belonging to a high-placed official. Ornately finished dark woods, chairs too delicate for a man who worked with his muscles, dark curtains to keep out the direct sun, an oriental carpet in a country where climate rots them. Decanters, crystal, silver candelabra, a map of the Caribbean and a disproportionately large portrait of dear old Louis XV.

Since Deschamps surely knew in his heart of hearts that he was an imposter, Michel often wondered whether he regarded all these trappings and the real nobles that inspired them as imposters, too, in their own way, offering little to the world except refining Machiavelli with each new generation of barons and bureaucrats. Michel thought so. His uncle said that unlike virtually every white person in Saint-Domingue, Deschamps would never want to move to France. He'd identified the colony as a microcosm, and being small, much easier to manipulate for his own purpose.

On other days, Michel would find the thought amusing, but not today. The life of his friend, sitting next to him before Deschamps' massive desk, would soon be in the hands of a master game-player.

Within the next hour, Michel realized he had sorely misjudged the game player. Deschamps became studiously businesslike when Michel started explaining his counterfeiting operation and its requirements. Noah required accommodation far from town, preferably on a plantation where he could work in secret and easily be provided with food and protection by the plantation owner, and have access to routes to other plantations for him to search for his woman.

Furthermore, Michel said, Deschamps would provide a letter bearing his seal to introduce Noah, guaranteeing him safe passage throughout Saint-Domingue. Should any misfortune arise, the letter would state that Noah and his equipment would be conveyed to him personally. He would also suggest in a postscript to his letter that Noah's mission was not to be spoken of because it was part of a strategy designed to be to the detriment of British forces in what promises to become a confrontation in the not too-distant future.

Deschamps had made precise notes as Michel talked. When Michel finished, Deschamps continued writing, scratching out previous passages and rewriting them.

"There. A rough. I can have a fair copy made tomorrow morning. Let us meet at noon, here. I will have arrangements to make. Fear not, I know what I am doing."

"I am indebted to you," Michel said.

"Yes, indeed you are, my young friend," he said, a smile growing by the second. "You could simply give me your cargo."

"No," Michel said, "I own but a share of it this time. However, I could provide you with cash to pay other merchants you might owe from the American colonies, or smugglers from there who I'm sure seek you out from time to time."

"All cash is good, Michel. It makes small transactions possible. It makes them quick and uncomplicated. Merchants hate waiting to find a cargo that will let them make use of their credit abroad. If I'm not misinformed, you can exchange your paper money for specie locally and buy the loveliest things from England."

Deschamps clasped his hands and leaned forward.

"I do believe £5,000 would neatly cover everything, my time and effort, our transport and the transport of your apparatus to the plantation, a handsome sum for the plantation owner, out of which would come comforts and necessities and protection for your friend here, plus the return to Cap-Français."

Michel had hoped to get away with paying half that amount until he remembered it was not only not his money but not even real money.

Noah handed Michel the sack. Michel counted the piles of notes and laid them neatly on Deschamps' desk.

"I myself," said Deschamps, sliding the money into a desk drawer, "do not hold with voodoo, but it is said that life unveils itself here in surprising ways if you are open to them."

The next day they met as scheduled at noon. Deschamps handed Michel the letter.

"I have not contacted the plantation owner I have in mind, but for reasons I'll not burden you with, I know he will be a willing participant in our piece of theater. There are mules already waiting for our backsides at the harbor. We will leave as soon as you remove your apparatus from your ship. It will be carried by porters. How many will I need?"

Michel looked blankly at Noah.

"It would be simpler with a couple extra mules. Otherwise we'd need four or five men."

Outside of his office, Deschamps sent the boy running away with a message.

"The extra mules will be waiting for us."

"Are you not going to change clothes for the journey, Origène?"

"Perception, sir, perception will carry the day."

Perception got rained on during the 20-hour trek through mango and palm trees, swamps and pine forest to the plantation. Noah several times stopped to make sure the paper was perfectly sealed.

As soon as he'd been presented to the plantation owner, Noah went to the hut he'd been provided with. It was located about 50 yards behind the Big House. There'd be no disguising the sound of the press, although he thought it likely that no one there had ever heard one. Furthermore, Deschamps said the owner would be told he was not to ask questions.

When Noah returned to the house, he wasn't sure how welcome he'd be. The man had one male and three female slaves attending to him in the drawing room. He was explaining how they were to conduct themselves with their temporary guest. One of the maids left the room, returning shortly afterwards with lemonade for everyone.

"Mr. Moreau…" It took a second for Noah to realize he now answered to another name. "Mr. Moreau, you'll have to present yourself at the house to obtain provisions since there are no shelves or cupboards for storing anything at your hut. I will often be absent in the coming weeks but you are free to eat here should you wish."

The plantation owner and Deschamps disappeared into another room. They were gone for almost an hour. Both were smiling when they returned. Deschamps was as good as his word. Michel couldn't help wondering how much Deschamps paid him. Probably not much. He was sure Deschamps had something over the man.

In the morning, when Michel and Deschamps came to say goodbye, Noah was already setting the components out in the same way Jacob had shown him when first teaching him how to assemble it.

"How do I get a message to you?" Noah asked Deschamps.

"Already arranged. Just ask the owner or one of the slaves directly. The owner has taken care of that eventuality."

Michel found the trip back much longer. While on the

surface everything seemed to have worked out far more smoothly than he'd expected, he felt an unease about that land. He pictured Noah in chains being dragged up the forest path. Days later, the closer the Chameleon got to New York the more he wished he could go back and drag Noah home.

CHAPTER 46

Another Ally

New York City
January 28, 1755

"YOU ARE instructed to report immediately to Miss Sarah Da Silva of Maiden Lane."

Michel burst into laughter at Jacob who saluted as he stood before him on the quay, rigid as a soldier addressing a general. While grasping Jacob's hand in greeting, Michel said:

"Tell milady I shall set a course for Maiden Lane within the hour, tide permitting."

Asser could have doubled his offer for Michel's cargo and it would have paled compared to the joy Michel felt at hearing Sarah's invitation. He allowed himself to feel sure she would have been at dockside herself had it not been for Noah's instruction not to be seen along the waterfront for any reason whatsoever. He had thought of her often as his ship made its way to what he now saw was a land of snow and cold. It had not been cold long, though. He'd seen no patches of ice along either shore of the East River. Noah had told him on the voyage to Saint-Domingue that many years before the river had frozen completely, imprisoning scores of ships for several days. Noah said the frigid temperatures had been followed by two weeks of exceedingly warm weather. Michel hoped for just that as he began the walk to Sarah's. Jacob had left him to return to New Street and the engraving atelier but promised to join them that night.

Nothing in the several markets he passed looked inviting under the dull gray sky. Vendors paced by their carts and tables to keep warm. He would arrive at Sarah's empty-handed.

He needn't have worried. No sooner had her door opened than she threw her arms around him. He lifted her off the ground and kissed her cheeks.

"You're so cold," she said after caressing his cheek with her hand.

"It's far colder standing in the bow of a ship today."

Sarah took his hand and led him upstairs to the kitchen and the hearth.

"Michel, tell me everything. I've been so worried about Noah, I haven't been able to sleep," she said. She had worried that he'd be enslaved again but Michel explained the arrangements he'd made with his agent to make that an impossibility.

"He's a hair's breadth from being under royal protection."

Michel knew he'd said that for his benefit as well as Sarah's. He told her a little about the agent offering that protection, but not everything. Despite the orderliness and refinements of the capital, the countryside harbored bloody secrets. Origène Deschamps, a native, admitted as such. He had said, "There are moments, my friend, when you taste it in the air."

Deschamps was a strange man. Michel remembered

that his next words had been,

"Have you had occasion to try the local snuff? It's excellent. You should include some in the cargo you take home."

What Michel did tell Sarah was that the greatest guarantee of Noah's safety was the exorbitant sum Deschamps had demanded and received to make arrangements.

Sarah seemed somewhat reassured and began to answer Michel's questions about how she had fared during his absence in the face of Croman's threats. To Sarah, the fear seemed distant now that Michel was back.

Jacob arrived just past 7.

"I hope you haven't eaten yet," he said rubbing circulation back into his fingers. Gloves were seldom necessary in France and he had yet to buy a pair in New York.

When Michel first arrived, Sarah asked countless questions while throwing together a soup. It ended up more like a stew. The men welcomed it and conversation all but ceased as they soaked up the last of it with bread. At last Jacob announced that he had news, or rather his friend Arnold Livstrom had.

"The fat man has put word out that he has holdings to sell in southern Pennsylvania. This must be the land whose deeds we forged."

"At long last," said Sarah. "How do we proceed?"

"We don't," said Jacob. "As I thought he might, Arnold has taken the bit between his teeth and wants to pursue Croman as if he were hunting down a fox for the sport of it. He says they do that in England."

Jacob wasn't the only one with news. Sarah announced that she'd finally gotten a chance to speak to Patricia's father.

"I told him the basics about what Croman did to us and how he's left me in fear for my life. When I told Mr. Van Huisen I wanted to get back at him he stood suddenly and said, 'I think you should leave.' He said he would never dirty his hands in a matter that would be before the authorities if any proof existed.

"I begged him to let me finish. I assured him I've never done anything illegal, except one thing, over which I had no choice. When I told him about the bogus deeds for property in Pennsylvania, he promptly sat down and said, 'Details, young lady. Details.'"

Sarah said Van Huisen was already aware of Croman's reputation for bullying and shady dealing.

"He said New York is becoming the capital of commerce in all the colonies but that, how did he put it? Yes, he said the problem was that 'As our economy grows so does our reputation for corruption.' He said Quaker businessmen in Philadelphia shudder at what goes on in this city. He said this has to end."

"What can he do to Croman?" Michel asked.

"He said Croman would have to actually sell the land to someone, and the buyer would have to come forward and accuse Croman. At that point, Mr. Van Huisen said he would be prepared to speak to the King's prosecutor, who is apparently his friend. The prosecutor could pass the information about the counterfeit deeds to a grand jury."

Sarah never ceased to amaze Jacob, and Michel's open mouth suggested he too had just had his sails taken aback by Sarah's tenacity.

"I have to wonder," Michel said, "if you had been a man whether this powerful provincial politician would even have let you finish your denunciation of a well-known merchant."

"I have my uses," said Sarah.

Jacob excused himself. Sarah had told him earlier there was a small shallop moored to the wharf the Commodore used. In it, hidden, were several casks. Jacob didn't want Sarah exposing herself by checking on it through the night. The Commodore was due to arrive the next day.

The longshoreman who'd pilfered the casks explained his early arrival to Sarah by saying the opportunity had been too good to pass up.

"There they were," the young longshoreman said, "the casks, sitting on a wharf. There was no ship tied up there. It was as if they'd been forgotten somehow. I watched for almost an hour. When no one claimed them I came alongside with my boat. Manhandled them aboard all by myself. It's a wonder one of them didn't smash right through the hull when I dropped it the last few inches. My arms gave up."

It had been a joyous day for Sarah. With Jacob's news about Livstrom's intentions, she might soon be able to be a she-merchant in the open, rebuild her warehouse and pursue bigger customers. Most important, she'd learned that Noah had been safely installed in Saint-Domingue with "royal protection". And Michel had returned.

After she heard Jacob close the door behind him, Sarah got up to clear the table. Michel rose, too. She put her right palm on his chest and kissed him on the mouth.

CHAPTER 47

Philadelphia And Beyond

ARNOLD Livstrom was taking a chance. His family was an old New York family, dizzyingly rich, and large. It was the latter factor that he was counting on. Being the youngest, he had yet to make a name for himself, or even attempted to do so in commerce or politics, or even in society. His appearances at functions were few. Only those at the very top of the social ladder could put a name to his face. So, Arnold concluded before leaving New York, it was a good bet that the fat merchant would not recognize him. Still, to avoid too many questions, he hoped they could conclude the sale quickly.

He had made his interest in the country property known to Croman by letter, in which he assured him of his bona fides and offered to pay cash should Croman wish him to do so. Arnold said he was from Camden, and suggested they first meet in Philadelphia, just on the other side of the Delaware River from Camden. From there, should he still be interested in selling to him, they could proceed due west to the lands in question along the Susquehanna River.

Croman agreed to the meeting. He arrived from New York by coastal boat crewed by men of the Yorkton, the ship of the co-owner of the properties, Captain Marcellus Flemming. Like Arnold, he hoped to conclude the affair quickly since his business was in need of cash. He told the crew to wait and stay sober.

"I should return in four days," he told them. The men later decided to drink in two-day shifts, meaning at least half of them would be perfectly sober on Croman's return.

Arnold had no trouble recognizing the merchant when he sat down at a table in the Benjamin Tavern on 4th Street, just below Market Street, the route he took from the harbor. After introducing himself, Arnold was invited to join Croman for a meal. Arnold declined, having eaten earlier. Mesmerized by the quantity of food the merchant consumed, Arnold had difficulty appearing interested in Croman's description of the lands. After all, his money would be returned to him once the forged deeds were exposed at trial.

Early next morning they rented three horses from the stable behind the inn. The third was for one of Croman's clerks.

"He has made sure all the papers are in order. Should you have any questions about the fine print, he's your man."

After the first few hours of riding, there was no more conversation to be had. Arnold sensed the merchant didn't like him, which was fine with him. More than halfway to Harrisburg they stopped at a tiny inn for the night. They arrived at Harrisburg before noon the next day and the merchant smiled for the first time at the prospect of leaving the horses behind and boarding a boat to take them the rest of the way down the Susquehanna. When Croman first decided the time had come to sell the land he arranged for a local merchant to act as an agent if necessary to provide a tour of the land. The boat let them off at a community of no more than 30 homes and businesses. The local agent nervously welcomed Croman and found them horses at the blacksmith's.

They rode south along a trail that followed the turns of the river. Arnold had to admit that the land was beautiful, but reminded himself that land was the last thing his family needed. Two hours later, the local agent announced that the entirety of the land for sale, close to 100 square miles, resembled what Arnold had now seen. Arnold pronounced himself delighted.

"Let us return to the inn in Harrisburg to sign the papers," Croman said grandly, as if the deal of the century had been concluded. When they arrived the inn had closed for the night but Croman's unapologetic banging on the door soon brought the proprietor. Croman ordered brandy and ham for them all.

The brandy revived Arnold enough to pretend to give each phrase in the contract his closest, most experienced attention. All he really wanted to do was make sure the document specified the land was in Pennsylvania. It did. After sufficient minutes to cause Croman's feet to fidget, Arnold said simply:

"Pen."

The innkeeper promptly provided it. Arnold signed and handed over £17,600. The amount was several thousand pounds less than the going price, Croman had said, and Arnold had thanked him. Now, at the sight of that enormous amount of cash, Croman betrayed a new respect for Arnold. Arnold let Croman order another bottle of brandy. An hour later they retired to their rooms as "friends" and "men of like minds".

Before his eyes closed, Arnold tried to remember how much of the cash he'd given Croman was Jacob's handiwork. Finally he decided on "at least £4,000". When Croman was eventually forced to pay him back, Arnold had already decided Jacob would get every shilling.

The following morning, as they headed back to

Philadelphia, the clerk was the only one to make a remark.

"Are there highway men about?"

Arriving in New York City the next day, Arnold had a message sent to Van Huisen's home requesting a meeting at the assemblyman's earliest convenience. Two evenings later, traveling by coach in a torrential downpour that had already melted every trace of snow, Arnold arrived at the house on Broadway.

Once installed in the sitting room, Arnold's Dutch Reformed Church host posed a question.

"Would a fine Bordeaux wine offend your Presbyterian sensibilities?"

"It's comforting to be back among civilized people," Arnold answered, greatly enjoying the jibe. Obviously Van Huisen shared his impatience with self-important churchmen.

Arnold produced the contract, then the deed.

"I believe Miss Da Silva has provided you with the circumstances of the forging of those deeds and stated her willingness, along with that of her brother, to testify to those facts."

"Indeed she has. Were she an attorney she would be a formidable opponent."

Arnold produced his receipt for the purchase, then handed Van Huisen a map of the land he'd purchased.

"What it fails to indicate is that the land actually lies in Maryland, not Pennsylvania."

Van Huisen knew of what was called Cresap's War. It had been going on for decades as settlers in Pennsylvania and Maryland battled each other with guns and fists over which province had the right to tax them.

"The boundary between the two has yet to be decided by the courts," said Van Huisen. "However, I think the seller should have advised you that the land you were buying was in disputed territory. The fact that he didn't testifies to his character."

After offering Arnold another glass, Van Huisen studied the documents. At last he put them aside and said:

"Let's strike before Croman can spend his windfall. I will endeavor to see the King's prosecutor tomorrow. He will keep you informed. Should the case go your way I will undoubtedly have words to say on the matter before the Assembly. The likes of Croman drive away business."

As unseemly as it was, Arnold dashed through the rain to his carriage.

"Maiden Lane, driver."

CHAPTER 48

Champagne

THE FAT merchant's trial began five days later, one day after his arrest. Jacob and Sarah sat nervously near the front of the courtroom. All Jacob could think about was the Irishman, Sullivan, who stood exactly where Croman now stood facing the jury of his peers, the ones who had the charges pressed against him following Arnold's complaint. Jacob then heard the voice of the judge sentencing Sullivan to death by hanging. He would never forget that moment.

Following Arnold's account of the land transaction, Sarah was called to testify. She had lost her nervousness. Her voice was steady and clear. Jacob knew that when it came to telling the truth, she was fearless. She described briefly how she and her brother came to be on the Yorkton, then detailed the clerking duties the captain imposed on them in return for comforts at sea and a shortening of their indenture contracts once sold in New York. She explained that she and her brother had grown up in the world of commerce in Bordeaux and consequently could write, keep books and speak all the languages commonly heard on the city's waterfront. She then handed the prosecutor the very documents the captain had long ago asked her and Jacob to "complete".

"What you have handed me, Miss Da Silva, are documents that are unsigned, undated and lacking any precise indication of the location of the land, other than the province of Pennsylvania. They purport to be from the Penn family of Bristol."

Emboldened further, Sarah began to describe her rape by the accused man. The judge quickly stopped her.

"Be that as it may, it is not the issue at hand."

Jacob's testimony was brief. He was asked only to corroborate what his sister had said.

Arnold Livstrom was then recalled to briefly testify as to the details of the transaction between himself and the accused. Communications between him and the accused, the deed to the land and receipt for payment were placed in evidence.

A final witness was called to speak on behalf of the accused. It was none other than Croman's longtime business partner, Captain Marcellus Flemming. The sight of his pinched mouth caused both Sarah and Jacob to shift in their chairs.

Before being asked a single question, the captain told the jury he'd never heard so many lies spoken in so little time. He was silenced quickly by the judge. Flemming then resorted to staring disdainfully at Sarah and Jacob, just feet away. The prosecutor drew laughter from the courtroom by reminding Flemming that he was not on a quarterdeck commanding this trial.

"Since you were not present at the sale of these lands to Mr. Livstrom, we cannot charge you as we have Mr. Croman. However, I for one, after viewing these documents, have little doubt that you behaved as Miss Da Silva and her brother have stated. You may indeed have known the late Mr. Penn of Bristol but nothing, absolutely nothing, suggests he presented you with deeds to even an outhouse in Pennsylvania."

The captain remained silent. The prosecutor continued:

"Very well, captain, can you think of any reason why you should not be charged as a conspirator in the deception, a contributor, if you will?"

For the first time the captain looked unsure of himself. He cleared his throat and said in a barely audible voice that he had tried to dissuade his partner at the last moment.

"Why would you have done that, captain?"

"Because he wasn't thinking straight. He hates the girl. He's obsessed with that woman. He thought he could silence her and the existence of the faked documents would never come out."

"Silence her?"

"Yes. His words."

"What do you think Mr. Croman intended to do to silence her?"

"I don't know, sir. But that's what he said. I will swear to that."

The judge then told Croman that he could call another witnesses on his own behalf, or testify directly to the jury.

As Arnold was to note later, Croman had obviously failed to appreciate how grave the accusations had become. As he spoke, his face was flushed with arrogance.

"I could waste the court's time by calling every great merchant in this great city to testify on my behalf. They would happily acknowledge that I set the standard for them, the example that will make this the most powerful city on the continent. I have nothing to apologize for. The girl makes these charges because she comes from nothing and resents all powerful men."

An hour later the jury returned. They found that Croman owed more than an apology. He was guilty as charged.

The justice ordered him to repay Arnold Livstrom the entire £17,600. If Croman failed to do so within a week, the court would see to halting the operations of his company until sufficient assets could be sold to pay Mr. Livstrom. Furthermore, Croman was ordered to pay a fine of £2,000.

"And," added the chief justice, "I suggest it would be wise to forget you ever heard the name Da Silva."

Sarah jumped into Jacob's arms before the judge's gavel fell.

Right behind her was Arnold:

"Too bad he wasn't sentenced to hang. I think that's one execution you would have attended."

At Arnold's insistence, Jacob and Sarah accompanied him to his home, just south of the Van Huisen mansion. It wasn't large by the neighborhood's standards but Sarah said the furnishings and artwork were worth enough to buy the province of Pennsylvania.

"You must learn not to exaggerate," Arnold said. "I could certainly buy all of Rhode Island, but not Pennsylvania."

Sarah and Jacob then proceeded to drink Champagne for the first time in their lives.

"It's French, you know," said Arnold with a straight face. "So, what other adventures do you two have for me?"

"None, I'm afraid," said Sarah. "Life should never be this much of a fight."

Arnold and Jacob toasted Sarah's words.

Arnold sent them home in his carriage. Before reaching Maiden Lane Sarah's mind had already been overrun with thoughts of Noah and her own captain.

CHAPTER 49

Revenge

"THEY'RE gone!" exclaimed Sarah.

"Who?" Jacob asked.

"Croman and Flemming. They sailed at dusk yesterday. They're apparently bound for England."

Sarah had decided to taste freedom. She walked down Water Street past Croman's office and warehouses for the first time since Noah's long-ago interdiction. Her purpose was twofold. She wanted to talk to Asser about investing in outgoing cargos.

She also hoped to come across some of the men who had brought her goods stolen from Croman in the past. The night before she'd awakened in panic at the realization that anything taken from the convicted merchant at this point would be out and out stealing. She couldn't justify that. She had been stealing from an evil man in order to survive. That was her rationalization in the beginning and she told herself she would do it again if she had to.

If only Noah weren't in Saint-Domingue. Only he knew

where to find his crew. She'd come across only one of them by the time she came to Croman's office. She stopped because a crowd was gathering. She made her way through the men, most of them well dressed, and saw a small notice in the window.

"This office is closed. Prop."

Sarah turned up Coenties Slip to Hanover Square where Croman's main office was. There was no sign and the front door was open. Seeing no one, she took the stairs to the second floor where she had worked. At the top of the stairs the first thing she did was look at the desk where Croman had raped her. She would never get over that.

Suddenly she turned to her right. A book of accounts had fallen to the floor with a thud. She raised her eyes and saw a middle-aged man wearing a threadbare gray vest.

"What's going on?" she asked, sounding as if she worked there still.

"He's gone and I have no job. None of us do."

"Have you checked his office?"

"No, I don't have a key," the man said, raising his arms to his side and letting them drop in a gesture of helplessness.

"I heard on Water Street that he has sailed for London. If he has it won't make any difference if we break in, will it?"

The man followed as Sarah rushed toward the office. She picked up a ledger and used it to break the glass in the office door.

"Lift me up," Sarah told the man. "Help me get through the window."

Once inside she used a heavy paperweight to break off shards remaining on the door frame. The man climbed through.

"What are you looking for?"

"Anything Croman may have overlooked in his hurry to flee. I used to work here. I spent more time than I wanted in this office late at night."

Sarah first went to Croman's outsized desk. To her surprise she managed to open a hidden compartment in one of the lower drawers on the first try. Croman had kept her forged deeds there. Reaching in blindly she pulled out a leather-bound notebook. She sat in his chair and rifled through the pages.

"Yes," she exclaimed. "This is a list of where he kept all his holdings, here, in England, in Jamaica. Even Madagascar. Was he in the slave trade?"

The clerk knew nothing of that.

Sarah clutched the notebook as if it were gold. Croman's holdings in the colonies at least would be more than enough for the court to sell in order to pay Arnold. Croman couldn't have possibly sold them before leaving.

Sarah continued searching the office. The main safe was empty but she knew there was a second, smaller one behind the armoire.

"Help me," she told the clerk and began trying to pull the heavy mahogany piece away from the wall. Frustrated, she tossed the contents of its shelves to the floor. She and the clerk then toppled the armoire.

Sarah returned to the desk and found the heavy key that opened the safe's padlock.

She couldn't reach the safe so she asked the clerk to climb on top of the toppled armoire. She then handed him the key.

"Money," he said. It was more of a question.

"Pull out everything," Sarah said.

The clerk handed it down to her, paper notes and specie. When he pronounced the safe empty, Sarah sat on the floor and placed it all on her lap. With practiced hands, she separated the denominations and then counted them.

She didn't announce the total. Instead she handed the sweating clerk £200.

"Do you have a family?" she asked.

When he nodded, she gave him £200 more.

"Will you be alright until you find other employment?"

"Heavens, yes, miss."

"Good, now go before we get caught."

Sarah waited a few minutes. She found a sack for the money and looked around one last time before leisurely descending the staircase. She closed the door behind her. She crossed the square and walked to the engraving shop. She was happy to find Peter not there. After relating the story of Croman's flight from New York, she handed Jacob the notebook. He said he'd close shop and take it straight to the office of the King's prosecutor.

"Afterwards," Jacob said as they stepped onto New Street, "I'll find Arnold and let him know that one way or the other he'll get his money."

When Jacob came to Sarah's house that evening he found her at the table with Michel.

"I have good news." He placed his shoulder pouch on the table and withdrew money, real money, lots of it. "Exactly £4,000, the amount of the forged money I'd given Arnold to help make the deal with Croman. He insisted I take it on the condition I give half to you, Sarah."

As she reached for her half, Michel put his hand gently on her wrist to stop her.

"That should pay nicely for your passage to Saint-Domingue. You can pay me now or later, my dear."

She put a £1 note in his tankard of ale.

"When do you sail?" Jacob asked.

"Soon. Within the week if all goes well."

"I wish you both God's speed," Jacob said, suddenly serious. "Noah has been there much longer than we planned." Sarah didn't need to be told that. Before Jacob arrived she'd been urging Michel to do everything in his power to leave earlier. It depended on Asser, Michel said.

"Then I'll talk to him tomorrow," Sarah said, her tone sharper than she'd intended.

CHAPTER 50

Course Due South

THE NEXT morning Sarah went straight to Asser's. They drank coffee at a new restaurant across the street from his office. The proprietor was French. Born in the fishing village of Callelongue, he moved to nearby Marseilles where he learned his craft as a restaurateur.

They spoke in French, enjoying their distinct accents. The proprietor said his main dish was bouillabaisse.

"My father was a fisherman and this is exactly what we ate. In the city rich people eat it but I don't know if they know that it is made from the dregs of the catch. Perhaps I won't give New Yorkers that information either."

"Well, sir, you already have two devoted customers, and you've just opened." said Asser.

When the owner returned to his kitchen, leaving Sarah and Asser alone at one of the five tables, Sarah pled her most important case. She described Noah's circumstances in Saint-Domingue and said testifying at the trial of Croman delayed their departure.

"Noah is my friend and he has been left alone there far too long."

Asser hastened to point out he would like to help but was obliged to await late-arriving cargo.

"Perhaps we can make a deal," Sarah told the veteran businessman.

"How so?" Asser had grown rich by keeping his ears open.

"You know that Croman sailed again on the Yorkton?"

"Yes," said Asser, adding that "people were saying all sorts of things all day outside his office, that he faced financial ruin, that he had raped a judge's wife, that his presence in London had been requested by the King himself."

"The simple truth," said Sarah, "is that he has simply abandoned his business. Apparently all his businesses. He has just washed his hands of New York, the city he believed was great only because of his efforts and acumen as a businessman. The pompous ass."

"An accurate characterization, Sarah, but what does this have to do with you and Michel sailing with a half-empty hold days ahead of schedule?"

Sarah told him about ransacking Croman's Water Street office and finding a secret list of all of Croman's holdings, a list that has been turned over to the Crown prosecutor to retrieve moneys the court has ruled he owes a prominent citizen of the city.

"Once that money has been recovered at auction," Sarah said, "I don't know what will be done with the other businesses. Perhaps you could inquire as to whether any might serve your purposes. I'm sure the authorities are eager to see the province's coffers enhanced."

Learning about the availability of viable businesses before the general public was incredibly useful intelligence, thought Asser. He sensed, however, that Sarah wasn't finished. Her father had taught her well. That woman could negotiate with the sultan of the Ottoman Empire and pick his pockets without him knowing it.

"After I had Jacob take the list of Croman's holdings to the prosecutor, I remember hearing that several of Croman's merchant ships were long overdue for returning to New York. I know that one went to the bottom in a hurricane. I don't know about the other two. They may have already come and gone. The point is, Asser, if Croman's ships return to port loaded with cargo purchased by Croman and other investors but they find Croman gone and his door locked, what will they do?"

"They'll be desperate to sell what they can to anybody who makes an offer," Assar answered.

"Exactly," said Sarah. "Here's a list of some of those ships. Some may be in port, others may be on their way home. No one else has this list. What I propose in return for the Chameleon's immediate departure is this: in my absence you buy as much of these cargos as you can afford. As we speak my warehouse is being restored and enlarged. What I would like is that you fill it with merchandise. Jacob will sign for it and issue promissory notes, which I will pay on my return. We hope to rescue Noah and be on the first tide back. In short, I would like to become your junior partner."

Asser stared at Sarah with admiration, as proudly as any father could. They came from the same worlds and spoke the same business language. Besides, he liked her and wanted her to do well.

"Yes, my dear Sarah, I will let you give me your gold mine in return for an early departure. I will pass word to the first officer that no more cargo will be coming aboard and the Chameleon's captain wishes her to be ready to sail as soon as possible."

One by one, Sarah had notified each member of Noah's band of Croman thieves that there would be no more stealing. She paid each the share they said they were owed and thanked them for all the risks they had run. Several of them corrected her.

"We did it for Noah, Miss." Sarah then finished notifying her network of clients that she was enlarging her warehouse space but in the meantime they would be unable to place orders from her. She'd revisit them when the work was done and the warehouse filled.

Two days after the meeting with Asser, on a March day that promised spring, Jacob and Geneviève stood on Asser's wharf and waved goodbye to Sarah and her captain. Jacob told himself that when Sarah was indentured to the fat merchant, he wasn't able to see her for more than two years. This absence, he hoped, wouldn't be as painful. At least she was not alone this time.

CHAPTER 51

News

Maroon Camp,
Parish of Limbé region, 19 miles SW of Cap-Français,
Saint-Domingue
April 12, 1755

AFTER two months at the plantation, Noah had begun to tell time by counting the number of forged notes he'd printed since sunrise. Such was the precision of the rhythm he'd developed to render the repetitious work less onerous: ink the plate, position the paper, haul on the star wheel, cut out the note, set it aside for drying. He also determined a pace that let him endure the heat all day long, much like the slaves dwarfed by the cane in the fields below his hut did.

Noah had lost count overall but he knew he'd printed more than double the money he and Jacob had set as a goal when the intended stay was about a month. His rough guess, more than £20,000. At the end of March, his second full month, he printed the final note. Occasionally he felt guilty about stopping. Then he would remember the supply of paper was almost exhausted. Jacob had made sure he had enough paper to account for damage by the weather but the plantation's elevation was high enough to keep the humidity bearable.

His visits to the Big House to eat soon earned him the trust of the slaves who worked there, serving the owner, who had disappeared for the first three weeks of Noah's stay. That fact was sufficient to relax the rules and allow easy conversation. After barely a week, Noah risked revealing the true purpose of his visit. He told them he'd been a slave before and had escaped. His escape was made possible by a group of Maroons who infiltrated the plantation at night and set fire to its main buildings, including the Big House and the large building that housed five huge boilers used to reduce mill-crushed cane to sugar.

He told the housemaids and cook that before his flight to the mountains with the Maroons he had been unable to find his wife. She worked and lived in the master's house, where Noah assumed she had been forced to become his mistress. She and Noah coordinated times when they could catch sight of each other, her on the porch, Noah near a tool shed. They rarely had a chance to exchange words. She was the most beautiful woman Noah had ever seen. He didn't know whether she died that night or was still alive working on a plantation.

The oldest servant, the cook, called Michel aside one day as she gathered herbs from the little garden behind the house.

"The Maroons visit us regularly looking for information that will help them plan attacks or poisonings," she said. "They also serve as a message system. They can get word to any plantation. I will have someone tell them about your presence and who you're looking for."

The wait for news was agonizing. On several occasions, a young field hand named Comé visited Noah at night. He said he had been brought from Ghana. The whites referred to Ghanaian slaves as Coromantees. Comé meant Sunday. He told Noah that in his homeland children were given day names, reflecting their day of birth.

Comé said he had heard from the Maroons several times.

"They have finally found someone who knew of your wife," he said. "They say the master married her but he died not long after. They say he wrote on a paper that the woman was free and that part of all the things he owned now belonged to her."

Noah wanted to run to the Maroon camp that very minute. Then Comé added:

"But someone else said she died. He said that before she died she had used her freedom to go to the Cap. That's all he knows."

Comé had saved him an immeasurable amount of time. A camp by camp search through the mountains could have gotten Noah killed. Among the slaves were those who would try to elevate their status with their owners by spying on Maroons. The trek could have lasted months. If exhaustion didn't kill Noah, starvation might. He didn't know the country at all. Because he didn't know where he'd been forced to work as a slave all those years ago, he had no idea where the Maroon camp that saved him was located.

"I have to meet this man, Comé," said Noah. "Please tell me how to get to the camp. Can you draw a map in the sand?"

Comé said he couldn't describe how to get there.

"I go tree by tree, ridge by ridge, ravine by ravine. I go at night when I can't be seen. I am much blacker than you. I am the night. You are the dawn, I think. At night I am not blind. You might be. You could not go alone even if I knew how to draw you a map."

"Can we go tomorrow?" Noah asked.

"No," Comé answered in his usual direct manner. He

never seemed to feel the need to qualify his words. "We will go Sunday night. As well as it being my name day Sunday is our day of rest. All we have to do that day is tend the gardens they make us keep to feed ourselves. I will be strong. You will see."

Noah didn't say anything but he suddenly worried about being able to keep up with a younger man, one who can see at night.

Noah spent the next day sewing shut a stout canvas sack containing his forged notes and the plate. He had piled the notes neatly on the bottom of the sack. The stacking made the bag less bulky to carry. He then cut a long narrow length of canvas, which he sewed onto the sack, creating a strap that would allow him to carry it across his chest or back, leaving his hands free to climb with Comé.

By telling Noah he would take him to the Maroons, Comé was making his own break for freedom. Noah asked him why he waited until now.

"I knew I was too young to survive on my own. Now I am almost a man. It is time."

Noah debated taking apart the press, but neither Jacob nor Michel's agent in Cap-Français had mentioned it. Perhaps that strange man, the agent, had plans to make use of it himself.

Noah ate little of the food he was served at the Big House that Sunday. He took much of it back to his hut and wrapped it in a cloth. He had no idea how long and arduous the night would be.

As he sat on the rich, dark soil surrounding his hut he remembered the smells of the "habitation" where he'd been enslaved years before. They were much like what he smelled now, except his plantation produced mostly tobacco. It was always in the air, mixed in with smells of mangoes, plantains and oranges. Now the ever-present odor of donkey excrement gave way to the smoke of the trash fires the slaves set every afternoon.

Comé slipped into Noah's hut around 11 that night. He didn't speak as he squatted and watched Noah do his last preparations for their trek. Noah's last task had been to sew the envelope containing his proof of freedom and his status as being under the protection of Monsieur Deschamps into the seat of his pants, cut loose for the climate. Shortly after arriving at the plantation he had used candle wax to coat the envelope and make it waterproof.

Comé stood outside the doorway, looking toward the Big House and listening. When Noah stepped out to follow him he turned back and saw what looked like hundreds of torches and small fires around the slave huts. When he turned back toward Comé he discovered his Sunday friend was already at the lip of the woods beyond the house.

For the first half hour they followed a narrow path that ended at a boulder. Comé climbed on top of it and extended his hand to help Noah up. Noah took his hand and used his feet to push off rocks sitting vertically to the side of the boulder as Comé had done.

After two hours Noah needed to rest. Comé didn't object but he clearly was in no need of catching his breath.

"How far from here?" Noah asked.

"We will arrive at dawn."

Although their destination was obviously at a higher elevation, there were long horizontal passages where Comé led him across the tops of ridges before slipping back into the woods to continue their vertical progress. As first light approached, Noah looked back at a ridge they'd traversed in darkness half an hour before. He knew he could not have crossed had he known that on the other side of the ridge was an 80-foot drop, the sight of which would have paralyzed his legs.

Minutes later two men with machetes blocked their path. Noah did not understand what Comé said to them but one of the two men nodded and began to lead the way to what Noah assumed was the camp. The other man remained in position on the path behind them. Noah couldn't help but notice that both men had deep scars running up and down their arms.

Despite the early hour few of the Maroons still slept. At the far end of the clearing, which was encircled by huts, at least 15 men sat on the ground listening to an old man who stood with the posture of a warrior. Finally, as the old man ceased talking, they stood in unison.

Comé whispered that the men were warriors. When they stood they revealed their weapons. Again in unison, they began raking their arms, drawing blood.

"They can now go to war knowing they will be protected. If they are wounded they will feel no pain. It is a voodoo blood rite," said Comé, not taking his eyes of the ceremony.

Noah and Comé sat off to the side of the clearing. Noah offered him some of his food but Comé said no.

Noah was feeling the need for sleep when a man of his own age presented himself. Noah stood.

"Are you the one who knew my wife?"

The man spoke good French and Comé didn't need to translate for Noah.

"Your wife survived the attack. Her face was badly burned. The right side. We cared for her at this very spot."

Noah mustered every ounce of self-control to let the man relate the story uninterrupted.

"She said she had just received her freedom. She had been the owner's mistress and the owner was an old man. He honored the Black Code. It was written by the King of France long ago. It stated that Frenchmen should do the correct moral thing and marry their mistresses. Most don't, but this man did.

"When your wife got better she showed us a paper, which she said proved she had received her freedom and had inherited the plantation. We were happy for her. She said she would not work the plantation and would give all the slaves their freedom if they wanted it before she sold it to a new owner.

"Your wife moved to the capital. She wanted to have her own business in the city. We then heard she got sick. I don't know whether that was before or after she heard that her late husband had a wife in France. When the woman learned of his death she claimed only she had a right to his inheritance. Your wife would have known that she had no chance of being awarded the inheritance when there was a white woman claiming it as her own."

"Have you heard of her since?" Noah pressed.

"I believe she died of her illness. I am sorry."

The man turned to go. Noah called after him.

"Did you ever know where she lived in the capital?"

He did.

Noah knew he needed to see it. He wanted to stand in front of it and imagine his wife inside, happy and free.

"Comé, how do I get to Cap-Français from here?"

"Tomorrow I will escort you out of the mountains. I will leave you at the flat lands, La Plaine-du-Nord. The plain will take you to the city. If you see the setting sun on your left that will mean you are heading in the right direction."

Noah shook the young man's hand firmly.

Comé said he now had to find out how he can serve the warriors. With that he turned on his heel and walked back to the top of the clearing.

Noah followed Comé out of the mountains that afternoon. Comé had chosen another route and it was much less arduous. By evening the plain stretched before him.

"Maybe someday you can join me," Noah said.

"Maybe." Comé smiled and turned back.

As Noah walked he realized that for all the time he had been back in New York after his escape he simply assumed that his wife was alive. Despite the precariousness of life in Saint-Domingue it would have been just as false to imagine that she were dead. He sometimes wished he was free of his daydreams of her. At other times, he swore he would never let them go. Now the truth had answered the question for him. All he wished was that he hadn't learned of her burns.

By evening Noah thought he could make out the red roofs of the city in the distance. It would serve no purpose to arrive late at night. He turned off the little road he'd been following and stepped into a farmer's field. He headed for a mango tree about 50 feet further north. He let his body sink down by the tree and reached for what remained of his food. He fell asleep before nightfall, his head resting on the money bag.

When he woke up five hours later, there was a full moon to light his way down to the city. Part of him wanted to run. He might get there in just a couple of hours. But the last thing he wanted to be was a homeless black man outside on the streets at 3 or 4 in the morning. Even in New York he wouldn't do that. On the outskirts of the city, the harbor was clearly in view. Ship lanterns made it look as if this was the most peaceful place on earth. Noah sat under a palm tree until the sun began to rise.

It being still too early to knock on doors, he wandered to the port to kill time. He also knew that the address where his wife stayed when she arrived in Cap Français was only a few blocks away from the port. After surveying the scores of ships in port, Noah strolled along Cours Le Brasseur, then down again to the quay. When he came to its end, he found himself looking across a small river that ran into the harbor. There was no way to cross. Noah had to content himself with just looking at the east side of the harbor.

In the distance, below a tall tree that stood out from the rest, he saw two ships hauled up the sandy incline of the shore. They were on their sides for careening. The more he stared at the smaller of the two vessels the more she looked familiar. He was too far away to read the name on the bow, but he could tell it was a single word, long and painted green, like that of the Chameleon. If only he could swim, if only he wasn't carrying a fortune in forged bills. He wanted to run along that beach and kiss her bow.

Behind him he could make out the sounds of the city waking. He needed time to think so he kept his pace slow as he worked his way back along the quay. Where would he find Michel? Would he be staying at an inn, or would he be staying as a guest of his agent? In any event, he didn't know where his home was. He knew only the office on Place Clugny. Finally he decided. Less than 15 minutes later he stepped into a narrow street just north of the market. He was told to look for a shop that made baskets. The house he wanted would be to its left.

Noah knocked, gently at first. After a minute he knocked twice more, more forcefully. A woman with a wrinkled brow and missing teeth looked up at him. She said nothing.

At last Noah asked if she ever knew a young woman named Malika.

"She had burns on her face," he said hoping that would jog her memory.

The woman's sad face nodded yes.

"Friend?" she asked.

"Wife. A long time ago."

The woman turned her back on Noah and entered a room on the left of the little hall. She sat on a small sofa facing the window. Noah sat on a stool, which he placed in the middle of the room. The room was painted green, a bit like the green Michel chose for Chameleon.

"I was told that Malika became a free woman."

"Yes," the woman said, her eyes fixed on Noah's. "But she died."

There was a long silence, which the woman broke.

"She survived less than a year. When she arrived she had the coughing sickness."

There was another long silence from the woman who had sat perfectly still the whole while.

"She was pregnant," the woman said. "Do you know her child?"

Noah felt as if he'd been broadsided.

"I didn't know," he said after remaining silent for several moments. "Did the child live?"

"Yes. She lives here, with me and my brother. She is six years old.

"May I see her?"

"Yes, but know that she is not your child. She's mulatto. Malika was…"

Noah finished the sentence.

"…very dark."

"Yes," said the woman.

She continued to stare at Noah, then eased herself upright. She walked out of the room.

"Come, child." She returned holding the girl's hand.

"What is your name?" Noah asked.

"Malika."

"Her mother knew she was dying. She wanted her name to keep living."

"Come here, Malika," Noah said gently.

Noah took her hands in his.

"You look like your mother. Do you remember her?"

The girl shook her head no.

"Well, Malika, I do. I remember her as if I saw her yesterday."

He released the girl's hands and she returned to the woman's side. Noah stood. He needed to move about. He had a wild thought. When he set sail with Michel he had dreamed of himself returning to New York with his wife. He knew it would take a long time to come to terms with the fact she was no longer of this earth. What if…

"Madame, I loved this girl's mother dearly. I have come a very long way to find her. I have now learned that she is no longer living. I don't want to go home alone."

It was Noah's turn to look intently into her eyes the way she'd looked into his.

"May I give Malika a new home? With me? In a great city called New York? I have money and friends. She would be free forever."

The woman got up and walked out the front door without saying a word. Malika sat calmly on the sofa looking at the big man. Ten minutes later the woman returned with a frail man of about her age. How different he was, thought Noah, from the powerful warriors he saw in the mountains. The man gave Noah a warm smile that accentuated his sunken cheeks, then looked at Malika. He saw that Malika was not afraid of this stranger.

"If you were married to her mother, then to me you are her family now," the man said. Noah had rarely heard such a kind voice. "Both her parents have gone. My sister says you want to take Malika far away where she will have a good life."

"Yes… Please." Noah felt his throat tightening.

The man turned to Malika.

"Would you like to go on a trip to a faraway land with this man?"

The girl grinned.

When no one spoke, she said, "Yes, please."

The woman got up, telling Noah she would wrap some of the girl's belongings.

When it was time to leave, Noah lifted Malika up so she could embrace the people who had raised her. To Noah's surprise, they seemed happy for Malika. He thought they'd resent giving her up. Then he realized they already knew too well what kind of life the girl would have in Cap-Français. They may never have heard of New York but they wanted to believe there was a chance Malika would have a better life there.

Now carrying Malika as well as her belongings and the big money sack, but with more energy than he'd felt since leaving New York, Noah hurried to Place Clugny. He didn't care that it was a rich man's office. His big fist thudded against the door.

When the butler answered, as well dressed as New York's high society, he seemed indifferent to the fact that the man who was uncouth enough to bang a door repeatedly was dirty, sweating, and carrying one huge canvas sack, a tiny yellow cloth sack, and a mulatto child.

"Monsieur Deschamps. Immediately, please. He knows me. He expects me."

The knowledge that he knew Deschamps and that he was expected didn't faze the butler.

"May I inform Monsieur Deschamps who is inquiring?"

"Tell him Noah…no, Normand. God dammit!" The expression drew a blank look. "A moment, sir," said the butler, closing the door.

The door opened and Sarah rushed to him with her arms spread wide. Suddenly she noticed the little girl and stopped dead in her tracks.

"Dear, dear Noah. You are alive! You have come back! We were desperate to find you. We could only, or at least I could only think the worst."

She touched the child's cheek and said to Noah, "Come closer, my dear friend."

Sarah ran her fingers over his head as if making sure he was real. She kissed his cheek over and over again. Despite the broadest smile Noah had ever seen from a white woman, tears flowed down her face. Noah put his big left arm around her and held her close. He didn't realize he'd lifted Sarah several inches off the ground. Sarah didn't mind. Malika giggled.

"Come, come!" Sarah said, leading him into the office.

"Monsieur Deschamps. Vite! Venez!"

When Deschamps entered the waiting room, the Adam's apple of his skinny throat did a double dip. However, true to his upbringing, he recovered quickly.

"I'd lost all hope, sir. Do you bring any returns from your journey?"

Noah, with Malika resting on his left arm, used his right toe to shove the sack closer to Deschamps.

"Ah, very good. You've been a busy man."

"That doesn't belong to you, sir, only a portion. Michel explained the agreement to me. I would not have worked otherwise."

"Quite right. I was merely expressing my delight at your success against what must have been formidable odds."

Noah wanted to strangle him. How Michel dealt with him over the years he would never understand.

"Where is Michel?"

The intensity of his question ended all pretense of polite conversation. He had gone through hell and wanted out, now. Deschamps blanched, aware of the danger emanating from a fierce man in his waiting room gently cuddling a child.

Sarah defused the moment.

"Michel is seeing to the careening of the Chameleon. When we arrived almost a month ago there was no word of you. We finally sent a messenger to the plantation and learned that you had disappeared. We had no idea where you were. Michel said we would wait as long as necessary. In the meantime, we unloaded our cargo, most of which Mr. Deschamps purchased sight unseen. We are eternally grateful to him for his assistance in this and other matters, Noah. He deserves our respect."

Noah stared at Deschamps.

"My apologies, sir. I have had a difficult time, not from the counterfeiting but from the search for my wife."

Turning to Sarah, he said:

"Only this morning it has been confirmed that she is dead. The little girl on my lap is her daughter. My voyage is complete. I wish to go home."

Sarah sat on her hands. Noah's announcement filled her heart. She couldn't take her eyes off Malika. Despite her light coloring, Sarah could guess what her mother looked like, the high cheekbones and the large dark brown eyes. Noah's love must have been stunning for those features to have survived the seed of a pathetic old Frenchman using his slave-owner's power to bed a black woman.

"Where was her mother from?" Sarah asked, still trying to calm the moment.

"The Ivory Coast." After a moment, Noah added softly:

"She must have been a queen, Sarah. If only you could have seen her."

"Undoubtedly," said Deschamps, anxious to move on. "We are in your debt."

Sarah explained that the gale he and Michel went through may have done more damage to the hull than Michel first thought.

"On our voyage he found the Chameleon sluggish, slow to respond," said Sarah. "That's why he wanted to profit from our wait here in Cap-Français to do the careening. He was told it would take a week. That week ends tomorrow. If the work is done he will still have to get towed back to the main harbor and dock there to take on a new load. We're here for at least a week longer."

Sarah held her arms out for Malika to join her.

"Mr. Deschamps, could you see to putting my dear friend and his daughter up at your home until we sail?"

"Mademoiselle, your wish is my command." He called for his secretary. When he arrived Deschamps explained that the house should be prepared for more guests. They will arrive within the hour."

Deschamps stood and excused himself.

"With your permission I have other matters of import

to attend to."

With Noah's arrival, gone was his chance to spend days alone with Sarah.

"Noah," Sarah said, "I hope someday I have a daughter half as beautiful as Malika."

They walked through the now bustling streets to Deschamps' château, each holding one of Malika's hands.

CHAPTER 52

The Creaking Bed

NOAH was exhausted. Though it wasn't strictly the case, he felt he'd escaped slavery for the second time in his life. His body complained as if he'd run from the mountains to the sea, holding his breath all the way. At the same time he felt he was beginning a new life, a strange sensation to have in a beautiful land that he associated with memories of desperation, misery and death.

When he awoke that morning, Malika lay curled at the bottom of his bed. She had gone to sleep in Sarah's bed in the next room. Neither he nor Sarah wanted the girl to feel alone. When he went to bed himself, he could hear Sarah playing with Malika. At one point, he heard the girl laugh. He knew nothing of children, yet he was amazed Malika could find it in her to laugh on the very day she was taken from the only home she'd ever known.

In his mind, as he looked at Malika at the bottom of his bed, he referred to her as "my daughter". To hell with "step-father". The longer he watched her, the more he felt joy. The spirit of his dead wife resided in the girl.

Deschamps had seldom been at the house since their arrival, but when he was he enjoyed demonstrating his refinement, dressing fastidiously for meals and proudly overseeing his servants as they covered the table with spicy versions of French cuisine. Though their host treated them as esteemed guests, they felt utterly out of place. Noah preferred being at Sarah's table.

Michel arrived on the third day. He had insisted on sleeping on the beach so he could observe every step in the careening. The Chameleon was his uncle's legacy.

"She will sail beautifully now," he announced to Sarah, who he took in his arms the instant he was through the door. When he released her, she smiled broadly and said:

"We have company." She turned on her heel and pointed down the hallway.

"Noah!" he cried, hurrying down the hall to embrace him. "The worry has been unbearable since Deschamps told us that you had left the plantation."

While gazing up at Michel, Malika took Noah's hand.

"Michel, may I present my daughter."

"Mademoiselle," Michel said, giving Malika a slight bow, then, squatting down to look at her in the eyes, he added:

"A pleasure to meet you."

As Michel stood, Sarah took his hand and all but hauled him into the sitting room

"Noah's story will break your heart, but first please tell us we will sail soon."

"Loading started this morning. I would venture to predict that we are spending our last week in Saint-Domingue. That will give us time to catch up. It appears there is much to tell, starting with the fact that when Sarah pointed down the hall towards you I expected to see a sack of forged money at your feet, not a lovely daughter."

"I have the money. Don't you worry."

When Sarah jumped in and told Michel that the amount Noah had printed was £20,000, he was stupefied. Jacob had told him he expected not even half that amount. Even that seemed like wishful thinking to Michel. In New France, money had gotten so scarce that the intendant authorized the use of playing cards as cash. He didn't know how many *livres* that many pounds represented but he suspected he could buy half of Quebec City for that amount.

"Did you tell Deschamps how much money you made?"

"Absolutely not," said Sarah. "How much did you say you'd give him?"

"I told him I'd give him a tenth part of what Noah produced. I said I estimated his share would be about £1,000."

"Well, let's keep him happy," Sarah said. "Very happy. Why not give him more, maybe £1,200? Tell him it's for his generous hospitality in putting us all up in his home."

While Sarah and Michel talked, Noah sat silent still trying to believe that he had a daughter. She seemed content sitting next to him. However, Noah was noticing that someone else seemed unusually content. Sarah. He was used to her energy and determination but this was different. She was almost playful.

Malika had chosen again to sleep at the bottom of Noah's bed. She had gone to bed immediately after supper. Noah insisted she be permitted to join the adults at the table when one of the servants took her hand to lead her to the kitchen. She probably would have found the conversation more interesting there.

Deschamps' gratitude for Michel's generosity was absurdly effusive. The night was extremely hot. Perhaps the wine had affected him more than usual.

Over *digestifs*, Michel asked Deschamps if he would like to complete their business by parting with a few *livres*.

Deschamps' eyes lit up immediately.

"Are you suggesting, Michel, that your engraver might

be willing to prepare me a plate for reproducing *livres*? I could use the press you kindly left me."

"Exactly. However he is a very busy man and I believe he would require payment in advance."

As she took in the negotiation, Sarah could barely contain herself, knowing full well that Michel already had obtained a plate for French money from the counterfeiter aboard his ship.

"Name your price."

"Let's say £150. Creating a perfect plate is a painstaking process, but once you have it… Need I say more?"

"Michel, allow me to raise my glass to the pleasure I take in doing business with you, as I did with your uncle. To further show my appreciation, I will make the price for the plate £200. After all, I never expected our arrangement to pay me more than the £1,000 we agreed upon. No one can say my generosity of spirit comes at a price."

It was late when the slaves cleared the table. Noah crept quietly into his room to not wake the girl. Despite the wine, he couldn't sleep. It didn't help that he couldn't stretch out because of Malika. As it was, he was longer than the bed. He was also increasingly anxious to see Cap-Français fade away behind them as they sailed for home. As the daughter of a freed slave, Malika would by law lose her own freedom when she became an adult. Noah wanted her to be as far away from Saint-Domingue as possible, as fast as possible.

While he lay thinking, he suddenly discovered the reason for Sarah's playfulness. From her room came the sounds of a couple making love.

CHAPTER 53

The Drop-Off

New York City,
May 2, 1755

EARLY that morning when the sun first appeared over the horizon, the ship's tender was launched and ordered to take position near the starboard bow where the best bower was being slowly raised. Two of the tender's four crewmen were in the bow, peering intently over the side until one hailed the deck:

"Belay!"

The anchor stopped rising. The bag was visible just below the surface. One seaman stood up in the bow and grasped the anchor line to keep the tender in position while the other kneeled at his feet with a dagger between his teeth. With both hands he reached over the side and wrestled with the knotted rope that held the canvas bag to the anchor line. Finally he managed to release the knot without having to cut the rope. He hauled the bag and the rope onboard and quickly released the second knot that had secured the bottom of the bag to the anchor line. Immediately, the anchor was lowered again. Fortunately there had been not the slightest wind to cause the Chameleon to swing round dangerously close to other anchored vessels while her anchor had been raised.

The tender was maneuvered from the bow back to amidships where the ship's ladder had been lowered over the side. The operation had been conducted on the starboard side because it faced Brooklyn where it was unlikely that an early riser would find it suspicious. Revenue officers boarded from the city side. Ten minutes later, convinced that no one on the Brooklyn shore had been watching, Michel descended the ladder. He sat in the stern. Sarah followed next and sat facing Michel. Finally, Noah descended slowly, Malika's arms wrapped tightly around his neck. There was also a rope slung around her and Noah's shoulders, like a harness. He sat next to Sarah.

When the ship's boat reached the wharf Asser was waiting. He had been informed the night before of Michel's late-evening arrival. The ship's boat had been sent to shore to ascertain whether Asser was ready to receive the Chameleon's cargo today.

To Sarah he said:

"So the same girl who swore she would never again board a ship has now returned from two more voyages, and she's smiling."

"I've learned that it all depends on the captain," Sarah replied, giving the diminutive merchant a tender hug.

Asser shook hands with Michel and Noah, then looked at Malika.

"Did the British charge duty for this lovely import to New York?"

Michel replied:

"It was precisely to avoid that that we brought her ashore before His Majesty had a chance to make our business his business."

"A man after my own heart," Asser said, before turning again to Sarah.

"Sarah, I summoned your brother some three weeks past. I had obtained merchandise I wanted to offer you first, to get you started. Also, I should mention that it came from a ship that arrived with cargo for Croman. I, of course, happily stepped in and relieved the captain of his burden. He now sails for me.

"But that is beside the point. When you were late in returning I wasn't sure quite what to do. Jacob seemed delighted about the goods. He said your warehouse has been fully repaired, and even enlarged. He signed for the merchandise and oversaw the unloading on Maiden Lane. I trust this complies with the general scheme we discussed before you left."

"I'm truly in business again. How can I thank you?"

"By doing more business with me, my girl."

"One more question, Asser. Any word of Croman?"

"None. He has truly vanished and his affairs here are in the hands of the authorities, I'm told. By the way, Jacob raised an interesting point when I saw him. He said Croman sailed off in the ship of the captain who betrayed him at trial. Your brother wondered who was at the helm when the ship reached its destination."

"I hope it was Captain Flemming," Sarah said.

Michel remained to talk to Asser when Sarah, Noah and Malika began their walk to Maiden Lane. Once again, Noah shouldered the sack of money. Sarah offered Malika her hand and she took it. Sarah had never enjoyed walking up Water Street more. She was now a full-fledged member of New York's teeming waterfront.

When they arrived at Maiden Lane, Sarah was so glad to be home that she went straight into the house without even walking around to the side to take a look at the rebuilt warehouse. She let Noah and his daughter pass before closing the door. Noah immediately started up the stairs towards the kitchen, but Sarah stopped him.

"Don't you want to see your room first?"

She pointed to the room on her left.

"My room?"

"Yes. Why not? Your other place is not safe for Malika, or anyone for that matter."

Noah looked around the room, stone walls, solid hardwood floor, a tall four-paned window. The makeshift place he'd made home had no windows.

"Sarah, I'd been planning on using my share of the money to get a suitable place. We could stay here until I do."

"What I'd really like is for you to make this your home. I did a lot of thinking on the ship. You are out working at all hours. You can't leave this little girl alone all that time. And I'm here most of the time, even more so now that this has become my office again. I would love Malika's company. I'd be there to feed her and talk to her while you're gone. And I can teach her things."

Noah didn't answer. He just took Sarah in his arms and held her so long Malika giggled.

"There are other changes I want to make, but we'll talk about that later. First I've got to see Jacob and talk to Michel."

While Sarah went to the market at the bottom of the street, Noah led Malika to the kitchen. She was still exploring it when Sarah returned with bread and milk. On the way back she opened the big warehouse door. The right half was piled high with merchandise, 10 times as much as she'd ever had there before. That amount alone would be enough for her to start being regarded as a serious merchant. The warehouse was still one room but the walls were now almost twice as high. She would need to have shelving built, and buy ladders, dollies and sack trucks.

After breakfast, Sarah began setting up the other first-floor room as her office, as it had been when she first got her home and what she thought would be freedom from the fat merchant. It contained a make-do mattress that Geneviève contrived when she arrived with the severely injured Michel. There were also a few crates and casks leftover from the days when she knew her life was in danger if she dared tried to sell them. The casks sill had Croman's mark on them. She and Noah rolled the casks to the warehouse. Noah then placed the crates on a tarpaulin he found in the warehouse and used it to drag them there. At Sarah's suggestion, he left to search for mattresses and blankets.

Before he returned, Sarah had swept away two months of dust, upstairs and down. She found an extra lamp and some candles and put them in a corner of Noah's room.

Michel arrived in the late afternoon. Unloading had begun and he was a free man for a few days at least.

He already knew Sarah had planned to ask Noah to share their home. They had discussed other plans as well. They were going to marry. At first they were unsure how to go about it. Michel, as ship's captain, could marry a couple but the idea of pronouncing himself husband and wife somehow took all ceremony out of the event. Would he stand as groom beside his bride while conducting the marriage, or stand facing her, officiating? It would be comic.

Michel was Catholic, by baptism only, and Sarah had never troubled to visit New York's only synagogue in the years she'd been in the city. However, she didn't want to become a Catholic. There were few of them and they were not welcome. The never-ending skirmishes with New France and outright wars between France and England saw to that.

It was somewhere off the Bahamas that Sarah and Michel independently arrived at the same conclusion. The Commodore, captain of the Citroen. He should marry them.

"This evening," Sarah said, "I'll ask Noah if he can sail

to New Harlem tomorrow to tell the Commodore I've returned, and ask him to come and visit me. If he agrees to marry us, we'll let the world know."

"I love you," Michel said. "Who shall we invite?"

"I said we'd tell the world, didn't I," Sarah said. "Come to think of it it's a pretty small world. Noah, Malika and Jacob, of course. Peter, but I don't think he'd accept. Asser definitely… You know, I'm going to invite Arnold. Then we could boast we had one of the richest men in New York at our wedding."

"Do you think he'd really attend?"

"No, but at least we'd end up with a note of congratulations bearing his signature."

Sarah abruptly rose.

"I'm off to fetch Jacob. Noah should be home soon."

Malika suddenly parked herself at Michel's side. He'd momentarily forgotten that this was now her house, too. Michel's uncle was the only family he knew. Now, since the demise of the fat merchant, the newly liberated Sarah had pulled a family together in no time at all.

CHAPTER 54

News From France

LESS than a month before the wedding was to take place, Asser sent word for Sarah to visit him at his office. There was no mention of a just-arrived cargo she might want to purchase, or an out-going one for which she might care to purchase shares to finance the voyage.

Sarah's commerce had been growing rapidly since her return, when she assiduously did the rounds of medium-to-large merchants to acquaint them with her inventory and prices. She-merchants were becoming almost commonplace and Sarah was able to compensate for the disadvantage of being young and pretty, and therefore frivolous, by a confidence born of a lifetime of experience in business. Her fast mind for math left many a man hesitant to try to pull one over on her. As they tried to complicate a deal with endless terms for purchasing this or that volume at such and such a price, and a different volume at yet another price, contingent of course on floating prices for each volume based on date of delivery, they soon found out that she could do the math faster than most of them could.

She and Asser never tried to play each other, except for the amusement finding out if they could. Asser had seen it all and actually taught her to recognize deals she should sail away from. After their customary pre-business coffee, Asser produced a letter dated more than a year ago. It came from a merchant in Bordeaux. It ended with:

"He is seen but rarely on the quay, but he is alive. I showed your inquiry to another agent and he confirmed my information."

Sarah had entered Asser's office floating. Every aspect of her life was unfolding better than she had a right to even dream. Only yesterday, Michel had purchased a marriage license. It was more costly than publishing banns but immensely more expedient.

Michel had made two more successful voyages to Saint-Domingue. On the last one Michel delivered what was supposedly Jacob's handiwork, the plate for French livres. In fact, it was the one seized from the French counterfeiter. While Michel had been in New York, Jacob was delighted to make a copy of it for future contingencies. Not knowing he'd been duped, Origène Deschamps said the deal for the plate was one that would bind the agent and Michel forever. Bonds are easily formed when you know each other's secrets, he said.

Sarah could hardly breathe. The news about her father was too good to be credible. How he must have suffered all these years thinking he was utterly alone in the world. At least she had Jacob all this time. He had no one.

"I don't know what to do," Sarah said, almost pleading for a right answer.

"First, dear girl, you must talk with Michel. Find out if he would risk sailing to France. Michel would be sailing under the French flag, and I must tell you that the British have already attacked hundreds of French merchant ships even though war has not been declared officially. The price of doing that could be the loss of his ship, not to speak of the risk to you and Michel personally. I don't advise it, Sarah. But it is Michel's ship, so you must talk to him."

Shaken, Sarah set off toward New Street. Maybe Jacob would have a solution. When she arrived, Peter let her in without greeting her. Instantly she saw that the two engravers were exceedingly busy.

"We're a day behind on an order for our most important client," Peter said.

"Then just a quick word with Jacob, if I may."

She walked around Jacob's press. She bent and whispered in his ear.

"Father's alive."

A small burin slipped from Jacob's fingers. He didn't bend down to pick it up. He stared up at his sister's face. He could see that she knew it as a fact. Otherwise she would not have come.

"What do we do?"

"I don't know, Jacob. I must talk to Michel. Asser says the British are attacking French merchant ships every day. We would be fools to sail there."

Catching an impatient glance from Peter, Sarah told Jacob to come as soon as he could.

Jacob ended up getting to Maiden Lane before Michel. They sat at the table with Noah and Malika. Noah had started to teach her English and encouraged Sarah and Jacob to talk to her in English.

"She'll need it here," said Noah.

As they waited for Michel, Sarah finally said what was on all of their minds.

"I don't know why we're counting on Michel for a solution. What can he say? I know he'd sail through an entire fleet of warships for me but that would be suicide."

Noah was the first to come up with a temporary solution.

"What's most important is to tell your father that you and Jacob are alive and well, that you couldn't be better. Tell him how happy you were to have only now heard that he is alive. Tell him you've been trying to reach him since the day you landed here. Tell him you don't know what to do because of the war. Write that letter a hundred times over and ask Asser to have it forwarded to France from every French port he deals with."

Sarah picked up Malika and sat her on her lap.

"Do you know you have a very smart father?"

By the time Michel arrived, the panic had disappeared.

Michel listened to Sarah's news and the great danger that Asser said would accompany any attempt to sail to France.

"Can you bring me some wine, Sarah?"

Before touching it he raised his glass.

"To your father. That is grand news."

After the others toasted, he said:

"Asser is absolutely right. I would not risk my own life let alone yours, Sarah, on such a foolish action. Start writing the letters as Noah said."

Sarah began serving a light supper. Most of the talk was conjecture about what their father's life had been like since the kidnapping. The talk helped Sarah accept the good news for what it was. Her own desperation to see her father was secondary for the moment.

After they'd finished, Michel spoke for the first time since the food had been served.

"This may be an equally foolish idea, but hear me out.

"What if we sail to England instead of France, then take a boat across the Channel and somehow make our way down to Bordeaux?"

He let the idea sink in a bit before continuing. He had their rapt attention.

"We would have to replace most of our crew with English

speakers. Many have already learned some English. Sarah you would take your business correspondence as proof that you are a New York merchant. Asser could provide something for me. My ship's papers are in English."

"What a relief," said Sarah, finally. "The man I am to marry, I thought he was only handsome. Now I see there's more to him."

Michel said he would speak to Asser of his idea the next day. It would be important for him to sail with a cargo to an English port where Asser knew traders, and, ideally, an agent who could fill the Chameleon's hold for the journey back to New York.

"Are you thinking what I'm thinking, Michel?" asked Sarah.

"I never know what you're thinking," he replied.

"I'm thinking we should get married as soon as possible. I want my father to meet my husband."

CHAPTER 55

A Good Investment

THE NEXT morning Michel felt uneasy as he walked to Asser's office. How safe would he and Sarah be traveling the roads of France? After crossing La Manche there would be at least 400 miles to cover by road in a punishing springless stage coach before they got to Bordeaux. He'd rather sail into a tempest. If Sarah's father was a frail as Sarah imagined him to be, he would never survive the coach journey across France let alone a sea voyage to New York.

Would the British even let them cross the Channel? His English had improved a lot but he could not hide his accent. Sarah spoke what sounded to his ear like perfect English, but maybe to an English ear there were signs of her French origin. Would they be suspected of being French agents?

With each step along the waterfront, Michel's enthusiasm drained away. He wanted to give Sarah everything she wanted in life, and what she wanted most was to see her father again.

The talk with Asser didn't make things better.

"This war has not yet been declared, Michel, but it will be huge. Every country in Europe is aligning itself to fight with either the French or the English for when the war does come. There is much talk of it in England. Just yesterday I spoke to a merchant who had just returned from England where he was trying to negotiate better prices from English exporters because of the dangers the war will pose for his ships."

"Did he get his better prices?" ask Michel.

"No. He was told, 'Royal Navy guns will soon have Frenchie blocked in at every turn.' In other words French ships won't be able to get out of port often enough to do British merchant shipping much harm. Is that arrogance on Britain's part? I don't know but I have a feeling it may not be."

"What am I to do?" Michel said. "Sarah is counting on me."

Most of the traders in Asser's far-flung network were Jews who'd fled war and or persecution somewhere, from Europe to South America.

"The world is not a friendly place, Michel. It is perhaps beautiful, but it is not friendly. You have traveled. You know that. When a man lands in a place where no one chases him with crosses, and no one shoots at him with guns, he has found home.

"To speak frankly, Michel, I would not take the woman I love to France, nor would I take myself there right now. I would pray her father lives to see the fighting stop, and then I would decide."

After a long silence, Michel asked if Asser had coffee. His arrival had been a surprise and none was prepared.

"So, I do nothing. I keep sailing under two flags so I can keep trading in Saint-Domingue. Is that it?"

"All this talk of war, it has made me think about that,

too, Michel. While you were sailing in the Caribbean, war got closer to home as well. Last year your troops from New France were humiliating the British everywhere and they keep building new forts in the Ohio River Valley to hem us in. But the British keep coming back. Just this summer they attacked Acadia and expelled the French from Nova Scotia. Then they intercepted a fleet of French ships trying to reinforce the colony and they sent them packing as well."

Asser sipped his coffee appreciatively. He enjoyed expounding his ideas. These were interesting times, he thought.

"What of your uncle, Michel? I would worry about him. I think the British will keep coming until they drive the French out. Everyone says the French king is weak, indecisive in every matter. I'm just a businessman but I think, for England, the time is right."

Michel had forgotten about his uncle's dream. It seemed meaningless at the time. But now? He told Asser that after his dream his uncle said he wouldn't want to wager on the future of bourbon lilies in the New World.

"Maybe you should think of rescuing him someday instead of Sarah's father."

"I should suggest it to him, Asser. You're right. But he is a stubborn man, and a tough one. Besides, he loves the land there, and he loves the great river below the city. He sailed it so many times. I don't think he'd ever leave it behind. We'll see."

"In the meantime, Michel. I told you I've been thinking about you and the Saint-Domingue trade. I will now explain. I spent all this time talking about British intentions because I think the best and safest thing for you now would be to start sailing under only British colors. Forget about Saint-Domingue. Make your ports of call England and Jamaica. I can set you up with agents in Bristol and Kingston."

Asser had saved the best for last.

"And here is something that will please Sarah, I suspect. I have spoken to most of the captains who once docked here in New York with cargos for a fat merchant. I have been lucky enough to rescue the cargos they carried and pay them. They now sail for me. I've told Sarah that she can invest in these voyages as well and I will keep her informed of cargos that might be of particular interest for her to add to the shelves of her warehouse.

"The good news for you, Michel, is essentially one of convenience. I have effectively adopted the men who once acted as Croman's agents. They will be the men you will deal with in England and Jamaica. You will always quit their ports with a full hold."

By the end of the morning, Michel's ship was being loaded with his first Bristol-bound cargo. The future of his business looked good. Ordinarily, making the agreement he did with Asser would call for a week-long celebration, but all he could think about was telling Sarah that seeing her father was impossible.

Sarah had left the house that morning with Michel. While he continued down the waterfront, she veered west to Geneviève's shop.

"Michel and I are getting married. I don't know what to wear?"

It took the dressmaker at least 10 minutes to release Sarah's hands and stop dancing her around the sewing room. Drawing Sarah near, she placed her palms on Sarah's cheeks and said:

"So you are marrying the man I found lying unconscious in the gutter imitating any number of other drunkards in this city."

"That's the man!"

Then Geneviève became all business.

"I know what you shall wear. Your dress will be dark blue, made of wool. Down the front, from bodice to ankle, will be an ever widening strip of bordeaux-colored silk. Bordeaux is not only your home but it is your color. It pairs magnificently with your black hair and dark eyes. The vertical stripe will make you look tall and regal. Many men will want to marry you that day. I promise."

"How much will such a dress cost?"

"Don't be silly. It is my wedding gift to you. Now leave, let me work."

Sarah thought her friend was joking, but she wasn't. When Sarah hesitated, Geneviève pointed to the door.

She and Michel had a wedding license. She would soon have the finest dress she'd ever worn. When Michel told her that evening that traveling to see her father was out of the question for the foreseeable future she calmly nodded to say that she understood. Michel took her in his arms and she hugged him back tightly.

At Michel's suggestion, they went to Jacob's café on Wall Street for supper. It was Sarah's first visit. She discovered she was the only woman present. Michel told her about the new business opportunities they now had thanks to Asser's contacts.

"The warehouse is already full and I have customers for most of it," Sarah said, happy to talk about how well things were going. "I now have enough money coming in that we no longer have to touch Jacob's money. That's amazing when you think about it.

"I'm also thinking the day will come soon enough when we will have to buy or build another warehouse. I want to ask Noah if he'd like to give up longshoring and take care of managing my warehouse for me while I tend to clients and seek out new business. He'd be closer to Malika at the same time."

Michel thought it was a wonderful idea.

"He's not getting any younger," Michel said. "I can tell you, I wouldn't last a day at what he does on the docks."

"He'd be good at it," said Sarah, "and there's no way

his longshoreman friends would let anybody 'misplace' my goods. He also knows how to make deals with several carters and that could work to our advantage when we need to pick up and deliver a lot of merchandise in a hurry."

When they paused to order food, the man sitting alone at the next table craned his neck in their direction.

"Pardon me, ma'am, for eavesdropping. It wasn't intentional, but I must ask, are you that woman, the one who served up Croman's you-know-what on a platter in court?"

Sarah laughed loudly.

"No offense taken, sir. None at all. I am that woman, and it was my greatest moment."

"No," said Michel, "your greatest moment is yet to come, when you marry me."

"As they say here on Wall Street," Sarah answered, "you strike me as a good investment."

CHAPTER 56

Love And The Walrus

October 17, 1755

THE Commodore fussed like a maid of honor. His boys from New Harlem had freshened the Citroen's paint and built an especially wide thwart amidships for the couple to stand comfortably on while he officiated the ceremony. Orange streamers flew from the mast. They were an afterthought, he said, and were orange only because they were the only ones he could find in New Harlem's largest store.

Commodore Barry also had his black seaman's jacket let out and the brown buttons replaced with silver ones. Though he claimed they once belonged to his grandfather, who had never risen above the rank of able seaman, he arrived aboard with his chest bedecked with naval medals and ribbons. His walrus mustache had been neatly trimmed.

The plan was to sail to the East River and down the middle channel before dropping anchor as close as the crowded harbor permitted to being abeam of Maiden Lane market. His first idea had been to have conducted the ceremony while serenely under sail but it was pointed out by several voices simultaneously that the positioning of the new marital thwart was such that the back and forth swinging of the mainsail's boom would catapult the as yet unmarried couple overboard. Michel diplomatically suggested an alternative. Since there were few witnesses to the marriage, he said, "Why not marry us in the middle of the continent's busiest harbor?"

Besides the crew and the Commodore, all of the family Sarah made was onboard: Sarah, Michel, Jacob, Asser, Geneviève, Noah and Malika. Malika wore a yellow smock, also made by Geneviève, who wore a pale blue gown she had originally designed for Patricia.

Peter had replied to the invitation but said that regrettably he couldn't attend because the idea of being on water left him in absolute terror, worse even than the thought of a republican uprising.

Arnold Livstrom expressed effusive joy over the coming nuptials and stated that he would be honored to participate, "but not in the traditional way." He went on to add: "Do not look for me at the ceremony, but be assured I will see you."

The morning had been chilly but by the time the Citroen was underway the temperature had climbed dramatically to the point it felt like a summer day. As they moved into the East River, the Commodore, manning the rudder, eyed the river and its occupants with suspicion, as if he had been charged with the safety of the King himself. Eventually, he had to carefully thread his way through clusters of ships, some Royal Navy vessels but mostly merchant ships.

"Reef sail!" As the boys jumped to the job he ordered, "Drop anchor!"

As the Commodore rose and stepped forward, Sarah stopped him and buttoned his jacket, which he'd opened to breathe more easily while manning the rudder.

"Thank you, *madame*," he said, stepping by her. *Madame*, it had a nice ring to it, Sarah thought.

Facing the couple, who now stood on the marital thwart, the boat bobbing only slightly, the Commodore raised a Bible between his thumb and index finger.

"I gather from the couple that there will be no need for this item today. Just as well because my eyesight is failing. I can spot a pirate at 20 miles but little squiggles two inches from my eyes are beyond my grasp. Let us proceed."

To the surprise of both Sarah and Michel, the Commodore didn't try to wax eloquent or pretend to render any of the traditional odes to the holy state of matrimony. Instead he spoke of the honor of being asked as a sea captain to perform the ceremony.

"In all my years at sea, this is the first occasion I've done so. It honors the institution of captaincy as well as that of marriage."

He then said he could not have been made happier than to be chosen by his new, but true friends to allow them to step forward in life as man and wife.

"You have allowed me to take part in your endeavors and you have invited me to your table. Before meeting you, I would venture to say I had retired from life. Thanks to you, I have rejoined the living. So, from the land of the living, I now pronounce you man and wife."

At that moment, the crew began ferociously ringing brass bells. Sarah and Michel kissed. In the din of the bells, they could barely hear the congratulations offered in turn by first Jacob, then Geneviève, Noah and Malika, who Noah lifted chest high to embrace the married couple.

Suddenly the harbor erupted. A 10-gun salute roared from a Royal Navy frigate only 100 feet to port. On deck Sarah and Jacob both recognized the waving man standing next to a ship's officer. It was Arnold. Who else in New York would have the inspiration and the influence to convince a high-ranking naval officer to so memorably acknowledge the marriage of an unknown couple of New York immigrants aboard a walrus-chinned boat? Cheers arose from surrounding vessels. Sailors and longshoremen in ships' boats raised their oars in salute.

Sarah elbowed Michel to draw his attention to the stern. Commodore Barry was facing his fleet and doffing his hat.

EPILOGUE

SARAH and Jacob continued to send letters to their father in Bordeaux. They never heard of him again.

After the wedding, Michel wrote his uncle in Quebec City to say he had married in New York and now sailed between New York, England and Jamaica. He asked Antoine to live with them in New York. As expected Antoine refused to leave "*mon pays*", Quebec. He replied that if New France was at last conquered by the British, Michel could simply add Quebec City to his trade route. "And bring your wife. I'd like to meet her. That woman sounds like a prettier version of me."

Despite Sarah's attempts to have him join the company formally, Jacob continued to pursue his first love, engraving. In 1763, his submission was chosen as the new £1 note for the Province of New York. Engravers had been asked to submit designs that would be impossible to forge. The following year he was hired as the royal province's official engraver.

According to the New York Gazette in 1764, "a former resident of the city, Mr. Zachariah Croman, has run for election to the British Parliament, and lost. There were reports in the British press that he was involved in a real estate scandal in Pennsylvania involving the relative of a former prime minister, Earl William Pitt."

As snow fell heavily on Broad Street in December of 1765, Geneviève was run over by the carriage of the Governor of the Royal Province of New York. She died that night of her injuries. Sarah did not hear of her death until eight days later when she received a message at her home from Patricia Van Huisen. It read: "Geneviève was to have arrived seven days ago for a fitting. The dress is required for the Governor's ball five days hence."

In the devoted company of his daughter, never having left the room on Maiden Lane, Noah lived with his wife's spirit for the rest of his days.

In the year that the King of England granted America independence, in 1783, the company's head office had moved from Maiden Lane to Hanover Square, and Sarah had judged Malika more than ready to take over all its operations.

Sarah and Michel had no offspring. In the end Sarah said it didn't matter. They had a family.

HISTORICAL NOTES

Every effort has been made to use the Manhattan street names in use at the time of the novel, 1748-1755. My source was primarily the following site:

A Guide to Former Street Names in Manhattan

http://www.oldstreets.com/

Information regarding street names (and almost everything else New York) was also verified in *Gotham: A History of New York City* to 1898, a Pulitzer Prize-winning history written by Edwin G. Burrows and Mike Wallace (Oxford University Press).

NYC Street Names Used in That Woman

Beaver Street: At the time of this novel, Beaver Street ran only between Bowling Green and Broad Street. The block between Broad and William was variously called Prince or Princess Street.

Bridge Street: Bridge Street

Broad Street: Broad Street

Broadway: Broadway

Crown Street: now Liberty Street

Dock Street: the portion of today's Pearl Street between Whitehall Street and Hanover Square

Duke Street: Now Stone Street between Broad Street and Hanover Square.

Hanover Square: Hanover Square

Maiden Lane: Maiden Lane

Mill Street/Lane: South William Street

New Street: New Street

Petticoat Lane or Pettycoate Lane: An alternate name for Marketfield Street east of Broadway

Queen Street: Now Pearl Street. Queen Street was sometimes called Great Queen Street to distinguish it from Little Queen Street, the present Cedar Street.

State Street: State Street

The Common: Now City Hall Park

Wall Street: Wall Street

Water Street: Water Street (after 1736)

William Street: The portion of William Street between Hanover Square and Wall Street was also known as King Street.

The Slips:

Fly Market Slip at the foot of Maiden Lane: The original slip was filled to South Street about 1820 and was made part of Maiden Lane in 1824. For years after the slip was filled in, the space between the new piers at that point continued to be called Fly Market Slip.

Coenties Slip was begun in 1696 and progressively enlarged and shifted outward with the expansion of the Manhattan shoreline. The slip was filled to South Street about 1880. Only the apex, between Pearl and Water Streets, retains its historic name.

Old Slip: The city's first slip, it existed by 1696 and was known as Old Slip by 1730. It was filled to South Street in 1834 but the filled in area retains the name.

Hudson River: At the time of this novel, the Hudson River was usually referred to as the North River.

Philadelphia Street Names

The two street names mentioned in the book, 4th Street and Market Street, exist today

Street Names in Bordeaux, France:

All streets names used in this book exist today. The Dijeaux Gate (porte Dijeaux) was also known as la porte Dauphine in the time of the previous king, Louis XIV.

Characters:

As stated at the outset, all characters in this novel are fictitious. I would like to note that while the character Arnold Livstrom is said to be from one of New York's two richest families, his actions in the novel are in no way based on any member of the actual Livingston family.

The fictitious character Commodore Barry is not the Commodore Barry who has a park named after him in Brooklyn. The park, formerly City Park and the borough's oldest, was named Commodore Barry Park in 1951, due to its location near the Brooklyn Navy Yard that Barry helped found.

Places:

New York City: by 1756 it had a population of about 13,046.

Saint-Domingue: today's Haiti.

Cap-Français: former capital of Haiti, now known as Cap-Haïtien or simply Le Cap or Au Cap.

Blackwell Island in the East River: today's Roosevelt Island.

Buchanan's Island in the East River: today's Randall's Island.

Fort George was originally Fort Amsterdam under Dutch rule. Under the British, its name was changed to reflect the current king.

The King's Arms was New York's first coffee house, built in 1696 on Broadway just above the Trinity churchyard at what was then Little Queen Street, now Cedar Street.

The forged land deeds used by Zachariah Croman refer vaguely to land that had actually been long under dispute between Pennsylvania and Maryland in what was known as Cresap's War (1730-67).

The Homeless Mule Tavern on Water Street is fictitious as is Noah's mill north of New Harlem.

A language note

In the last chapter the Commodore teasingly addresses Sarah as "*madame*" before she was actually married. That usage of "*madame*" represents a bit of literary license on my part. In reality, a woman was always addressed as "*mademoiselle*", even when married. "*Madame*" was reserved for women of high aristocracy, even when not married. This practice ceased after the French Revolution.

About the Author

Wayne Clark is a Montreal writer and author of the international award-winning literary fiction novel he & She. In addition to writing fiction he has worked as a journalist, copywriter and translator.

Photo credit: e.v.

www.ingramcontent.com/pod-product-compliance
Lightning Source LLC
LaVergne TN
LVHW020648110826
845149LV00012B/1948
* 9 7 8 0 9 9 2 1 2 0 2 6 9 *